Praise for the Hendees' Novels of the Noble Dead

Thief of Lives

"Readers will turn the pages of this satisfying medieval thriller with gusto." —*Booklist*

"Fans of Anita Blake will enjoy this novel. The characters are cleverly drawn so that the several supernatural species that play key roles in the plot seem natural and real.... Supernatural fantasy readers will enjoy this action-packed strong tale because vampires, sorcerers, dhampirs, elves, fey-canines, and other ilk seem real." —*Midwest Book Review*

"*Thief of Lives* takes the whole vampire slayer mythos and moves into an entirely new setting. The world the Hendees create is ... a mixture of pre-Victorian with a small slice of eastern Europe flavor.... Magiere and Leesil are a really captivating pair.... [The Hendees] handle the ideas and conventions inherent in vampires really well. While, thanks to the clever setting and characters, they make it feel like a very different twist on the subject." —*SF Site*

"A great fantasy adventure, an intriguing mystery, and a chilling gothic tale, weaving a complicated but ever-alluring literary fabric. If anything, this one was even better than [*Dhampir*], which is no small feat." —*Sequential Tart*

continued ...

Dhampir

"*Dhampir* maintains a high level of excitement through interesting characters, both heroes and villains, colliding in well-written action scenes. Instead of overloading us with their world-building and the maps and glossaries typical of so much fantasy, the Hendees provide well-rounded characters that go a lot further than maps in making a lively fantasy world."
—*The Denver Post*

"Take Anita Blake, vampire hunter, and drop her into a standard fantasy world and you might end up with something like this exciting first novel. . . . A well conceived imagined world, some nasty villains, and a very engaging hero move this one into the winner's column."
—*Chronicle*

"This *Buffy*-like story in a medieval setting won't disappoint vampire aficionados."
—*Booklist*

"Barb and J. C. Hendee have written a refreshingly innovative horror novel . . . The plot is meaty and juicy with unexpected turns so that readers are anticipating the next surprise."
—*Midwest Book Review*

Don't miss the exciting beginning of
Magiere, Leesil, and Chap's adventures in

Dhampir
Thief of Lives

SISTER OF THE DEAD

A NOVEL OF THE NOBLE DEAD

Barb & J. C. Hendee

A ROC BOOK

ROC
Published by New American Library, a division of
Penguin Group (USA) Inc., 375 Hudson Street,
New York, New York 10014, USA
Penguin Group (Canada), 10 Alcorn Avenue, Toronto,
Ontario M4V 3B2, Canada (a division of Pearson Penguin Canada Inc.)
Penguin Books Ltd., 80 Strand, London WC2R 0RL, England
Penguin Ireland, 25 St. Stephen's Green, Dublin 2,
Ireland (a division of Penguin Books Ltd.)
Penguin Group (Australia), 250 Camberwell Road, Camberwell, Victoria 3124,
Australia (a division of Pearson Australia Group Pty. Ltd.)
Penguin Books India Pvt. Ltd., 11 Community Centre, Panchsheel Park,
New Delhi - 110 017, India
Penguin Group (NZ), cnr Airborne and Rosedale Roads, Albany,
Auckland 1310, New Zealand (a division of Pearson New Zealand Ltd.)
Penguin Books (South Africa) (Pty.) Ltd., 24 Sturdee Avenue,
Rosebank, Johannesburg 2196, South Africa

Penguin Books Ltd., Registered Offices:
80 Strand, London WC2R 0RL, England

First published by Roc, an imprint of New American Library,
a division of Penguin Group (USA) Inc.

First printing, January 2005
10 9 8 7 6 5 4 3 2 1

Copyright © Barb Hendee and J. C. Hendee, 2005
Map copyright © Penguin Group (USA) Inc.
All rights reserved.

Cover art by Koveck

ROC   REGISTERED TRADEMARK—MARCA REGISTRADA

Printed in the United States of America

Pronunciation Guide

All non-English languages are presented with a shared set of English letters, characters, and marks for a common standard in pronunciation. There are no silent letters; all letters are pronounced. All vowels are generally in the English "short" manner, though exceptions not noted do exist. At first, languages may appear similar in print. The table below explains the more basic rules of pronunciation, and by sound and syntax, you will note the differing flavor of individual languages.

`	Grave Accent	An English standard "short" vowel, but its voiced duration is short, as well. It is little more than a way to shape the transition between surrounding letters. Example: ì = *i* (nearly unvoiced) as in *bit*.
´	Acute Accent	An English standard "short" vowel in most cases, but the voiced duration is elongated. Example: á = *a* in *ban* (slightly longer).
¨	Umlaut	An English standard "short" vowel of standard duration, but with the back of

		the throat open, producing a wider or deeper sound. Example: ä = *a* in *father*.
^	Circumflex	An English "long" vowel of standard duration most often followed by a short *i* as a diphthong. Example: â = *ai* in *rain*.
'	Apostrophe	Indicates a brief pause in voiced pronunciation, similar to a brief catch of air or voicing before continuing. Sometimes used to clarify syllabic separation in complex words.
-	Hyphen	As for English, it occurs in compound words or for the use of a specialized prefix or suffix, as well as showing correct syllabic separation when the hyphenated term is pronounced as one word.
hk		In the Suman language (Sumanese), pronounced as represented in a "breathy" manner. In Belaskian, it is more quick and sharp. In Elvish, it is the *ch* in the Gaelic word *loch*. However, the sounds are similar, and any will do for basic reading.
chk		Occurs mostly in Elvish and Dwarvish. At the end of word, it is pronounced as written. Similar to the ending of the word *latched*, where the *e* is unpronounced and the *d* becomes a *k*. When it appears midword, it is a syllabic separation; the *ch* ends the previous syllable and the *k* begins the following syllable.

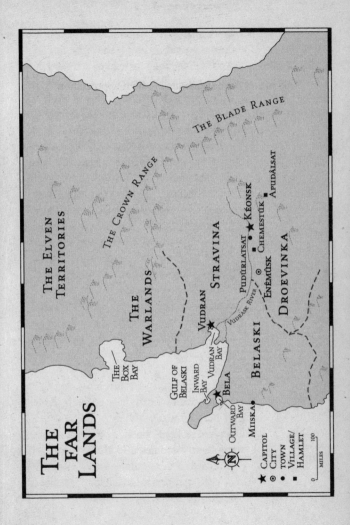

This one is for our parents . . . with appreciation.

Prologue

Amber light spread across the dirt floor from a fireplace embedded in the cottage's sod-and-timber wall. It barely illuminated a rough table and stools, two low beds with patchwork quilts, and other hand-me-down fixtures so old, no one remembered whose father's father or mother's mother had first acquired them. And on the tail of nightfall, a tall and black-haired woman in her twentieth year lit but one candle upon the table, for even that was a luxury.

She was straight-boned, with deep brown eyes beneath eyebrows that arched high, and strands of hair escaped her long braid. Beneath her wool coat, she wore an age-stained apron covering a blue dress. She swung a cook pot out from the fire on its iron arm so the stew wouldn't burn, then stepped to the cottage's one front window. Brushing aside burlap curtains, she cracked the shutter to peer anxiously up the village path.

Few villagers moved among the huddled huts, carrying in firewood or heading for the common well, buckets in hand. She closed the shutter, let the curtain fall into place, and returned to the table to set out two clay bowls and wooden spoons. From the shelves she gathered a cloth-wrapped bundle and a knife, then settled upon a stool. She unwrapped a loaf of rye bread to cut away the dried end. There was nothing more to do, and she watched the fire's flames recede.

When the knock came, she sighed in relief.

Before she stepped to the door, a hollow voice growled from outside. "Enough pleasantries!"

The crack of shattering wood filled the small hut as the door slammed inward. Its top leather hinge broke away, and splinters skittered across the dirt floor. She backed into the table, nearly tripping over a stool.

Three shadowed figures stood in the opening, their features hidden by cowls and cloaks. The tallest lowered his foot as the broken door ceased shuddering.

"That was not necessary, Father," said the one next to him. Dressed in a charcoal cloak and hood and crafted riding boots, his gloved hand was still raised to knock again. He let it drop to his side.

The third figure hung back as the father entered and, in three strides, grabbed the woman by the throat.

She clutched the table for balance as he bent her backward. His thumb levered her chin sideways to face his companions as he studied her profile. Even with her head tilted, she kept her gaze upon her assailant.

Candlelight partially exposed his face inside the hood. Nearly colorless crystalline eyes stared back at her, and his features were paler than those of her own fair-skinned people. A long aquiline nose ran down to a thin-lipped mouth. He wore steel vambraces on both forearms, and beneath his cloak was a crestless, burgundy tabard over a shirt of mail. She fumbled for better support on the table, and the base of her palm scraped something sharp.

"This is the one?" he asked, but his question was not to her.

The one who called him Father took a step into the hut, allowing the third figure to drift toward her.

His long, hooded robe swirled like black oil as he glided across the cottage floor. Firelight made faint markings and strange symbols shimmer in and out of sight upon its folds. Where his face should have been was a mask of aged leather that ended above a bony jaw supporting a withered mouth. The woman saw no eye slits in his mask. He reached toward her, as if he "saw" her, but his gaunt fingers stopped shy of her cheek as she struggled to pull away.

"Get out of my home!" she shouted. No one gave her notice.

"Yes . . . ," the masked one whispered with a voice like windblown sand. "The one shown to me. The one sent into my dreams by our patron."

The father glanced back to his son.

"You should be pleased," he remarked. "She'll make you an attractive bride."

The woman's eyes widened. She wouldn't be the first or the last to suffer the whims of a vassal lord assigned to a fief, but nobles did not take village women as wives.

"Bride?" said the son. "I doubt, Father, that your lackey"—and the masked one hissed over his shoulder—"would bother with the customs attached to such a title. Take her and let us leave. The sooner done, the better."

The masked one's fingers inched forward, and she felt her captor's grip tighten to pull her up. At the touch of fingertips on her cheek, her hand closed about the knife on the table.

The robed one recoiled to the room's far wall before she even moved. She twisted forward, thrusting low and upward. The knife blade slipped into the side slit of her captor's mail shirt and buried in his abdomen.

His grip clenched harder about her throat. No one in the cottage moved.

Her rage drained when she stared into the father's face and saw no hint of emotion in his eyes. He pulled her upright by the throat, not bothering to remove her hand from the knife hilt. The masked old man glided evenly toward the door and out into the night. The father pulled her along by the neck as he followed the old man.

She staggered and regained her footing. The son turned away as she passed, and she caught no glimpse of his face. Two large horses waited outside in the village path. The son mounted the closest, a tall bay, and the father lifted her up behind him as if she were no burden at all. Shouts rose out of the dark.

Villagers emerged from cottages and huts, but most stayed well back. A few held torches or candle lanterns that barely illuminated the path between their homes. Three young men came forward in smudged and grimed field clothes, armed with hoes and hay rakes. Two hesitated, but the third showed no fear. Even in the dark, the woman recognized his brown unwashed hair hanging loose around angular features and a square, dark-shadowed jaw.

"Adryan, don't!" she called, as much in anger as concern for his safety.

A villager who assaulted a noble was a corpse sooner rather than later, and no one of importance would question it. The young man barely glanced at her, his attention shifting between the masked figure and the tall, armored father.

"Release her!" he snapped. "She's mine."

"You fool!" she shouted back. "Stay back. There's nothing to be done."

She was about to slide off the horse, but the son swung his arm back to block her.

"You should listen to her," the son said.

Adryan rushed the father. The tall nobleman brushed back his cloak to expose the knife handle protruding from his abdomen. The young man faltered, and the masked old one slid forward into his way. The robed figure slapped Adryan across the cheek with one gnarled hand.

Adryan buckled and fell backward to the ground, screaming and clutching at his face. As he writhed, the father gripped the knife hilt and withdrew the blade from his own flesh as if from a sheath. He tossed it to the ground beside Adryan, and the young man's two companions backed away.

The masked one closed on Adryan.

"Enough," ordered the father. "We've no more time to waste here. Meet us at the keep."

The robed figure turned and nodded agreement. His arms stretched out to the sides at full length, palms up to the sky, and his breath came out in a long, audible exhale. The air in the village path began to churn.

Sitting upon the horse, the woman watched leaves and twigs swirl on the ground in a circle about the dark robe. Flickering shapes shimmered in the turning breeze. The light of the villagers' lanterns and torches caught something taking shape in the air.

Faces with sunken cheeks and hollowed eye sockets, flesh shrunk across phantom bones, materialized in the whirling air. Their translucent hands clutched at the dark robe on all sides, and the masked figure faded from sight as the whirlpool breeze died.

The night's cold sank sharply into the woman's body as she stared at the empty space.

The father mounted his horse and turned down the path into the forest. The keep was some distance beyond the trees to the top of a knoll. The son turned his horse to follow, and she heard a shout from behind in the village. Smothered in despair, she didn't hear it clearly and looked back, grabbing hold of the son's waist as the horse stepped into a trot.

Up the path came another woman, stout and black-haired,

wearing a purple dress. She was running after the horses with the fallen knife clutched in her hand.

Gripping the horse's sides with her knees, the woman shouted, "Bieja, no!"

Relief filled her. Her older sister had once again come home late from the market in the central village to the north. The horse lurched forward into a gallop, and she tightened her hold on the son's waist, no longer able to look back. She heard her sister call out again.

"Magelia!"

Chapter 1

Magiere sensed the instant of dawn, though the inn's small room was dark and shuttered. It called her from sleep. This first night with Leesil in her arms lingered in her memory, his shoulder beneath her cheek and her outstretched palm on his chest beneath the blankets. She still feared for him, but perhaps if she kept him always this close, she could keep him safe even from herself.

A more troublesome thought wormed into her awareness. She fought it down, recalling the scent and taste and touch of Leesil in the night, until they'd settled into warm slumber. But the thought wouldn't leave, and perhaps in part it was Leesil's closeness that fed it strength.

Magelia—and Nein'a.

Two mothers waited. One dead, but the second still lived, or so she hoped—for Leesil's sake.

Magiere opened her eyes to see her fingertips peeking from beneath the blanket's edge across Leesil's chest. When she lifted her gaze past his shoulder, still bandaged from their battles, she found his amber eyes looking down at her.

"You're awake," she said.

"I like watching you sleep. It's the only time you're peaceful."

Did he always have to make jokes? Magiere tried to sit up, but his arms closed around her.

"Not yet," he said. "It's early. I don't think the sun is even up."

"It will be soon," she lied, and relaxed back against him.

Her dhampir nature had grown more pronounced in recent days. She felt the sun's presence even when indoors. In the night, the heat Leesil stirred in her made her heightened senses open wide. With only a sliver of moonlight through the window's shutter crack, she'd clearly seen his white-blond hair, narrow face, and lithe body. His amber eyes, almond shaped from his half-elven heritage, were locked upon her. At most times, her unnatural senses frightened or sickened her for what they revealed, but in that night, she hadn't cared so long as all she sensed was him. She was in Leesil's arms, and little else mattered.

Except for two mothers, who'd each left her child with a dark and bloody heritage.

"Did you sleep all right?" she asked.

"A little," he answered.

She knew he might be lying. He often had trouble sleeping, now that he'd stopped drinking. This, as well, was linked to a mother he'd thought dead for years. Magiere peered about the room.

"Where's Chap? Did he stay out all night?"

Leesil smiled. "For once, he showed some manners."

Magiere scowled. She rolled over to reach for the sulfur stick on the bedside table and lit the one candle resting there. The night before, they'd taken this room at the first inn outside Bela, the capital city of Belaski. The three of them had often slept outdoors in past years. Their dog, Chap, would be well enough on his own, but it bothered Magiere that she hadn't thought of him all night.

She rolled back to find Leesil leaning up on one elbow above her. He slid his fingers between hers, a striped pattern of flesh in the mingling. Half-elf and half-undead, they were a strange contrast with his golden-brown skin and white-blond hair and her blood-tinted black tresses and pale flesh. A mischievous smile crossed Leesil's lips, and Magiere lost all concern for the moment. Chap could wait a little longer.

The candlelight revealed their surroundings more clearly.

It was all simple, neat, and pleasant, but it wasn't home—wasn't the Sea Lion tavern in Miiska. Her falchion leaned against the bedside table, close within reach beside the bed on which they lay. Their travel chest and belongings sat under the window, reminding her that soon they would be on the move again.

"What?" he asked.

"Another journey," she answered.

Leesil settled back on the bed, comfortably close as he brushed stands of hair off her face.

"The sages gave me some supplies, but as we get farther north and into the Warlands, restocking could get difficult. More so as we move on to the northern mountains and the Crown Range between there and the elven lands. We'll need more before we leave."

Magiere hesitated. How could she make him face her new choice?

In youth, he'd fled from slavery as a warlord's assassin, knowing his escape would cause his own parents' execution. For years afterward, he drank himself to sleep each night to smother guilt-spawned nightmares. Even Magiere hadn't known, until he'd confessed but a few nights ago. Then an assassin named Sgäile—one of the elven *anmaglâhk*—had come to take Leesil's life. Leesil's mother had betrayed her own caste by teaching him and his father the *anmaglâhk*'s cold-blooded ways. The assassin changed his mind and let Leesil go. From this encounter, Leesil suspected his mother still lived, imprisoned all these years by her own people.

Now that he had hope, Magiere had to make him wait even longer.

"Before we seek your mother, if she still lives," she said, "we need to go to my home village in Droevinka."

She'd fled from there nine years ago at the age of sixteen, and the thought of returning made bile rise in her throat. Her discomfort vanished when Leesil's smile faded.

He rose up in the bed. "If she lives? What does that—?"

Magiere quickly covered his lips with her fingers as she sat up.

"I didn't mean it that way. I want to believe as much as you . . . but I had a mother, as well, and a past neither of us knows. I need answers, too."

Twice they'd been manipulated into battles with the undead. The last time they fought, in the king's city of Bela, had left them both with more questions than answers. Magiere learned more of her nature—dhampir, hunter of the dead—in being coerced into ridding Bela of its undead predators. In the end, Welstiel Massing, whom she'd once thought an ally, revealed himself as a Noble Dead akin to the ones he'd pitted her against. He'd staged the encounters to train her for his own purpose in acquiring an unknown artifact supposedly guarded by ancient Noble Dead.

Welstiel had been less than forthcoming or even knowledgeable about her origin, but his actions stirred Magiere's desire to know.

Leesil's eyes betrayed a twinge of dismay as he looked at her. "No . . . no." He shook his head. "It's been too many years—"

"Please, listen," Magiere cut in. "This isn't just for me,

but for both of us. There's so much we don't know about my past compared to yours."

"And we'll get answers," he said, "but the living come first."

"I wasn't made by the living!" she snapped. "An undead used my mother to make me—to kill its own kind. I need to know why."

Leesil fell silent. Guilt over lashing out at him made Magiere calm herself before continuing.

"Before we can head north through the Warlands and beyond to the elven territory, we must travel eastward and inland, around the Gulf of Belaski. That's halfway to Droevinka and my past, so close to my answers and less than a third the distance we will travel north."

She put her hands upon Leesil's cheeks and leaned in close until her forehead touched his. When she lifted her head again, he stared downward, not looking at her. His expression softened as his hand slid down her cheek, her long neck, and across her breastbone, and finally gripped her hand.

"All right, it makes sense. If my mother is alive after all this time, likely she's in no danger. It makes no odds if we take a little longer to reach her."

Magiere scooted forward and wrapped herself around him, flesh to flesh, and held him. He understood, but it made her feel no better for having forced it upon him.

"And I swear," she whispered in his ear, "once we learn what we can for me, we'll hurry north for your mother."

She pulled back enough to look into his sad but resolved eyes. Although she spoke calmly, the scope of their impending journey left her feeling small and lost. He was about to answer when the thud of a door and running feet echoed from somewhere out front in the inn, and footsteps grew louder.

"The innkeeper is up and about," Magiere said, wanting to push away the outside world a bit longer.

Leesil shifted her out of his lap and reached for his breeches as he swung his legs over the bed's side.

"No," he said. "It's probably—"

The little room's door burst open and slammed against the wall.

"Magiere . . . Leesil! I'm coming with you!" Wynn cried out, and she twisted the latch and shoved the door open with both hands. "Domin Tilswith gave me leave!"

The instant the door struck the wall, Wynn Hygeorht, apprentice for the Belaskian branch of the Guild of Sagecraft, stopped cold.

All her excitement drained away.

Leesil clutched a blanket as he grabbed for his breeches, his wiry torso dark gold in the candlelight. Startled, Magiere jerked the blanket back over her own specterlike body. The blanket snapped from Leesil's hand, and he lost his grip on the trousers, as well. His amber eyes widened, and Wynn's cheeks flushed as all thought scurried from her mind.

Leesil stood before her, stark naked.

"Oh . . . ," Wynn stammered. "Oh . . ."

The door recoiled from the wall and struck her shoulder, and Wynn stumbled back into the opening. A low grunt made her glance down long enough to see Chap standing beside her. A few burrs and twigs stuck in the dog's long silver-gray fur, and his crystalline eyes widened as he looked into the room.

Wynn lifted her head again, and embarrassment overwhelmed all good sense.

"Forgetful gods, Wynn!" Magiere snapped, still clutching the blanket as she stood up. "With all that learning, didn't those sages teach you to knock?"

With a sudden inhalation, Wynn slapped her hands over her eyes at the sight of an exposed Leesil and an incensed Magiere heading straight for her. In less time than it took to announce her presence, she had lost the good graces of everyone she intended to join on the coming journey. How much worse could this possibly become?

"Get out!" Magiere snarled.

Wynn fumbled for the doorframe, too mortified to open her eyes. Two large paws thumped against her rear, and she stumbled into hallway. She heard the door slam shut behind her as she caught herself on the passage's far wall.

When she turned about to peek between her fingers, Chap sat before the closed door. His translucent blue eyes were filled with something akin to an elder's disappointment. Wynn slid down the wall to slump upon the floor.

"You should have warned me," she said.

Chap cocked his head, unblinking. His expression was too much like that of an old master sage waiting for a slow pupil to see the obvious answer to a stupid question.

Wynn stared back at the closed door. "Oh, my," she groaned.

Chap grunted and licked his nose.

"Oh, be quiet," Wynn snapped.

Leesil belted on his breeches and pulled his shirt over his head. "Well, now neither of us has any secrets from Wynn."

"You knew she was coming," Magiere said in the same biting tone she'd used on Wynn.

Leesil saw the accusing wrinkle of Magiere's brow as her own white shirt dropped around her neck. It was difficult to decide which response would spare him the worst of her coming assault. An uncovered lie would be dangerous later, but so was the truth in the moment.

Looking at Magiere's uncanny beauty, at her black hair

loose over her shoulders, and her pale face and dark eyes, such a choice was exasperating. Only the day before, he'd thought their previous night together could never have happened.

As much as Leesil adored her challenging nature, and even goaded it at times to watch her smolder, this wasn't the time for another clash with Magiere. And worse, with the lingering memory of her pressed against him, he couldn't think of a convincing lie.

"Yes, I knew," he admitted. "I gave Wynn a necklace to sell, and she's brought us the coins from it."

"Necklace? What necklace? Leesil, what did you—?"

"I took it from Sapphire's body before we burned her corpse in Bela. We've a long way to go, and we're not going to get there on your bad temper and my charm."

He jerked the door open before she could come at him again.

Chap sat before the open door, his tail thumping. Wynn slumped against the far wall, her face buried in her hands. Barely twenty years old Wynn had a round face and brown braid hanging over one shoulder, and the sage's traditional long gray robe had been replaced with a shorter one that hung to the thighs of her new breeches.

Her little hands slid down from her eyes and she peeked up at Leesil, her olive cheeks flushed, and she covered her face again.

"You two get in here," Leesil ordered.

Chap trotted in, and, at the sight of Magiere's stern expression, he slipped past the travel chest and out of the way. Wynn entered more slowly.

"I am so truly sorry," she whispered.

Magiere crossed her arms. Leesil tensed as he shut the door, waiting to see if she would continue with him or turn her ire elsewhere.

"What's this nonsense about coming with us?" she snapped at Wynn. "You're supposed to be on your way to Miiska with our payment from Bela's city council."

Leesil and Magiere had been well paid for their services. Wynn had promised to take a bank draft to Miiska with a letter to their friend Karlin explaining their plans and other matters.

"Domin Tilswith will go in my place," Wynn blurted, plainly relieved that her poor manners seemed forgotten. "Your town council can begin building the community warehouse. He asked me to travel with you to the elven territory and serve as your translator. The elves here are different from those of my continent, so reclusive and secretive, and—"

"You're *not* coming with us," Leesil cut in, astonished. Wynn was little more than a sparrow barely out of its mother's nest—too innocent and naive to get involved in what he and Magiere didn't fully understand. "Now, did you sell the necklace I gave you?"

The young sage stood silent. With only a brief hesitation, she frowned, pulled a pouch from her robe's pocket, and handed it to him.

Leesil looked into it and found a fistful of coins, half gold and half silver, and mostly sovereigns. It was more than enough to see them through the coming seasons, or so he hoped.

"I received a good price for it—and I am coming with you," Wynn said. "Domin Tilswith assisted you both more than once and gave you shelter in Bela. He wishes me to—"

"I doubt it was his idea," Magiere scoffed.

"We have other more immediate plans," Leesil said. "And when we do turn toward the elven territory, it may well be winter. Wynn, you aren't fit for such a journey, and we don't have time to coddle a scholar on the road."

Wynn straightened her back, head up, embarrassment replaced by stubborn indignation. Leesil had seen this more than once during their time in Bela.

"And how will you get your answers?" she asked. "Do you speak the elven language? Does Magiere?" Wynn pointed at Chap. "Ah, he does. Perhaps Chap can translate for you."

Leesil's annoyance was getting the better of him. "This is going to be dangerous. We're walking blind and don't even know who or what is toying with us, let alone why."

"And still," Wynn said, "how many languages do you read and speak? Not that of your mother's people. Magiere can barely read at all. I can translate for you and speak with and for Chap, as well. In return, I will bring back new knowledge for my guild. I traveled nearly a year across land and ocean to reach this country with my domin and the other sages. I do not need you to—"

"Aren't you listening?" Magiere asked. "We're not heading north. First, we go inland to my old home in Droevinka, which means a longer journey than you thought. There are places in my homeland where they don't speak Belaskian, and you'll be the ignorant one. So much for your services."

Leesil saw a strange concentration, or perhaps eagerness, fill Wynn's expression at the mention of Magiere's homeland. The sage's gaze fixed upon Magiere's face for a moment before she spoke.

"All the more to learn of . . . this continent's people and cultures. Language is my strength as a cathologer, a sage skilled in the nature of knowledge itself. One more to learn is one more benefit of the journey. There is no choice in the matter. Leave without me, and I will only follow you."

Chap groaned, and his furry face wrinkled like Magiere's scowl.

Leesil exchanged glances with Magiere, but neither of them said a word.

Though half-elven, he'd never known his mother's people or learned their language. Wynn might prove useful, once they turned north out of Droevinka. But by the way the stubborn little sage reacted to Magiere's homeward purpose, there was more to Wynn's interests than fabled lands and foreign tongues.

"Let's pack up the wagon and pay the innkeeper," he said. "Save the rest of the talk, as we have to go back into Bela for more supplies."

The barest smile settled on Wynn's lips as she turned toward the door. "Come, Chap. I brought something for you."

As she stepped out, Chap glanced up, but Leesil shrugged. The dog whined and loped after the young sage as Magiere shook her head in disbelief.

Leesil gathered their few belongings, carrying their chest with Magiere's help. Outside by the road, he shivered in the chill autumn air and spotted Wynn's pile of belongings stacked beside the inn's front door. He led the way around the side to the stable, a rickety shake roof on poles that leaned against the inn's weathered wall for support. Crude railings divided its weed-strewn space into stalls, and therein were the two horses for their nearby wagon.

Wynn crouched upon the ground with a large piece of tanned hide rolled out before her. Its edges were cut square, and its length and breadth matched the reach of one arm. On it were rows of elegant and curved markings and symbols, either singular or in groups, and all drawn with ink. Some were organized into columns, and a few groups of symbols like scrawled words or phrases were set off to either side within small circles and squares.

The markings were strangely familiar to Leesil, though for a moment he couldn't remember when or where he'd seen them. Then he remembered Wynn scribbling with chalk upon the floor of the sages' barracks. They'd stumbled upon

Chap's little secret, a hint to his true nature as a *majay-hì*, a Fay in a dog's body. Wynn marked words and letters upon the floor so he could paw out answers to her questions, though the process had proved less than efficient.

Leesil stepped closer, as did Magiere. The hide Wynn had made was more compact and orderly but still as unreadable to Leesil as the chalk all over the barracks floor.

Chap cocked his head and began pawing at the hide.

"Not bad," Leesil commented. "But we need to get on with the day."

"I only wanted to show it to him," Wynn said with puzzlement.

She watched Chap's awkward pawing, and as she tried to catch up, she spoke in the odd lilting and chopped tongue of the elves.

"A'bithva, Chap? A'bithva jeannis?"

Chap pawed more symbols, and Wynn followed with her eyes, lips moving silently. The dog stopped, poised on haunches, and looked up at Leesil and then Magiere.

Wynn stood up with her small hands clenched.

"You left him outside . . . all night?" The words caught in her throat as if she couldn't quite get them out. "How could you? With no food, no water!"

Magiere stiffened and spoke so quietly that Leesil was immediately on his guard.

"Is this what we can look forward to? That mutt gets to use her for his endless whining and begging?"

Chap wrinkled his muzzle; then he licked his nose at Magiere. Leesil hoped it wasn't some kind of gesture, or at least that Magiere wouldn't think so.

"I'm sure it will prove more useful than that," he said.

Despite her outward anger, Magiere rummaged in the back of their wagon until she procured some dried meat and a water flask.

"At least we can question him more easily," she said, and set out strips of jerky and a tin mug of water for Chap.

Leesil wasn't so confident, as Chap hadn't been forthcoming so far. He kept this to himself as he helped Wynn haul her belongings to the wagon. The sage dug in her leather pack to bring out a waxed parchment. When she unfolded it, Leesil smelled the mint before he saw the wad of tiny leaves within.

"I thought we were leaving, not setting up house," he chided.

"I left in a hurry to catch you this morning," she said. "I assume none of us have had breakfast."

Magiere shook her head. "We'll get something in the city while we gather supplies."

"No," Wynn argued, digging out yet another parchment pouch. "I need my tea. We can ask the innkeeper to send hot water to your room. A proper start for the day."

Leesil rolled his eyes and headed back to the inn to see if the old proprietress was about.

"Please ask for three clean mugs," Wynn called out, "so we need not unpack any of yours."

Leesil bit on his lower lip as he shoved the inn's front door open. So much for Wynn needing no coddling—and she'd been with them barely since dawn.

That night, as the sun dropped below the horizon, Chane opened his eyes. His internal awareness was unusually precise, even for a Noble Dead. He fell dormant at sunrise and woke at sunset, but for the first time in memory, he felt a moment's uncertainty of his surroundings. Then he remembered.

He was in a country barn that his new companion, Welstiel Massing, had led them to the previous night. An iron pitchfork, shovel, and hoe leaned against the weathered wall

near the double doors, and the place smelled of stale hay,
rust, and dried dung. In place of livestock, all he sensed were
small lives, perhaps mice, and his own rat curled inside his
cloak pocket. Sitting up in the loose pile of old hay, he
watched a fat spider above him crawl across a web glistening
with evening dew. The egg sac it approached seemed ready
to burst with a hundred new lives.

Chane had never awoken in such a place or such a state.
He had plotted the death of his own master and creator to
achieve freedom. Now he grew nostalgic for his clean cellar
room in the lavish home back in Bela, regardless of the servitude and enslavement that had come with it. He pulled his
cloak tighter about himself, though he felt no cold. Freedom
had its price, so it seemed.

"Welstiel?" he said, voice cracking the silence of the decaying barn.

"Here," a cultured voice answered.

Chane started at the movement in the stall across from
him. A figure stirred, arose, and stepped from those deeper
shadows and into the open space between the stalls.

As always, Chane sensed nothing of his new companion.
Both of them were Noble Dead, both adept in their arcane
arts. Welstiel could be seen, heard, and touched, but even to
Chane's heightened awareness, nothing of his life force, or
rather its lack, could be sensed. Chane did not know how this
was so, and that unnerved him further.

Welstiel brushed the straw from his black wool cloak. Of
medium height and build, he appeared to be in his early to
mid-forties by human standards. He wore his dark brown
hair combed back, revealing his most distinguishing feature
of two sliver-white patches at each temple. He wasn't wearing his gloves, and Chane's eyes strayed down to the man's
one tiny oddity—the missing half of the little finger on Welstiel's left hand.

Chane was taller, in his mid-twenties by appearance, with pale skin and red-brown hair halfway to his shoulders, which he tucked behind his ears. They had spoken sparingly the night before upon their first direct encounter following all that had happened in Bela. Now Chane was uncertain what to say or what came next in their newfound association. He reached for his sword nearby, pulled his cloak back as he got up, and strapped on the blade.

"Where to now?" he asked.

"To the inn where Magiere and Leesil slept," Welstiel answered. "We will pick up her trail from there."

Chane hesitated before asking, "Why are we following her?"

Welstiel studied him closely, as he had done on the night before. He stepped closer.

"Why are you here? Why join me?"

His dispassionate tone betrayed only mild interest, but Chane knew his answer must be convincing. He had lived in Bela with his "master," Toret, a lowborn little vampire who had managed to turn a noble like Chane for protection and moderate wealth. Forced to obey this creature that had raised him from death, Chane's first goal had been to find a way to destroy Toret. When the dhampir and her half-blood arrived to hunt Bela's undead, Chane had finally arranged for Toret to lose his head. Yet nothing afterward had occurred as expected.

"I was imprudent," Chane answered. "I sought to be free of Toret, but I had not anticipated losing my home, my inheritance, and—"

"Your welcome at the Guild of Sagecraft?" Welstiel offered.

The halting conversation of the previous night had given Chane a handful of wary moments. Welstiel's awareness of all in Toret's household was unnerving, particularly how much he seemed to know of Chane.

Chane nodded.

"Is that where you sought to spend your time, once free of Toret?" Welstiel asked. "With the old domin . . . Tilswith, I believe, and his little apprentice, Wynn?"

Chane repressed a flinch and remained stoic.

He had counted on retaining the house, retrieving his inheritance, and keeping his undead nature a secret through long years in calming company at the sages' guild. Magiere had exposed him, and though he had escaped slavery, all had been lost—including his welcome in Wynn's company.

He had nowhere else to go.

Welstiel had a purpose in seeking the dhampir, and all that Chane had left was the longing for revenge for what Magiere had cost him. He would bide his time with whatever reasons might satisfy Welstiel.

"I am here now," Chane said. "And you are tracking the dhampir. Why?"

"She is unique and critical to my objectives," Welstiel replied. "But you are young in this existence. Your mortal family must still be alive. Why not go home? If they wish to be rid of you, they could replace part of your inheritance."

Chane shook his head. "I cannot go crawling home for coins. If my father learned how I lost . . . I cannot."

Welstiel scanned their surroundings until his gaze returned to the small brass urn hanging upon a chain around Chane's neck. He pointed first to Chane's sword, then to the urn.

"You are skilled and resourceful, so you may be useful to me. I offer you a bargain. I will pay you enough to travel west across the ocean, to Calm Seatt in Malourné or from there to the Suman Empire and the capital of Samau'a Gaulb. Both cities have longstanding branches of the Guild of Sagecraft. They are like nothing you can imagine compared with the meager offerings in Bela. I will prepare letters of introduction for you to certain connections I have. You have time on your side. In thirty years, few here will even remember your name, and you can return, if you wish. Time is the one true advantage that our . . . kind has."

The last words were spoken bitterly, and this gave Chane pause. Did Welstiel despise his own existence? He pushed the question aside.

"And in exchange?"

"Assist me and be rewarded," Welstiel replied, and then his voice lowered. "And put aside any foolish notion of revenge."

Welstiel's offer still smacked vaguely of servitude, but some of the fog clouding the future lifted from Chane's mind. He longed to speak with Wynn even once more, but this was impossible now that she knew what he was. The prospect of finding a place in another sage's guild was at least a second-best enticement. It filled him with anticipation akin to warm blood flowing from a fear-filled victim. And if Welstiel should forget this arrangement, there remained the smaller pleasure of revenge upon the dhampir, and thereby against Welstiel himself for any deceit.

Chane nodded his acceptance.

Welstiel pulled on his black leather gloves and started for the barn's doors. Chane picked up the sack and leather-strapped chest that held his remaining possessions and followed. They did not speak again while walking.

The woods were not dense between the farmland fields, but Welstiel kept to the trees and off the road until they were almost upon the small inn. It rested amid its scant neighboring buildings beside the main road out of Bela. Ill-kempt, weathered, and with a side stable that leaned severely into its eastern timber wall, the inn had the look of a place rarely visited. Few incoming travelers would stop here so close to a city where better options waited. And once leaving the capital, likely at daybreak, fewer still would pause for the night after traveling such a short distance.

Welstiel knocked at the front door. When no one answered, he knocked again. The door eventually cracked open, and a squat woman with graying hair peered out. She took in Welstiel's wool cloak and opened the entry a little farther.

"Didn't expect no one after dark tonight," she said in a muffled voice, and she frowned at the fine patrons upon her doorstep. "Got a room, but it ain't been cleaned."

Chane stepped closer. It was unlikely a room should remain uncleaned all day in an establishment this small. He caught the scent of cheap liquor beneath stale sweat on the woman's skin. Not expecting further business, she'd probably taken her payment from Magiere, purchased a jug for herself, and spent the afternoon drinking. He wrinkled his nose in disgust.

"We are not seeking lodging," Welstiel said politely. "We arranged to meet friends here but were delayed and have become separated. She is a tall, young woman with black hair traveling with a blond-haired man and a dog. Did they stay here?"

The innkeeper's brow creased over bloodshot eyes, and Chane realized she wasn't as witless or drunk as she first appeared. Her faded brown dress was stained but not dirty, and while wisps of graying hair escaped her braid, it was still reasonably well bound. She glanced at Chane.

"You gentlemen are friends of that rough woman—and that half-blood? He didn't fool me none with the scarf. I saw his eyes."

Welstiel's calm expression never faltered as he held out a

silver shil, far more than a night's lodging would cost in a place like this.

"Could we see the room? Perhaps they left a hint as to where they were going."

The woman's eyes widened for an instant. She grunted, taking the coin, and reached back inside for a lantern. "This way."

She led them along a narrow side hall. Chane followed behind, wondering what Welstiel expected to learn from an unmade bed or a full chamber pot. The old woman opened a lone side door in the hall. The bed indeed was unmade, and the room was bare from what Chane could see as Welstiel and the old woman stepped in ahead of him. Chane heard the pulse beating beneath the innkeeper's flesh in the dim room.

In Bela, he'd often hunted in the poor sectors for concealment. If sustenance was all that time allowed, he was not choosy about slovenly or inebriated prey. He stepped through the doorway and closer, as the old woman followed Welstiel, and he reached for the sagging scruff of her neck.

Welstiel turned, surveying the room by the woman's lantern light, and his gaze stopped on Chane. He slowly shook his head once.

Chane willed his hand down to his side. A flash of anger passed through him, growing upon the smoldering hunger. The innkeeper, as if suddenly aware she was alone with two strange men, turned to look at him.

"Where were they going?" Welstiel asked.

"How should I know?" she retorted. "I ain't no eavesdropper or peeper!"

"Of course not," Welstiel said apologetically and opened his purse again. "Perhaps you heard something in passing that might be helpful?"

Again she grunted. "The half-blood said something about

resupplying in Bela, and the woman talked of the inland road around the gulf. That's all I remember."

Welstiel gave her another silver shil and put his hand on her shoulder. He steered her toward the door as Chane stepped out of her way.

"You have been most helpful, madam," Welstiel said. "If you could leave us, we will be on our way momentarily."

Two coins in hand, the innkeeper glanced at him once and did not argue. "Good night, sir," she said, as if remembering her manners.

"Good night," Welstiel answered, and closed the door behind her.

When the woman's footsteps faded down the hall, Chane turned on Welstiel.

"There is no one else here to sound an alarm. Who knows when we'll have a chance to feed again?"

Welstiel leaned threateningly toward Chane. "You will not leave a trail of torn bodies like some rabid animal. Control your urges or be gone."

Chane did not relish servitude to a new master now that he was free of Toret, but he remained silent. Hunger's heat faded too slowly for comfort, leaving his senses fully open to cast about the small room. The scent of life thinned in the old woman's absence, and something more subtle took its place.

Sweet, almost refreshing, it brought him the memory of quiet moments, ancient texts and scrolls, and a cold lamp gleaming brightly from a tabletop. He pictured Wynn sitting beside him and could almost smell the herbal aroma that followed her everywhere. But the fragrance was not hers.

"So, what now?" he asked, looking about the room at the disarrayed bed, the small stool, the bedside table with its half-melted candle and three mugs.

"We go into Bela and purchase horses," Welstiel replied. "Magiere is beginning a journey. I suspected but was uncertain until now. Purchasing supplies in a large city likely took until noon. They cannot be more than half a day ahead of us, and we might close the distance before sunrise. We must hurry to find a stable still open now that night has come."

Chane barely heard Welstiel's words as he fixated upon the three pottery mugs. He stepped closer to the bedside table, and the strange scent of memory surrounded him. Dread crept into him as he picked up one mug.

At its bottom was a single mint leaf among scant tea grounds.

It had been an evening at the guild barracks, filled with quiet company and the curiosity of a scroll from The Forgotten, the lost history, when Wynn had last offered him such a cup. Sage and scholar, she did not waste her precious existence in the drudgery of the masses, the cattle of the humanity. She was unique, a living treasure.

Wynn had come to Magiere and Leesil.

Had she joined them? It would be a delicate matter to play along until he could decide to take revenge upon Magiere or continue to serve Welstiel's vague agenda. What if Wynn were there, caught amidst all of it and unable to fend for herself?

His hand shook as he set down the mug, and he felt Welstiel's attention upon him.

"What is it?" Welstiel asked.

"Nothing."

The number of mugs was not lost on his companion, and Welstiel stepped closer to pick up the same one Chane had examined. Welstiel turned it slowly, studying the remains in its bottom.

"I doubt they shared tea with the dog. Who was the third person?"

Chane held up his open hands as if he had nothing to offer.

Welstiel returned the mug to its companions upon the table. "Shall we go?"

Chane's attention hung one moment longer upon the mug, with the scent of mint still filling his head.

The city of Bela had faded from sight, and Chap darted through the roadside brush in the dark chill air. Nightfall had passed, but Magiere still pressed them onward, as if half a day in the city had delayed their journey too long, and they needed to make up ground. Chap heard the wagon rolling along the road behind him.

His companions had purchased heavy winter cloaks, a few extra shirts, and ample supplies, though perhaps not enough of the smoked mutton that Chap had found in an open market. They were well stocked and back on the open road once again. It should have been a joyful change. He could not stop this journey, nor would he wish to if it would lead them to the answers they sought. But seeking Magiere's past was another matter.

Chap ran, feeling his body's strength and speed as wild grass pulled at his silver fur. He slowed to circle into a sparse grove, paws treading across the mulch floor of the small clearing therein.

A breeze lashed his coat, striking downward from the sky instead of through the trees. The answering hushed chatter of branches did not follow immediately. He heard the forest's whisper all around him.

Chap spun about with a low rumble in his throat.

The clearing was loosely walled with scattered spruce and beech trees grown tall from roots sunk deep into the earth. Branches reached out to one another, like interlacing a circle of sentinels holding hands. He peered between them into the dark woods beyond, searching, but there was nothing out of place. Yet the wall of trees thickened in places where he had looked away too long and back again. Movement within their branches made the limbs sway ever so slightly.

Fool . . . miscreant . . . betrayer!

Whispers lashed into his thoughts from all around, and Chap snarled, kicking up needles and leaves from the forest floor as he spun about.

Eyes glittered at him from dark shadows beneath the branches, like stars pulled from the sky and held captive amid the foliage. A flutter of wings passed overhead, and Chap ducked instinctively. Claws skittered on bark as some small creature raced up the trunk of the largest of the trees now ringing him in.

Chap turned toward the ancient sentinel with its gnarled bark and full spread of crooked limbs, not yet cowering under the shame rising inside him. The movement of unseen living creatures made the dark spaces between its branches open and close like mouths taking in breath to denounce him with every exhalation.

Fallen is our kin in his flesh. So distracted from purpose.

Chap shrank back with his eyes upon his accuser. He felt its sentiment echoed by unseen others all around him.

His kin gathered here.

All around in the forms of the forest they came. Within leaf and needle, branch and trunk, and small bright eyes peering out at him from the dark spaces. Even within the air and earth was the growing presence of them—of the Fay—until he felt them in the tingle of his skin beneath his thick fur.

The ring of woods about him thickened with their presence, and all attention was upon Chap alone.

He answered back. *I have not failed yet.*

The crackle of wood filled up the clearing. *But you permit the child of the dead to wander the path you were sent to turn her from? Turn her aside!*

Chap flinched, standing rigid before the old tree, and he dropped his head. *How . . . What more could I do?*

A flight of birds darker than the night broke from the tree limbs to dive at him. Chap leaped aside, and their screeching echoed well after they dispersed back into the woods.

Force her . . . , came the answer.

Chap backed away one step—*No.*

Charm her. . . .

A low rumble escaped his throat as outrage washed away shame. He had been sent to keep Magiere from the past, from the truth of her origins, but his kin asked too much. He would not force Magiere's decision. He would not influence her mind.

Never.

The clearing's air began to churn. Chap darted to one side, but the whipping breeze followed. Leaves and twigs, dirt and pebbles ripped from the forest floor to lash at him. He crouched down upon the ground with closed eyes as sorrow coursed through him. He would not force Magiere, not dominate her like a slave, but neither would he leave her.

I am with her always to guide her. I have not failed yet.

The churning air quieted, and the pelting of his body ceased.

Silence lingered until Chap thought he was once again alone, but he still felt his kin all around, quiet and contemplative until the acknowledgment came. *We cling to hope.*

Chap heard his own labored breathing, felt the pounding of his heart and the cool earth beneath his belly. All else in the woods was quiet. Even the tingle on his own skin had faded.

A light breeze made the branches sway and rustle. No longer a wall of limbs and shadows, they were as widely scattered as when he'd first entered the clearing. When Chap lifted his head, his kin were gone, and all that remained was the living world around him.

"Chap!" Leesil's voice called out. "Where in the seven hells are you?"

He turned and loped toward the road but stopped short to look back, then sat down to wait halfway between road and clearing. When the wagon rolled up, Magiere pulled the horses to a halt.

"No more running off," Magiere grumbled at him.

Wynn clambered out of the wagon's back, wobbling slightly as she rubbed her stiff legs. Outfitted in breeches, stout little boots, and a white shirt, her hooded short-robe did not quite reach her knees. She looked strange, perhaps less solemn, without her long gray robe.

"I do not care how far you want to get from the city," she said on an exhale, and glared up at Magiere on the wagon's bench. "This is far enough for one day, let alone part of a night."

Before Magiere could answer, Leesil hopped down from his place beside her.

"I have to agree," he said. "And Chap's already found a decent clearing to camp for the night."

"We could have booked passage on a schooner," Magiere said, and tied off the reins. "That would have taken us straight across the gulf to the Vudran Bay and the mouth of the Vudrask River. Then we needn't bother with this wagon—or camping at night."

"I told you," Leesil responded, "I have no intention of ever voluntarily climbing back onto some floating casket. Watching my food come up over and over again is not my idea of entertainment."

An old argument, but its familiarity brought Chap no comfort. And yet, he had made his point to his kin. He would not fall from his way, and he would not dominate or enslave

Magiere's will. Persuasion was another matter, and there was
time left to change her path.

As Wynn unpacked and Magiere tended the horses, Leesil
walked toward Chap with his waterskin in hand. He patted
Chap on the head as he passed, then stopped with a wrinkle
of his nose.

"What have you been rolling in?" Leesil muttered, and
wiped the dirt off his hand from touching Chap's head.
"You . . . a Fay? My splinter-ridden backside! Less than a
day out, and already you need a bath."

Chap lay down in that very spot and watched over his
companions until late into the night.

Chapter 2

Over a half moon later, Magiere reined in her shaggy pony with a sigh as she waited for a sullen Leesil to catch up.

"Half-mad bag of bones," he muttered once again to his mount.

From Bela, they'd traveled inland down the Belaskian peninsula and south of the Inward Bay, then eastward along the Gulf of Belaski's lower coast. When they reached the head of the Vudrask River, Magiere had decided to sell the wagon and horses to buy passage upriver on a barge. Wynn was indifferent with fatigue, but Leesil quickly agreed. As much as he despised sea travel, rivers didn't roll endlessly, making his food rise in his throat. The barge's smooth glide was also preferable to jostling along upon a wagon bench. Even against the mild current, at most times the barge was as quick as traveling by road. The riverside paths were clear and close, and teams of mules were set ashore to pull the barge as they headed southeast upon the Vudrask toward Magiere's past.

The quiet voyage brought Magiere tranquillity as she huddled beneath a blanket with Leesil. Wynn and Chap stayed close together, as well. Their trek inland seemed a blur of lost memory rather than recent events, and Magiere pulled close to Leesil that first day on the barge.

"We haven't had much time to ourselves," she said to him. "One night. That's all."

Leesil smiled at her. "There'll be time enough in this life. I'm in no hurry on that journey."

She remembered the night he'd first kissed her, taking her by surprise as they'd argued in the sage's barracks following the end of their hunt in Bela. The words he'd spoken just before the touch of his mouth still lingered in her thoughts.

"I've lived three lives," he'd said. "As a child in the Warlands, knowing only deceit and death. Then roaming the countryside alone but for Chap. Finally, the game with you, from the night we met . . . with Chap's meddling. I'm looking at a fourth life now. Any life begins by stepping forward to live it. And I say again—I won't die on you."

So little time had passed since they'd curled together the following night in the first inn on the road out of Bela. This new closeness was awkward and strange, but she clung to it. For his sake more than her own, she wished this fourth life to be his last and longest.

Leesil's hand rested upon her thigh beneath the blanket as the barge slipped along the river. She put her hand on top of his, thumb wrapping around his wrist. She felt the scars there from her own teeth—from the long lost night in Miiska when he'd saved her life with his own blood. Those marks made fear crawl through her, but she refused to pull her hand away.

Magiere watched the autumn-gilded world glide by, saw its changes not only in season but in the land itself as they passed through the far reaches of Belaski on the south shore and Stravina to the north side. After seven more days, they passed beyond the well-kept ways of Belaski and into another world, where the river became a border between Stravina and Droevinka. Neither country had Belaski's wealth or organized government to oversee even the main land routes along the Vudrask. As the river narrowed and its current increased slightly, the bargemen switched their own mules for ox teams chartered from local farmers eager for income during the fallow time. Passage became difficult and slow. After spending one day to cover four leagues, they stopped at a large village.

Magiere intended for them to ride the barge a bit farther, but her home village, Chemestúk, was a three-day ride away. This stop would be the last place to purchase mounts. When she suggested this to Leesil, he threw a fit.

"Horses? Trust my neck to some flea-bitten bag of muscle lunging around on four stick legs, and lurching at every windblown leaf? I'd rather puke my way up the coast on a cargo schooner!"

The following quarrel made the barge crew cease their dockside duties and stare—not to mention villagers close enough to overhear. In the end, Magiere purchased three sturdy ponies and a pack mule, then bullied Leesil into the saddle, while Wynn finished repacking their supplies.

That had been three days ago, and Magiere now waited upon her pony for Leesil to catch up. He'd barely spoken all day except to mumble colorful curses at his shaggy mount, which ignored most of his demands.

Magiere surveyed her dank homeland. Old trees were dotted with moss that dangled in scant beards from the branches. The ground was perpetually moist in the chill air, and beneath the aroma of loam and wild foliage was an ever-present scent of decay. The thickened forest nearly blotted out the cloud-coated sky, with only a brief respite whenever the puddled road swerved closer to the open riverbank. Droevinka was held in perpetual dusk by its shadowed and twining trees. Even when rain didn't fall, the murky canopy dripped upon them.

Magiere looked back for her companions. Wynn followed last with the tethered pack mule, Chap trotting along beside her mount. Leesil's charcoal-gray scarf, now spotted with drizzle, sat askew on his head, exposing a tangle of white-blond hair and one slightly pointed ear.

"Of all the idiotic ways to cross land," he grumbled. "My backside will never be the same."

"We're close," Magiere half whispered, "but we'll stop for the night."

He quieted in surprise and looked up at a patch of gray sky between the treetops. Magiere knew it was unusual to halt this early, and Leesil studied her, all traces of irritation gone.

"There's still a bit of light left," he said. "Are you all right?"

"Yes . . . ," she started. "Only . . . I've stayed away from this place for so long."

He reached out and grasped her wrist, slender hand warm against her skin.

"It's a little late to ask, with a long road behind us," he said. "But are you sure you want this? We can turn back, head north through Stravina and into the Warlands."

The urge to follow him away from this place made Magiere tense at the suggestion. The desire to flee her past as she'd done years ago—this time with Leesil beside her—was so strong. But there were questions to answer.

What am I? . . . Why am I here?

Why was I made . . . by an undead to hunt its own kind?

Wynn pulled her pony to a stop behind them and slumped in the saddle. Magiere still regretted allowing the sage to accompany them. The damp chill was taking its toll on Wynn, though she never complained.

"We'll stop," Magiere said, pulling her wrist from Leesil's comforting grip. "Wynn, pick a spot and rest. Leesil will start the fire while I tend the ponies."

Wynn lifted her head, brown braid darkened by the misty air. "I will be fine . . . once I prepare some tea."

They busied themselves with their tasks. Chap followed Wynn about as she as unpacked bedrolls and filled the tin teapot. Leesil took out an oilcloth sack of dry kindling and sparked a small fire that sputtered and smoked from the damp wood he fed it. He scrounged small twigs to dry by the flames so he could replenish his kindling. Magiere tethered the ponies to a stout spruce near a patch of grass and brought them oats and water. The road they'd traveled was little more than a mud path, and the going hadn't been smooth.

"A king should pay more attention to the kingdom's roads," Leesil muttered, pulling biscuits and apples from a burlap sack.

"Droevinka has no king," Wynn said.

Leesil handed her an apple. "What?"

"There is no hereditary monarchy, only a grand prince."

Leesil snorted. "What's the difference? A king by any other title . . . is most often still a tyrant—or at best, oblivious."

Magiere knew the distinction in her homeland well enough, though she'd never cared to comprehend rulers and their ways. It would have changed little in her early life.

"I've read some of the Belaskian histories," Wynn said, sitting and gathering a blanket around her legs. "There is a considerable difference. Droevinka is divided among houses, each one headed by its own prince in a bloodline claimed to be noble. Most are descended from the peoples who migrated here or invaded this territory in the far past. Many of the houses are named for their original people, and they all serve the grand prince. A new grand prince is chosen every nine years by the gathered nobles. For over a hundred years, no one has claimed the title of king."

"A few have tried," Magiere said, too preoccupied to feel bitter. "Their constant plots and schemes leave little attention for anything more than each house keeping a throttlehold on its province. Villagers pay taxes and pray their lords don't become ambitious. Better to scrape out a living as a serf than to die and rot as a conscripted soldier in their prince's bid for a king's crown."

Chap whined, and Wynn reached into her pack for the large hide parchment with its elvish symbols.

"So who rules the land we're on now?" Leesil asked.

"The Äntes," Magiere answered.

"They hold most of the land closest to the river," Wynn added. "One of the oldest houses. Magiere would know more."

Leesil raised a blond eyebrow at Magiere.

"They would be your heartless tyrants," she whispered. "That's all you need know."

Leesil frowned as he checked his kindling drying beside the fire.

Wynn turned to Chap. *"Ag'us a'wiajhis tú oijhchenis?"*

After so many nights, Magiere knew this one phrase, though there wasn't really a need for Elvish to ask the dog what he wanted to eat. He'd eat most anything dangled in front of his nose, and the choices were limited anyway. Chap scooted close to the sage and reached out a paw to touch a few symbols on the talking hide.

"Dried fish," Wynn interpreted, following the thumps of the dog's paw. "A skinned apple. Leesil, I need a knife."

Leesil's frown deepened. He rolled his shoulders as if the shirt beneath his wool cloak itched. Magiere tried to ignore his reaction.

Such exchanges with Chap still bothered Leesil. In all

honesty, now that the dog's nature was partially revealed, Magiere had begun to appreciate how well Wynn communicated with Chap. Rather than begging or carrying on in his usual dramatics, Chap pawed at Wynn until she brought out the hide. Yet beyond this simple chatter, he revealed little more concerning his nature as a *majay-hì* or his reasons for meddling in Leesil's life to bring him into Magiere's company years ago. He ignored the talking hide whenever Wynn raised such issues. Chap's longstanding deception still grated on Leesil's nerves, and troubled Magiere. Sooner or later, Chap would have to answer for this.

Leesil pursed his lips, handed over his knife, and then pulled out some smoke-dried fish. Wynn went to work peeling an apple.

Staring into the fire, Magiere's hand settled absently on her falchion's hilt, middle fingertip tracing the small glyph in its pommel. The blade injured a Noble Dead like no other weapon. This, her studded hauberk, and two amulets had been left to her by a father she'd never known upon the death of a mother she'd never met. During the battle in Bela, she'd given Leesil the topaz amulet that glowed yellow when an undead was near. She no longer needed it; her dhampir senses were enough to warn her, and the amulet might well warn Leesil of danger if she couldn't.

The other trinket remained a mystery, in part, but she wore it in plain view. A small half-oval tin backing held a chip of bone with mysterious fine writing carved into its surface. It had been used only once, and she'd been unaware of that until too late. Welstiel had told Leesil that a dhampir could absorb life from blood only if the bone touched her skin while she fed. Leesil had recklessly done just that, feeding her from his own wrist when she'd been wounded during their first hunt for Miiska's undead. She touched the amulet now and wondered how dependable Welstiel's words might be. The bone amulet felt warm, perhaps from the fire, and she scooted back to sit against a tree trunk.

All traces of daylight disappeared, and darkness closed around the camp. Leesil picked up a wool blanket and came to settle beside her. As he covered both their legs, Magiere reached around him and pulled him close until he leaned into her arms. His warmth against her burrowed deeper than the heat of the flames, smothering her chill. Leesil leaned his head back on her shoulder, watching Wynn feed Chap slices of a peeled apple.

"She's spoiling him," he whispered.

Magiere almost smiled. Tomorrow, they reached Chemestúk, her . . . home? No, not anymore. Her home was far away, at the Sea Lion tavern in the port town of Miiska, where she lived a peaceful life with Leesil. How long would it be until she was truly home again?

For this moment, she held on to Leesil's warmth and the sight of a large wolfish dog sloppily chomping pieces of apple.

Welstiel rolled in his dormancy, the sleep of the undead, trying to hide his dream-world eyes from the black-scaled coils swirling on all sides of him. Like dunes of obsidian sand in a windstorm, they undulated with no beginning or end. In this dream place he returned to so often, his eyes would never close, and watching the coils for too long made him tremble with nausea.

He had thought his dream patron would be angry, but he felt no ire or irritation surrounding him. He felt nothing but alone—and watched.

"Please . . . give me your counsel," he whispered.

The answer echoed into his thoughts from far away.

Continue . . . follow.

Welstiel rolled again in dormancy. His patron's black coils

faded to the monotone darkness of sleep. He thrashed over on his side and out of slumber, fully conscious.

He sat up on the floor of an abandoned shrine on a forgotten trail off a back road in Droevinka. Stone walls were stained by age and grime, and the pillared archway had lost its door to rot in years past. He and Chane had taken refuge here before dawn as they tracked Magiere inland. The altar behind him was devoid of statuary or emblems, any such likely stolen long ago after devotees had abandoned this place's spiritual patron. Leaves, blown soil, and debris had thickened in the corners and crevices, and spindly weeds sprouted here and there.

He stood up, still shaken from communing with his dream patron, and looked about. "Chane?"

His companion was gone. How long had the sun been down? Lately, when rousing from his vivid communions, Welstiel's internal awareness of the sun became less and less acute. This disturbed him as he stepped outside.

The thick forest was quiet except for the infrequent call of a bird and the patter of drizzle. There wasn't even a breeze to rustle brush and branches. He remembered they had passed a tiny village—barely a collection of huts—shortly before dawn. Chane had been restless. Had the fool gone to feed?

Welstiel stepped back inside to gather his things and don his cloak, preparing to search for Chane, and then he stopped. He was alone, and while traveling with a companion, such moments would be rare.

He had not quite realized how difficult it would be to track Magiere, as she could move freely during the day while he had to take shelter. After the past few nights' journey, he had an unpleasant idea of where she might be going.

She headed southeast at first, which had confused him. He expected her to leave the Vudrask River and turn north into Stravina. He almost lost track of her on the night after she abandoned the barge, and he sent Chane on an errand in order to gain a few moments' privacy to scry for Magiere's whereabouts.

He couldn't waste another moment alone.

Kneeling in the shrine, Welstiel removed a brass dish from his pack and placed it on the mulch-strewn floor with its domed back facing up. Murmuring guttural words, he drew his dagger and sliced a shallow cut in what remained of the little finger of his left hand. He watched his own black fluids drip once, twice, three times to collect in a tiny bulge at the center of the plate's back. The stub of bone in his little finger felt warm. It took a moment's focus of his will to close the tiny wound.

The dark droplet upon the brass plate's back began to move. It ran slow in a short line away from the center, heading east by southeast.

Welstiel cleaned the plate and dagger, tucked them away, and stepped back outside, prepared to hunt for his errant companion, Chane.

There was no longer any doubt. Magiere headed toward Chemestúk.

Wynn watched Magiere and Leesil across the fire as they whispered to each beneath their blanket. Foolish though it was, this familiar sight made her lonelier with each passing day. She did not wish to invade their newfound closeness, but it made her feel like an outsider.

Nothing on this journey was as she had imagined.

It never occurred to Wynn what life might be like without the constant presence of her mentors and fellow sages. Orphaned as a child, she had been taken in by the Guild of Sagecraft in the kingdom of Malourné across the ocean. In the excitement of the journey's start, Magiere's smoldering demeanor and Leesil's constant humor were an enticing change from all she had known. But after so many days of travel, she missed Domin Tilswith and the comforts of the sages' barracks. At least Chap was constant as her main companion. She ran her fingers through the fur on the dog's neck and heard his rumble of content in return.

She had envisioned herself as the useful scribe and translator for Magiere and Leesil, not unlike the journeyman sages assigned to some noble's house and fief back in her homeland. She would record the details of these foreign lands for the guild's records, expanding upon the vast knowledge the sages swore to safeguard for civilization. But Magiere and Leesil spoke the language of Belaski and had not needed her skills, and now to her frustration, they were in Droevinka. Magiere was the only one fluent in the local language, but even Leesil spoke it well enough to get by.

Wynn, who spoke seven languages, did not speak Droevinkan. Not yet.

Leesil tried to tutor her, but she was at a loss every time they had passed through one of the local villages. Worse, Magiere pressed them onward at a tiring pace. There had been little time to record anything of note—of what little there was to note. The weather was cold and wet, and she did not think she could choke down one more dried biscuit for breakfast. She longed for intelligent conversation and a bowl of warm lentil stew with tomatoes and rosemary. And watching Magiere and Leesil, she wondered what it would be like to nestle beneath a blanket, exchanging whispers of forgotten histories and faraway civilizations . . . with Chane.

Wynn stiffened.

She pushed away such an unsettling notion. Loneliness was getting the better of her. Self-pity was as pointless as pining for a past moment lost forever.

Weighing more heavily upon her was a growing sensation of betrayal, now that she had spent so many days in the com-

pany of Magiere. She had not exactly lied about her reasons
for making this journey, but she had omitted the fact that
Domin Tilswith placed upon her the task of observing
Magiere. This had been his reason in sending Wynn, since
she had already established a connection with Magiere. He
wanted specific accounting of every aspect of the "dhampir"
badly enough to send his apprentice off with two hunters of
the undead—three, counting Chap.

At first, this unique task was the promise of adventure,
and her domin's confidence filled Wynn with pride. She had
been raised by the sages, who cared for her health and hap-
piness, and could provide the guild with something no one
else could. But the reality of secretly studying a traveling
companion and then documenting her findings made Wynn
feel like a spy. Once she had almost told Magiere the whole
truth but thought better of it at the last moment. She could
never predict how Magiere might react to anything, and
Wynn feared being sent back on the first available barge
headed downriver.

Wynn reached inside her pack and pulled out a squat cold
lamp. She lifted its tin lid and glass cylinder and removed the
small crystal it held in place of a wick. She rolled the crystal
between her fingertips. There was little to note regarding
Magiere, as yet, but they had been in Droevinka for some
time. At least she might document the climate and land so far.
Standing, she tried to smile at Magiere.

"I think I will scribe some notes for a while."

Magiere nodded. "Then get some sleep. And try to stay
close to the fire. The nights here will keep getting colder."

Wynn retrieved her materials and, with the cold lamp and
crystal in hand, stepped a short ways off to sit upon a downed
tree. She gently rubbed the crystal between her palms and returned it to its holder in the lamp. Its light burst out to push

back the dark and illuminate the tools of her trade resting upon her lap.

Unstrapping a flat, folded leather bundle, she shuffled the loose parchment sheets within to expose a blank one and carefully uncorked her ink vial to dip a quill. She set to documenting the vegetation they'd encountered, noting where along their path the changes occurred so they could later be referenced upon maps of the territories. It seemed she had written only a few lines when Leesil's voice broke the silence.

"Forgetful gods, Wynn!" he called. "That lamp is brighter than the fire. Put it out so we all get some sleep."

Her writing hand flinched, fouling several characters in spattered ink.

She glanced over to see that Leesil and Magiere had settled for sleep in their bedroll and then looked down at the mess upon her notes. They had rushed all day, and now she was to be rushed through her few useful moments of the evening.

"Sorry," she called back.

Gathering her things, she closed the lamp's shutter to smother its light.

Wynn settled into her bedroll as two tears slid unbidden down the bridge of her nose. Something bumped against her feet, and she peered over the blanket's edge.

Chap panted lightly at her feet, silver coat tinged red gold in the firelight. He stared at her, translucent blue eyes full of sympathy. His tail switched once across the ground, scattering clods of tree needles and wilted leaves.

Wynn held up the blanket's edge, and Chap belly-crawled in beside her. He snuggled against her with his head pressed into the crook of her neck, and she wrapped her arms around him, fingers clutching his long fur. At least Chap was constant.

*   *   *

Since his rise from death to a Noble Dead, Chane had never experienced true hunger. He had never before gone for two weeks without feeding. He was starving for blood, for life to fill him up once again, as he crouched in the brambles a stone's throw from a small cluster of huts.

Upon waking to Welstiel rolling on the floor, whispering to himself again, Chane knew he had to get out and hunt. He could not ride all night again with this emptiness inside him. So, he slipped away while his companion lay dormant.

He could smell living flesh . . . and blood . . . with all his senses opened wide. It was close within those timber and thatch hovels. The scent clotted his mind with memories of split skin in his teeth and salty, warm fluid spilling through his mouth and down his throat. Then followed the sound of a heartbeat that slowed and dimmed in concert to the life energy that rose inside him.

Should he wait for someone to come out, perhaps for firewood or to check one last time on the pen of geese around back? What if no one emerged?

A cottage door opened, and a portly man reached out to grab a few logs from a firewood stack. Chane tensed, but the man never stepped completely out before a woman's shrill voice stopped him.

"Close the door, Evan! You're letting in the cold."

The door closed.

Chane had not developed the mental abilities his master, Toret, had displayed, but he did have a gift for locating the "presence" of others if he concentrated. He focused upon the hut and felt the separate lives of five mortals. There were too many in one place, so he turned his attention to the next domicile and sensed only two.

He walked to the door and knocked. A wrinkled old woman with a long gray braid peeked out. Chane folded his arms around his chest as though chilled.

"Forgive me, old mother," he said, "but my horse threw me half a league back on my way to the next town. I could not find an inn before nightfall. I asked across the way, and Evan told me to see you about a late supper and a spot by the fire."

Her brown eyes were sharp, but he was clearly no brigand in his long tailored cloak and well-made boots. He hoped she would take him for a young merchant.

"No inn here abouts," she said with courtesy more than sympathy. "Evan sent you? That's just like him. The lazy lout barely cares for his own."

"Who is it, Grandma?" came a voice from inside, young and feminine, and Chane's jaw twitched.

"A young man who's lost his horse," the old woman said, chuckling; then she opened the door wide. "Best come in. We'll feed you, but Evan and Olga must put you up for the night. My granddaughter's not married, and we don't need to give idle folks any more fodder for gossip."

So many new sensations surprised Chane of late. True hunger was something he had never experienced while serving Toret, and now he felt genuine relief at being invited inside.

The interior was shabby, as expected, but the stone fire pit in the back wall was a comfort, as was the iron teapot hanging above the flames on an iron swing arm. For a brief instant he thought of fresh mint leaves, and then all such thoughts dissolved as he saw the hut's other occupant.

About fifteen years old, plump and curvy, with a smattering of freckles and wild curls of red hair, she returned his stare with curious eyes.

"Should I fetch Evan?" she asked her grandmother.

"Soon enough, Adena, dear. We'll reheat that stew first."

The old woman walked with effort, as if her bones and joints ached. Chane waited until she reached the fire pit and the girl joined her. The girl picked up a folded rag and lifted the teapot. When the two were close together, Chane stepped up behind the old woman and snapped her neck with one quick jerk.

Her body crumpled to the floor.

The girl dropped the teapot, and water splashed across her dead grandmother. Chane had his hand over Adena's mouth before she could inhale to scream.

She clawed wildly to remove his grip as he leaned close. Her hair smelled of musk and straw, until the fear leaking from her pores overpowered all other scents. He wanted to let her struggle a bit longer until that smell made his head swim with bliss, but he had been too long without the taste of blood and lost control of himself.

He shoved her against the wall and bit into her throat. One outward rip of teeth opened the wound, and he bit down on her throat again. The rush of warm blood flowed into his mouth, down his throat, filling him with life.

At first she struggled, her choked screams muffled beneath his palm. She soon grew silent and stopped moving. Normally, Chane lost himself in euphoria and did not truly taste the blood itself. This time, its flavor engulfed his tongue and gave him a satisfaction he had not experienced before.

He applied more pressure and fed until her heart stopped. When she died, life no longer filled him with each swallow, and he dropped the girl's corpse.

Chane paused to steady himself against the wall. His body was having trouble absorbing life so quickly. No matter what happened with Welstiel, he would not deny himself again for so long.

In this moment, his entire existence seemed one long path of obedience. First his father, then Toret, and now Welstiel. Even filled with warmth and strength from the girl's blood, he shuddered at the thought of his father, Viscount Andraso.

The man was a master of masks. Everyone outside his family and close retinue found him charming, all smiles and good humor. Behind closed doors, he wore another face. His only pleasure derived from domination and cruelty. Chane's mother was a small, bird-boned woman who loved books and music, and she was Andraso's favorite victim. Chane loved her, but every year he watched her disappear further inside herself. He feared his father so much that he never defended his mother. This failure still weighed upon him. But on the day he came into his inheritance, he fled to Bela to find a new life, never realizing what new existence would find him instead. He later learned that his mother had died by her own hand. He did not return home for the burial.

Standing in the hut, feeling stronger than he had in weeks, Chane resolved never to become Welstiel's puppet. They would use each other, and that was acceptable, but the choice to obey or not would be his.

He left grandmother and granddaughter where they lay and walked out into the dense forest. With luck, Welstiel would still be rolling on the floor, mumbling to himself. Chane wondered exactly what sort of creature Welstiel might be. Noble Dead had to feed four or five times in a moon to retain full strength, and to the best of his knowledge, they did not dream.

Chane detested the constant mist and dampness of this somber forest. Who would ever choose to reside here? He started back for the shrine when a figure stepped though the foliage directly in front of him.

"Where have you been?" Welstiel asked.

Chane had not even sensed Welstiel nearby. His traveling companion was not in his usual meticulous state, and his uncombed hair hung in tufts down his forehead. His gaze dropped to Chane's chest with an expression of disgust.

"You have blood all over your shirt."

Chane looked down to see that his shirt was soaked.

"I had to feed," he said, "or I would have been no use to you by morning."

Westiel stared at the blood a moment longer and then straightened himself. "Did you at least get rid of the body?"

"No, I let them lay. No one saw me, and we'll be far gone by morning."

"Them?" Welstiel's jaw tightened visibly as he glared through the dark toward the village. "Which hut?"

Chane heard the creak of leather as Welstiel clenched his gloved hands.

"The second one . . . on the right," he answered.

Welstiel pushed through the brush toward the hut as Chane followed. He opened the door, glancing at Chane as if he were a revolting animal.

"I will take the old woman," Welstiel said. "You carry the girl, since your shirt is already ruined."

This seemed pointless to Chane, but he did not argue. He picked up the girl's body and returned to the forest with Welstiel. They discarded both bodies halfway to the shrine in a growth of dense brush, covering them with mulch from the forest floor.

"Scavengers may finish this, and perhaps no one will know what happened," Welstiel said.

Chane suppressed disdain. He was free and masterless, with strength flowing through him that brought clarity. "Have you discerned which way the dhampir has gone?" he asked.

"Yes," Welstiel answered, not looking at him.

"Then I should change my shirt . . . while you saddle the horses."

Welstiel did not reply as he led the way toward the shrine.

Chapter 3

Leesil reined in his pony at the cluster of dingy huts ahead. In the damp weather, the pounding of villagers' feet and scant livestock had turned the center path to a muddy passage between squat structures with shake or thatched roofs. Lean strands of smoke arose from rough clay chimneys or simple smoke holes. The log post walls were streaked gray where rainfall had washed away the wood's natural color. Beneath the forest scent were the smells of cow dung, soot, and dank hay. Bleakness lingered like a fungal stench in the clearing that held the village captive.

This was Chemestúk.

"We are here?" Wynn asked Magiere. "This is your home?"

"It was," came the answer.

Magiere dismounted, as did Leesil, and Wynn followed their example. Daylight was fading.

"We walk from here," Magiere instructed. "Unexpected visitors need to be noticed well before they enter a village."

Leesil clutched the leather reins and pulled his pony forward. The knot in his stomach tightened as they passed between the outermost huts, and his mind held but one thought.

This is where my Magiere grew up.

She kept no secrets from him. Whatever he asked, she answered, but he'd never inquired, "What was your home like?" or "Who were your people?" Perhaps because he didn't care to think about his own past, and if he had asked her . . .

A way with words wasn't among Magiere's notable skills, and even so, it wouldn't have been enough for what Leesil saw.

Braids of garlic and henbane hung beside doorways with other herbs and dried plants he couldn't name. Strange symbols were carved into the outer walls and doors of most dwellings. Some were faded, while others appeared more recently gouged.

To the south was another clearing, smaller than the village space, where weathered planks, erect stones, and debarked wood shafts sprouted from the ground. Some bore garlands of wilted flowers. Leesil noticed a glitter of light through the tree branches, where a lantern hung from a tall pole.

When one of their own died, these backwoods peasants bought oil before food. They starved to keep lanterns burning for as many nights as possible, in fear of unseen things the recently deceased might attract.

It was all far too familiar, and a shudder of revulsion and shame assaulted Leesil. Around him was the living inspiration for the game that he and Magiere had used to prey upon villages for so many years.

Hunter of the dead.

He'd never imagined Magiere as one of those they'd swindled and cheated. When he glanced at her walking beside him, studying her pale and smooth profile, she looked out of place. It seemed impossible that she'd grown up in this murky world soiled with damp and ignorance. Muddied below the ankle, her boots were sturdy for wear and soundly cobbled. Her black breeches and wool cloak were travel-marred but a far cry from the threadbare clothing of the villagers. She'd pushed back her cloak, sheathed falchion in plain sight for all—perhaps as a subtle warning.

Eyes peered from doorways and windows. A few people in the open stared warily at this trio of trespassers.

Up the road out of the village's west end loomed a squat keep upon a rise lifting out of the surrounding forest. Even at a distance, its dark profile looked worn and ill-kept, like the village. Its upper rim was uneven, perhaps with broken stones, leaving gaps like missing teeth. Leesil felt the chill air sink into his bones as two more thoughts settled upon him.

Magiere's mother had died in that place.

And Magiere had grown up beneath its shadow.

A crack of wood made Leesil jump. He spun halfway around, his hands slipping up opposing sleeves ready to draw his stilettos.

A bearded man in a soiled cap stopped splitting wood and cradled his ax as the strangers passed by. Whispers and mutters grew as more peasants returned from the fields they worked nearby in forest clearings or stepped from cottage doors. Some seemed frightened, while others were openly cold to the point of anger. Half of them carried hoes and spades.

"Night spawn!" an old woman hissed in Droevinkan, and then spat on the ground in Magiere's path.

Chap growled back at the woman, fur rising on his neck as his step quickened. Leesil brushed his fingertips across the dog's head, and Chap slowed to stay behind him.

Magiere wasn't a stranger here, and was even less welcome than they were.

Leesil forced all somber thoughts from his mind. His punching blades were packed on the mule, and stilettos wouldn't do well against this many opponents. To protect

Magiere, he'd have to be fast—and vicious enough to make fear his better weapon.

"Magiere, what is wrong?" asked Wynn. "What did that woman say, and why are they looking at you this way?"

"Stay close," Magiere answered, then whispered to Leesil. "None of your charm. It won't work this time."

Obviously, he thought. Two men approached, and before Magiere could argue, Leesil stepped in front of her.

He assumed the one in front was a village leader. Perhaps sixty or so years but still muscular, he had disheveled gray hair, and a few days' growth of beard. The wrinkled bags beneath his eyes made Leesil think of fungus lumps on a gnarled tree. Little distinguished him from the rest of those present, but his companion's face trapped Leesil's gaze.

He was in his late forties, unwashed hair hanging around his angular features and stubbled jaw—but only half stubbled. One side of his face was a mass of scars up to his eye, as if a torch head had been pressed to his cheek and jaw. The injury made one side of his mouth twist into a permanent grimace, and a wisp of madness flickered in his hazel eyes.

Leesil slipped his hands behind his back, out of sight, and opened one wrist sheath's strap to let a stiletto drop into his palm.

Chap's growl returned, and the closest of the mob pulled back.

"Greetings, Yoan," Magiere said to the elder, and then gave the scarred man a nod. "And Adryan . . . I've come to see my aunt."

Her flat tone puzzled Leesil but not enough to distract him from studying the positions of all around them and any avenues through the crowd. Before Yoan answered, the one called Adryan stepped closer.

"You're not welcome here, you misbegotten *cóshmarúl*!"

he spat out. "You're nothing but darkness, and we've enough of that already."

Magiere had always been quick to return threats in kind. When no response came from her, Leesil turned slightly without losing sight of the two men. Magiere was calm as she stared at her accuser.

Adryan took another step, this time too quickly, and Leesil lunged at him. By the time Adryan's eyes fully widened, Leesil held the flat of his stiletto tip against the man's throat. Gasps and shouts rose among the villagers as most retreated, even those who were crudely armed. Leesil guessed the last thing they truly wanted was a fight with armed strangers.

"I don't care for your manners," he said to Adryan.

Yoan clenched his teeth and glared at Magiere, casting all blame her way. Adryan's surprise faded as he looked back at Leesil.

"And I don't care for the company you keep."

Leesil remained poised, trying to keep track of all movement around him, but he didn't start as Magiere's hand settled on his shoulder from behind.

"Leesil, don't," she whispered.

Before he could argue, a shout carried over the mob's murmur.

"Magiere?"

A plump woman in a faded purple dress pushed through the villagers, swatting and shoving them aside. Gray-streaked black hair was pulled into a braid, much like Magiere often wore. Her deeply lined, round face cast her expression in a perpetual state of ire, and from the way her neighbors stepped aside, it was likely a true enough state. At the sight of Magiere, she stopped with one hand covering her mouth. First disbelief and then joy fought her dour expression.

"Oh, my girl. Is it you?"

Leesil barely heard Magiere's shallow-breathed response. "Aunt Bieja."

"She cannot stay," Yoan said. "You know that."

The plump woman closed on Yoan with crossed arms. "And where'd you be without her? Whose coin paid for that new ox . . . and that steel plow blade you all been sharing since last year? You can chew on my wide leathery backside, you grizzled boar!"

Leesil blinked, too bewildered to smile over the tasteless retort. Magiere had been sending money home? He shoved Adryan back but kept the stiletto held out in warning.

Aunt Bieja slipped past him and wrapped Magiere in a fleshy hug. Magiere stiffened, but her aunt kept murmuring, "My girl, my girl," and Magiere's arms finally clasped the woman in return.

Leesil watched in silence, losing track of Adryan and the village mob for a blink. Chap ceased growling and watched, with perked ears. Wynn glanced about worriedly, and Leesil remembered she couldn't understand much of the Droevinkan being spoken. He sighed through a smile and nodded once to reassure her, then stepped closer to Magiere.

"If this is your aunt, can she cook?" he asked. "I'm sick to death of biscuits and jerky."

Bieja turned to assess him, and joy vanished into suspicion.

"My companions," Magiere said. "This is Leesil and Wynn."

"The four-footed beggar is Chap," Leesil added. "Don't let him near the cook pot."

Glancing at each of them in turn, Aunt Bieja smiled again at Magiere, cheeks pulling back to reveal deep dimples.

"They're all welcome, but I still can't believe you're here." As she led Magiere away by the arm, she shouted back to Yoan. "I'm taking my niece home! Have someone see to their ponies . . . instead of standing about like witless hogs."

Leesil helped Wynn pull their belongings off the pack mule, and then Bieja led them off between two huts. No one tried to stop them. The thought of hot food and a roof to keep off the forest's drip improved Leesil's mood, but not so much that he didn't glance back.

Yoan put a hand on his scarred companion's shoulder, but Adryan jerked free to shamble away. Leesil saw Adryan's wisp-mad eyes watching them before the man slipped from sight through the village.

Welstiel awoke from the black coils of his dream patron, his thoughts upon Magiere. There was no need to scry for where she had gone. Then he realized he lay upon a bed and, across the room, Chane gathered their belongings, his gray rat crawling in and out of the pack as if playing a game.

Finding shelter from daylight became more difficult the deeper they traveled into Droevinka. Abandoned shrines and empty barns or sheds were not common, as the people here tore down anything unused for fuel or other pressing needs. Several times they came dangerously close to being caught by the dawn. As much as Welstiel detested burrowing beneath the forest's rotting mulch for protection from daylight, he preferred to avoid inns, as well. Anyone who slept all day drew attention.

On this evening, however, Welstiel awoke in a bed.

He loathed speaking to these peasants, but as the previous dawn had become a real threat, they'd chanced upon a small village. Chane proved his worth, introducing them as merchants who had traveled all night in a foolish rush to reach their destination. Professed exhaustion, offered coins, and his broken use of the Droevinkan language made his story more convincing. Chane did not use many words, but his manner won peasants over in a way that Welstiel would have found difficult to achieve. There were moments when Chane's sly nature reminded Welstiel of Leesil.

"Are you awake?" Chane asked.

"Yes. The bed was a pleasant change," he answered, sitting up on its edge. "I did not have the chance to thank you for your quick thinking. I manage well with the citizens of Bela, but the people here do not seem to trust me."

Chane continued with his packing.

"It's those white patches in your hair, and your skin is paler than mine. You act too much the noble, and you appear too much the superstitious hearth story told to frighten children. I look the part of a young, struggling merchant."

This was certainly true.

Welstiel noticed that Chane hadn't finished dressing yet. He wore breeches, but his shirt lay on the bed. The skin on his arms was smooth over long muscles, but his bare back and shoulders were covered with a mass of scars. White crisscross marks, so deep they appeared layered, reached from his lower back up to his neck.

"What happened?" Welstiel asked.

"Hmmm?"

"Your back. Our kind should heal of such things."

Chane glanced absently over his shoulder. "My father. Our bodies heal of injuries only after we're turned. This happened before."

Welstiel studied the layers of scars. Lines that crossed created lumps where previously healed wounds had been newly split open at later times. These had been inflicted over a period of years.

"Your father did that to you?" he asked.

Chane ignored the question.

"The horses are ready." He grabbed his shirt and pulled it

on. "The villagers are in from the fields, and we should leave soon."

Welstiel arose, unsettled yet again by his failing sense of time. "How long has the sun been down?"

"Not long."

Welstiel stepped outside. Chane followed, giving thanks and farewells to the peasants lingering near the common house. Once again, they mounted and rode into the night, side by side.

"I was able to buy some grain for the horses," Chane said. "Our supply was low."

Welstiel nodded, the image of Chane's back lingering for an instant in his thoughts. He did not wish to know of Chane's past any more than he wished to share his own. What mattered was their present course.

Wet trees bordered the road leading into the dark, and in that null black ahead, his mind drifted to the abandoned life he had spent in this land. Droevinka had not changed, nor had the people who lived here. Nor his distaste for this place.

"It is time we spoke more candidly," Chane said calmly, as if commenting on the weather.

"Pardon?"

"You were talking in your sleep again."

Welstiel heard nothing from the forest, not an owl or even a squirrel skittering through a tree. He and Chane were alone. He had no response—or not one he was willing to share. Communing with his dream patron took up more and more of his dormant hours, leaving him drained during their night travel, yet revealing less of use concerning what he sought or how to find it.

"Why are we heading east?" Chane asked, reining in his horse. "I have followed you without question, but you said Magiere would turn north, and that was many days back. So why are we heading deeper into Droevinka?"

Welstiel had no intention of discussing his plans, yet Chane had proved useful. Welstiel reined in his horse.

"I believe she has gone to her home village, searching for her past," he said. "Then she will continue on the path I spoke of."

"Her past?"

"She has only recently discovered her nature and little beyond that. I believe she seeks to find out why she exists . . . perhaps even her unknown parentage."

"Then she doesn't know who sired her?" Chane asked. "And will she find those answers?"

"No."

A half-truth, but the best answer to give. Chane's curiosity had to be diverted, and Welstiel needed to retain control. Chane took something from his cloak pocket and turned it slowly in his gloved hand. Soft glimmers of light escaped his fingers.

"What is that?" Welstiel asked.

Chane opened his hand, revealing a small crystal that produced a dim glow. His voice became strangely soft.

"A simple cold lamp crystal . . . made by the sages."

Welstiel urged his mount onward, and he heard Chane following behind.

There had been three mugs at the inn outside Bela, with their remnants of tea and mint, and then there was the young sage called Wynn. How distraught she'd been when she had learned Chane was one of the Noble Dead. And Chane, for a sadistic monster, showed a penchant for the companionship of sages.

Perhaps there was already something that Chane found diverting.

*   *   *

Magiere ducked her head and stepped through the low doorway of Aunt Bieja's hut. She felt a chilling familiarity. So little had changed.

The one room was dimly lit by a small fire crackling in the stone pit set into the right sod-and-timber wall. Over the flames hung a blackened pot on an iron swing arm. The rough table and stools before the hearth were exactly as she remembered, though in place of the candle was a small tin lantern with a cracked glass. Below the front window was the same low bench, but now accompanied by an old spinning wheel, its wood dark with years of use. Pots and cooking implements hung on the far wall beyond the fire. Canvas curtains were nailed to rafters as a partition for Aunt Bieja's bed. In youth, Magiere had always slept on a mat near the fire.

"Looks much the same," she whispered, more to herself than to anyone else.

"Well, you don't . . . you and that sword." Aunt Bieja patted Magiere's cheek before heading for the shelves across the room. "I'd part with a copper chit or two just to see old Yoan falter again at the sight of you."

She chuckled and pulled out two squat candles, lit them from the lantern, and set them on ledges in the wall to spread more light.

Chap, Wynn, and Leesil stepped around Magiere and into the tiny room. Leesil's hand slipped briefly across her back as he passed. She longed to be home again, but her home in Miiska, not here.

Adryan had called her *cóshmarúl,* an old-tongue word for an unseen spirit that sat upon the sleeping and unaware to crush the life from them. The hut's dark walls were suddenly too close for Magiere, this one room smaller than she remembered. Chemestúk was the *cóshmarúl* of her childhood, and it had been waiting for her to come back within its reach.

She'd been perhaps five or six years old when the pain began.

Aunt Bieja had told her of Adryan's hopes concerning her mother, before Magelia had been taken to the keep. When she was a child, Magiere wondered at the burn upon Adryan's face that few would speak of. Never knowing her mother, and not yet old enough to understand why the villagers shunned her, it was easy then to imagine Magelia as someone much like her aunt. Only taller and more graceful.

Late one day, Magiere had wandered from the field, in which Aunt Bieja settled to hoeing, and clambered toward the village graveyard. She'd snatched up wildflowers along the way, for mothers always liked flowers. Most children shied away from the graveyard, but Magiere had no fear of the dead, as yet. Why should she, when her mother was called "the best of people" and she was dead?

It had taken a while to reach her mother's marker under a tall tree. All its lower branches had been pruned away, and the higher ones spread wide in a roof overhead. It was like sitting in her mother's house. A quiet place away from everyone who shouted or made ugly faces at her.

Magiere heard the scrape of footsteps as someone walked nearby with big feet. At first, he lingered out of sight, beyond the clearing's edge. She glimpsed a muslin shirt, gray breeches, and brown boots as the man strolled beyond the trees. Maybe someone else was visiting his dead mother's house, and that was a good thing to do. The boots stopped, and a hand parted the branches. Magiere scooted closer to her mother's marker at the sight of the visitor's scars.

Adryan stepped halfway through the branches and then paused to watch her. Magiere tried to ignore him, tucking more flowers around her mother's marker.

"Come looking for your mother, little thing?" Adryan asked, one hand gripping the branch he'd pulled aside.

It was a friendly question, and why not? Adryan, even with his frightening scars, would have married her mother. Magiere smiled a little at him, for it wasn't often that anyone but Aunt Bieja spoke with her instead of at her.

"I know where she is," Magiere replied, as if the question were just a teasing one. "She's right here, in her house."

The skin around Adryan's eyes wrinkled like his scars.

"No, you haven't found her . . . yet," he said, and his words sharpened like those of the other villagers. "I can send you to her. That's where you belong."

He took another step out of the trees.

The branch slid through his grip, and green needles tore away to litter the ground. His other hand hung at his side, and something in it glinted once in the fading daylight.

Magiere couldn't breathe. She stared at his hand. Not the one with the strange glint, but the other . . . slowly stripping the branch bare as bone.

"Magiere, where are you?"

When her aunt's voice called out her name, Magiere gasped in a breath and looked back the way she'd come, but Aunt Bieja was still too far off. She turned back, and Adryan was gone.

The bare branch quivered in the air. There was no house anymore with her mother waiting in welcome. . . .

A squeeze on Magiere's upper arm startled her from memory. Leesil's fingers circled her arm, and concern marred his tanned features. He leaned close enough that she heard his quick breath in her ear.

"What is it?" he whispered.

Magiere shook her head, tried to smile, but this only made Leesil frown in suspicion.

Wynn dropped her pack by the table and inhaled deeply as she examined the cooking pot.

"Are . . . this . . . *esoni tjèto* . . . are these *shoshovitzí*?"

Her jumbled speech with its mixed-in Belaskian broke the moment, to Magiere's relief.

There were few of her thoughts that she could explain to Leesil while others were present. When she looked away from him, she found Aunt Bieja watching the two of them. Magiere's discomfort rekindled.

Her stout aunt cocked an eyebrow at Wynn's words. Magiere was grateful that it offered a way to avoid both Leesil's and her aunt's curiosities.

"Are these lentils," Magiere translated for the young sage. "Wynn doesn't speak much Droevinkan as yet, only Belaskian."

"Ah, we don't get much of that foreign tongue this far off the main ways," Bieja replied. "I remember a little of it, but I'm half a life out of practice."

The young sage pointed to the cook pot as she looked to Bieja for approval, who nodded. Wynn grabbed a folded cloth nearby with which to grip and lift the pot's lid. She smiled broadly, replaced the lid, and set to digging through her pack and pulling out small pouches.

"May I?" she asked Aunt Bieja in Droevinkan, and switched to Belaskian as she spoke to Magiere. "Tell her this one is rosemary."

Magiere did so, and Aunt Bieja chuckled as she examined each of Wynn's herbs. The two women exchanged one- and two-word questions and answers in mixed tongues. Chap inched closer to sniff the pouches, though this turned out to be a ploy to nose his way toward the cook pot. Leesil stepped in to grab Chap's haunches and pull back the struggling dog.

Bieja still wore the same purple dress Magiere remembered, though now it was far more faded. Several times Magiere had sent money when she was fortunate enough to find a land-bound merchant heading inland toward

Droevinka. She should have known Bieja would give such coins to the village instead of spending it on herself.

The sight of her aunt's kind face, with its broad dimples and wrinkles, filled Magiere with guilt. She'd never sent word of purchasing the Sea Lion, yet nine years later, her aunt welcomed her as if she'd been gone but a moon.

Magiere felt Leesil's hand slide up her back again, and he whispered, "You all right?"

"It's good to see her," she answered.

It was a half-truth and the lesser part of all her thoughts. When she reached up to touch Leesil's shoulder, Aunt Bieja glanced at them again. Magiere neither pulled away from Leesil nor removed her hand. Leesil, not noticing they were watched, stripped off his charcoal scarf and shook out his white-blond hair.

Magiere tensed, forcing herself not to look toward her aunt this time.

Superstition ran deeper here than even the back ways they'd worked in Stravina. She wasn't certain how her own flesh and blood might react to someone of Leesil's unusual ancestry.

"Whatever you're making smells wonderful," Leesil said.

Chap yipped in agreement, which earned him a pat on the back from Wynn. The sage looked happier than Magiere had seen her in some while. The hut was warm and dry, and the scent of lentil stew was mouthwatering.

"Supper for all, though we'll need to stretch it a bit," Bieja answered, and after a moment's hard appraisal of Leesil's hair, she turned to gather more things from her shelves. "Then I think you have much to tell me."

Magiere took a deep breath.

She hauled the bench to the table for Leesil and herself, and they were all soon enjoying the luxury of well-seasoned stew, some late pears, and a loaf of black forest bread. Wynn made small noises of contentment as she ate. Magiere realized the meal was not far from the food served back at the sage's guild. Only halfway through the meal, a loud belch came from under the table, followed by the licking of chops. Chap had finished before anyone else.

The closeness around the fireside table wore away Magiere's first impressions upon stepping into the hut. She'd barely finished a few spoonfuls when Leesil pushed his emptied bowl back.

"So, what exactly was that mob about back there?" he asked of Aunt Bieja.

Magiere stopped eating and stared at him.

"Magiere hasn't told you?" Bieja asked. "About why she left?"

"She wasn't happy here ... wasn't well liked because of her father. But she didn't mention anyone trying to run her off with pitchforks."

Magiere dropped her spoon into the bowl, shifting on the bench. "Leesil—"

"No, I want to know what's going on."

Wynn's attention swung back and forth around the table as she tried to follow the conversation. However, Bieja's glare was purely for Leesil.

"Auntie," Magiere said, hoping Leesil would remain quiet, "we've come to find answers about my mother ... and my father. And there's much to tell you—"

"I can see that for myself, girl," Bieja answered, and folded her hands upon the table.

"I'm not sure where to start," Magiere continued. "For now, we need to know what you know. Things you might not have told me. Little things that seemed not to matter might help. Especially about my father ... anything from the first time you ever saw him."

Magiere waited as her aunt pondered for a moment.

"Perhaps family matters are best left to family," she finally said.

"No." Magiere settled her hand on Leesil's forearm. "They are part of this. . . . It's not just me anymore."

Again, Bieja hesitated. "There were three of them."

"What?"

"I told you . . . your father took your mother when he first came here as lord of the fief, but three of them came that first night. Two noble . . . but the last was a masked thing in a char-colored robe. He's the one who maimed Adryan with no more than a slap."

"Adryan's face?" Magiere asked. "His scars . . . no one would talk about it."

"You can blame that on Yoan," Bieja growled. "Along with the rest of the hog swill poured out over the years. Oh, some truth was well known enough, but he said we'd best keep quiet or invite more misery. And all else that followed, I was forced to obey." She shook her head and mumbled something under her breath. "Adryan tried to protect your mother. They were betrothed—at least he thought so."

Magiere sat silent, chilled inside even near the fire. Through the childhood suffering, the one person she had trusted was Bieja, but her aunt had kept secrets.

"What do you mean *forced*?" she asked. "I've never seen you give in to anyone's wishes unless they fit with your own."

"I lived in fear for Magelia," Bieja said. "My sister was my only companion, and they took her. Sometimes servants came and told us stories of her walking in the courtyard, heavy with child, but she was never allowed out, and we weren't allowed in. I tried many times, sneaking as close as I could, but never saw her and got beaten down twice by patrolling guards. The rest concerning your father you already know. One night, one of those noblemen who took Magelia came to me. His shirt was stained with blood when he brought you within hours of your birth, as well as the armor, the amulets, and that sword. He said they were gifts from your father. He also brought Magelia's blue dress for you. That frightened me more than anything else. The next day, a man-at-arms brought your mother's body down for me to bury, and that was the last we saw of anyone from the keep. I guess they left in the night, though we didn't know it for a while. Not for certain until the next lord assigned to this fief arrived a half moon later."

Bieja closed her eyes a moment.

"I tried to hide you at first and managed for a time. When Yoan found out, he wanted you exposed, cast out in the woods to die for fear of what ill-fortune you'd bring down on the village. I used your sword to hold him off, and told him the village might face worse if we killed a noble's child, forsaken or not. I would have said anything to save you, but fear is the only thing these fools understand. So Yoan and the others let you be—for the most part. But you were still a reminder of those men's ill-favor upon us, especially to Adryan."

Magiere looked away, not wanting to hear any more. Bieja had lied to her for years, but Magiere couldn't escape the image of her aunt holding Yoan off with the falchion.

"I'm sorry," Magiere said. "But you should have told me."

"You were too young, and why burden you more? You'd enough to deal with as a child."

"What was this lord's name?" Leesil asked.

Bieja shook her head. "That was a long time ago, and we weren't worthy of such information. We just called him 'my lord.'"

"Was it Massing?" Leesil pressed.

Wynn straightened, recognizing this one word. Magiere felt as if she'd been struck in the face and turned on Leesil.

"It had to be said," he whispered in apology.

"Perhaps others heard it," Bieja said, pondering the name for a moment. "I can't remember."

"Who is the current lord?" Leesil asked. "Maybe there are still records or some other mention to be found at the keep."

"No lord," Bieja answered. "I guess the Äntes couldn't find anyone willing. Our zupan, Cadell, was appointed as overseer. He and his wife are at the keep now. Cadell is a good man, at least. You can go speak with him tomorrow."

Magiere barely heard her aunt's response. Each time she sought plain and direct answers, the truth, like all else in her life, became muddied.

"Enough for tonight," Leesil said. "Your aunt is right. We can go to the keep tomorrow."

Wynn had been trying to follow the exchange, and Magiere assumed she'd probably understood some of it. The sage sat up straight, on the point of speaking, then appeared to change her mind. She slid off her chair to the floor and began whispering to Chap. The dog looked at her and pawed at the sage's pack. Wynn pulled out the Elvish talking hide, and the two of them went to sit in the corner by the spinning wheel.

"What in the world are those two doing?" Bieja asked.

Magiere sighed. "A long story."

"The long ones are the only ones worth telling," Bieja responded, and her attention turned once again to Leesil. "And I've a few questions of my own."

The older woman got up to pull a tin kettle from beside the fire. She poured tea into unglazed clay cups for the three of them, and Leesil started to fidget.

"Well, it's sort of . . . We have this . . . ," he began.

Bieja clunked the kettle down and snatched up the side of Leesil's long hair, exposing one oblong ear.

"Hey!" was all Leesil got out.

"I knew you were wrong somehow!" Bieja shouted. "What do you think you're doing with my niece, you imp?"

She lunged to the shelves and grabbed an old notched carving knife. Leesil sprang to his feet, both hands going up his opposing sleeves, reaching for his stilettos.

"You may have charmed her wits, but I see you clear." Bieja said. "I know of changelings. I know a forest spirit, right enough."

"What—?" Leesil sputtered. "I'm not—hold off a breath!"

Before Magiere could grab Leesil or try for her aunt, Leesil's surprise and reluctance undid them both. Instead of drawing steel on Magiere's only relative, Leesil back-pedaled. The bench caught behind his legs, toppled, and Magiere tumbled over backward to the hut's floor.

"Auntie—no!" she shouted, and kicked the bench out from under her legs.

Bieja rounded the table, closing on Leesil, who scooted backward across the floor as fast as he could. She stomped on his outstretched leg, pinning one of his feet.

"And you aren't taking her into your *zûnû* world," she snapped, "like some lost maid in the woods!"

"Magiere!" Leesil yelped.

He sounded more pathetic than she'd ever heard before, but it was Wynn who scrambled across the floor on all fours, waving her hands up in front of Bieja.

"No, not . . . bad . . . friend," was all Wynn could get out.

Bieja shoved her off with little effort. "Get your addled wits out of my way, girl. He's charmed you, too."

The delay was enough for Magiere to regain her feet and grab Bieja's wrist.

"Auntie, stop it! He's not some lecherous spirit trying to drag me off. He's just an elf."

"I am not," Leesil snapped, pulling up his stomped foot and holding it with both hands. "My mother was."

"Bog swill!" Bieja spat. "No such thing as elves—that's just foreigners' tall tales. No such creature has ever been seen hereabouts."

"Oh, deceitful deities," Leesil muttered.

Chap let out a yawn from the corner, where he still sat throughout the ruckus. Wynn whispered harshly at the dog in Elvish. Magiere wasn't certain what the sage had said, but Chap looked away, dropping his head.

"You're a big help," Leesil said to the dog.

Chap huffed and lay down on the floor.

The irony of Bieja's exclamation hadn't escaped Magiere. She wanted to pour out the whole story to her aunt, who still loved her without question, who had held off a village elder with a sword and assaulted the evil forest spirit trying to beguile her niece.

But she couldn't speak of everything.

Not that she and Leesil had spent late summer and early fall hunting vampires of myth and superstition. Not that she was descended from these same Noble Dead who preyed upon the living. And certainly not that for years she'd made a living—and even sent home part of the coin—from swindling villagers out of their savings using their own fears against them.

"Leesil and I own a tavern . . . but that came later," she said. "And elves are flesh and blood, though few have seen them. Leesil's mother was one of the few who've lived among humans. For the rest, I don't know where to start."

Bieja eyed Leesil, clearly uncertain if her niece was of her own mind. "How did you meet this here . . . elf?"

"I'm not an elf," Leesil muttered.

"He tried to pick my pocket," Magiere said without thinking, and her aunt glared at Leesil with malicious intent.

"That's not what happened," Leesil blurted. "Well . . . sort of."

Magiere sighed and carefully lifted the knife from her aunt's grip. Some things had to be explained, if not all.

Chapter 4

Leesil awoke the next morning to a chilly room. The fire had died in the night, and there was a chill in his stomach, as well. Today, they visited the keep where Magiere's mother had died.

Magiere woke beside him on the dirt floor and pulled back their blanket. Her stoic front couldn't hide the dread in her eyes. The sooner they finished with this, the sooner he could take her from this place.

She remained silent through their light breakfast, and this bothered Leesil as never before. Perhaps because there were so many unanswered questions concerning Magiere's past or even questions he couldn't yet imagine. However, now that Aunt Bieja was certain he wasn't going to spirit off her niece, she sat and chatted with him, explaining all she could of local affairs. The zupan tending the keep and fief wouldn't be available until midafternoon. Still but a commoner himself, he had his own lands and household to tend, so he preferred dealing with fief matters in the early afternoon, and left any audiences for late in the day.

"Fief matters?" Leesil asked. "What exactly does he do?"

Bieja smiled. "We're more fortunate than most clanships.

Cadell handles the accounting himself and checks to see how the villages in each zupanesta in the fief are faring. There are five villages alone for our clan's zupanesta. If disaster strikes any village, and they cannot pay all their taxes, he faces the collectors of the Äntes house himself."

Leesil's fondness for Aunt Bieja grew steadily, although she could be a little daunting at times. Strong and sensible, she was knowledgeable in spite of a lifetime of superstitions. After the previous night's misunderstanding, it was plain that lightning tempers coupled with protective natures ran in this family's women.

"Well, if we can't visit the keep until later," he said, "what can we do around here? By necessity, I've gotten handy at mending roofs and old furniture."

"I understood some of that," Wynn said, clearing bowls from the table. "If we have the morning free, I would like to wash out some clothes. Magiere?"

Magiere nodded as she shook out her black hair and began to braid it. "We'll tend to our own needs while we can. There's no telling when we'll have another chance."

"Here, let me braid that for you," Bieja said, stepping around behind her niece.

Magiere stiffened, but Bieja smoothed wayward wisps of hair back from her face. Magiere relaxed as her aunt's nimble fingers weaved and plaited.

Leesil tried not to stare but kept glancing over again and again. Bieja took her time, perhaps making up for the years she'd been unable to care for her niece. With an ache in his chest, he got up to step outside.

The rest of the morning was spent washing and repacking. Leesil split firewood for Aunt Bieja and stacked it beside the hut. They avoided the other villagers as much as possible, and no one stopped to visit. The day would have been peaceful if not for Chap's fretting and scratching at the door. But whenever Leesil let him out, he'd look around the village and whine pitifully.

"What's wrong with him?" he asked Wynn.

Wynn tried speaking to the dog with the talking hide, but shook her head. "He keeps saying *horses* and *journey*. He wants to leave."

Leesil patted the dog's head. "Hopefully tomorrow."

This only made Chap more irritable. He growled low under his breath as he slunk back to the hut's far corner and lay with head on paws, watching all of them. Leesil didn't know what to do for him.

At midafternoon, Magiere looked out the front window and heaved a sigh. Her jaw tensed as she turned to Leesil. "It's time."

He nodded and looked at his punching blades lying upon their bundled belongings in the corner. Their forward ends were shaped like flattened steel spades with elongated tips and sharpened edges all around. At their bases were crosswise oval openings, allowing the blades to be gripped by their backsides for punching. A gradual "wing" curved back from the outside edge of each blade head and ran the full length of his forearm, ending where his elbow would be. He'd had special sheaths designed so he could strap them to his hips.

"Blades . . . or just stilettos?" he asked.

Magiere hesitated before answering. "I'd rather not look ready for a fight, but I don't care to be unarmed either. Can you cover the blades with your cloak?"

She'd already donned her own cloak and pulled it around to hide her falchion, though the sheath's tip peeked out from behind.

"Fair enough," he replied, and followed her example as he shifted into Belaskian for Wynn. "Try to get Chap to stop whining. He's making my head ache."

Wynn was dressed in her breeches and a red shirt borrowed from Leesil, as her white one was still drying. The shirt was much too big, but she'd managed to tuck it in. She pulled on her hooded short robe, but before she answered, Chap lunged for the open doorway.

The dog spun around to stand in the way, blocking it. Whining shifted to growling. The daylight spilling through doorway cast his silver-gray fur in a gossamer blue glow. His crystalline eyes filled with desperation as he bared his teeth and looked to Magiere.

"Stop that!" Leesil ordered. "What's wrong with you?"

He reached out to grab the dog by the scruff, and Chap turned on him, snarling.

"He does not want us to go," Wynn said. "Each time we mention the keep, he gets more upset."

"I don't want to go either, but we must," Magiere said in a sad voice, and she stepped closer to the dog. "There is no other choice if we want answers."

Chap barked twice, his arranged reply for *no,* and growled louder.

"Wynn, can't you talk some—?" Leesil started, but a small realization occurred to him. He shifted back to Droevinkan as he spoke to the dog. "All right. You win. We'll pack up the horses and leave."

Chap's attitude didn't change, as if he hadn't understood a word said. Leesil turned his back to the dog, facing Aunt Bieja behind the table. She looked quite put out by the dog's outburst.

In all their years together, Leesil had spoken almost nothing but Belaskian around Chap. It was the most common language spoken in the coastal lands, even in the backwoods of Stravina. Elvish was the only other language that he knew Chap understood. It seemed even a Fay in a dog's body had to actually learn languages like anyone else.

Chap didn't understand Droevinkan any better than Wynn. Perhaps less.

Leesil smiled, which made Aunt Bieja frown in puzzlement.

"Do you have someplace we can lock him up?" Leesil asked quietly.

"There's a shed out back," Bieja offered. "The door could be barred, but how will you get him there?"

Chap remained on guard, and Leesil gave Magiere a knowing look before he turned to Wynn, shifting languages yet again.

"Let's not leave our gear in the way. We'll take it out back to the shed." He hefted his pack, while Wynn and Magiere followed suit, and turned back to Chap. "Get your mangy backside out of my way. You've been a pain in my head all morning, and I've had enough."

He shoved Chap with a swing of his leg, hoping he didn't get nipped. Chap shuffled aside with a rumble, and Leesil pushed Magiere out the door ahead of himself.

"Quickly," he whispered to her.

Magiere gave him a perplexed look but took off at a jog around the side of the hut. Chap lunged forward, but Leesil blocked the dog as he ushered Wynn out. He didn't want to anger Chap further, but he needed to throw the dog off balance.

"Valhachkasej'â!" Leesil snapped, using one of the few Elvish phrases he knew. "You deceitful mutt."

And he slipped out the door. There was only a moment's silence before he heard an indignant snarl from Chap.

Leesil sped around the hut to find Magiere and Wynn standing beside the open shed door. He pulled up short to flatten himself against the hut's rear wall. When Chap skidded around the corner, he saw only Magiere and Wynn at first. The dog lunged forward, spotting Leesil too late. Leesil stepped in behind Chap, grabbed the dog by the haunches in midlunge, and shoved. In a clatter of wood scraps, hoes, and racks, Chap crashed into the shed's enclosure.

Magiere swung the door shut, and Leesil threw his back against it, digging his heels into the ground. The snarling and battering from inside began immediately.

"Could you, um . . . find something to brace this shut, please?" he asked Magiere.

She gave him a scowl that said this was another of his more idiotic schemes, then picked up a stout spade left outside and braced the shed's door with it.

Wynn's small mouth dropped open, as Chap continued to thrash about inside the shed.

"How could you do this to him? As a Fay, Chap may know far more than we do of the world. If he does not want us to be here, he must have a reason."

"And he's not giving it to us," Magiere answered. "Until he does, this is the only place where I might find answers. If he won't help, he can stay out of my way!"

Wynn flinched at her harsh tone. "Perhaps I should stay with him?"

"No, I'll need you if we find records," Leesil said, and he stepped away from the shed door. "I can read some Droevinkan, but you're the scholar."

Leesil led the way out of the village and toward the keep. They passed a few nervous villagers on the way, but none spoke to them. The keep disappeared from sight as they trudged the road through the forest. Climbing a final rise, Leesil felt the previous dusk's tension return as the keep reappeared at the crest of the hill, and he paused at the break in the trees.

It was a simple fortification, and more than a bit worn with age. Moss grew between lichen-spotted stones on its lower half. To one side was an undersized stable, while the other held a small abandoned barracks with a clay chimney. Around all the grounds was a stone wall decayed over the years to half height, and its gate doors were missing. The surrounding forest had been cleared away from the wall for thirty paces on all sides.

Wynn stepped close to Leesil, shivering in the dank afternoon. She was so small that she could have stood beneath his chin. With her hood up over her hair, only her oval face showed, making her anxious eyes seem rounder as she looked up at him. Magiere stood to his other side, unblinking.

Two men stood inside the courtyard near the keep's front doors. They talked quietly to each other, while a third led a horse to the side stable and a water trough.

"Are we still going in?" Wynn asked.

"Magiere . . . you know the way," Leesil said.

"No," she replied. "I don't."

He raised an eyebrow.

"This is as far as I've ever come," she said. "I was forbidden to come here. . . . No one from the village ever came here by choice."

"But you spent your whole childhood living nearby," Wynn asked in surprise. "You must have—"

"I sneaked up here alone a few times," Magiere said, "but never farther than the tree line."

Leesil put his arm around behind Magiere and walked forward slowly. As he and Magiere passed through the doorless gate, the two men near the keep stopped talking. Each guard carried a spear, as well as a long-knife sheathed on his belt, but their clothes were plain and threadbare. They were likely no more than locals engaged by the zupan.

"Can I help you?" the shorter one asked, and his tone suggested that they state their business quickly.

"We need to speak with the zupan," Leesil said.

"Is he expecting you?"

Leesil felt Magiere's hand clench his with a shudder. She let go and stepped forward, her voice polite but cold.

"We arrived only last night. It's important that I see him."

The man shook his head. "Leave your petition with me, and I'll see that he gets it. If you come tomorrow, perhaps he will—"

"Oh, stop with your pretense, Cherock," a deep voice called out. "Father missed lunch, and he's having an early supper. Today's no more exciting than the rest, and he won't mind a few visitors."

Leesil turned, searching for the speaker.

In the keep's open doorway stood a slender man with coal-black hair that hung to his shoulders in a wild, unruly mass. His dusky complexion almost matched Wynn's olive tone, unlike the pale villagers and the would-be guards. He wore russet breeches with high boots and a baggy shirt of sea green with the cuffs rolled halfway up his arms. In one hand he held a fiddle, and in the other he lightly gripped a player's bow. The instrument's finish was worn away where the man's chin would rest. He smiled openly as he gestured them inside with the bow, and Leesil saw nothing behind the expression but a friendly welcome.

"Come, come," the young man called. "Cherock is doing his little duty, but my father doesn't stand on ceremony. Join us."

Such a relaxed invitation was unexpected, but Leesil and Wynn followed Magiere to the doorway. The young man looked over all three visitors but gave Wynn a longer appraisal as his smile broadened.

"I am Jan. Cherock acts as if my father has the schedule of a capital potentate, but we're not quite so overrun. Before we took to the keep, we lived in my father's central village or visited among my mother's people . . . and I'm dying for any company besides these courtyard hang-abouts."

As Leesil stepped past Jan to the keep's doorway, he noted a series of three silver hoops in the young man's left earlobe.

"And when was the last time he held an audience?"

Jan paused a moment. "Late summer, I think. One village needed coin for a new mule. I don't suppose you need an ass for your labors?" He nodded toward Wynn with a conspiratorial whisper. "I could give you a bargain on Cherock, if you like. A little exercise might improve his nature."

Wynn backed toward Leesil as she eyed the young man and tried not to smile.

"She's not familiar with the local language," Leesil said.

"Ah, lost in foreign lands, are we?" Jan opened his arms in a grand gesture. "My mother's people are well traveled. *Vídaty vravètí Belaskina?*"

Wynn seemed charmed and relieved that the zupan's son had formally asked her if she spoke Belaskian. However, it made Leesil suspicious about how a backwoods peasant had become so fluent in the language.

Jan ushered them through the short entryway into the keep's main hall, chattering at Wynn all the while. The main hall was little more than a large chamber, and it felt overly hot to Leesil after the chill outside.

Stairs circled up along the wall to the left, and matching ones went down below to the right. The timbered ceiling was twice a man's height and less aged than the stone, likely having been expanded well after the structure had been first built. The original fire pit in the hall's center was filled in with newer floor stones, and a hearth large enough to crawl into had been added to the far wall. A fire blazed therein, its smoke drafting up through a mortared chimney. An older man and woman sat at a table eating flatbread and roasted mutton.

"Visitors," Jan announced, plopping into a spare chair. "Cherock nearly turned them away. Father, you must speak to that man. Give him something more important to do than run off anyone of interest."

Jan's father looked up with a chunk of bread halfway into his mouth. Unlike his son, the zupan was a barrel of a man with pale skin, fading freckles, and cropped red hair peppered by gray flecks. He turned a discerning gaze upon Leesil and Magiere before pulling the bread strip from his mouth as he stood up.

"My son's good nature overbears his good manners," he said. "I'm Cadell, overseer of this fief and zupan to one of its clans. This is my wife, Nadja."

The woman stood, offering a smile, and motioned them to sit. Her manner was closer to that of Jan, and the son's resemblance to his mother was striking. She, too, was slender with wild black hair, and her complexion was darker than Wynn's. She wore gold earrings and a cyan dress tied at the waist by an orange paisley sash. Around one forearm wrapped a bracelet of ruddy metal, possibly a mix of copper and brass. It wasn't until they stepped near the table that Leesil saw the detailed engraving upon it of twining birds with long tail plumes and flecks of green stone for eyes.

Wynn turned her head several times between Jan and Nadja.

"You are mountain nomads . . . the Tzigän?" she blurted out in Belaskian. "I read a brief mention of your people. What are you doing so far south? What do you eat in those barren mountains? Is it true that you can read future happenings?"

Leesil let out a sigh that turned to groan before he could stop it. He and Magiere had rarely traveled the mountains, but he'd heard enough of the Tzigän to be wary. Not that they were dangerous, but things had a way of turning up missing when these people were about. Both Nadja and Jan blinked in surprise at Wynn's barrage of questions, and Jan burst out laughing. He set his fiddle upon the table and patted the chair nearest his own.

"Come sit with me, little one, and I'll tell you all. First, that we prefer the name Móndyalítko. That Belaskian word is . . . somewhat unflattering."

It certainly was, thought Leesil, but appropriate for vagabond thieves. This situation was getting out of hand, and he turned to Zupan Cadell.

"That isn't why we came." And he nodded to Magiere. "My companion and I seek information and hoped you could help."

Nadja watched Magiere with open curiosity and held out her hand. "Come, sit. What is it you wish to know?"

"My father," Magiere answered, and shook her head at the offered chair. "I'm looking for some way to trace him. He held this fief twenty-five years ago when I was born, and that is the last I know of his whereabouts. The few villagers who knew of him don't remember his name or won't talk. I hoped you'd have records."

Nadja's olive brow wrinkled as she turned to her husband. Cadell rubbed his wide jaw as he stared down at the table a moment and then shook his head.

"When we arrived, the keep was in shambles," he said. "Some furnishings had been looted. No lord had lived here for nearly two years. Neither had any taxes been collected. I agreed to manage the fief on the condition that Prince Rodêk forgo the lost taxes and allow me time to reorganize."

The idea of a fief left without an overlord for two years was far too strange for Leesil's taste, but he shook his curiosity off to deal with the matter at hand.

"There must be something," he said. "Accountings, ledgers . . . anything?"

"Not that I have found," Cadell answered. "Likely the last overseer took any such back to the Äntes estate or else they were looted. I've had to begin anew, even to re-counting the local households among the villages and reckoning what is due."

Magiere's face fell, her gaze dropping to the floor. She gripped the back of a chair.

A small part of Leesil was disappointed. A larger part was relieved, which in turn brought a heavy guilt. Whoever Magiere's father had been, Leesil suspected her mother had faced an uglier death than dying in childbirth. He was no longer sure Magiere should learn of this. And worst for his guilt, if this ended Magiere's search, perhaps they would be back on the road north in search of his own mother. Magelia was gone, but there was a chance that Nein'a still lived.

"Where would the records be taken, if they were removed?" Wynn asked.

Cadell frowned. "The Äntes castle is in Enêmûsk, the main city for this province, but I'd guess the records would end up in Kéosnk, the capital. Prince Rodêk Äntes reigns as grand prince for another three years, and he will live on the royal grounds for his term. From what I guess, he doesn't trust his younger brother, Duke Lúchyan, with care of their family's holdings. If records exist, you might find them in the capital, but there's no guarantee. With all the civil skirmishes between noble houses over the years, Kéonsk is always the center of conflict. Buildings have been burned and records lost."

As Cadell began, hope rekindled in Magiere's eyes, but by the end of his words, Leesil saw it dwindle again.

"May we look around the keep?" Wynn asked. "I will not disturb anything, but there may be documents hidden in places that others have overlooked."

Leesil was dubious, and Wynn seemed to catch this in his expression.

"Cathologers among the sages," she said, "like myself and Domin Tilswith, are experienced in both the protection and care of records. I do know what to look for."

Cadell consented, provided that anything found was brought to him first. And the search began.

In addition to the main hall, there were storage rooms and a kitchen on the main floor. Upstairs were sleeping quarters, one such room converted into a study. Leesil had trained as a youth in the art of hidden spaces, and he, too, knew what to watch for. He walked each room, scanning walls, floor, and ceiling for telltale cracks or unusual structure. Wynn inspected furniture, checking their undersides and pulling out drawers to look behind and beneath them. She even checked to see if chair and table legs were loose, a suitable space for hollowed-out hiding places.

Neither of them found anything.

"Do not give in yet," Wynn reassured Magiere. "I thought we should start up here, as Domin Tilswith says to exhaust upper floors first. But most archives are kept in lower levels, where they are more protected from fire and illicit removal."

Leesil agreed. Back down on the main floor, Jan waited for them by the main entryway.

"Can I help?"

"Can we go to the cellars?" Wynn asked.

Jan retrieved a candle lantern from the table. "Follow me, little one."

Wynn pulled a cold lamp crystal from her pocket and warmed it in her hands until it glowed brightly. The sight of it raised Jan's curiosity so sharply that Leesil became wary again. The young man asked no questions as the four of them walked down the curving stairwell and into the darkness below.

The stairs emptied into a square space at the head of a passageway running beneath the keep, and the air was as chill as outside. Jan led the way with Wynn just behind him, and he stopped briefly to light two oil lanterns on the walls.

Along the passage were six doors, three to a side, of thick wood and rusted iron fixtures. Between them were support arches of larger stones across the passage's roof. At midway, Jan pointed downward in caution to a floor grate so no one would trip upon its hinges. Leesil took Wynn's wrist and steered her crystal down closer to the grate.

Beneath it was a hollowed-out square chamber that smelled of stagnant moisture—the keep's dungeon for prisoners. For a moment, Leesil thought he saw gaunt faces peering up at him from below. He pulled away.

These were only old guilts resurfacing in Leesil's mind. How many had he helped put in such a place—or worse—beneath Lord Darmouth's keep in the Warlands?

"What is in these rooms?" Magiere asked. She pushed on the first door in the passage's left wall, but it would not open.

"One holds stores we've gathered," Jan replied. "Another has surplus goods collected for taxes in place of crops and coin."

"And nothing was found here when you first came?" asked Leesil, studying Magiere's obstinate door with its rusted latch.

"Nothing of note," Jan answered. "Old crates with moth-eaten cloth or tin plates, probably from when the barracks were manned. I didn't look in all of them myself."

"Time to do so," Magiere said, and pointed to the doors. "Are these locked?"

"This one isn't," Leesil offered. "Give it a shove."

Magiere joined him to push. The door shifted enough for Leesil to work the latch.

"They should all be open," said Jan. "There's nothing here worth locking up."

Wynn stepped in behind Leesil, holding out her crystal so that its light spread through the doorway. The room was large enough to lie down in, but it was empty. Leesil took the crystal and scanned once along all four walls before shaking his head at Magiere.

"It's an old keep, and not one of importance," he said regretfully. "We'll look carefully, but don't expect this forgotten place to hold many secrets."

"Next room," she said, ignoring his forewarning.

They proceeded one by one through the doors along the passage. Some opened more easily than the first. Cleaned and swept, they held recently added goods delivered by villages for taxes due from the fief. A few loose or broken wall stones had been replaced or remortared. There was nothing else of note.

Leesil studied the stones of the hallway. Cracked or broken ones had been replaced over the keep's history, and the walls were a patchwork of shades and textures. Likely wet weather and dank earth had combined with the weight of the keep to wear away at the understructure. There were signs of other erosion by time, repaired or not, and also hints that the lower level had been slowly expanded since the keep's first construction. The stones at the passage's end were not as aged as those nearest the stairs and the landing's chamber.

Only the last two rooms on opposing sides held anything interesting. Inside were stacked crates, which contained wares likely stored from the long-abandoned barracks. Leesil stepped out into the passage to face Magiere.

She glared down the passage of open doors as if searching for an enemy that would not reveal itself.

"There's nothing here," Leesil said.

She turned on him, expression cold like the stone surrounding them, as if neither his words nor his presence affected her. Her resistance faltered as she inhaled deeply. "Finish with the crates," she said, and turned away to walk back down the passage.

Leesil returned to the last room, where Wynn looked at him with sad eyes.

"Go through them all," he said, gesturing to the crates stacked around the small chamber's walls. "Empty them all . . . and then we're done with this."

Wynn nodded, and even Jan remained silent as he pulled the first crate down to the floor and opened it.

Leesil was about to follow Magiere but thought better of it. She sat on the bottom stair with her head down, elbows resting upon her knees. Her fading desperation would be covered by her usual anger. Anything he said would only make it worse.

"Leesil, come look at this," Wynn said.

"What is it?" he asked, stepping back into the room.

Wynn shook her head. "I am not certain. This room holds barracks equipment from many years past. Perhaps there was a military contingent here once. There is a parchment in this first crate. A list of some kind."

The worn parchment was frayed at the edges and torn along one ancient crease, where it had been folded in quarters. Leesil couldn't see the writing itself directly as Jan silently mouthed the words on the yellowed and dingy sheet.

"Just an account of the room's contents," Jan said. "From many years past. My father wouldn't have an interest in packing lists or inventories too old to be helpful."

Wynn studied the sheet and looked around the small room. She shoved the parchment in her pocket and opened another crate. With Jan's help, she searched the remaining crates but found nothing else noteworthy.

Jan looked at Leesil and shook his head.

"That's enough, Wynn," Leesil said, and gripped the young sage's shoulder. "We're done here."

Wynn pulled away, not ready to give up. She removed the parchment from her pocket to stare at it again, even though she couldn't read the language.

"Let's go," Leesil said.

He led the way out and down the passage, pulling each door closed as he passed. He could hear Wynn counting under her breath as she followed behind him—"One, two, three . . . five, six, seven"—until they reached the landing chamber.

Magiere looked up at him. There were no words of comfort he could find that wouldn't sound like hollow excuses. He held out his hand to her, and after a lingering silence, she took it and stood. Leesil headed up the stairs.

"Seven?" Wynn murmured from behind. "Leesil . . . there are seven."

When he looked back, she stood below in the small chamber facing the passage. Leesil couldn't see her face, but her head bobbed as she looked to the parchment and back down the hallway again.

"If this parchment accounts what these rooms once contained . . . ," she muttered. "Seven lists . . . for seven rooms."

Magiere's grip tightened on Leesil's hand. She let go to scramble down the stairs and grab the parchment from the sage. She stared at it but a moment, and then looked up at Leesil. If there was hope in her eyes, it was smothered by fear of another misdirection.

"The seventh room could just be the chamber here at the stairs," suggested Jan.

Wynn's shoulders slumped, but Magiere kept her eyes on Leesil, waiting.

Leesil stepped back down to join her and tried to keep his

expression impassive as he held his hand out to Wynn. "Give me the crystal."

Wynn's crystal in hand, Leesil dropped to one knee and inspected the chamber's floor. Strangely, along its center he found shallow traces of lines where something heavy had been dragged along the chamber floor and into the passage. The scarred lines were packed with dust and dirt, so were quite old. Closer to the walls were circular stains that suggested large barrels full of liquid had been stored here at one time, and he pointed them out.

Jan was looking at the list over Magiere's shoulder and shook his head. "There's no mention of barrels here, just crated goods," he said.

Leesil took a deep breath, careful to let it go silently before looking up at Magiere.

"Be certain," she said to him.

He stood up and let his gaze wander from the stairs to the ceiling, along the passage of doors, and down to the hallway's end with its blank wall. There was just this one cellar storage area and one dungeon under the keep.

Leesil looked up once again to the stone ceiling. Above these cellar chambers was the main floor of the keep, surrounded by its thick stone walls. Any hollowing below the keep to produce this passage of chambers would've been done with thought for the support of the upper building.

"Wait here," he told the others.

Leesil counted his steps as he climbed the curving stairs up to the main floor. With the exceptions of the entryway, the kitchen out back, and the stairs leading up and down, the main room's wall was the keep's outer wall. He paced the same number of steps back along wall until certain he stood directly above the cellar's landing chamber below. From there, he stepped out the distance to the other side of the keep—fifty-eight paces. He returned to cellar's landing chamber and looked down the passage of chambers.

"What is he doing?" Wynn asked.

"Be quiet, and let him think," Magiere answered.

Leesil's stomach rolled at the rekindled spark of hope in Magiere's eyes. This was all a hunch at best, but she nodded for him to continue. Leesil paced out the distance down the passage between the six rooms. At forty-two paces, he reached the end wall.

The passage was short of the distance across the whole keep along the same line.

This meant little, other than perhaps the cellar's end had been kept short of undermining the keep wall. The stones of the passage's end wall were newer than elsewhere but still well aged. It confirmed his earlier appraisal that the cellars had been slowly expanded over time from when the keep was first built many decades ago. He studied the end wall— and suspicion grew.

The stones were aged more uniformly than he'd noticed in his early inspection. There were no signs of patchwork here. He held the crystal close as he moved back and forth across its surface. The stones were fitted solidly up to the edge of the passage's side walls in both corners.

Leesil held his breath. He heard Magiere and the others moving in closer behind him.

"What?" she demanded. "You found something. . . . I can see it in you."

He held the crystal close to the corner.

This end wall's stones had been cut off to fit inside the passage's side walls.

Something at the passage's end had been blocked off long ago, as the passage had originally been longer. Leesil took off his cloak and began unstrapping his blades.

"We need tools," he said. "This wall was added, and the passage runs beyond it."

"Hold there," Jan said. "Even if my father agrees, you can't start knocking down walls. Remove the wrong support, and the place could collapse on us."

Magiere grabbed Jan by the shirt. "Just do as he says!"

Leesil reached out and grasped Magiere's wrist, pulling her away from Jan.

"This wall was a later addition," he explained, keeping an eye on Magiere. "It isn't supporting anything. Get your father, and find us some tools! Wynn, go with him."

Jan turned away, muttering under his breath, and Wynn followed. Magiere's gaze was fixed upon the end wall.

"There must be something . . . ," she whispered. "I can't . . . I can't leave here with nothing."

Her voice was so full of desperation that Leesil wrapped her in his arms. Magiere slumped forward, her face buried in his shoulder. He felt her tremble, and he rocked her slowly. What if there was nothing behind the wall? And what if there was something leading into Magiere's past? There was little hope either would bring her any relief.

Jan and Wynn returned with Cadell. It took some convincing, but once Leesil showed the zupan the wall's structure, Cadell was reasonably convinced it was safe to break it open. He seemed as disturbed by the discovery as Leesil. Jan had brought a pair of prybars and handed one to Leesil. The two of them set to breaking out the wall's top-center stones first.

The stench that wafted through the opening made all of them step away, gagging and coughing. Cadell caught Wynn as she stumbled, retching, and his face twisted in disgust at the scent of decay assaulting them.

Leesil's fear mounted. All he wanted was to drag Magiere from this place and never return. He thought he saw this same thought on her own pale face, but Cadell broke the silence.

"Finish it. Tear it down."

Leesil and Jan rammed through stone and mortar with their prybars to widen the opening. When enough of the wall fell away to allow him to step through, Leesil found the dark cavity where the passage continued, but it reached only a short distance. Another wall obscured by darkness stood before him, and he held Wynn's crystal out.

"The seventh room," Wynn said from somewhere behind him.

The door in the revealed wall was severely decayed, and the air smelled of rotted wood over the top of something more rank. Magiere tried to step past Leesil, but he held her back with a shake of his head, and began carefully inspecting the seventh door.

There was no sign of anything unusual, but the years had eaten at the wood. He hooked the door's latch with his prybar, stepped as far back as he could, and pulled. The door collapsed outward as it broke from its hinges, and the fetid stench mounted until he could taste it in his mouth.

Leesil heard Wynn moan as his own stomach lurched.

Magiere stood close behind him as he held the crystal up in the doorway. The crystal's light, undiffused by a lantern glass, was so sharp that it deepened the room's shadows as much as it revealed pieces of what lay within.

The back wall appeared to be old mortared stone. It barely caught the light, so the room was quite large. Near it, Leesil spotted what he thought were the shattered remains of a large wooden crate or box. One strut remain vertical, its height above his own waist. There was another slightly smaller crate to its right.

Leesil stepped in and spotted a large crusted vat to the left. Next to it was a crumpled mass, and other such piles appeared here and there on the floor along the wall. As he approached the vat, shadows turned around the walls as the crystal's light moved with him, making the dark heaps upon the floor shift like animals disturbed from slumber in their unearthed burrow.

One appeared to roll its head, and as Leesil stopped, the shadows froze all around him.

A mass on the floor in the left front corner took shape in the light as Magiere gripped his shoulder.

It was a body in a sitting position. Rotted clothing partially obscured the bones but not the skull. It narrowed toward the dangling lower jaw, hinting at a triangular face it once wore. Its dark eye sockets were larger than those of human skulls Leesil had been forced by his parents to study in his youth. And upon it still clung wisps of white-blond hair. Slender fingers too long for a human rested on a narrow rib cage.

Leesil didn't need a closer look to recognize the tall lithe stature. This elf had died and been entombed without ceremony in the dark forests of Droevinka, far from its homeland.

Magiere's other hand flattened against Leesil's side. Her grip on his shoulder tightened as she pulled him around to face the chamber's back wall again.

Around the base of the walls were the remains of more bodies.

Chapter 5

Thinly veiled by a night mist, the keep appeared to have aged a century in the brief decades since Welstiel had last seen it. From beneath the branches of a spruce at the clearing's edge, he watched two men with spears walk slowly across the courtyard.

"She is inside?" Chane asked. He crouched nearby, and moonlight peeked through a break in the clouds to wash over his pale features.

Welstiel nodded. He peered about the forest with his senses open wide, letting not only sight but also sound and scent flood into him. Being this close to the keep, this close to the beginning, made him wary. Magiere was inside—of that much he felt certain—but what concerned him more was who else might still have a keen interest in this place, and in any visitors from the past.

"We wait," he said. "Stay close to me if she appears, or I will not be able to hide you from her awareness."

Chane looked at him expectantly, waiting for an explanation of how this could be accomplished. Welstiel silently kept his attention upon the keep.

The two would-be guards walked the grounds' circumfer-

ence together rather than separately. Simple villagers, their
presence was one more hint that this place might well have
been forgotten by all who knew what had happened here.
Somewhere inside those stone walls, Magiere wandered, unaware of the ghosts of her own past. Welstiel willed that she
remain ignorant.

As the guards passed from sight around the stables, the
crumbled keep appeared still as a headstone in a forgotten,
hallowed place. This illusion of peace and serenity masked a
long-ago madness, and Welstiel's mind slipped back. . . .

It was nearly twenty-six years earlier, and Welstiel's father dragged Magelia from her village home. She rode behind Welstiel, clinging silently to his waist all the way to the
keep. Her sister ran after them as far as she could, screaming
Magelia's name in a frenzy of fear and anger.

Someone loves her, Welstiel thought without feeling.
Someone was frightened for her.

It hadn't mattered. It hadn't changed anything.

Lord Bryen Massing was tall, but Welstiel had not inher-
ited his father's imposing height. They shared dark brown
hair, square faces, and the shallow bump at the bridge of their
noses, but heritage and a few features were all they had in
common. Most notable to all who saw them together, the father did not have the white patches of hair at his temples that
the son wore.

The fief his father had been assigned was primitive compared with others they had tended over the years, with a squat
tower keep of mortared rock with crude barracks and stable
attached, built near the central village of Chemestúk. Welstiel rode into the keep's muddy courtyard that night following his father. Their family retainer, the robed and masked
Master Ubâd, stood waiting for them.

The torch-lit courtyard was alive with activity. Men-at-arms and a few conscripted villagers attempted to unload the contents of five sturdy wagons. Along with family baggage, each wagon carried a square crate at least two-thirds the height of man and covered by a thick canvas tarp. Seeing the lord and his son arrive, the men grew openly nervous and too hurried in their tasks. They pulled a tarp aside to reveal one of the crates.

It was constructed of oak held together with steel straps and bound to the wagon bed with chains instead of rope. As two guardsmen unhooked the chains, a deep muffled voice howled out from within the container: *"Shaïrsnïsâg mi, na mi tâitägâg cräiùi ag shiùi ag chêr!"*

The words Welstiel heard sounded Elvish but were more guttural, and he could make no sense of them. A thunderous boom issued from the crate's walls, and it slammed sideways into one guard. The impact crushed the man's legs against the wagon's side with an audible crack of bone. His companion leaped out the other side and scrambled clear. The guard screamed and toppled over to dangle against the rear wheel with his legs pinned against the vehicle's sidewall.

Master Ubâd glided toward the wagon. His dark robe showed no sway from footsteps.

"Fools!" he hissed, ignoring the trapped man's squeals of pain. "The contents are worth more than all your lives. Take care—and have all five crates brought to the lower chambers."

Ubâd's face was covered by an aged leather mask with no eye slits. Only his withered mouth and chin were visible. When he moved, strange markings shimmered briefly across his char-colored robe in the torchlight.

Welstiel heard less articulate growls coming from the crate, as the men returned to pulling it free from the wagon. All were careful not to pass too near Master Ubâd, who

watched them closely. The maimed guard was quickly
dragged from sight.

Welstiel and his father dismounted, and Lord Massing
lifted Magelia to the ground and grasped her wrist to drag her
inside. Her black hair hung in waves to the middle of her
slender back, and her blue dress made her skin appear ivory.
She struggled and tried to jerk away, but her captor kept
walking, unhindered by her efforts.

Master Ubâd's bony hand motioned Welstiel to follow, as
he moved smoothly toward the keep's main doors. Welstiel
abhorred being so close to the creature, but he had little
choice and followed.

"I can walk on my own!" Magelia shouted. "Leave me
be."

Some part of Welstiel was capable of pity, but this woman
was just a peasant. He found these unfolding events more
and more distasteful. They entered the main hall, furnished
only by an aged table, a few chairs, and dusty rushes covering the floor. Welstiel shivered in the cold. He was always
cold in this foreign land and rarely removed his cloak even
when indoors.

His father suffered no such discomfort, not since Welstiel's youth and the first appearance of Ubâd in their lives.
Lord Massing released the woman and removed his own
cloak with one hand, tossing it onto the table.

Magelia backed into the nearest wall, and Ubâd's head
turned as if he could see her clearly through the leather covering his eyes.

"Do not allow your guard to drop, Bryen," he said. "She
must not escape."

It grated on Welstiel that this creature spoke to his father
in such a manner. Welstiel called him "Father," of course, but
all others conducted themselves with suitable decorum, even
Prince Rodêk of the Äntes. At the counsel gatherings of the

house's nobles, his father was announced as "Lord Bryen Massing."

Ubâd did not show his father the proper respect.

Withered, faceless, conjurer of spirits of the dead—such rare specialization earning the title of necromancer—Ubâd's forecasting ability was questionable at best. He amounted to little more than a servant in Welstiel's eyes and yet addressed Welstiel's father in a familiar way.

Lord Massing raised a hand to his temple. His left eyelid twitched as he whispered inaudibly to himself.

Welstiel no longer asked what troubled him. His father's unnerving habit of speaking to himself was becoming common. Ubâd did not hesitate, sliding closer.

"Your son can lock up the woman until all is arranged. You should rest . . . slumber . . . and commune."

Bryen Massing stared blankly into Ubâd's mask, then nodded.

"Yes, see to matters here," he said, and turned toward the stairs curving up the inner wall, his vacant gaze passing briefly over Welstiel. "Lock her in the cellar and assist Master Ubâd as needed."

Lord Massing walked heavily up the stone steps, leaving Welstiel to handle Magelia. He did not want to touch her for any reason, even on the orders of his father. This arranged joining was not of his making or desire. He pointed toward the stairs leading down the opposite way to the lower chambers.

"Go," he said.

Beneath the fright in Magelia's dark eyes was anger, and she was watchful, studying everything around her. Welstiel noted for the first time that her face was attractive, with a long straight nose and delicate jaw framed by her mass of black hair. Her wrists and fingers were slender to the point of fragility. He pitied her as he might pity a sack of kittens just before they were thrown into a river.

With a tilt of his head, he motioned again to the stairs and took a step toward her. She slid away from him along the wall and proceeded on her own. As they reached the stairs, a crate was pulled in through the keep's doors, and Welstiel glanced back.

It was not the one that had crushed the man-at-arms. Built like a cage of wooden struts, thick canvas panels were stretched inside its bars to hide or protect what it held.

As Welstiel descended behind Magelia, he heard the thrash of beating wings against the canvas.

Late the same night, Welstiel descended into the cellar passage. He passed the doors of the six small rooms, the first of which held Magelia locked within. He did not stop, but walked on to the end and the seventh room. Inside, he found a flurry of activity.

Five crates had been unloaded. Several conscripted villagers and a few men-at-arms were settling the crates in place and removing their tarps.

First the steel-bound oak box containing the muffled rage of its occupant, and then the framed canvas with its soft sounds of fluttering misery within. The third was cedar, and silent inside, while the fourth was a framework of oak surrounding an urn large enough for a man to crawl inside. The latter's weight was three or four times that of the others and, when moved, it sloshed liquid inside. Even when the box sat undisturbed, Welstiel occasionally heard liquid lap against the leather-sealed opening at its top.

The fifth container was by far the most unsettling and intriguing.

It measured less than half a man's height in all dimensions and was made of bound steel plates that were discolored and blackened. Steam rose with a sizzling crackle from the damp floor when it was set down, and erratic scraping came from within the metal walls. The frantic noise grew until a screech from the steel made everyone in the room flinch. Every nerve in Welstiel quivered at the sound. Then the crate sat silent.

A villager was freeing a chain used to drag it along and brushed a hand against the discolored metal. The sizzle of his flesh filled the room and he cried out and pulled back, putting his hand to his mouth. He crumpled to the floor, whimpering, until a man-at-arms kicked him into motion again.

Welstiel left the seventh room. He stopped outside Magelia's locked door for a moment, and then walked back up the curving stairs.

Several nights passed. Welstiel had come down for supper in the main hall when a roaring and clanging resounded from the cellar below. He hurried down the stairs, taking them two at time. Ubâd's screeching voice echoed in his ears before he reached the landing chamber.

"Alive, you fools. He must remain alive!"

Welstiel ran to the passage's end. The door to the seventh room was ajar. As he grabbed its edge to swing it open, he looked through the crack. A body leaned in the near left corner.

Fingers crooked in anguish, the elf's hands rested limp upon his chest. His head tilted back into the corner, and his eyes gawked unblinking at the ceiling, wide balls of white with amber centers. The hanging gap of his mouth was mimicked by a slash across his throat so deep that it had split through to his windpipe. Little blood seeped from the wound, and the corpse was too pale for one of the forest people.

Welstiel's view was suddenly blocked as a man-at-arms crashed into the chamber's front wall. He pushed the door wide.

Near the center of the room, Ubâd stood behind a large brass vat with his bony hands clenched.

"Get up!" he shouted. "Break his legs, if you must."

The guard clawed up the wall to his feet, and he rushed across the room with an iron bar in his hand.

Among the shattered remains of the oak crate stood a man, or so it appeared, struggling with Lord Massing.

Bryen's opponent was thick and gnarled, his muscular limbs sprouting from a torso almost twice the width of a human's but only two-thirds as tall. His bushy brows and beard were coarse like chestnut horsehair around bulky rough features that made it hard to see his eyes. Iron shackles encompassed his wide wrists and ankles, but their connecting chains had been snapped and dangled loose.

The guard stepped in, swinging the iron bar low into the prisoner's leg.

The squat man's bare foot did not even move. The thudding impact had no more effect than striking a column of stone. He slapped the guard aside with little effort. The guard's body smashed headfirst into the back wall, and he fell to the floor, his neck broken. The iron bar rolled away.

The prisoner roared out through yellowed teeth. *"Mi ko'eag a'grùnn ta gowl shiûn ämbi' shiû fuiliâg mi!"*

Everything happened in a few blinks of the eye, but Welstiel felt locked in an eternity.

Bryen punched the gnarled man's face, and Welstiel expected the prisoner to crumple. The man barely flinched and drove his larger fist into Bryen's sternum. Bryen buckled, and the prisoner crouched low and heaved him up into the air. Welstiel lunged forward to snatch up the iron bar, but he could not close the distance in time.

The prisoner slammed his father down, and Welstiel felt the impact through the floor stones. He hesitated in fear, as he had little skill at arms. His chosen method of conjury was artificing, the making of objects and tools, and not spellcraft. Even so, what could he possibly conjure or summon of the elements to aid his father now?

The air in the room began to swirl. It kicked up dust from the floor that made Welstiel blink as he looked for the source of the sudden wind in this underground chamber.

Ubâd, in his whipping charcoal robe, hovered above the floor.

Wisplike eddies appeared in the swirling air around him, each twisting and curling, until translucent faces appeared at the head of each wisp. Their sorrowed features blurred in the air. Spirits of the dead gathered about the withered necromancer and, one by one, they broke away and dived at Bryen's opponent.

The first spirit struck through the prisoner. He shuddered but kept pounding down upon Bryen with huge fists. Another wisp pierced the wide man's flesh, and another, until he finally screamed in pain.

"Assist me—now!" Ubâd shouted. "Take his breath!"

Welstiel blinked once before understanding. Such a simple thing, he should have thought of this himself, but spellwork was not his strength in conjury. He held out his cupped hands, palms facing each other, then lifted them until they framed his sight of the prisoner. Forming the lines, shapes, and symbols in his mind to overlay what his eyes saw, he began to chant.

The air between his palms pushed outward, but he held it in place like a small entity trapped within a conjuring circle. He loathed following Ubâd's commands but was determined to save his father.

Another spirit struck the wide man. He opened his mouth to yell, but no sound issued, and he buckled, grasping his throat.

Welstiel's head ached with concentration as he summoned

the air from out of the prisoner's lungs. Free of the wide man's assault, Welstiel's father struck upward into his opponent's bearded jaw as two more spirits pierced the man's body.

The prisoner's eyes rolled as he gasped for air, and he toppled over. Bryen was up and on him in an instant, pinning his thick arms back with the dangling chains.

"Leave him alive," Ubâd commanded.

Welstiel ceased chanting. His father pinned the captive's stomach against the brass vat and forced the man to lean forward over it. Before Welstiel understood what was happening, Ubâd slashed open the prisoner's throat with a curved dagger.

The hulking man bucked at the blade's passing and thrashed wildly. Bryen put his full weight on top of his captive. It did not take long for the prisoner to go limp as his blood drained into the vessel. Bryen stood up, releasing the body to flop heavily upon the floor.

Welstiel saw the prisoner's eyes, smaller and darker than the elf's, staring blindly up at the ceiling. His mouth was clenched shut in a permanent grimace, and the thick beard was matted to his chest with his own blood.

"Well done, my son," Bryen said. "One dwarf is far more trouble than we expected."

Awareness filled Welstiel like a winter chill spreading from Bryen's approving gaze. His father lived an unnatural existence, but this spilling of blood without thought shocked Welstiel. The thing that stood before him, offering dispassionate praise, was far less his sire than he had ever before realized.

"We must not delay," Ubâd said urgently. "Now that it's begun, preparation must be finished immediately."

Bryen cast the necromancer an annoyed glance but nodded agreement. Without another word to Welstiel, he stepped to the wood-framed crate with its canvas walls. Drawing his own dagger, he slashed open one side. The canvas separated and fell away.

Welstiel saw the prisoner within.

Bound with leather straps instead of shackles, she was delicate. Even curled in fright at the container's rear, he could tell she would barely reach his sternum when standing.

Her face and build were as lithe and slender as the last prisoner's had been hulking and wide. She would have been slight even standing next to the dead elf. Her two eyes, staring out in wide terror, had no irises. They were fully black like a sparrow's, and the dark rings around them showed she had not slept in days. From narrow feet to her head of feathery hair, her pale flesh appeared downy, though there were places where it had molted or been rubbed to bare cream skin.

And bound down to her naked torso were wings of mottled grays and whites sprouting from her back. Her attempts to free them were likely what Welstiel had heard when he had first seen this container.

Bryen grabbed her bound wrists, dragging her out and holding her up to dangle from his grip as he walked toward the vat.

"You should retire," Ubâd said to Welstiel. "There's still much to do here, and you've exceeded your stamina."

Welstiel got to his feet. He was about to approach his father, but Ubâd slid into his way as the necromancer followed Bryen across the room. Welstiel suddenly felt isolated and alone.

He turned to leave. Behind him, the sound of a frantic scream was cut short. He thought of Magelia, locked in her cell, forced to listen, and he turned his eyes away as he passed her door.

Once in his own room, Welstiel locked the door and sat at

a small desk lit by the three dancing flickers in his orb. There he remained for the rest of a sleepless night with his eyes closed, flinching at the sounds of two more screams that echoed up from the seventh room beneath the keep.

Chapter 6

Cadell and Jan brought additional candle lanterns, and the room was illuminated around Magiere in yellow light. The stench was still so thick that she could taste it. Before her was a small heap of remains amid an old wood frame with decayed shreds of cloth still bound to it.

At first, she thought it was two bodies, for there were too many bones for a single being. Yet there was only one skull, human shaped, but too small and narrow, with oversize eye sockets like those of the elf. There was only one set of hands and feet, with toe bones that were too long. Its limbs had been bound with leather straps now crusted hard with age, as well as another hanging loose around the frail rib cage.

In the filth surrounding it were the remains of rotted feathers.

"Wings?" Wynn whispered as she drew closer, holding up a crystal. "It had wings . . . like a bird. Perhaps female—if its make is similar to other races."

Magiere's gaze traced the tangled bones until the illusion of two bodies was dispelled by the memory of once seeing a dead hawk in the woods. A few feathers lying before her still held their mottled gray and white color.

"What is it?" Jan asked, though he kept his distance a few steps away, near the large vat they'd discovered.

Wynn shook her head and looked up, but not at the zupan's son. Magiere saw fear in the sage's unblinking eyes. For an instant, all Wynn's horror turned upon her, and Magiere backed away.

"There's another over here by this iron box," Leesil called from the right side of the room. "But it's . . . something else. I'm not sure what."

The words barely entered Magiere's thoughts. What did the remains of this sealed chamber reveal concerning the death of her mother? Had something been done here to Magelia in order to bring her unnatural daughter into this world?

Magiere saw her whole life infested with the dead and undead. Even her birth was somehow forecast with these bones, yet she couldn't fathom what they told her of the past. She sensed—somehow *knew*—that the contents of this room were connected to her.

There were only more questions, and no answers.

Beside the crusted vat lay the second body they'd found. Wynn had partly cleared the hardened leather clothes from it, telling them it was—had been—a dwarf. The sage knew of these people from a *séatt*—dwarvish for a city stronghold or fortified haven—across the bay from the capital of her homeland, Malourné. That capital, Calm Seatt, had been named out of respect for the dwarven people who'd helped to build its first keep.

Neither Magiere nor Leesil had ever met one of his kind. Wide framed and wide jawed, with a skull as large as a soldier's helmet, his thigh bones were as thick as her whole wrist. Slightly yellowed with age, the bones had speckled shadows in them like a hint of granite.

"If any of this bears upon the past you're looking for,"

Cadell said, "I don't care to know any more of it. We've enough troubles of our own."

"More than you thought," Magiere replied bitterly, but she didn't explain.

Whatever happened here had been done in haste and then sealed up. Few but Leesil could have uncovered its existence. But if she had come looking, who else might do so, as well, once word traveled of what had been found here?

Magiere couldn't bear looking at anyone in the room. She turned her attention to the vat, and hunger churned inside her.

The vat's outside was tarnished. Wynn had scraped away dust and grime to reveal engraved symbols, each no larger than a coin, across its entire surface. She had asked Jan for paper and charcoal to make rubbings for later study. At one side of the vat, dark stains ran down it as if the contents had been poured out or had spilled over.

When Magiere looked inside the vessel, a thicker stain covered the bottom third of its depth, creating a dried and cracked layer. She took the crystal from Wynn, startling the sage, and lowered its light into the vat. The cracked layer in the bottom had a distinctive dark brown color, like liquefied earth dried out. When her hunger stirred again, Magiere knew what it was from instinct more than anything else.

"They were bled . . . here," she whispered.

When she stood up, she faced the elf's corpse lying in the chamber's front left corner, and she looked down at the dwarf's.

"Sacrificed," Wynn whispered.

"How long ago . . ." Magiere trailed off and turned to Wynn. "How old are these remains?"

Wynn looked away, and it took a moment for her to answer.

"It's impossible to be exact. But from decomposed animals I've studied in the past, I would guess no more than thirty years, perhaps less."

The sage backed toward the far side of the room. Her hand shook visibly as she pulled her short robe more securely around herself.

"So," Magiere asked in a hard voice. "Twenty-six years would be as good a guess? About the time I was conceived."

Leesil came up beside Magiere, glanced once at the vat, and tried to pull her away. Magiere jerked her arm out of his grip.

In all, six corpses had been found. One was human with leather armor and a sword, perhaps a guard during the time when her father had been lord of this place—a father who might not be as unknown to Magiere as she'd once thought.

Welstiel had posed as an ally during the fight with Miiska's undead, but that conflict, as with the one in Bela, had been of his making. From the beginning, he'd known of her dhampir nature, as well as the falchion and the amulets. In Bela, he'd claimed to be preparing her to assist him in gaining whatever ancient treasure he sought.

Visions . . . in Bela, there had also been horrible visions.

By accident, she'd stumbled upon another attribute of her dhampir nature—to experience the moment of a kill through an undead's perspective. To lure her to the capital, Welstiel murdered the council chairman's daughter and left the girl's body on her own doorstep. By chance, Magiere had walked in his steps at the death scene while holding a scrap of the girl's dress. She relived that moment, felt the victim's flesh tear in Welstiel's teeth as if she were him.

How much more would she see with an innocent's bones in her hands? At least she would know if he had been here . . . if he was the one she'd come here to find.

Magiere knelt down and wrenched the dwarf's skull from its carcass.

"What are you doing?" Cadell said, and took a step toward her. "Enough of this. You will not desecrate—"

"Stop it!" Leesil snapped, and he was on her from behind, grabbing for the skull. "Whatever happened here, you don't want to see it . . . not like that!"

Magiere cradled the skull with one arm and snapped her shoulder back into Leesil's chest. She followed with her arm and sent him sprawling. Before he got up, she looked into the skull's sockets, the grit of bone against her bare palms and fingers.

"No!" Leesil called.

Magiere closed her eyes.

Darkness. The sounds of voices around her and quickened breaths behind curses. The stench of the cold chamber filling her head.

Nothing more, as Magiere opened her eyes again.

"I'll have no more of this sacrilege, defiling the dead," Cadell growled, and he stepped threateningly toward Magiere. "Get out of here."

Magiere tightened her grip on the skull as she raised her eyes to Cadell. She wasn't going anywhere, not without answers. She rocked back on her heels and stood up. Leesil stepped in front of her, snatching the skull from her hands.

"Leave," he told her. "Now. Go back to your aunt's, and wait for me."

"Yes, all of you go and leave this to us," Cadell said.

Jan looked upset but didn't speak, and Wynn remained quiet at the back of the chamber.

"We're not done here," Leesil replied, and returned his attention to Magiere. "Wynn and I will join you shortly, once we've finished examining the bodies."

Magiere looked about the room. As she received no vision by touching the dwarf's skull, she didn't believe he died by a vampire's attack. Some part of her felt relief at the thought of escaping this place. She didn't even acknowledge Leesil when she turned and walked out.

Outside the keep, the two village men paid her little attention as she strode through the courtyard and back down the road. More corpses had been found in her life's wake, yet they'd revealed nothing. One more of the dead still waited.

Chap had long since ceased battering the shed's door and walls. He spent even longer trying to claw up the rough planks on the floor. Neither approach gained him an escape. Mounted to the hut's side, the shed proved sturdier than it appeared, and he couldn't get his thick claws into the floor cracks.

He peered through a crack in the wall and saw that night had come. With time, he could break free, but Magiere and the others had already been gone too long. He had to try another way, and he began to howl in long mournful tones.

He kept at it as loud as possible, hoping to disturb someone. In a short while, footsteps approached outside, and a woman's stern voice came from beyond the shed's door.

"Fê lênêshte, tú êmpórtún córchêtúru!"

He could not understand her words but reached out to touch her thoughts. Surfacing memories flashed through his mind.

Magiere arriving in the village.

The inside of the hut . . . and an image of himself curled alone in the corner that morning.

Magiere's relative, Bieja, stood outside the shed's door.

Chap could not delve into a being's thoughts further than the memories that came to the surface of its mind. All living things remembered their pasts in scant pieces. He could also use these memories to poke and prod an unaware being's choices or actions . . . nothing more than a mental suggestion.

The only other way was to dominate the being's spirit, suppress its will, and take control of its body directly. And this he would never do.

Gently, he recalled for Bieja her memory of him curled silently in the corner as he mixed his howls with piercing whimpers and feeble scratches at the door. Outside, Bieja heaved a deep sigh, her voice filled with resignation.

"Tót dreptate, tú fê sósê . . . dar you óptêm cómpórta tú."

Chap heard a scraping sound, and the shed door began to open. When it was wide enough for his head, he bolted.

The door flew open, a startled Bieja jumped out of his way, and Chap raced off into the night. Her angry shouts followed briefly behind him, but he ran out the side of the village and turned toward the keep.

Chap kept the road in sight for a guide as he raced through the forest with his senses reaching out into the night. No one passed along the road, and the forest ahead on the slope showed signs of thinning near the crest.

A door slammed shut, and Chap froze with ears poised as he looked through the trees and toward the keep.

Magiere came down the road at a steady gait, her cloak loose in disregard of the night's chill. Her pale face was expressionless, all emotion suppressed or turned inward. Chap caught an old memory of a grave in the forest that surfaced in her thoughts once, twice, again and again. Each time, he sensed Magiere recoil from this image, smothering it with other more recent memories.

In a hidden chamber beneath the keep were secrets and death.

Chap's panic sharpened.

Magiere was one step closer to the truth, yet she did not realize it. And he was one step closer to failing—to losing her—and in the end, Leesil, as well.

Chap went wide through the forest to get ahead of Magiere, as he raced back toward the village.

Chane did not enjoy standing in the woods, in the dark, to keep watch over a decayed keep in the middle of nowhere, but he did not complain. To make matters worse, Welstiel was fixated upon the old structure, lost in thought, and offered little reason why they waited. He did, however, insist Chane never move too far away from him.

Whenever they had needed to hide from the dhampir or the dog, Chane had noticed that Welstiel absently touched the brass ring on his finger.

Chane saw movement coming from the village, and he focused. A flash of silver fur passed through the trees near the road.

"It's Chap," Welstiel said. "Magiere's dog is coming."

To Chane's surprise, Welstiel reached out and grasped his cloak, pulling him close. "Get down."

Chane did not care for the idea, but obeyed. He heard a door slam shut. The rat in his pocket began squirming, so he took it out and let it sit on his shoulder. It wrinkled its whiskers and sniffed at his face.

Magiere strode out of the keep's courtyard and down the hill toward the village. She looked pale and defeated. The sight of her made Chane's jaw ache. Her smooth skin and black hair drew his full attention. Victims who fought back excited Chane, and no one had ever fought like Magiere. She drew closer and walked right by their position. Welstiel was studying her face as she passed.

"We should withdraw," he said. "There is nothing we can do."

"Was there something you planned to do?"

Welstiel ignored his question. "Look at her face. Her search here is over, and there is nothing more for her to seek.

I suspect she will leave this place in the morning. We should find a place to rest for the day. When we wake tomorrow night, I believe she will finally head north."

Chane looked down along the road, but the dog had not joined her. It had disappeared. Welstiel backed into the trees holding tight to Chane's cloak, keeping them close together.

Wynn completed her rubbings of the vat's symbols. The millweed paper Jan had brought her was too rough for the work, but she made do, her hands shaking as she'd worked the charcoal against the paper. It was unlikely that Cadell would allow them to remain long enough for her to scribe out all the vat's markings, and she did not wish to be here any longer than necessary.

Somehow, all of this was connected to Magiere's birth.

Magiere had been sired by an undead, birthed to be its enemy and predator. That much they knew, but now it seemed that a vampire had committed a blood sacrifice for that purpose. The brass vat was a conjuring vessel of some kind, but its size and the number of victims were baffling. What was truly needed to birth the child of an undead?

"If you're finished, we should go," Leesil said as he paced, glancing at an impatient Cadell near the room's entrance. "I don't want to leave Magiere on her own for too long."

Wynn had not studied the last two strange remains. Her sage's nature and need for all pieces of the puzzle were greater than her own dread of the answer.

"Another moment . . . ," she said. "I need—"

"Isn't this enough?" asked Jan.

His charm and attention toward her had waned, and Wynn saw him staring at the tarnished vat and the roll of rubbings she held close.

"Yes, I think you've got quite enough," Cadell said. "It is

no wonder there have been few masters of this place with such tragedy hidden beneath it. I must report this to the Äntes."

"Then you're a fool," Leesil said, swinging his arm in a wide arc, indicating the whole chamber. "Or do you think you'll remain caretaker long after bringing this to their attention?"

"How can I not?" Cadell asked. "You've unearthed a curse upon us, and I'm at a loss for how it will ever be cleansed."

Wynn recoiled at the zupan's words. She felt responsible for placing him in this situation.

"He is right, Father," Jan said. "Prince Rodêk would send one of his vassals, and even troops perhaps, and you would never regain stewardship of the fief. Your presence is far more important to the people here than some noble servant of the Äntes. No, we will keep this to ourselves, and not even our own clan should hear of it."

"How is that possible?" Cadell asked, turning his anger on his own son. "Look about you!"

Jan did so, with one last brief pause at Wynn. "I will see to it, gather and contain the bones. Mother can send word to her people. They will take me into the mountains, so I can lay these remains to final rest where no one will disturb them."

Cadell regained composure from his son's words. "All right then, we will do as you say," he answered, and turned to Leesil. "Now get out, and let us deal with this."

"Soon . . . in a moment," Leesil answered with forced calm and a frown at Wynn. "Finish, please."

Wynn returned to the winged remains among the wooden frame with its shreds of aged canvas. What would Domin Tilswith do if he was faced with these bodies . . . with these sacrifices? He had sent her on this journey with his deepest trust. She was determined to try to act as he would. There was still something lost in her memories that stirred when she looked at the physical make of this winged body, and, as she knelt with her back to the others, she did something that shamed her.

She quietly loosened one of its finger bones to secret it in her palm.

Wynn kept her hands in front of herself, so the others could not see. She lingered long enough to note as much of it as she could for later recounting in her journal, and then she moved on to the fourth and fifth skeletons.

They had fallen near each other. One lay before an open iron box the height of her leg, and the other near a huge clay urn lashed into a wooden frame, likely for hauling. The urn was as tall as her head, and its side had been smashed in.

The insides of the iron box had gouges in the metal, visible even beneath the grime and thin coat of rust. The bones of the creature next to it were more disturbing than the winged one. In place of teeth, its jaws had sharpened ridges, and the final bones of its toes and fingers ended in sharp curved points. The creature, locked within the box, had tried to claw its way out.

All its bones and dried flesh were tarnished with streaks of red grime so thick, it made them look pitch black. Another sense of the familiar stirred in her mind. Keeping her back to the others, she pretended to lean in for a closer examination. Removing a loose toe bone with its claw, she palmed it along with the winged creature's finger.

The fifth body rested near enough that she did not have to move. Slender but solid of build like the elf, the creature had strange rows of spikes stuck out along the back side of its forearms, from each vertebra of its spine, and along its crested skull. The bones were cream-white and had not yellowed beneath its decayed filth. Its teeth were also ridged, but with regularly spaced points.

She made a hidden reach for one of the smaller spikes springing from the front of its shin. She took one of these off and added it to her collection.

Her gaze returned to the spikes on its spine, longer near the upper back but growing shorter toward the tailbone.

Like the fin of a sea creature.

Wynn stumbled as she got up and began shaking.

"We will leave you, zupan, to tend your own . . . ," Leesil started to say, and then his eyes widened as he looked at Wynn. "We're done. It's all done. There's no need for tears."

Jan took a step toward her, suspicion and mistrust washed away with concern.

Wynn pulled away from him, suddenly afraid to let anyone near her in this place. She had not even been aware of her own tears, only that she could not stop shaking and found but one word for her thoughts.

"*Úirishg!*" she said in a whisper tinged with hysteria.

Her gaze passed over one remains to the next, out of control—elf, dwarf, a creature of the air, one of water, and the other . . . of fire?

"Take her out of here, you fool," Cadell snapped. "This place has driven her beyond wits, as it might do us all."

Leesil reached out and steered Wynn toward the entryway. She let herself to be pulled along, as her mind did little more than reiterate her earliest lessons in the structure of creation.

The elements are Spirit, Earth, Water, Air, and Fire . . .

Showing states in Essence, Solid, Liquid, Gas, and Energy . . .

To manifest as Tree, Mountain, Wind, Wave, and Flame . . .

And within the chamber were an elf of the forest, a dwarf of the mountains . . .

She did not know the names for the other three. They were so lost back beyond The Forgotten that no one knew them as more than part of the myth of the *Úirishg,* as the elves called them. The sages translated that word as akin to "Fay-blooded" or "Children of the Fay," but the word was so old that its literal meaning was uncertain.

Old recovered texts revealed scant hints of a myth among her lands that humans were the oldest race. In primordial times, they mingled among the first Fay, and their offspring were the beginning of five new races. It was a legend that tried to explain their origin, perhaps with some hidden truth, though the elves of her continent found it little more than an amusing tale.

It should not become real, not like this . . . in blood and ritual sacrifice.

Before Leesil guided her all the way up the stairs, Wynn jerked free and ran the rest of the way to the keep's front doors. When the cold night of the courtyard outside wrapped around her, its numbness sank through to her own bones. She collapsed to her knees on the damp ground, sobbing. There was no sign of the two guards.

Leesil caught up to her, crouching to take her by the shoulders.

"Wynn . . . what did you find?" he asked, and then he saw the three bones in her limp hand. "Oh, for all the dead saints! What have you done?"

Wynn raised her head to look at him.

Leesil reached around her to pull up her hood. He closed the short robe's front more securely around her.

"You have to tell me," he said. "I don't understand what's wrong."

"Úirishg," she whispered again, and held up the three bones.

With effort, she told him of the Children of the Fay who were the five forgotten races. Only two, the elves and dwarves, were known to truly exist, and in that it should have all been but a myth. Leesil listened with the bones between them in Wynn's palm, and in the end she saw there was some understanding in his eyes.

"All right," he said. "But we have to go. I need to find Magiere."

He tried helping her up to her feet, but Wynn began to shake again at the thought of Magiere waiting for them in the village below.

"No more," she cried. "I do not want to know any more."

Leesil gripped her arms and forced her up. She was surprised by the strength in his hands.

"I understand," he said, "but you have to pull yourself together—now! Magiere is already on the edge, and I need you to stay with me."

"What is she?" Wynn asked.

"Don't start that with me," Leesil returned. "She had no more choice than you or I in how she came into this world. She was born a dhampir and—"

"Is that all you think she is?" Wynn said. "I just told you what we found in that room. The vat was so large, it would have taken a long time to make, to engrave. It was left and discarded, as if it could be used only once . . . because of what it was used for. Have you ever wondered why a Noble Dead—a vampire—for an unknown reason, would labor to create its own kind's hunter?"

Leesil's temper flared. "That's not what she—"

"Yes, she is," Wynn nearly shouted. "It is her nature . . . but only its thin outer surface. Those victims in that chamber . . . Leesil, someone searched the world to find them, and three are but a myth so old, it had been forgotten. They were brought here to be slaughtered for Magiere's birth and then sealed in rather than risk disposing of the evidence in another manner."

She shoved him away, and her voice softened. Not in sympathy but in disbelief at his blindness.

"What was done here is close to impossible. And you still think it was just to create an enemy of the Noble Dead?"

Leesil stared back at her, looking lost amid her words. "I have no choice in this, I love her . . . and I can't turn away. If you don't help me, then I'm alone. Not even Chap seems willing to tell what he knows or why he brought Magiere and me together."

He stepped closer, looking tired and desperate.

"I need you," he said. "You have more knowledge than any of us. All I have is cunning and my past, and that may not be enough. I need you now."

Leesil's plea made Wynn's knees tremble. This was not the world she wanted to live in. She feared these first steps into Magiere's past would inevitably lead them to worse places. In Chap she had found a Fay taken to flesh, who had befriended a half-elf with a black past she still knew too little of. The dog had steered Leesil to Magiere, and they had stumbled on to more of Magiere's nature than Chap wanted anyone to know.

Beneath the city of Bela, Wynn had kept Magiere from killing Chane, though he was revealed as a monster. And she adamantly defended her choice, believing that even Chane might have some good in him . . . what she felt, how different he had been in the quiet study of the sages' barracks.

Leesil pleaded with little more than his blind faith in someone he loved.

"We had better go," she said.

He blinked in relief. He took her hand, gripping it gently, and pulled her along as he headed down the road.

"Say nothing to Magiere," he told her. "If what you suspect has any truth in it . . . for now, we'll keep this between us."

*   *   *

Magiere faltered as she passed Aunt Bieja's little home. Even with the shutters closed on its one front window, soft light leaked through the cracks.

Few villagers were about, and those few quickly became none, now that she stood amid the cluster of squalid buildings. When the sound of the closing doors and sliding wooden bolts ended, she was alone in the dark. For the moment, it was too much. She wanted one warm touch of life before her next task. Magiere opened the hut's door and stepped inside.

Aunt Bieja stood before the burning fireplace, the cook pot's lid in her hand as she stirred its contents. She looked up as Magiere closed the door.

"I wondered when all of you would return," Bieja said with annoyance. "Already added water twice to keep the stew going. Where are the others?"

Magiere decided to say as little as possible. She'd wanted only to see a friendly face not marred by the hidden past that surged toward her.

"They're still at the keep," she answered. "They'll be along shortly. I just stopped to let you know . . . I'm on my way to see Mother."

Bieja closed the pot, and her expression softened. "I wondered if you were going or not. I haven't been there myself in a long while."

Her aunt's words surprised Magiere. Tending those who'd passed on was at least a yearly ritual for the people here. Still, it was best that Bieja had moved on, as had Magiere . . . until this return.

Bieja paused a moment. "So, did you find anything at the keep?"

"A little," Magiere lied. "We'll leave that for later. I don't want to keep everyone waiting too long, so I'd better go."

"Take your time, dear," Bieja answered, wiping her hands with the old rag she'd used for a hot pad.

Magiere stepped out into the night once again.

The graveyard was a ways off into the trees but not so far it couldn't be seen. This was the usual way, as if the dead should still have a home among the living. The lantern that had glimmered within the plot on the first night they arrived was gone. Magiere was forced to call upon her night sight, letting her dhampir nature trickle through her flesh enough for her vision to open wide. It seemed a whole lifetime since she'd last been here, and she stepped slowly through the trees, uncertain of the way.

Village graveyards in Droevinka were little more than a series of spaces in the woods kept reasonably free of low growth. Tree branches were thinner here, letting in the night sky, but the moon wasn't high enough for much light. She made out a few markers sprouting from the earth here and there, with evening mist a vaporous carpet between them.

Some were made of planks and posts. A few newer ones were stone. Recent lapsed taxes and missing overlords may have afforded the coin for such. It was ironic that the changing fortunes of the living were marked by remembrances for the departed.

But it wasn't her own memories she hunted among the dead. She came for those of her mother . . . or at least as seen through her killer's eyes.

Magiere stopped short.

She could neither continue nor flee but only remember the skull she'd so recently held in her hands. In Bela, she'd envisioned a girl's last moment by walking in a Noble Dead's footsteps with a scrap of the girl's dress in her hand. She'd lived inside Welstiel's moment as he tore open the girl's throat without even feeding.

Magiere would have to walk every passage and room of

the keep, over each of its stones if need be, to find where her mother had died. But a scrap of clothing wouldn't remain for her carry now. Not after all these years in the ground. She would need bones.

"Forgive me," she whispered, and drew her falchion. "I have to know . . . to see if it was him, Mother."

There wasn't time to find a spade without drawing attention, so the blade would have to do. She stepped forward, searching for anything that sparked memory of this place— of her mother's marker. Sweat built beneath her grip around the sword's hilt.

The spring before she'd left home, Magiere had gone with Aunt Bieja to a woodwright's shop in a neighboring village of the zupanesta. Her aunt paid for a new marker, the old one having weathered to where it no longer stood up in the earth. The two of them lost half a day's fieldwork in the journey.

Magiere stopped again, looking about.

She remembered that the marker was on the south side of a large fir. She crouched near the base of the nearest tree. There was no marker she recognized by make or the name upon it.

Her dread for her task withered beneath a rising fear. Where was the marker . . . her mother's grave? She stood up to look back, wondering if she'd come too far. The markers in this present clearing were older, so Magelia's grave should be near.

Magiere heard softly shifting branches nearby, perhaps from a breeze high above that had penetrated down into the woods. She gazed ahead along her original path, but saw nothing besides the thickened forest. This was the last graveyard clearing. She backtracked, anxiety quickening her step.

In the previous clearing were a few smaller stone markers. Nothing appeared familiar to her. She heard the breeze again, nearer this time, and it whistled sharply in her ears.

Magiere's instincts surged, and she ducked around a tree. A long shape whizzed past her and cracked against the trunk, and she heard bark tear away under the impact.

A shadowed figure appeared around the tree's far side. Magiere stepped out and away. Starlight was enough for her to make out the disfigured side of his face.

Adryan held a long staff, overly thick at its upper end. He shifted its weight with both hands, slowly swinging the end back and forth through the air like an inverted pendulum.

"Looking for your mother again," he said softly.

It was not a question. Anger stirred dhampir hunger in Magiere's stomach, and her vision sharpened further. Rather than open rage, Adryan's expression was a mix of anguish and anxious hope. He mirrored her movements as she side-stepped farther into the open, tilting the staff from side to side.

"What have you done?" she asked, glancing about. "Where's my mother's grave . . . where's the marker?"

The barest wrinkle appeared on his brow, but it was enough to see he didn't understand what she'd asked.

"You're the last of it," he said. "Magelia was mine, and he took her. When he left, that should have been the last reminder. And then you came, little thing, crawling out of a thieving noble's bed."

The staff's end leveled as Adryan turned his whole body to power his swing. Magiere dipped her blade to catch it.

A dull clang sounded on impact as her sword was slammed away and the staff struck her side. Magiere went down hard, stumbling over a stone marker in her fall. Pain spread through her side.

It was only a staff, and Adryan was only a villager without skill at arms.

When she looked up at him, she was just a child beneath the high branches of the graveyard. All she saw was his scarred face leering at her from the trees on the last day she'd ever found her mother's house.

"I'll send you to her," Adryan said, nodding his head as his cheeks glistened with tears. "And I'll never have to look on you again."

He swung the staff at her, and Magiere shrank away as she'd done so long ago beside her mother's grave. It glanced off the stone marker with a crack.

Magiere rolled back and chopped down with her falchion upon the staff, hoping to break it. A louder metal clang sounded, and the sudden stop of the blade jarred her wrist. She took her eyes from Adryan just long enough to glance at the staff.

Bound to it with nails and straps were thick iron strips longer than her forearm. They formed a sheath around the staff's upper end, creating a crude great mace. Magiere kicked out at his shin.

His foot slid on the wet sod, and he dropped to one knee. Before she could scramble away, he pushed up from the ground and lifted the iron-shod staff. Twisting his body, he brought it round at her again, like a scythe in a wheat field. Magiere leaped back out of its reach toward the next tree.

"Pin her down!" Adryan screamed in frustration.

His words confused Magiere for only an instant, but even that was too long.

Another twinge shot through Magiere's injured side as someone grabbed her wrist from behind and jerked her sword arm back around the tree trunk. Her wrist was held tightly out of sight as a hand clawed at her fingers, trying to take her weapon.

The staff arched toward Magiere's head, and she ducked as low as she could. The bark above her crackled as the staff hit.

Before she could spin to her right and free her sword, a

pitchfork came from nowhere. It skimmed her left ankle, pinning her foot to the ground between its prongs. Its wielder was barely visible around the side of the tree, pressing the pitchfork down with his weight.

Fear gathered in Magiere's stomach and began to burn. Adryan spun around, gathering force into his next swing. His eyes glowed with the hope of an injured man who saw relief within reach.

A scream rang out from behind the tree. Adryan faltered at the sound, and his swing came low as Magiere felt her sword arm come suddenly free.

She threw herself against the pitchfork, not caring that she fell or what had become of the second attacker who'd held her arm. The third man clung to it as he tumbled with her to the ground. Adryan's staff struck the tree's side and recoiled, and he stumbled under the jarring force.

Magiere's fear turned to hunger and ran out of control from her stomach into her head. An ache built in her jaws. It sharpened as her teeth pressed apart and her mouth filled with saliva. Her vision opened even wider, and the night brightened enough to hurt her eyes.

Magelia had been taken away by a Noble Dead. But it had been Adryan in the graveyard clearing who'd taken the last of a mother from a forlorn and frightened child.

Magiere bit into the arm of the man grappling for the pitchfork. Her teeth sank halfway through thick wool cloth and into flesh. He cried out, and wet heat spread across Magiere's lips. The taste of salt seeped through the wool and into her mouth. She smashed her fist down on the man's head, and he went limp.

Magiere arose, tears in her eyes. She snarled, the blood still in her teeth, and rushed at Adryan.

*   *   *

Leesil followed Wynn into the hut, expecting to see Magiere waiting, but he found only Aunt Bieja fussing over her cook pot.

"Finally," she huffed. "Now, if that niece of mine would bring herself back again, we can eat whatever hasn't caked itself to the bottom of this pot."

Leesil settled Wynn at the table, and the sage hunched there with her head down. That Magiere had come and left again fed Leesil's worry. Bieja told him where she'd gone, and this calmed him somewhat.

He'd wondered when she might visit her mother's grave, realizing she might prefer to do so alone. So he would wait, but not for long. When Bieja added the tale of Chap's escape, Leesil slumped at the table with a groan.

He'd spent years drinking himself to sleep at night to hide from the nightmares conjured by his past. Those torments, resurfaced in newfound sobriety, lessened when he lay in Magiere's arms at night. The long-hidden secrets of the keep hinted at things as dark from Magiere's own past. And to top it all, he would have to find Chap before the dog frightened unsuspecting villagers.

All he truly wanted was everyone here under his watchful eye, safe, so he could forget what he'd seen at the keep, if only for a short while. He didn't even want to hear more of Wynn's insights. She sat staring blankly at the tabletop, lost in her thoughts.

"You want to tell me what's going on?" Aunt Bieja asked. "From the look of you two, that niece of mine is being as closed-lipped as ever."

Leesil shied away from the elder woman's gaze. "I think it's best to wait for her. It's not my place to—"

"You'd better start filling my ears with something I want to hear," Bieja warned. "Unless you'd like those ears trimmed down to a respectable size."

Leesil was in no mood for parental threats.

"That skull in her hands . . . ," Wynn whispered.

"What's she saying?" Bieja insisted.

Wynn lifted her head like a child on the verge of sleep but troubled by a sudden thought. The sage's words made about that much sense to Leesil. She wasn't even looking at him.

"What about it?" he asked, raising a hand for Bieja to wait.

"What was she doing with the skull?" Wynn asked, seeming afraid of any answer that might come.

"Seeking a vision, I think," Leesil answered. "In Bela, she had to hold something from a victim at the place of death. It let her see through the killer's eyes, if it was a Noble Dead. I can only imagine what it's like for her. I couldn't let her do that . . . not with what we saw in that room."

"Are you going to tell me anything?" Bieja interrupted.

Before Leesil could stall her further, Wynn continued. "But where is Magiere?"

"She went to visit her mother's grave," he answered.

"Now . . . in the dark, after holding that skull . . . after all of what we found?"

Wynn looked away in puzzlement, lips moving as she mouthed something to herself. She turned back to Leesil. "No, she would not. . . . Do not let her—"

"*Valhachkasej'â!*" Leesil cursed, and he was off the bench and heading for the door.

Aunt Bieja shouted from behind him, but he was already out into the night and running for the graveyard.

In the keep's sacrificial chamber, Magiere's actions had terrified him more than what they'd found. She was obsessed with finding her undead sire and had tried to reach back to relive the slaughter.

The moment she'd stared into the skull's empty sockets

was shadow and dust compared with what he feared she did now in the graveyard.

A male voice screamed from somewhere ahead in the dark.

Leesil leaped and dodged through the grave markers of the first clearing as another voice cried out. Two more clearings, and he still couldn't find Magiere. He heard a snarl from nearby, and he stumbled, trying to pick out its direction.

He followed it into the next clearing, and what he saw brought him no relief.

Magiere grappled with a tall man at the clearing's far side. Her falchion was missing. Even in the dark, Leesil saw her mouth forced wide by teeth like a wolf's. The two struggled for control of a thick-ended staff, until Magiere wrenched it sideways, pulling herself closer to her opponent.

Her head twisted, and she bit into the man's shoulder.

Leesil sucked in cold air. He drew one of his blades as he closed on the two and slammed full speed into both of them.

The impact sent all of them sprawling, and Leesil tumbled up against a tree. His scarf had fallen off, and he stripped his cloak, as well. When he rolled to his feet, Magiere was facedown to his left across two broken markers, and then he spotted the body.

Pitchfork across his limp hand, a man lay still where he'd fallen, eyes closed, mouth slack. Leesil looked at Magiere.

She rolled to a crouch. The saliva running from the corners of her mouth was darkened from stains on her lips and teeth. Her eyes were wide with irises full black, and her face was wrinkled in a snarl. She didn't even look at him and glared back at her opponent. When he arose, Leesil recognized him.

Adryan, half-scarred and half-mad, stood with his eyes locked on Magiere.

Magiere had succumbed to rage, slipping deep into her

dhampir half. In such a state, Leesil feared she wouldn't stop until Adryan was dead. What could there be between these two that had kept this kind of hatred alive for so long?

Adryan swung the staff high, bringing it down toward Magiere's head, and she made straight for him, lunging to her feet from all fours. If Adryan missed, Magiere would tear him apart, and if he didn't . . .

The staff's end came down, and Magiere swerved around it without breaking stride.

Leesil leaped in to cut her off. His left foot landed upon the slant of Adryan's grounded staff, and he kicked out with his right into Magiere's shoulder. She tumbled away, and he stomped down with his full weight upon the staff. It snapped, and Adryan stumbled back with the splintered half in his hands.

Leesil stood with both feet planted, the staff's heavy end trapped beneath one foot. It felt thick, and he glanced down to see its iron-shod end.

In his youth, he'd seen shorter, single-handed versions used by Lord Darmouth's mounted riders to disperse crowds. Whoever didn't fall beneath the horses' hooves had their heads split open by those swinging iron-shod clubs.

Adryan had come here to kill Magiere.

Leesil stepped toward him, lifting his one blade.

"Get gone," he rasped out. "If you want to live."

Adryan stood there a moment, claw marks on his face, his shirt and vest shredded and stained with his own blood. Leesil saw the remnants of a strange hope in his eyes, and then it faded as the broken staff dropped from his grip. He put his hands to his head, turned, and fled into the trees.

Leesil turned toward Magiere and remained perfectly still. She clawed wet earth to pull her feet under herself and get up.

"Magiere . . . come back," he whispered.

Face soiled from the ground, her head jerked around at the sound of his voice.

Black irises fixed upon Leesil. There was blood on her mouth, in her teeth. Her hands were stained, as well, and her fingers were hooked, ready to grab for him. Beneath the blood, her nails appeared extended beyond her fingertips.

Leesil knew she didn't see him. Not him . . . just some thing in a predator's path.

"Please," he said softly. "Come back to me."

Ever so slowly, he crouched downward, reaching with his free hand for the shod end of the broken staff.

"Magiere . . . Magiere," he whispered over and over.

With hands outstretched toward him, she froze there, and Leesil stopped, too.

The creases of her snarl faded from around her eyes. Her mouth closed until only her long canines were visible between parted lips. She looked down with her black eyes at her bloodied hands and began to shudder.

"It's all right," Leesil said. "Let it pass."

He started to rise again, and she flinched. She saw him. He tensed and swallowed hard, knowing what returning awareness would bring to her.

Still feral in all her features, Magiere's expression twisted in horror as she looked at him and at her own hands. She began backing away.

"No . . . Leesil. Not again."

Her words were barely understandable with her mouth so altered. She choked between whimpers and collapsed to her knees before Leesil could reach her. Hunched over, she covered her head with her forearms rather than hands. Leesil dropped before her, tilting her up by the shoulders.

He saw the change pass over her.

Between clenching spasms of her jaw muscles, Magiere gagged as if trying to clear her mouth and throat. She bucked in dry heaves each time, and all he could do was steady her and wait for it to pass. Her teeth receded until only the canines remained slightly long. It was her eyes that shifted last, color flooding in from the outside edge of her irises. Magiere stared back at Leesil, her face stained by tears, soil, and blood.

She began pawing at him frantically.

She pulled his shirt up, nearly tearing it apart. Everywhere she touched left stains of blood from her hands, and that increased her frenzy.

"Enough!" he said, and grabbed her wrists to stop her. "It's not my blood. I'm all right."

Magiere closed her eyes and leaned forward until her head thumped against his shoulder. It didn't take long for her pull away again. "Adryan?" she asked weakly.

"Still alive," Leesil answered. "But there's another body across the clearing. Did you . . . kill him?"

Magiere jerked her arms out. Leesil was startled how easily she broke his grip. She ran across the clearing, and he followed. When she couldn't bring herself to touch the prone figure, Leesil put his hand near the man's nose and mouth and detected shallow breathing. He gave Magiere a quick nod of assurance.

"Leave him," she said. "Let him wander home on his own."

Leesil picked up his scarf and cloak from where they'd fallen. Magiere sat down and leaned tiredly against the tree, dragging the falchion to her from where it lay nearby.

"If this ever happens to me again," she said, "stay away from me."

"I can face you," he answered, "any way you—"

"I can't," she cut in. "I couldn't face hurting you again. And I don't want to even think about what you saw in me tonight."

"I've told you more than once, I'm not that easy to kill . . . and I can face you, any way you are."

Leesil crawled over to kneel before her. Now that she was safe—from herself, as much as anything else—his fear faded to be replaced by anger.

"What I can't face is why you came here," he said. "Where's your mother's grave? What did you do?"

Magiere looked out through the ruined graveyard, markers shattered, broken, and uprooted.

"I couldn't find it," she whispered.

At first Leesil wasn't certain of her answer. But if she'd done what he'd feared, vision or not, he believed he would have seen its aftermath in her face.

"I have to know if it was Welstiel," she said.

"Not like that." He shook his head. "Whatever happened, you don't want to feel your mother die in your hands. And you don't even know where she died. What were you going to do, wander the entire keep?"

Magiere's gaze was still distant. There were clear paths through the grime and blood on her face, and Leesil realized she was silently crying.

"You saw what was in that chamber," she said, and turned away from him as if hiding in shame. "What am I?"

Leesil knew it wasn't a question she expected him to answer. He shifted closer and grasped her arms, turning her toward him. Using his scarf, he tried to wipe some of the blood from her lips. When he'd done as much as he could, he leaned in and kissed her softly on the mouth.

He sat back and looked in her astonished eyes.

Chap watched from the thicker forest beyond the graveyard as Leesil led Magiere away. Panting in the darkness, he hung his head in relief and licked the remnants of blood from his jowls.

He had nearly run out to Magiere and given himself away when the scarred man appeared. So fixed upon Magiere and her opponent, he had not even sensed the approach of the others. When the two skulking peasants tried to hold Magiere against the tree, he rushed in from behind to seize the one holding her sword arm by his leg. Grinding flesh in his jaws, he dragged that one screaming into the woods. He released the man to hobble away only when he was certain the peasant would flee rather than return to the fight.

Chap then ran through the trees around the clearing, trying to find an avenue to strike Magiere's opponent without being seen by her. His evasion of Wynn's questions had already stretched everyone's patience. If Magiere saw him in this place, or anywhere near her mother's grave, she would expect an explanation.

Leesil arrived, and Chap pulled back as the fight ended, but he kept Magiere and Leesil in sight.

Neither of them should be here . . . in this place, on this path. The further Magiere pressed on into her past, the less likely it was that Chap could ever stop her. As she and Leesil left the graveyard together, Chap circled back once again to a marker left lying in the woods.

It was strange how mortals clung to the dead. To remember them was one thing; to hold on to them like a possession was another. For Magiere it presented a temptation he could not allow. Seeing her mother die as if by her own hands could strip Magiere of hope. And then, even Leesil's presence might not be enough to keep her from falling into darkness.

So Chap had raced ahead of Magiere to the graveyard and found what she had sought. He did not understand the spoken language of this land, but its written markings and symbols were similar enough to those of Belaski. Speaking furtive wishes to the grass, he asked the blades to grow and creep. They filled in and covered the hole left at the grave's head, and he dragged Magelia's uprooted marker into the forest.

Chap stepped into the ruin of the graveyard, markers toppled and broken all around from a conflict of festering old hates and anguish. When he passed Magelia's grave again, all signs of its presence or the missing marker obscured, he paused on instinct and sniffed the earth.

It was undisturbed, but this he already knew. Magiere had not found her mother's true resting place. He sniffed again, scent filling his head, as if this were the way to sense what was missing beneath the odor of damp loam, grass, and slivers of old wood caught in the earth. Even the dead carried a lingering essence of the life once held.

There was nothing.

Chap stared down at the earth. Whatever had been done here had happened so long ago, there was no trace of how or when.

But Magelia's bones were gone.

Magiere lay in the corner of her aunt's hut, curled in the unfolded bedroll. While Leesil had tried to clean them both up at the village well, she asked him to tell her aunt whatever he thought was necessary to explain this night. When they'd returned to the hut, Aunt Bieja put Wynn into her own bed, and Leesil had settled Magiere in the corner to rest.

Tomorrow, they would move on to Kéonsk, though Leesil was reluctant. They would leave early, before word of what happened in the graveyard spread through the village.

She half heard Leesil's low voice as he sat at the hearthside table talking with her aunt, but her fatigue-fogged thoughts drifted elsewhere.

She'd been so lost in rage but remembered Leesil's face.

The night had been brilliant in her sight, but his luminous

hair had burned her eyes like the sun. Confusion rose as she reached out her hands, ready to tear him.

And then doubt . . . followed by strange longing.

He spoke, and at first she heard only one word. "Magiere."

She remembered. This was her name.

The eyes that watched her were like amber stones she wanted, would hide away, and keep to herself.

That face, those eyes . . . had a name. Both were framed in her sight by her own hands, blood appearing to run from his flesh down her fingers. She could taste it in her mouth. It made her choke with despair.

"No . . . Leesil. Not again."

Terror followed.

Until he leaned close, kissed her tainted mouth, and she looked in shock at Leesil's face to find no revulsion there. The same face that had called her back from hunger.

As Magiere lay in the bed, a scratch came at the hut door. She was vaguely aware of Leesil speaking in sharp tones as he let Chap in. The dog looked about, walked over to her, and sniffed her head. When Magiere rolled to look at him through half-open eyes, her thoughts ran in a blur, and for no reason, an odd memory surfaced.

She walked south on the coastal road of Belaski. They were just approaching Miiska for the first time. Its north-end market was filled with people out for the day buying and selling the necessities of life. In the air was the smell of baked goods and smoked fish and other simple things.

Magiere looked up again into Chap's crystal blue eyes. "No, not yet. We go on."

The dog wrinkled his jowls and trotted over to drop beside the bed where Wynn slept.

The room darkened, and only the low fire spread a red glow through the room. The blankets lifted as Leesil crawled under them. He lay close to her. Magiere slid her fingers into his hair, letting her palm come to rest against his tan cheek.

"I want to remember your face," she whispered. "It keeps me from the dark."

Chapter 7

They awoke before dawn at Aunt Bieja's urging, and gathered their belongings to leave before anyone saw them. Magiere was quiet the whole while, and said only a few words when she bade her aunt good-bye. She watched Bieja with worry as the elder woman exchanged token packets of herbs with Wynn. Leesil lingered back by his own pony.

The night before, it had surprised Leesil how little Magiere's aunt reacted to what he'd told her of the keep and the graveyard, though he'd said nothing of why he'd gone after Magiere. Aunt Bieja wasn't blind to the changes in her niece and remained sadly silent through Leesil's tale, only nodding now and then.

As they prepared to mount up, Bieja came to him last.

"Mind yourself," Bieja told him quietly, away from the others. "Between instinct and knowledge"—she nodded toward Magiere and then Wynn—"you'll need wisdom to balance things out."

To be taken so quickly into the gruff good graces of Magiere's one and only relative brought a lump up in Leesil's throat.

"You don't have to stay here," he said. "We have our place in Miiska."

Bieja's expression darkened like the Droevinkan sky. "This is my home, for better or worse."

"Think about it, please," he said.

Placing his foot in the stirrup, he swung up into the saddle and look down at her. The elder woman's face, for all its stoutness and darker color, wasn't far different from Magiere's.

"I'll think about it," she answered.

"Think hard," he said, and handed her a folded scrap of paper. "Or we'll be back to cause you more trouble."

Bieja frowned in puzzlement and took the parchment.

While the others had slumbered that morning, Leesil had torn a spare page from the back of Wynn's journal. He wrote a brief letter of introduction to Karlin and Caleb back in Miiska—with six silver sovereigns wrapped in it for Bieja's traveling money. He hoped she would heed his wish.

"If you change your mind," he said, "travel to Miiska and ask for Karlin or Caleb, and show them this letter. Either should recognize my scrawl, and it tells them you're Magiere's aunt. They'll get you settled at the Sea Lion. And this isn't charity. Caleb could use the help."

Aunt Bieja looked once more at the letter. She tucked it into her apron pocket, and her brown eyes grew warm as she patted his leg.

"Take care of my niece," she said.

And the next part of their journey began.

Three days later, Leesil felt little relief upon reaching the Vudrask River once again. His thoughts mixed upon themselves with all that had happened in Magiere's village, from the morbid discovery in the keep's hidden chamber to the chilling realization of Magiere's loneliness as a child. She had been shunned and despised for sixteen years, yet for all the cruelty, she'd had one person in those days who truly loved her and was willing to let her go her own way. It made him wonder if his parents had loved him, and if they had ever considered letting him choose his own path.

Part of him wished he and Magiere shared such thoughts more easily. In spite of their newfound closeness, they'd spent so many years avoiding any discussion of their pasts. Habit was quite hard to break.

When they reached a village along the Vudrask, it was late in the afternoon. They bought passage on another barge, east to Kéonsk, the capital city of Droevinka. Cloak over his arm and charcoal scarf covering his ears, Leesil stood on the bank of the river. Its wide gray water flowed under an afternoon breeze that rushed across his face.

Down by the docks, Magiere haggled with two men from a passing caravan, trying to sell the ponies. Her cheeks glowed white under the overcast sky. When the sun peeked through the clouds, red glints surfaced in her black hair. Both men slowed their heated barter to stare. Even Leesil caught his breath, but not for the same reason.

Magiere didn't look like a creature of this world. She was too beautiful, her contrasts too severe. She frowned at the men as Leesil approached.

"I paid four silver sovereigns apiece for those ponies," she said, "and they're offering five for the lot."

Leesil looked at the men with lined faces and calculating eyes and wondered if they were brothers. "We're not in the trade . . . just looking for a fair price."

"If she paid too much for the beasts," one of them replied, "it is not our loss to bear."

Leesil glanced at Magiere. They had money to spare from the necklace Wynn sold off in Bela, but her stingy nature would not let this go.

The price settled at seven silver sovereigns for the ponies and the mule. Magiere wasn't satisfied, but the barge was leaving. Leesil pulled her away as he took the men's final offer. Once the barge left the shore, he settled with Magiere under their blanket. She was still annoyed.

"I'm not a miser," she said, though he'd made no such claim. "That was robbery." She wrapped her hands around his leg beneath the blanket.

Wynn sat cross-legged on Leesil's other side. The young sage looked physically healthier for two nights indoors and eating Bieja's lentil stew. Her mood was another matter, though she wasn't half as withdrawn as Chap. The talking hide was laid out before him, but Chap showed little interest in conversation. After days on that troublesome pony, the barge's flat deck was such a relief to Leesil's backside that he didn't care. There was little reason to think Chap would be any less secretive than always.

And Leesil's mother waited—or so he hoped.

This urgent desire made him understand Magiere's desperation to discover her past even more. It also made him anxious to head north and trace what had happened to Nein'a. But the better part of him would still leave no stone unturned for Magiere's sake, and so they continued east, deeper into Droevinka.

Clear roads paralleled both riverbanks, and a stout oxen team on the south bank pulled them at a steady pace until dusk. Although they'd planned to sleep aboard the barge, at nightfall the vessel docked at another waterside settlement large enough to be a small town.

The trees nearby were too faded for this wet land, lacking the typical dark green, yet full winter was still a ways off. Between the clusters of huts spreading along the river to both sides of the landing, taller wooden buildings stuck up at the village's center and near the river. Along the road out the

town's west end was a stable with a smithy. Just shy of this
was one large, well-lit building.

"Is that an inn or common house?" Leesil asked one
bargemen, and then he added to Wynn. "Perhaps we don't
have to sleep outside again."

Wynn sat up expectantly and chattered to Chap in Elvish.
The young bargeman looked at Leesil hesitantly.

"This is Pudúrlatsat, a regular stop," he replied. "It's a
strange place. Townsfolk will bring out any cargo in the
morning."

"What do mean by *strange*?" Magiere asked. "If there's
trade here, we should try to resupply."

The bargeman shook his head with a shrug. "Suit yourself, but this place is too dull for my taste, even when we land
at midday."

Leesil raised an eyebrow, looking to both Magiere and
Wynn.

"I prefer to sleep inside if possible," Wynn answered.

Magiere folded the blanket and picked up her falchion.
"We'll see what they have to offer. There wasn't an opportunity to gather stores while we stayed with my aunt."

Leesil strapped on his punching blades and fastened his
cloak so the weapons wouldn't attract attention. He didn't
expect to need them, but the past few days had him on edge.
He looked the place over as they walked up the dock and toward the sloping path to town.

Street lighting was scant as they approached the center of
town. Oil pots hung from tripods at the four corners, where
the dock path crossed the main road running through town.
Wynn was a step ahead of Leesil, cold lamp crystal in hand
to the light their way.

Chap growled softly and moved out ahead of her.

A tall wolfhound limped around the corner to peer at them
from beside a tripod lamp. It didn't growl in return.

Leesil saw the animal's gaunt build and dull eyes coated in a film of age. He stepped up next to Chap, ready to grab the dog. Chap reacted to other canines in varied ways, sometimes friendly and at other times attacking without warning. Leesil never knew what to expect. Chap sniffed toward the newcomer and offered a soft whine.

"I think we should go back to the barge," Wynn said.

A trickle of fatigue washed over Leesil. He couldn't fathom why, and shrugged it off as he stepped onward past the wolfhound. "Let's at least check for an inn."

Once in the town's midway, Leesil made out signs above one shop for a leatherworker and another for a woodwright. There were a few people about, closing up for the day and going off to their homes or elsewhere. Most appeared to be old or middle-aged, moving slowly with a tired gait. He was about to head for the well-lit building they'd seen upon docking, when he realized Magiere was no longer beside him. She'd stepped beyond the intersection and stood looking down the main road the other way.

"What?" he asked, joining her, then noticed her worried expression.

"I'm . . . it's nothing," she answered. "It's a bit dreary compared to Miiska."

"You figure that out all by yourself?" he chided. "What tipped you off?"

She didn't even snap at him. As she turned around to head up the road, Leesil sighed and followed, waving Wynn on ahead of him.

Several villagers paused as they passed, but no one gave them much notice. The most distinct expression Leesil caught was a weary curiosity from a man with a burlap sack over his shoulder. He looked back once, for the man moved too slowly for his age, as if walking were an effort. The villager trudged along with his head down. The buildings around them gave way to small huts and cottages, and ahead Leesil caught the charred scent of the smithy.

"What can we do for you?" a voiced called from his left.

Leesil slipped his hand down to one blade strapped on his thigh. Magiere turned toward the voice as Chap circled back.

From a side path stepped a short, compact man in a leather hauberk wearing a sword sheathed on his hip. In the glow of Wynn's crystal, his eyes were light brown and alert, but his sand-colored hair showed hints of gray. Beside him was a petite young woman so pretty that Leesil blinked.

She resembled the man in coloring, but where his short hair was dull and lank, hers hung in a wheat-gold wave to the small of her back. Her eyes, round and large above a tiny nose, were nearly gold in the crystal's light. Her dress was the color of a sunflower, less drab and dingy than that of the other townsfolk.

"We're passing through on a barge," Magiere said, "and hoped to sleep indoors tonight, if you have an inn."

The man didn't answer at first, gaze dropping to her sword sheath peeking from beneath her cloak. "I am Geza, captain of my lord's guard," he said. "This is my daughter, Elena. The inn closed up a while ago, but there's the old common house."

He pointed to the well-lit building Leesil was steering them toward.

"The inn closed?" Leesil asked. "On a main route to the capital?"

"The proprietor passed away with no one left to take over," Geza answered.

Elena took a step closer, staring at Magiere's sword, as well as her bone amulet. She smiled at Wynn and Leesil.

"You are welcome," she said. "Father and I live near the manor, though I often come down with him on his rounds. I will help you settle in the common house, if you like. It's seldom used but for our own gatherings. Bring your dog, and I'll find supper for you."

"We can pay," Magiere answered.

"Of course," Elena replied.

She led them onward, and Geza followed behind, surveying all they passed along the way. There were fewer folk about and far more homes with scant light slipping through shutter cracks. Chap paused once along the way, head up and ears perked.

Beside a wide lumber cottage with a split shake roof was a small pen, its fencing made of scavenged branches bound by grass twine. The three thin goats within the enclosure made no sound, not even shuffling nervously at Chap's presence. Leesil noticed that the tall wolfhound was still following behind Chap at Geza's side.

"This is Shade," the captain said, and passed by to open the common house door. "She's a good dog, a fine hunter."

Leesil patted Shade's head, and the wolfhound wandered into the common house ahead of everyone. Wynn followed with Chap, but Leesil turned around. The road back through town was empty. The bargeman had called this place dull. A severe statement coming from one who lived in this land.

"I hate this country," Leesil muttered. "Oppressive and depressing, no matter where you turn."

"Figured that out, did you?" Magiere retorted. "And what was your first clue?"

Leesil ignored her teasing. Things here didn't fit together well. He'd seen no young people about except for Elena. Nothing but thin old goats, thin old dogs, and thin old people trudging about.

"Come inside," Magiere said. "We'll be on our way in the morning."

Leesil joined her, but the man with the burlap sack and half-hidden face lingered in his thoughts. There had been something wrong with that face. Like Geza's, it hadn't been quite old enough for the person who wore it.

Late in the night, Chap lay with his muzzle on his paws and his eyes on the common-house door. The place was little more than a large room with a simple kitchen out back and a few benches and tables. The dying fire still crackled in the wide stone hearth.

Magiere and Leesil had layered their bedrolls together and slept near the far wall. Magiere's leg was wrapped around both of Leesil's. Her head rested upon his shoulder, and her blanket of black hair spread across his chest. Wynn lay just behind Chap, curled under her own blanket, and Shade nestled against Chap's side.

Chap had never spent close time with another animal. Shade's eyes occasionally opened, and he licked her head, lulling her back to sleep with her own memories of warm hearths, wide fields, and mutton stew. But he would not close his eyes.

From the moment he had stepped across the town's threshold, a familiar discomfort nagged at him. His skin tingled, and he was on edge. It was not quite the hole he felt in the life of the world when he fixed his awareness upon an undead. Yet it was close. Then there was Shade, not as old as she appeared, who suffered the waning of essence that came only in late life.

Chap longed to hunt, to find what lingered in hiding here, but there had been no tangible scent or sense of what plagued this place.

So he lay with his eyes on the door.

Long past midnight, it creaked open.

Chap raised his head barely above his paws, scooting his back feet under himself, ready to lunge.

Shade's wiry head lifted. Instead of apprehension, Chap

felt a weak glee from the wolfhound as she struggled up. Her
tail switched slowly, and she stepped in front of him. Chap
did not expect this and tried to maneuver around her. A wink
of yellow in the dark caught his eye, and Elena slipped
through the doorway in her sunflower dress.

He sensed only sorrow in the girl.

Shade went to Elena, haunches wagging as much as her
tail. The girl dropped to her knees, and the hound licked her
face. Chap stepped closer, looking directly into Elena's eyes.

"Help us," she whispered.

She thought he was a mere dog—yet she begged for his
aid.

Chap trotted over to awaken Magiere.

Something wet pressed against Magiere's face.

She raised her hand to push it away. One eye opening, she
stared right at Chap's nose. He grunted and dragged his
tongue over her cheek again.

"Stop it," Magiere mumbled, wiping her sleeve across her
face.

As she turned her back to the dog, her senses sharpened.

Chap would never wake her without a reason.

"Leesil, up," she whispered.

Next to Chap stood the tall wolfhound, Shade, and kneeling nearby was Elena. Her yellow dress was soiled from dust
on the floor and her calm, friendly manner was replaced with
urgency.

Leesil sat up beside Magiere. The soft sound of voices had
roused Wynn, as well, and she rolled out her blanket, rubbing
her eyes.

"You're the hunter," Elena whispered. "The one who kills
the dead?"

Magiere felt heat drain from her flesh. No one they'd met
on this journey had mentioned such things or connected her

to the old backwoods rumors. She wanted nothing more of peasant superstitions.

"Help us," Elena said. "Please."

"Why do you think you need my help?" Magiere snapped at the girl.

Elena shrank back. "My lord sent me . . . to bring you to the manor to speak with him. Please help him. He'll pay whatever you ask."

"We're taking the barge to Kéonsk tomorrow," Magiere said. "We don't have time."

Two tears slipped down Elena's face. "Just talk to him. That's all I ask."

"Now?" Leesil asked.

"He's waiting. He wants this kept a secret, so as not to give our people false hope."

Chap barked once. He trotted to the door and glared back at all of them with a low rumble.

"Oh, he actually wants to do something," Leesil grumbled. "He's been dragging his tail since we left Bela, and now he wants us to go with this girl."

"He thinks there's something to hunt," Magiere whispered.

She looked at Leesil, and though he was wide awake, he appeared haggard and exhausted. They'd shared a bed for nearly a moon, and only a few times had she awoken in the night to hear him mumbling in his sleep or feel him clench and twitch under an old nightmare. She would gently shake him and pull him close until he settled again into quiet slumber. But not this night, yet he looked as if he hadn't slept at all. Wynn swayed as she stood up.

"Are you all right?" Magiere asked.

Wynn rubbed her eyes again. "I am . . . just tired."

Magiere grabbed her boots and sword lying at the head of the bedroll. "Elena, what is going on here?"

The girl shook her head. "I don't understand it all. You must speak with my lord."

Magiere wished she'd listened to the bargemen and stayed out of this town.

"All right," Leesil said. "Give us a moment."

He pulled on his own boots and strapped on his punching blades. As he fastened his cloak, Magiere saw him pull out the topaz amulet she'd given him so it hung in plain sight.

"Wynn, bring the talking hide for Chap," he said.

Moments later, they hurried out into the night. Magiere took the lead, falchion unsheathed, and Chap trotted beside her. Elena and Wynn followed, with the wolfhound between them. Leesil fell back to the rear.

"How far is this lord's manor?" Magiere asked.

"Only a little ways," Elena answered. "It's not too far to walk."

When they reached the town's midway with the tripod lamps, Elena directed them inland. The dock path extended past its meeting with the main road and widened a bit as it headed through the trees and away from the river. Magiere glanced back every so often to see Leesil watching the side ways between the buildings. Once beyond the town, he looked through the trees to either side, all the while fingering the topaz amulet.

The land rolled slightly, but it wasn't as sharply hilled as around Magiere's home village. They came to a wooden bridge with railings that spanned a stream running over a rocky bed. The bridge was sturdy and wide enough for two horses to cross abreast. At the far side, a branch hung low in the way. Magiere pushed it aside to pass, and the limb snapped off. A cascade of pale needles fell loose to litter the bridge flooring.

The branch seemed dead, but it had withered and rotted so quickly that its needles had no time to wilt off.

"Something's out there," Leesil whispered.

Magiere looked back to see him watching the forest upstream.

"Wait here," he added.

As he slipped over the bridge's side, Magiere tightened her grip on the falchion. She glimpsed Leesil's cloak in the dark before he vanished from sight around a tree. When he didn't reappear on its other side, she stepped closer to the railing, trying to spot him again.

Leesil reappeared upslope from the stream and nearer the road beyond the bridge. As he stepped out into the open path, he waved them forward. Magiere urged Wynn and Elena on, and Chap ran ahead. When they caught up, Leesil gestured for Magiere to follow him.

"Chap, stay and keep watch over Wynn and Elena," he said.

Magiere followed Leesil into the forest. Any undergrowth was all but gone here, with patches of bare muddy earth all around. They headed downslope through the thinning trees, until Leesil stopped and pointed.

"Close to the water, this side of that large embedded rock," he said.

At first Magiere wasn't certain what to look for. Then she spotted a scattered handful of cattle by the water. They were so still.

"Didn't even jump when I came out of the trees," Leesil said. "Not surprising, from the look of them."

Magiere let her night sight open up.

The cattle were thin. Even from this distance, their ribs stood out against sagging skin. Their large eyes were half-closed, nether asleep or fully awake. What were they doing wandering loose in the woods, as if no one cared what happened to them?

"These are the worst," Leesil said. "The goats in the town were similar, and so are the people."

"I don't understand." Magiere sighed, and Leesil shook his head in agreement, but his handsome face looked tired, like everything and everyone else here. She reached out and touched his cheek, letting her finger run down to his chin. "And I'm worried about you. I don't like this."

"Me neither, but we should find out what's going on."

She led the way back to the others, and they headed inland once more. Their destination appeared after only two more curves in the road.

While it wasn't a proper keep, the square building was two stories of fortified stone. Perhaps this deep into the country, away from the borderlands, there was no need for more. Other wooden buildings were set off to its sides, one tall enough to be a barn but with a peaked shake roof. A low stone wall encircled the grounds, and the road curved by a side path up to its large iron gate. Geza was waiting there.

"You came," was all he said, and he waved them through. The captain led them on to the doors of the large stone manor. Once they passed inside its entryway, there was a change.

Magiere felt jarred, as if in one step she'd crossed a distance to another place far away, separated from the world right outside. The interior was suitable for a fief noble or vassal lord, but it wasn't the luxury of their surroundings that brought this strange sensation. Something else had just happened, and she peered suspiciously back as Geza shut the doors.

"This is much better," Wynn commented, rolling her shoulders.

Braziers hung from the walls at the entryway's sides, and there were lanterns down the hallway ahead. Geza had them kick off their muddy boots in a small side room before he led them down the hallway. Over the stone floor was a dark blue carpet with fringed ends and patterned borders of maple leaves.

"It feels different here." Leesil sighed in relief. "Less oppressive."

Geza gave them a quick side glance but didn't comment. "This way."

Magiere noted her companions' reactions. Both Leesil and Wynn looked more awake. Not fully rested, but alert. The captain ushered them through an open archway and into a large chamber.

Tapestries of hunting scenes were illuminated by old-fashioned iron braziers mounted in the stone walls. A walnut table with stiff high-backed chairs ran end to end across the room. On its other side was a large, arched fireplace. Piled logs crackled therein, sending a wall of heat across the chamber to its entrance. There were no servants, and Magiere had seen no other guards on the grounds besides Geza.

One chair was pulled near the blaze. In it sat a tall man in his early thirties staring blankly at the flames. He wore simple breeches and soft clean boots. His shirt, what Magiere could see of it, was dull white and in need of a wash, and he clung to a blanket wrapped around his shoulders and covering his arms.

Magiere couldn't imagine anyone feeling a chill in this sweltering room, and she stripped off her cloak to drop it over a chair.

The man's hair was sandy, like Geza's, but longer and ill-kept. Thick stubble on his jaw didn't suggest a beard so much as many mornings of forgotten grooming. Elena hurried over to him, putting her hands protectively on the back of his chair.

"They're here, my lord," she said, but when he didn't respond, she added, "Stefan . . . the hunter is here."

Magiere winced at the word *hunter.* She watched Elena's hand settle on the lord's shoulder and gently slide up to his neck into the back of his hair. Leesil tapped Magiere's arm and raised his white-blond eyebrows.

Was Elena serving as mistress of this house?

"You asked for us?" Leesil said.

The man blinked and turned his head to look at them. The lost expression in his eyes faded, but he didn't stand up. Instead, Elena motioned to wooden benches placed near the fire.

"It's so warm in here," Wynn said, and the lord sat up straight at her words.

"You may call me Stefan." He spoke in Belaskian. "We lost the need for decorum a while ago, as prisoners do not have titles."

Stefan's gaze wandered to Magiere's sword and to Leesil's blades as he tossed his cloak on top of Magiere's before circling to the hearth. Magiere followed, ushering Wynn and Chap before her. Stefan's eyes rested a moment on Chap, and his mouth formed the beginning of a smile.

"I see my Shade has found a friend. All the dogs but mine were the first to go."

He slipped his right hand out from under the blanket, the other still tucked away, and Shade walked stiffly over to lick his fingers.

Magiere remained standing, while Leesil straddled a bench, loosening his shirt collar. Wynn sat down with Chap beside her.

"What about the other dogs?" Leesil asked.

Stefan didn't answer, but his faint smile remained as he studied Wynn more closely. The hide of Elvish symbols was half-unrolled beside her upon the bench.

"Who are you?" he asked. "It's difficult to imagine such a bookish girl involved with these other two."

"I help as I can," Wynn answered.

Magiere folded her arms. A few moments in this lord's languid presence was enough to stir her dislike of the man. He was likely useless and found himself far too tragic.

"Why don't you get to the point . . . why you called for us," she said.

"It's a rather long tale, but if you can help, I will pay anything you ask."

"Just tell us what plagues these people."

"My replacement," he said.

And he began his story.

Lord Stefan Korbori's wife, Byanka, wasn't beautiful, accomplished, or overly rich. He was a soldier, son of a second-generation noble who'd died in military service to Prince Rodêk's father. Distinguished by only a minor title, he possessed both the ambition and the ability to lead, but he considered himself most fortunate to have won Byanka's hand. She was blood kin of the Äntes house, favored second cousin of Ivanova, half sister to Prince Rodêk. And Rodêk was reining Grand Prince of Droevinka.

In Byanka's company, Stefan surfaced from the ranks of lesser nobles to the attention of Baron Cezar Buscan, Prince Rodêk's chief counsel and Protector of the City in the capital, Kéonsk. After quelling a peasant uprising over grain tax, at the age of twenty-eight, Stefan was rewarded with the Pudúrlatsat manor and its coveted fief, only two days' travel down the Vudrask River from Kéonsk.

He took his new responsibility seriously, and Byanka served well as his lady without complaint at being taken from court. She shared his ambitions and knew the fiefdom was a stepping stone toward favor with the Grand Prince himself. After two years in the fief, Stefan celebrated the birth of a son. In that hour, he felt affection for his wife that had nothing to do with her royal blood.

Crops flourished, his son learned to walk, taxes were collected on time, and the fief's commerce grew. After excelling in arms of war, Stefan showed his worth in orderly governing. Life was good as he returned home on a quiet night from a neighboring village. Byanka sat in the main hall by the huge hearth, teaching their son to pet Shade more softly and not pull on the dog's fur.

Stefan smiled. "Any luck?"

"Not really," Byanka answered. "It's fortunate she's so patient with him."

Stefan's wife was short, plump, and plain, with mouse-brown hair, but she paid careful attention to proper appearances. She had engaged Geza's daughter, Elena, as a personal maid to dress her hair every morning, though she rarely left the manor. Her idea of a good day was raising their son and enjoying a dinner with her husband, when they might discuss the future together. He appreciated her calm demeanor and understood her sacrifice in marrying him, and he promised himself she would never regret such a choice. In the years to come, he would surely be appointed to serve on the prince's counsel at court.

Geza, the captain of his guard, entered. "My lord, you have a visitor from Kéonsk."

"Taxes aren't due for a month. Who is it?"

"I don't know him, my lord," the captain answered. "He calls himself Vordana and says he was sent by Baron Buscan. Should I show him in?"

"Vordana? No title?"

"None that he mentioned, sir."

This visitor was unlikely to be of serious importance and perhaps was only a messenger. Until he was certain, Stefan thought it best to receive this Vordana privately.

"Byanka, why don't you take the boy upstairs?"

With a smile for her husband, she whisked their son away. Soon after, Geza escorted the visitor in and left the room. Stefan didn't bother to mask his surprise.

Vordana was of medium height and slight of build. Unarmed, he wore a shin-length umber brown robe that swished when he walked, and it was tied closed by a scarlet cord. There was no mud on his boots. His clothing, unusual for travel, was not the most remarkable thing about him.

Around his young face of twenty or so years hung hair as white as that of an old man in his final days. It lay unbound across his shoulders, reaching to midtorso, and glowed vividly in the firelight of the warm hall. He wouldn't be thought handsome, with his thin-lipped mouth and deep-set eyes, but he was striking.

Stefan didn't know what to say and forgot even a polite greeting as Vordana circled the room, looking at everything but Stefan and nodding in approval.

"Yes," he said in a hissing slur, "this will do nicely."

"You are from Kéonsk?" Stefan asked. "Baron Buscan sent you?"

Vordana turned as if seeing Stefan for the first time, or perhaps as one forced to take notice of another's presence. "Yes," he said again.

"You didn't come alone? Do you have men who need barracks for the night?"

Vordana stared at him through black eyes. "I have, two guards outside. I required no others, as those stationed here will serve my needs."

Stefan tensed, disquiet growing inside him. "My people will see to your needs for the night. Perhaps you should state your business."

"Business?" Vordana stopped near the hearth with his arms folded. "I am to assume the stewardship of this fief. Is that

not part of Baron Buscan's authority, to award the fiefs of the
Äntes?"

At first, Stefan suppressed his rising alarm, wondering
what he could possibly have done to fall out of favor. All was
in order in the fief, and more so, it had improved in his care.
He stilled his thoughts and stood his ground.

"I oversee this fief," he said, "and Baron Buscan has sent
no word to the contrary. By your own address, you aren't
even titled."

Vordana smiled with teeth as white as his hair. He coiled
one hand into his robe and pulled out a rolled parchment.

"Here is the order signed by the baron. You have been re-
assigned to the cavalry under Baron Lonâes, on his way to
Stravina concerning border matters. I understand you have a
wife and child, so you are welcome to wait until morning to
take your leave."

Stefan snatched the parchment from Vordana's hand. It
bore the Äntes seal.

He tore it open and scanned the contents twice to confirm
every poisonous word. It ended with the rough signature of
Baron Buscan. Stefan had somehow fallen from favor.

"It has all been arranged," Vordana said. "I am told you
are devoted to the grand prince and the Äntes house, and that
you would respond with good grace and duty."

Stefan remained completely still for a moment. Then he
jerked his sword from its sheath. Vordana's smile didn't have
time to vanish before he ran him straight through the heart.
Stefan's voice was quiet and sharp as he whispered to Vordana.

"Here is my good grace to you."

Vordana's smile faded. He tried once to gulp a mouthful
of air and died before his body struck the floor. Dark red
blood spread outward through the white shirt beneath his
robe. From out of the shirt's collar tumbled a small brass vial,

some strange token hanging by a chain, and it dangled over his shoulder upon the floor.

"Geza!" Stefan shouted.

His captain ran into the room, sword drawn, for Stefan never shouted. "My lord—?" Geza began before he saw the body.

"Where are his guards?" Stefan demanded.

"Outside, in the courtyard," the captain answered. "Waiting with the horses."

"Find men you trust for discretion, and send them to the stables. Tell those two guards to take their horses there. When they are out of sight, have your men kill them both. Dispose of the bodies and mounts in the forest where they will not be found. If anyone comes to ask, we have had no visitors from Kéonsk. Do you understand?"

Geza stared at him, but Stefan knew his captain would obey. Geza's own success in the ranks depended on Stefan's position. With a brief hesitation, the captain hefted Vordana's body over his shoulder and left once more.

Stefan took two long, slow breaths to quell his anxiety, then stood up straight. If Buscan truly wished to replace him, he would know soon enough, but something about the parchment felt wrong. It was unprecedented for a fief steward of title to be replaced with no prior word—and certainly not a lord in good standing. And not by some untitled miscreant. He would wait for further word from Kéonsk.

A month passed, and nothing came.

Stefan began to relax. Geza showed some disquiet in his presence, but otherwise life remained ordinary. Until the night Byanka screamed.

Stefan sat in the hall by the fire and heard her horrified wails from the upper floor. He ran up the stairs, following her voice, and found her standing in their son's room, ripping at her hair.

In the bed lay his son, or what had once been his son.

The little face and hands were shriveled husks above the covers, and his eyes were open but dried and sunken. He looked like one abandoned in a wasteland to die of starvation and thirst, transformed into a dwarfish, withered old man. Stefan had kissed his son good night just hours before, and now the boy was dead.

Byanka cried out like a madwoman. "I hear the guards whispering. The visitor who came that night . . . What have you done to us?"

When Stefan reached out to give her comfort, she shoved him away and began howling again.

In the days that followed, her mood remained unchanged. One evening when Stefan again tried to calm her, he saw lines in her face and the darkening rings about her eyes. Fear filled him at the thought of an unknown plague spreading among them. He closed the manor to outsiders and kept his guards out of the villages as much as possible. Byanka continued to wane over the next three days. No matter how much water or broth she drank, she suffered from a terrible thirst. When she finally died, Stefan wept, crouched by her bedside, where she lay as withered as their son had been.

Within a moon, the peasants and animals of Pudúrlatsat began dying.

Crops and trees withered along with them. Geza followed orders without question but wouldn't look his liege lord in the eyes. At the month's end, Stefan rode to an outlying village of the fief and found it thriving. Only the town nearest the manor, on the river to Kéonsk, suffered this mysterious blight. He returned home that night at a loss for what could be done.

He feared sending word to Kéonsk for assistance. He feared an inquest. Once in the courtyard, he handed his horse to a guard, walked to the manor's main hall, and froze in its archway.

A cloaked and cowled figure stood by the hearth. It took effort for Stefan to breathe evenly as he entered. Someone had come looking for Vordana. When the figure turned his way, Stefan's anxiety turned to horror.

Fair skin was as gray as Stefan's dead wife and son when he had buried them. The man's shin-length robe was soiled all over, as were his boots and bloodstained shirt. Stark white hair hung out of the cowl in dirty, lanky clumps. His eyes peered out from sunken sockets.

Stefan tried to speak, but his voice caught in his throat.

Vordana stood by the hearth.

Yes, came the word with its taint of reptilian slur, but Stefan was uncertain if he actually heard it aloud. He jerked out his sword and rushed around the hall's table.

Laughter surrounded him, and he stopped before the pale figure of Vordana. Disbelief made him dizzy as he held out his sword.

I am already dead, and that will not help you.

Vordana's dead lips never moved.

I could drain you to a husk, like your mate and offspring, but I want you to live a long, painful life . . . my puppet! Even your guards I will leave . . . for a while.

Stefan rammed the blade through Vordana's chest. The man lurched back one step, but that was all.

Unintelligible words, like a hum, built to an ache inside Stefan's head. His vertigo increased with those sounds in his skull, and he lost control of his body. His hands dropped limply to his sides, and his legs buckled until he knelt upon the floor.

Vordana did not bother to remove the sword from his chest. Stefan watched helplessly as the man's pale, begrimed hands clamped about his own head. Over the hum in his head came words he could understand.

I can maintain my watch here just as easily behind a puppet, but for my broken life, yours is forfeit. You remain in the manor, and by my command, if you step beyond the threshold, you will die in that instant. You will do whatever I instruct but always while locked within your stately cage. I will drain your town and land as I need to sustain myself. When they are gone, I will turn to you and your household.

And before you think that death is your escape, you will not join your son and wife by such an act. Look upon me to see what lies beyond your death if you attempt to take your own life.

Stefan lost awareness of the room, of himself, and of Vordana, except for the words that subjugated his own thoughts over the chant buzzing within his skull.

Then all was sudden silence, and he opened his eyes.

The hall was empty, as was the passage through the archway. He ran along it to the front door and pulled it open. There was no one outside.

In that quiet moment, it seemed his fevered imagination, fed with guilt and loss, had conjured him a nightmare. Had Vordana even visited him? Light-headed, he put his hand on the edge of the doorway to steady himself. A chill bit his hand through to the bones, and he fell back with a scream.

"What happened?" Wynn asked abruptly. "Could you not leave the house?"

Lord Stefan closed his eyes and shook his head. He opened the blanket wrapped about him and held up his hands. Or rather one, for the other was missing. All that Wynn saw of his left hand was a scarred stump of wrist.

"We had to cut it off," Geza said in Belaskian.

Wynn jumped at his voice. She had forgotten his presence across the room while she listened to Stefan's tale.

"It had to be removed before the rot of dead flesh spread," the captain added.

"Your wife and child," Magiere asked of Stefan. "Were there any wounds or other marks on their bodies?"

Elena shook her head, answering for him. "They just faded, the life draining from them."

"How did Vordana survive two thrusts through the heart?" Leesil asked. "And how did he trap this lord in the manor? What are we dealing with here?"

There was long pause.

"We hoped you would tell us," Stefan said.

"Well, he was certainly an undead, judging from your description," Leesil said. "Perhaps even a type of Noble Dead we haven't heard of."

"What is that . . . a Noble Dead?" Stefan asked.

"The highest, most powerful of the undead," Wynn answered. "They retain more of who and what they were in life than simple spirits of the dead. They move freely in the world under their own volition, but must feed on the living to sustain themselves. They can learn, grow, become more than they are, like the living."

Magiere grunted at this last comment, but Wynn did not respond. They never spoke of their disagreement over Chane in the sewers of Bela, but Wynn knew Magiere had been wrong. It stood to reason that if not all humans were the same, then not all vampires were the same either. Lord Stefan's replacement was certainly another matter.

"So Vordana is one of your Noble Dead," Stefan said, pulling the blanket around himself again. "He gained a title after all."

"By what you described, he's a mage," Leesil said. "We've run into such among the undead before."

Wynn caught Leesil's glance toward her. Obviously Magiere was not the only one to recall that moment in Bela's sewers.

"Could he do this to himself?" Leesil asked her. "Raise himself from the dead?"

Wynn shook her head. "I don't know. At my homeland guild, we study many things to prepare for becoming journeyman sages. Domin il'Samaud was my instructor for arcane arts, but I never heard mention of anything like this. There was talk of life-theory, and how some conjurors focus on spirit work. A few to the extent of reanimating the dead."

There was one small detail of Lord Stefan's tale that surfaced in Wynn's thoughts.

"You mentioned that Vordana wore something around his neck."

Stefan nodded. "A small brass vial on a chain. A token of some kind, I assumed."

"Some conjurors use brass containers," Wynn continued, "to trap conjured or summoned elemental material, including that of spirit—even a human spirit. But to do so as preparation against one's own death, or to reconjure one's own spirit back from death . . . It would be impossible."

Wynn felt Chap pawing at her leg. The dog snatched the rolled hide sitting on the bench and pulled it to the floor. She reached down and finished unrolling it, and Chap began tapping upon it with his paw.

"What is he doing?" Elena asked.

"It's a bit much to explain," answered Leesil.

Wynn followed his movements until he stopped and looked up at her.

"*Tôlealhân'* . . . will-craft?" she asked in puzzlement.

At first it made no sense, but when clarity struck, she wished it had not.

"Sorcery," Wynn whispered. Chap barked once to confirm

it before she continued. "I know what was done. Vordana placed a *hàs* upon Lord Stefan."

"Sorcery is outlawed," Leesil said. "And what do you mean? . . . What's this *hàs*?"

"It is Numanese, my language," she answered. "I do not know a Belaskian word for it. *Tôlealhân'* is Elvish and could refer to a mage of the mental realm. That is sorcery, just as the arcane of the physical realm is thaumaturgy, and that of the spiritual is conjury. In the Elvish of my continent, *hàs* translates to *gyeas*. It is a task set so deeply into one's mind that the victim would 'will' its own death rather than fail to accomplish it."

She looked at Stefan, and though there was twisted justice here for what he had done to keep his position, she pitied him.

"Magic does not hold a *gyeas* in place," she said to Stefan. "It becomes part of you, your thoughts, like a hidden memory you refuse to forget. Deep inside, you believe beyond doubt what will happen if you fail to obey. Only a countering *gyeas* might break this."

"And that would require a sorcerer, like Vordana," Stefan replied, his gaze distant.

There was nothing more Wynn could offer, and the following silence bore down on her. Leesil finally changed subjects.

"Your replacement was sent by the prince's man," he said to Stefan. "Why didn't someone come to investigate when you never reported for your new duties?"

"Perhaps it was all a lie, and Baron Buscan didn't know." Stefan pulled the blanket tighter, shaking his head. "And all I did was for nothing but fear."

"That seems unlikely," Magiere said. "Anyway, all that matters is what we can fight."

"Sorcery is not just used upon victims," Wynn cautioned.

"It can be used to expand the powers of the sorcerer's mind. It is the most insidious of the three magics, but it is not what brought Vordana back. To do this, he would also have to be a master of conjury, with power I have never read of. Even in studies with Domin il' Samaud, there were few legends of individuals who mastered and combined all three magics into what is called 'wizardry.' "

"Oh, lovely," Leesil groaned. "Then there's someone else who did this for him."

Magiere's expression hardened as she paced once before the hearth's expanse, tossing her head toward Stefan.

"So, now we decide . . . whether or not we help a murderer."

Wynn's own surprise at such harsh words was broken as Elena spat back with equal venom.

"How dare you? You've no idea what he's suffered. Will you help our people or not?" Her tiny hand remained protectively on her lord's shoulder.

Stefan raised his one hand to cover hers. "Enough. It's all right."

Wynn stared up at Magiere. "It is the people here who need our help."

"We need to discuss this ourselves," Magiere said bluntly. "Alone."

Stefan nodded and stood, heading for the archway. Elena followed him with Geza close behind.

Until leaving Bela on this journey, Wynn had always lived with the sages and worn simple gray robes. For a moment, watching Elena with her lord, she wondered what it would be like to have a mass of wheat-gold hair, to wear a dress, and to have a man grasp her hand. She pushed such thoughts away.

"Magiere, you know we can't refuse," she insisted. "Vordana may take his time in torturing Lord Stefan, but he does so through the people of this fief. Sooner or later, he will kill everything here and perhaps move on to another settlement."

"I'm not so sure . . . about moving on," Magiere said. "And we have no way to find this Vordana. I've sensed nothing since we docked here, and Leesil's topaz has shown no sign."

"Perhaps Vordana is too far off, somewhere else," Wynn argued.

"No, he's close," Leesil answered. "With what this lord has told us and what we've seen, he's near enough."

"Could Chap track this thing?" Magiere asked.

The dog barked three times.

"That means *maybe*, so he is uncertain," Wynn said. "But he might not need to. I am not a mage, but there may be something I can try . . . a small mantic trick. Connections exist between all things, especially the living. If Vordana sustains himself by absorbing life energies around him, I might be able to see it happen, as it affects the layer of Spirit in this place. I could find him."

Leesil shook his head. "Wynn, this sounds like—"

"It would be like watching the surface of a lake," she cut in, "when a trough has been gouged somewhere along its shore. The whole surface shows signs of movement in the direction of drainage—in the direction of Vordana. I have some notes from my studies, and I think I can do this much. We have to try. Is this not what you do? Hunt the undead?"

Wynn fell silent. Once, in Bela, she had tried to focus her own life energies to speed the healing of Leesil's flash-blinded sight. It had seemed to work, but she was forthright in stating that she was no mage. What she proposed was more than bolstering the natural processes of life. But what choice did they have? She could not believe Magiere was ready to walk away from this on the moral grounds that Stefan was to blame, even if he had murdered two innocent guards.

Magiere closed her eyes in resignation and nodded. That was enough answer for Leesil.

"We'll try it your way, Wynn." Leesil reached out to pat her hand. "We'll try it your way. But there's one more thing. By Stefan's tale, Vordana said he was here to watch. But for what and why?"

"I caught that, as well," Magiere said, "but I'm not certain what it means."

Elbows on knees, Leesil folded his hands and leaned his forehead upon them. "A spy . . . perhaps a scout, someone preparing a foothold for war."

Wynn sat up straight and spoke out too loudly. "That makes no sense. Belaski is prosperous, and Stravina is on constant guard from the provinces in what you call the Warlands. Who would invade—?"

"Not from outside . . . from within," Leesil said. "A civil war. If Buscan did send Vordana, then why hasn't he followed up? Unless he can't do so openly. Or it's possible someone else tried to place Vordana here on watch for a reason."

"It's not our concern," Magiere said, though Wynn saw Leesil's words working upon her. "So, do we assist Lord Stefan . . . all three of you? This may get ugly in ways we can't foresee, and I want to be in agreement."

Chap yipped once, and Wynn nodded.

"No matter what Elena says," Leesil growled, "that lord is a self-serving bastard. Make him pay until it hurts. And as much as this pains me, make him throw in some horses. That barge isn't going to wait for us, and we'll be back to traveling by land when this is over."

"We'll gather our belongings from the barge in the morning," Magiere said. "We stay on the manor grounds tonight.

It seems to be the only place Vordana doesn't touch, and judging by the change in you and Wynn since we entered the manor, I believe that much."

"Yes," Wynn said in relief. "I will tell them we are staying."

Magiere picked up her cloak and turned back to Wynn. "I'm glad you're with us.

Wynn's face flushed. "I am, too." To her surprise, she meant it. She only hoped that when the time came, she could do what she claimed.

Chapter 8

Leesil finished the most depressing day of his life. Well, perhaps not the most, but it ranked high in recent memory.

The barge master was surprised that they planned to stay and offered to return most of their passage fee. Leesil took it, thanked him, and helped Wynn unload their belongings. He sent her back to the manor to prepare what she needed to find Vordana.

Magiere hoped to catch Vordana in the forest, but they couldn't count on this, so they spent the morning in Pudúrlatsat getting the lay of the place. Dead-eyed townsfolk and bone-thin animals made Leesil wish they'd never left the barge the night before. Anywhere outside the manor grounds, a nagging exhaustion plagued him. They returned to the manor so he could regain his strength before nightfall, guessing that Vordana could move only at night. Unless Wynn presented reasons to the contrary, they decided to proceed in the same manner as they had always hunted before.

Geza provided them crossbow quarrels, and Leesil prepared a pot of simmering garlic water. The cook, a stout older woman, didn't care for him in her kitchen, and she cast angry glances his way. Leesil offered her his most charming smile without effect. Once the garlic water was ready and partially cooled, he set the quarrels to soaking and asked that she leave them be. He filled flasks with oil and prepared torches, then went to see how Wynn was progressing. She sat at the main hall's table with her journals and a few unrolled parchments. Chap, Magiere, and Shade were already there.

The hall was a pleasant place, if Leesil forgot the outside world that awaited them. The fire roared, and fresh mint tea and bread were on the table, so he helped himself.

"Have you found anything?" he asked.

Magiere sighed. "Nothing that helps."

Wynn raised an eyebrow, her lips pursed as if holding back a retort. She turned all her attention to Leesil as she answered. "Conjurors can bind a spirit, but the body is still dead. I think Vordana's body is more a vessel for his spirit than anything. That means his body may not last. From Stefan's description, Vordana's body does not revivify like a vampire's would, but it also means taking his head may not be enough."

Leesil swallowed a mouthful of bread and leaned closer to peer over Wynn at the journals and parchment scattered before the young sage. The writing was in a language he couldn't read. On one parchment were strange diagrams and symbols, and a list with one word written in Belaskian— *dhampir*.

"So cutting his head off won't work?" he asked.

Strands of brown hair escaped Wynn's braid to curl in wisps about her tired face. "No, it might destroy him, but I'm not certain. At worst, severing the head would separate his vision from his body, making his continued actions more difficult."

Magiere rubbed her forehead. "Why didn't you just say that earlier?"

Wynn sucked in a deep breath and held it. When she finally answered, it was with a measured, forced calm that didn't quite hold. "Because I have no idea what Vordana truly is! I am making the best guesses—"

"What about garlic?" Leesil cut in.

Any diversion, no matter how annoying and weak, was better than these two taking out their frustration and fatigue on each other. Wynn shrugged and shook her head, and Leesil returned to sipping his tea. At least the sage had developed a backbone in dealing with Magiere's seething nature.

"The trouble I see," he said to Wynn, "is that he'll leech you and me on sight. Magiere and Chap don't seem affected by the consumption in the village."

"Yes," Magiere replied, "and I don't want you and Wynn facing something you can't fight."

"Don't even think about taking on Vordana by yourself," Leesil warned.

Wynn rolled up her parchments, slid them into a leather cylinder, and tucked the case into her pack upon the floor.

"Though Vordana drained Stefan's wife and child quickly, this would likely have required focus—again, only a guess. If Magiere and Chap can engage him immediately, he might not be able to center upon Leesil or me, and then perhaps Leesil can get to him."

"Sensible," Leesil said. "All you need do is point the way, where and when he comes."

The young sage closed her journal, one thumb rubbing repeatedly along its leather spine. She stared at the tabletop, lost in thought.

Leesil's wariness grew as he watched Wynn still worrying absently at the journal's spine. Before he could say anything, Elena entered, carrying a canvas satchel with both hands.

She wore a freshly pressed dress of forest green, and her

wheat-gold hair seemed to bounce on the air as she walked. "I'm sorry for the delay," she said. "It took all day to raise the money."

Magiere sat upright. "What do you mean 'raise' the money? Stefan is paying out of his own coffers."

Elena looked at them all with confusion. "Stefan has no fortune. What Lady Byanka left him is beyond reach while he is trapped here. A small portion of the taxes supports the manor. For your fee, he contributed household money set aside for stores, though we have grain and crushed oats to keep us. Then this morning he also had two horses sold at a neighboring market. The rest of your fee was gathered from the townsfolk. They've been told of you and were glad to help pay."

Sounding neither bitter nor angry, Elena tried to explain as if she'd made some sort of mistake. The dhampir had come to save them, and Elena was openly grateful to live on porridge all winter to pay the agreed price.

Leesil looked away, unable to the meet the girl's eyes, and his gaze passed over the pewter pitcher of red wine that rested beside two goblets on a side table. It took all his effort to keep from striding across the room to drown his frustration. A quick glance from Magiere was all the confirmation he needed before he took the bag from Elena.

"How much did Stefan get for his horses?" he asked.

"There was his war stallion and riding horse. I think forty silver shils, or about nine sovereigns, among what is here. Is it not enough?"

Leesil knew little of the price of horseflesh, but it sounded like less than half of what such animals were worth. He reached into the satchel, counted out forty shils worth of coins, and handed the bag to Elena.

"Buy proper food for the household, and give the rest back to your people."

"But, the dhampir said—"

"Never mind." Leesil dumped the coins in his hand onto the table. "This will be enough."

Elena looked at the pile and then at Leesil. Her perplexed frown didn't fade when she nodded and left the hall, satchel in hand.

Leesil offered Magiere a halfhearted smile. "Nothing ever changes."

"Not in this world," she replied, then shook off the moment and got up from her chair. "The sun is setting, and we should get to the edge of the town. Wynn, I want to keep this away from the people, if possible."

"Of course," the sage agreed. "But I cannot be certain where Vordana will come from until I sense him."

Leesil strapped on his studded leather hauberk and belted his punching blades as he watched Magiere prepare. She put on her own hauberk and made certain her falchion slipped easily from its sheath. Her black hair tied back with a leather thong, its red glints matched the firelight tinge on her pale face. He wished he could watch her a little longer like this. There were two crossbows, and he handed the smaller one to Wynn.

"Strap this over your back . . . just in case. I'll get the quarrels and meet you outside."

They walked out the manor's gate toward Pudúrlatsat. As they neared the village, Wynn stopped in the road that led through its center to the river dock and knelt down. She rolled the cold lamp crystal between her trembling hands until its light burst forth, and set it beside her on the ground with her crossbow.

There was so much to remember from years past. She recalled theories and processes she had studied in her homeland guild, recorded in scant notes throughout her journals. It was little more than what all apprentice sages learned of the arcane, among all other subjects studied. All theories, summation and postulation, but it would have to suffice.

"I must focus," she said, "if I am to tune my sight to the element of Spirit that pervades this place and see any shift within it."

A simplified explanation. She wished it were as simple to accomplish.

"Get to it," Magiere said. "We'll keep watch."

Wynn clenched her hands to stop their trembling.

Ritual was the safest method, as she did not have the experience to hold all the symbols solely in her mind, as with a spell. It would also bolster potency and provide stability. She scratched the sign for Spirit in the earth with a wide circle around it, and then kneeled within the circle. She traced a smaller one around herself, and in the border between the two circumferences, she added shorthand sigils.

Wynn remained still, pushing down uncertainty, and silently recited the processes scribed in the earth. Shutting her eyes, she placed her hands over them.

She focused on letting the world fill her with its presence, its essence. She imagined herself breathing it in, and then made the essence flow through her palms and into her eyes. In her darkened sight, the scribed sigils appeared and rushed at her . . . into her . . . until her inner awareness spun with vertigo. Time stretched until she forgot how long she had knelt there, repeating the process until she felt her face—her eyes—begin to tingle beneath her hands.

"Wynn?"

"Shush . . . Leesil, leave her be."

"This is taking too long," Leesil muttered.

Wynn slumped, and her hands dropped to flatten on the ground and brace her up. She opened her eyes.

Across the world's night colors lay a translucent mist of

off white, just shy of blue. Its radiance permeated everything like a second view of the world overlaid across her normal sight. Within the buildings' dead wood, the radiance thinned, leaving shadowed hollows in the shapes of shacks, huts, and shops. The glimmer thickened near the earth and was even brighter in her hands upon it. She looked out through the forest, and the ghostly mist became a net through the branches, leaves, and needles of trees and brush.

But even there, Wynn saw the waning essence as in the town structures.

A nearby tree with barren limbs had lost nearly all its inner sheen, its frame like a skeleton of deep shadows. It was almost dead. She swallowed hard and breathed deep to quell the urge to vomit.

"Wynn . . . did it work?" Leesil asked. "Can you see anything?"

She turned, and the sight of Leesil startled her. He shimmered like a ghost illuminated from within. He shone most where his dark skin was exposed and least where his hauberk and clothing covered him. His amber irises were like stones caught in sunlight, so brilliant, they pained her eyes.

"Yes . . . ," she answered, her voice heavy with effort. "I can see."

Leesil's radiance blurred ever so slightly.

Wynn sat upright, though her stomach lurched. She looked about the forest and at the town ahead along the inland road. Nothing changed.

Then she saw it again. A perceptible shift in the glimmering mist. It moved.

"It . . . He is coming," she rasped.

"Where?" Magiere demanded from behind her.

Wynn looked both ways, along the town's landward side and through the trees, trying to discern the mist's flow. It was slowly building momentum. Its currents aligned, moving in the same direction.

"To the east," she said, and heard Chap's low snarl in answer. "In the trees back beyond the town."

"Leesil, cut through the town, and try to get past him," Magiere said. "Chap and I will draw him back toward the road and try to ambush him this side of the bridge. We'll at least keep him off balance until you come up from behind. Wynn, stay behind Chap and me, and keep out of sight if possible."

Wynn reached for the dark shape of her crossbow.

The mist's currents in the earth changed before her eyes. Still heading east, they paralleled the riverside road through town.

"Wait," she blurted out. "I think . . . think he moved on to the main road."

Leesil hissed under his breath. "*Valhachkasej'â!* He's walking straight into town. All right, same as before, but I'll head east through the woods and backtrack toward him. Try to keep him occupied."

Wynn watched Leesil snuff his torch and take off into the trees. His own glow mingled in the forest's web of essence, and then he was gone.

"That's enough, Wynn," Magiere said. "We know where he is. Come on."

Wynn arose and stepped from the circle.

The world remained a distorted overlay of the ghostly and solid slurred across each other. It should have ended the moment she stepped free of the symbols scratched in the earth, but it did not.

Her vertigo sharpened. She crumpled to her knees again and vomited up her supper.

Two hands grabbed Wynn's shoulders from behind, holding her upright.

"What's wrong?" Magiere said.

"It should have stopped," Wynn gagged out. "I cannot . . . make it stop."

"Close your eyes," Magiere said. "Don't look at anything. But we have to go, now!"

Wynn was jerked around before she could close her eyes.

Trails of radiance flowed through Magiere, as in Leesil, yet without his strange brilliance.

And tangled as well within Magiere's essence were lines of shadow, like those of the dying tree. Ribbons of black wove through her glimmering blue-white essence, and . . .

They moved.

Wynn saw her hands clasped on Magiere's forearm and saw the glow from her own essence—her spirit—creeping toward Magiere's flesh. She lifted her gaze upward, but did not find the amber sparks of light she had seen in Leesil.

Magiere's eyes were pits of darkness.

Welstiel sat up without disorientation that night. For once, he had no dreams, no momentary lapse trying to remember the previous dawn.

Chane had procured a large piece of heavy canvas and, as sunrise approached, found a dense copse. He hid the horses and rigged an enclosed tent, which he covered in branches until it blended with the land.

"My father taught me," he explained. "When hunting, we often slept outside."

Upon waking, Welstiel heard the soft sounds of creaking leather outside the tent and assumed Chane was saddling their horses for the night's travel. In spite of peaceful rest, Welstiel could not escape the memories evoked by the sight of his father's keep and all that happened there. He sat in the makeshift tent, torn between relief for a moment's solitude and wanting some distraction to pull his thoughts from the past.

"Are you awake?" Chane asked from outside.

Welstiel twitched. "Yes. I'll be with you in a moment."

He closed his eyes and tried to clear his thoughts, but his frustration over Magiere's mysterious path wouldn't fade. This was the fourth nightfall since leaving Chemestúk, and still she traveled east.

He pulled the brass plate from his pack and placed it on the ground with its domed bottom surface facing up. Murmuring soft words, he cut the stub of his little finger and let a drop of his black fluids strike the dome's center. It clung there for a moment then shifted slightly across the surface to the east. Welstiel roughly wiped the plate clean and repeated the act, but the result was the same, so he tucked the plate away and crawled from the tent.

Chane stood waiting with the horses.

"Is there a village nearby?" Welstiel asked. "Have you checked the area at all?"

"There is smoke rising east of us," Chane answered. "Since the dhampir travels upriver, I assumed that's where we would head next. What is wrong?"

"I'm not certain," he answered. "I think she has stopped again and not far off."

Chane frowned but mounted up, waiting for Welstiel, and the two moved off through the forest. It was not long before Welstiel noticed the first dead tree—and then another.

They emerged to see a settlement next to the river almost large enough for a town. The main road ran directly through it. Fading smoke rose from shops at the near end, as well as from a few other chimneys up the way . . . too few chimneys for this cold time of year.

Welstiel looked back over his shoulder. In the distance down the road, the forest was lush.

Chane's horse stumbled and wheezed.

"Can you feel it?" he asked, and the tall undead slid from his saddle, clutching his mount by the bridle. "Whatever is happening here, it's affecting the horses."

Before Welstiel could answer, a familiar sound carried down the road—the eerily drawn-out howl of a dog.

"They are here," Welstiel said. "On a hunt."

Chane was already back up on his horse, urging it forward.

Magiere suppressed the urge to charge from around the shop's corner where she hid. She peeked out to see the lone figure walk steadily down the center of the main road. Leesil needed time to circle around behind their target, and she hoped to get in at least one strike before Vordana could act.

She had dragged Wynn behind a water trough across the way, and Chap waited there, too. Wynn was still sickened from what she'd done to herself to spot Vordana's approach, but Magiere could do nothing for her at present. She told Chap to hold until she emerged to face what came, and the dog grunted once in agreement.

Hunger grew in Magiere's stomach, but it was different from before, wrapped around a cold core rather than heated rage rising into her head. She let it seep out until her night sight expanded and the approaching figure became clear.

Grayed, emaciated flesh stretched over the bones of his face and hands, and filthy white hair hung in mats out the sides of his cowl. The front of his white shirt beneath the soiled umber robe was stained dark by old blood. There was no sign of the brass vial Stefan had mentioned in his tale.

Magiere grew wary and uncertain. Among her fights with the undead, this was the first time one walked into the open with no concern for revealing itself. Falchion in one hand, she held her torch back and low behind her. The tripod braziers at the town's crossroads provided enough light that the torch shouldn't give her away.

She peered farther up the road to the town's east end, but she saw no sign of Leesil. Whether he was there yet or not, Vordana was only a building's length away. She leaned back, counted five more of his steps, and spun out from hiding.

Chap's savage wail cut the silence.

Vordana turned toward the sound, and Magiere swung her blade at his throat. Without a glance back, he stepped away, and the blade tip passed in front of him. Magiere swung the torch around at his midsection, and Vordana was forced to retreat again.

Up close, his eyes were filmy and clouded in sunken sockets. He glared back at her and raised a hand.

Chap dashed out and leaped, snapping at the outstretched arm. Vordana jerked his hand back, and the dog landed to wheel back to the left. Magiere inched forward on the right.

"Stay wide!" she shouted to Chap. "Don't let him face us both at the same time."

Behind Vordana, a flicker along the rooftops caught Magiere's eye for an instant. It had to be Leesil closing in.

She rushed Vordana, swinging falchion and torch in wide arcs to drive him toward the right side of the road. Chap stayed left, but he was a snarling mass of jowls and teeth. Magiere didn't know how long the dog would hold off.

A shape dropped from the dark above. Though Magiere knew it was Leesil, the image slowed her for an instant.

Both blades drawn and arms outstretched for balance, he leaped from the roof's edge like a steel-winged bird, one leg drawn up. As his extended foot hit the ground, both blades arched forward at Vordana's back.

Again, the walking corpse shifted instantly out of reach.

Leesil's blades bit the earth as momentum brought him into a crouch. His crossbow hung over his back, and the topaz hanging about his neck glowed brightly. Chap ceased wailing and dashed in from Vordana's left, snapping at the sorcerer. A flinch of uncertainty passed through Magiere. Vordana used something beyond sight to follow their movements. Then anger set in, and her night vision sharpened.

This was just another undead. Strength flooded through her limbs on a wave of hunger.

Vordana's dead face turned toward her.

Magiere felt a sharp ache in her body, as if something were being torn from her insides. A rush of fatigue followed the pain. She shook herself, clinging to her hunger, and the sensation vanished.

Vordana's filmy eyes widened. He sidestepped another snapping lunge from Chap, but his gaze never left Magiere.

You . . . you are what we've been waiting for?

Magiere heard his words though his lips never moved. She swung the torch at his face.

Leesil spun in his crouch and kicked at the undead's legs, trying to knock him off balance. As Vordana hopped clear, Leesil rose up, driving a punching blade toward Vordana's throat. The creature twisted away, and the blade's tip snagged and tore through the side of his cowl.

Vordana's head cocked to the side like a dead owl, inspecting Magiere with startled interest.

All this time, watching . . . and this is how we find you again. You've come home to us!

He grinned, yellowed uneven teeth jutting from receding gums.

Magiere stood her ground. Who had been watching for her? Was she what Vordana spoke of when he'd told Stefan he could keep his watch behind a puppet?

Vordana's gaze shifted toward Leesil.

Leesil gasped, staggering to one knee, and Magiere saw a

shudder run through his body. He tried to strike out with a blade but only fell to his knees.

Magiere charged in, but Chap got there first, slamming into Vordana's legs and knocking him off his feet. The dog scrambled around, snapping for his face. The undead raised his arm in defense, and Chap's sharp teeth bit into the dead flesh. He began thrashing his head to tear it.

Magiere stepped in to aid Chap. Vordana snatched Chap's rear leg, and with the dog's jaws still on his arm, heaved Chap at her.

All she could do was swing the falchion and the torch out of the way as Chap crashed into her. They fell back together in a tumbling mass. As they rolled apart, Vordana stepped toward Leesil's crumpled form.

Fear for Leesil washed away Magiere's rage, and she rushed in front of him as Chap charged straight for the sorcerer. Vordana stopped short, backstepped, and both his hands came up with fingers crooked.

Magiere's head filled with humming words she couldn't understand. Vordana's whole intent was fixed on Chap. Magiere thought she saw a spark flash in the undead's eyes.

Chap skidded to a stop, turning about to stare up and down the street. He whimpered. As he ran back and forth across the road, the whimper grew into a snarl.

"Chap, get back!" Magiere shouted.

The dog didn't seem to hear her. He spun around, eyes glaring at nothing in the spaces between the buildings. With a mournful howl, Chap took off down the inland road toward the manor.

For an instant, Magiere froze in shock, then she rushed Vordana, slashing with the falchion.

He dodged, but this time alarm flashed over his face. Magiere followed with the torch, hoping to light his cloak on fire, but again, he managed to duck and back away.

Your elf is nearly gone, but he'll sustain me for a long while.

Magiere flinched and glanced back toward Leesil. He was getting to his feet, no longer as stricken as he'd been just moments ago.

She realized her mistake. When she whirled back, it was too late. Vordana had both of them in his sight line.

A tingle crawled over Magiere's skin. She didn't understand the chant that echoed through her skull, but it fed an emotion into her flesh and bones that made the world fade.

Fear.

Wynn stood up on shaky legs, struggling with the crossbow, still dizzy with the blue-white mist that permeated everything she saw. Chap had fled, and her spellbound sickness had cost Magiere and Leesil. Both appeared to go mad before she could lift the crossbow to fire.

Leesil dropped his blades and turned about, searching the night. He stumbled off between the buildings.

Magiere backed away from Vordana. She did not seem to see him as she cast about, eyes wide in fear of something Wynn couldn't see. All Wynn saw was Vordana's presence. Unlike the dying tree with its lingering essence, he was completely shadow within.

The world's glimmering essence drifted toward him. Where it touched him, it was consumed like water into a black pit. Trails of the blue-white currents clung briefly to the moving ribbons of shadow in Magiere and then pulled away to drift on to the undead sorcerer.

"Magiere!" Wynn called out.

Vordana turned toward her.

His eyes, like Magiere's, were ebony pits even darker than his form. His composure returned, and so did his grin. He stepped toward her, and his voice filled her mind.

A treat . . . before I return home with good news of my find. I can taste you from here!

Wynn heaved up the crossbow and fired. She tried to aim for center mass as Leesil had once instructed her, but when she pulled the lever and the bowstring snapped forward, the crossbow bucked in her grip.

The quarrel struck Vordana in his right eye. His head jerked to the side on impact, and the quarrel head punched out of his temple. Vordana cried out, grasping at it as smoke sizzled from the wound to envelope his face.

Wynn did not wait and turned to run. In her spellbound sight, she stumbled along the buildings hedging the main road and nearly tripped over a tripod brazier. Its flame blinded her for a moment—but an idea flashed into her mind.

Magiere and Leesil used fire to fight the undead.

The iron vessel was too hot to touch. It looked too heavy to lift by its suspension chains, and there was nothing about that she could light in its flame. She remembered one place where she might find something of use.

Wynn stumbled on toward the smithy down near the common house. They had seen smoke rising from its chimneys when they had arrived the night before. If a smith lived and worked here, there might be smoldering coals left from the day's labor. As she reached the forge room door, she panted in relief. It was not locked. She heard footfalls pounding from behind as she slipped inside.

Chane bullied his weakening horse toward the town's inland side, forcing it to run through the trees. He heard Chap's eerie wailing and needed a vantage point to see what was happening. He did not care if Welstiel followed or not.

The dog's voice fell silent.

The land here was flat, but he found enough of a rise to let him see over the short buildings around the crossroads. With his sight opened wide, Chane saw a bizarre scene play out in the town's midway.

Dressed in her hauberk, with a torch in one hand and her sword in the other, Magiere faced a soiled figure in a short, hooded robe. Chane focused his whole awareness on the dhampir's adversary. What he sensed disturbed him.

The figure's presence wasn't blank, like Welstiel's, but there was no life in this man. Not like one of his own kind, but a lingering deep emptiness of death he'd never encountered before . . . at least not in anything that still moved.

Chap charged into the creature's legs, tumbling it to the ground, and turned to snap his jaws closed on its arm. Leesil was on the ground, but Chane couldn't tell if he was injured. Suddenly, the creature threw the dog at Magiere, and she fell under its weight. Both dog and dhampir were quickly up again. The dead man was already on his feet and stretched out his hands in the air, gesturing at Chap.

The dog whirled several times, and then ran off wailing up the inland road. As it passed out of sight, Chane dismounted and jogged down to the same path between the buildings for a better view. Magiere swung at the creature again, and Chane found what he sought.

Wynn huddled behind a water trough across the main road, a loaded crossbow in her hands. As he looked back to the fight, the dead man gestured at the dhampir standing before the half-elf.

"Magiere!" Wynn shouted.

Every sinew of Chane's body clenched as she gave her position away.

Magiere and Leesil ran off in separate directions between the buildings and inland through the forest. They abandoned Wynn, and the dead man turned to look at her. She fired the crossbow.

Chane got up to run toward Wynn, but something snagged his cloak from behind.

"Stop!" Welstiel ordered.

Chane whirled around, slapping away Welstiel's grip. "She's alone down there!"

"The sage is not part of this," Welstiel said. His dark cloak cast him as a deeper shadow within the dark. "Magiere is in danger. We must go after her."

If Wynn's need were not so urgent, Chane would have set upon Welstiel right then—and severed his head. He took two steps back, turned, and ran between the buildings into the crossroads.

Chane halted between the braziers and searched about. He heard running footsteps to the west along the main road and followed them. Ahead, he saw Wynn disappear into the wide door of a building, and the dead man was close behind her. The air around the building smelled of char and metal. Chane drew his sword as he reached the smithy's open door.

Looking inside, he saw the creature as it peered into the empty stalls to one side. In the center of the room was a brick forge pit of glowing coals.

"Wynn!" he called out. "Wherever you are, stay down!"

The cloaked creature spun around.

Chane had tossed aside many a corpse in his short time among the Noble Dead, but it had been a long while since he'd seen one that had succumbed to decay. The quarrel Wynn had fired into his left eye was gone, leaving a blackened hole that oozed down his gray and sunken cheek.

"You like spells?" Chane asked. "Come try one on me."

A mere boast, since he had no clear idea what magic this thing had used upon Magiere and Leesil. Yet he did have a few tricks of his own.

The undead took in Chane's fine cloak and sword and smiled with shriveled lips. His one eye narrowed in concentration. For an instant, Chane felt a pulling sensation from within his flesh; then it vanished.

The corpse stopped smiling.

It looked down from Chane's face to his chest, and Chane followed its gaze to catch the object of its interest. His own brass urn for binding familiars lay in plain view.

You think you can match me . . . vampire?

The words filled Chane's thoughts.

Through long years of study, Chane knew of few reputed methods of conjury and thaumaturgy that might produce projection of thought. He froze for a moment, at a loss for what to do.

He was facing a sorcerer.

And that meant he was in serious trouble . . . as was Wynn.

Chane lunged forward and swung, burning up the life energies he had consumed in past nights to bolster his speed and strength. He needed to take the thing's head without warning. The creature ducked under the blade, not even startled. It seemed to know what he planned even as he began to move.

The creature grabbed a smith's heavy iron hammer from the wall and swung back at him. It was not skilled at combat, but the action took Chane by surprise. He stumbled back into the forge, and his hand pressed briefly through the ash into hot coals. He snatched it away at the sound of searing skin.

Perhaps it needed time to cast, as Chane would when the moment came. When it swung clumsily again, Chane backed away, his thoughts turning quickly.

Crafting lines of scarlet light with his thoughts, he visualized them overlaying his view of the creature and began whispering his chant. First the circle, then around it a triangle, and into the spaces of its corners appeared glyphs and sigils, stroke by stroke. He sighted through the diagram's center at the ground beneath the sorcerer's feet.

And he heard the creature's laugh inside his head.

A conjuror? And I worried you might be dangerous.

Suddenly, Chane could not move. He could feel his body, and there was no ridid clench of muscle, but it would not answer his will to step away.

As the last of his incantation rolled off his tongue, he shuddered at what he saw through the diagram in his thoughts.

All the room's fixtures shifted in his sight. He saw the forge that should have been behind him and the smithy doors. He saw himself viewed from the room's far side, as if he looked through the eyes of someone facing him . . . the eyes of the dead sorcerer.

A flicker of elemental flame ignited from the ground beneath his own feet, instead of his target's.

The creature had slipped into his thoughts, fed him its own sight, and Chane had unwittingly turned his own conjury on himself. Searing heat filled his boots as the hem of his cloak ignited. And he still could not move.

Then the sorcerer's face contorted, and his mouth opened wide into a silent scream.

The creature's arms twisted around behind his back, reaching, as smoke rose behind him.

Chane felt control return to him. He dropped to the floor, rolling in the dirt to extinguish his cloak. The brief flame he had conjured was already gone, but his breeches were blackened and seared above the tops of his smoldering boots. He scrambled up again, suppressing the pain in his feet.

Wynn stood in the forge room's back corner near a narrow workbench holding an empty crossbow. She leaned against the wall, trying to reload, but her grip kept slipping, and she blinked her eyes repeatedly. A jangling sound pulled Chane's attention back to his adversary, flailing to remove a smoking quarrel from his back.

The sound came from a brass vial on a chain about his neck. It fell into view from the sorcerer's shirt amid his frantic struggle.

Sorcery required no conjuring vessels, so why was this undead wearing one?

On impulse, Chane snagged the dead man's cloak and pulled him around. The sorcerer, shocked by pain from the quarrel, did not respond quickly enough, and Chane grabbed the vial. A hard jerk broke the chain, and he threw the brass urn onto the forge's hot coals. The dead man's expression shifted from pain to horror as the brass began melting.

No! I can't . . .

The sorcerer lunged for the forge with outstretched hands, and Chane slashed out with his sword. The undead dodged aside, still fixed upon the brass vial. It caved in over the coals' heat, and a puff of vapor was released with a snap. The dead man's one filmy eye opened wide as his mouth gaped. He looked wildly about the room.

A word—or was it a name?—screamed through Chane's thoughts.

Ubâd!

Whispering, unintelligible sounds filtered through Chane's mind. Afraid that the undead sought to cast his own spell, Chane rushed him again, but the room filled with swirling clouds of gray. He lost sight of his quarry and couldn't see anything. As he thrashed about, the vapor began to thin almost as quickly as it had appeared, and the clouds vanished.

The sorcerer was gone. There was only Wynn staring at him from her corner before she slumped to the floor.

Her brown eyes wide with disbelief, the image of her oval face hit Chane as if he'd run into a wall. It had been so long since he'd seen her. He stumbled over to drop down beside her on the floor.

"You are burned," she whispered.

There was a sickly pallor to her skin, something brought on by more than fear, and she kept blinking her eyes. Her hands shook as she clung to the crossbow.

"It is nothing that I can't heal on my own," he said.

"Is he gone? Is Vordana gone?"

"Yes, I believe so . . . though I'm not certain how or why. A sorcerer has no use for conjuring vessels. I hoped it was something he needed to maintain his existence."

Chane reached out to help her up, and she shrank away from him. Her gaze wandered over him as if she were looking for . . . looking at something on him. He glanced down to his scorched boots and breeches.

"I will be all right," he assured her.

The reality of his presence seemed to dawn upon her. "What are you doing here?"

"I saw that thing coming after you. I couldn't let him—"

She shook her head, brown braid slipping from her hood. "That is not . . . you know what I meant."

How could he lie to her, keep her from telling the dhampir? How could he find some gladness in her eyes at the sight of him? The only times in his new existence he had been truly content were those sitting at a study table with her, delving into ancient parchments and sipping mint tea. He clung to the truth buried in a half-lie and held out his hand.

"I came after you," he said. "This backward country with its ignorant peasants is no place for you. I have a good horse that can carry us both back to Bela and your guild. I am not what you think, and with your help, we can make Domin Tilswith understand."

Her round eyes widened even more.

"Please. I would do anything you ask," he said, "if we can just go back to Bela and try to live as we did before."

Chane had never begged in his life.

One tear ran down Wynn's cheek. She dropped the crossbow in her lap and put her shaking hands to her head.

"Do you still feed on human blood? Do you still hunt and kill for your existence? Would you stop this for me?"

Chane tensed. How could he make her understand that most mortals were cattle not worth her concern? They meant nothing. Only the few, such as her and Domin Tilswith, truly mattered.

When he did not answer, Wynn wiped her face with her sleeve. She stopped crying but wouldn't look at him.

"Did you see where the others ran off to?" she asked quietly. "Do you know what Vordana did to them?"

For an instant she had shown concern for him, but now her thoughts were for her companions. He had poured out his most honest desire, and she spoke only of Magiere and Leesil and their dog.

"They were panicked. I would guess that creature played their thoughts against them, perhaps buried them in false impressions, even fears."

"I have to find them," Wynn said, and another tear slid down her face. "You cannot follow us. If Magiere knows, if she sees you, she will try to take your head. So will Leesil."

Now she was telling him what to do?

"Don't you miss the guild?" he asked. "Our evenings together?"

"Oh, Chane." Her voice broke as she dropped her head low. "Go away! Even if I do, it was not real. You lied about what you are, and now I have to lie to Magiere and Leesil for you. Get on your horse and escape while you can."

Wynn stood up, bracing herself with one hand on the workbench. When Chane reached out to steady her, she froze for a moment. She did not pull away from his touch but neither would she look at him. She put the crossbow strap over her shoulder and walked to the door.

"I know everything has been spoiled and lost for you," she said barely above a whisper. "And I am grateful you were here tonight, but you must go away. Get as far from us as you can."

Wynn left him standing there, and Chane did not try to stop her.

Chapter 9

Shadowed silhouettes flitted between the trees to either side of Magiere as she ran through the woods trying to escape. Each time she swerved to chase one down, it faded back into the forest beyond her reach. These skulking companions made hunger burn in her throat. When her night sight widened, she saw the glint of crystalline eyes in each dark presence.

Undead trailed her every move.

"We hunt," a voice whispered off to her right. "And you hunt."

"We hunger," from her left. "And you hunger."

One of the dark shapes appeared ahead of her between two wilting fir trees. Magiere slid to a stop, her grip tightening on the falchion's hilt.

Its eyes were like stars dragged down from the sky and entombed in the forest. They fixed upon her.

"You belong with us . . . you know this."

Magiere darted away and thrashed through the low branches. Night's chill ate into her but didn't slow her down. She ran faster, as if loss of body heat freed her. More shapes appeared in the trees, but these huddled upon the ground, alone or together. She heard their snarls, and beneath, the smothered whimpers of their victims.

They were feeding.

Magiere's rage grew. She swerved toward one shadow crouched by a cluster of bushes and raised the falchion to strike it down.

It vanished, and her hunger swelled instead of receding.

What remained was a young man prone upon the ground, limbs flailed out and vacant eyes staring up into the forest canopy. Beneath his slack jaw, blood leaked from his torn throat, and forest needles slowly fell upon him from above. She sensed a remaining trickle of life within him and saw her own hand reaching down for his throat.

Magiere lurched back.

Bodies lay everywhere upon the forest floor. Men and women, old and young. One girl child with eyes wide open sat limp against a tree like a doll on a shelf . . . like the stuffed doll the girl held in her lap. Bite wounds across her pale body showed through tears in her dress and wool sweater.

"No more left," came another whisper through the trees. "No more blood . . . but you still hunger. We still hunger."

All around Magiere, corpses decayed in the mulch.

"Must find more . . . more life . . . and we follow if you lead. Lead us on, little sister. Your time is coming."

Magiere's hunger surged again. Holding it down forced a whimper from her.

"Leesil," she whispered, over and over with eyes closed, until his face filled her thoughts. When she opened her eyes again, the dead were still there, all about in the forest.

A white flicker passed through the trees ahead, appearing briefly here and there between the rotted trunks. Magiere's senses opened wide in fright.

She heard soft breathing and the barest rustle of footsteps

in the mulch. The pound of its heartbeat seemed to vibrate upon her skin.

This was all she heard—no other sounds, no living thing in the forest. Not even herself. Only one heartbeat instead of two, for beneath the cold spreading within her, her own heart had stopped.

She was dead—and she was starving. The voices of the undead in the dark had whispered for her to find blood . . . to feed.

The figure slipped from the trees and into the clearing where she stood.

Leesil stared at her with amber eyes, white-blond hair hanging loose around his tan face. He held out his left hand like an offering.

Magiere saw the scars of her own teeth upon his wrist. Inside she recoiled, but her body crept forward.

"No, Leesil," she sobbed.

The words were difficult to say as her teeth grew and her jaw expanded. Magiere tried to halt, but her feet stepped forward until she felt the heat of Leesil within reach. Rage surged through her for no reason. Hunger deepened in a spasm that made her drop the falchion.

"Stop me, please," she begged him. "You have to . . . once and for all."

"You are alone in this thirst," he said, and Magiere heard the undead gathering, closing in around them through the bone trees. "I'm all there is. And my blood is all that's left for you."

Magiere seized Leesil's arm, tears blurring her vision, and pulled him sharply toward her. Her jaws widened as she buried her face in his throat.

*　　*　　*

Welstiel crashed through the brush in search of Magiere. He wasn't certain why she had suddenly fled into the forest, but he suspected.

That dead thing in the crossroads had slipped something in her thoughts.

Magiere had fallen prey to a command, a suggestion or impression now fueled by her own thoughts and emotions. Lost in her own mind, she was capable of anything, from cutting her throat to drowning herself in the river. He had to find her.

Welstiel stopped, listening, trying to sense for Magiere's presence. He heard thrashing amongst the trees off to his right. Branches ripped at his cloak as he ran toward it. He slowed to a stop in the forest when he spotted Magiere ahead in a clearing. Bloodied scratches marred her arms and face from running through the brush.

He hesitated, seeking for any way to approach her unseen, and circled wide through the trees to get ahead of her before she bolted again. She spun around, frantic as she looked about the clearing, then closed her eyes tight as she whispered.

"Leesil . . . Leesil . . . Leesil . . ."

Her eyes snapped open, and she stared directly at Welstiel. She saw him.

Welstiel ducked through the trees, hoping it had been happenstance, but her gaze followed wherever he went. All his plans melted in that moment. She would not continue this journey or the quest he hoped to steer her toward. Instead, she would turn to tracking him. There was nothing more to do but resolve this crisis.

He stepped from the trees to face her, holding out an empty hand. Hopefully he could stall long enough to free her of the phantasm clouding her mind.

"No, Leesil," she sobbed.

Welstiel froze. In her delusion, Magiere thought he was her half-elf—and hunger and dread were plain upon her pale, scratched face. If Magiere ever believed she had fed upon—killed—her closest companion . . .

His mind worked quickly. There was opportunity here.

She could never face what she had done—thought she had done—or return to Miiska and the pathetic life she had tried to build with Leesil. Magiere would be adrift without purpose. Grief and self-hatred addled a mind, made a person most pliable.

Welstiel carefully wriggled his hand from his glove, snatching it with thumb and forefinger before it fell. He worked the brass ring off his finger, knowing what this would do to her. Without the ring's protection, her instincts would sense his nature immediately.

Magiere shuddered.

Welstiel knew this was dangerous, but the possible advantage outweighed any cost. She certainly could not kill him.

"Stop me, please," she begged. "You have to . . . once and for all."

"You are alone in this thirst," Welstiel said. "I'm all there is. And my blood is all that's left for you."

Her irises full black, tears ran down her face as she seized his outstretched arm and pulled him close. She buried her face in his neck.

Welstiel tensed, waiting for her to bite into him.

A muffled moan rose out of Magiere that Welstiel felt through his chest. Her hands clenched tightly on the shoulders of his cloak.

Magiere shoved him away hard.

Welstiel grabbed at tree branches to keep from falling. His shock became frustration. Magiere collapsed to hands and knees like an animal trying to restrain itself. The sight was pathetic, distasteful.

She looked up at him, a hint of confusion in her feral features.

"Leesil?" she whispered with uncertainty.

Welstiel realized he had pushed too far. There was nothing more to do but what he had come for in the first place. He drew back his hand.

"Wake up," he snapped, and struck the side of her head with his fist.

Magiere spun backward, falling facedown in the wet mulch. Welstiel slipped on his ring and ducked out of sight behind the nearest trees.

He watched her from hiding to make certain the blow was enough to break this fear-driven obsession. She choked a few times, rose to her hands and knees, and looked wildly about the clearing.

"Leesil!" she screamed out. Magiere clawed her way to her feet and began running toward town.

Welstiel sank to the ground. Any relief he felt was smothered in bitter disappointment.

Leesil stood alone in the forest. There was blood on his hands, on the stilettos in his grip.

He dropped the blades, backing away, uncertain of where he was, what he'd done, and to whom. He glanced down at his arms. His sleeves were of thick cloth, colored a soft charcoal gray with a hint of green. A cloak of the same shade hung about his shoulders with its hood up over his head. Across his nose and mouth he felt a scarf wrapped to obscure the lower half of his face.

He had seen these clothes before. Sgäile of the *Anmaglâhk* had worn them, the elven assassin who'd hunted him in Bela.

Leesil turned but stopped short before he could flee.

Between the trees ahead of him stood a tall man with his back turned. Narrow framed and square shouldered, black hair cropped short in a military style, he wore an indigo silk dressing gown. Leesil stepped closer, one hand reaching down for a punching blade. It wasn't there.

As he drew close, he saw a strange wound at the base of the man's head below the stubble of his hair. Blood seeped out, running down the man's neck to soak the robe's collar.

The man reached back to touch the spot, then looked at his hand and smeared the drop of blood between thumb and fingertip. He peered over his shoulder at Leesil. His long face was accented with chin beard and scant mustache below prominent cheekbones and a bony shelf of brow.

Leesil's throat closed up at the sight of Lord Progae's hazel eyes. He had never forgotten his first target.

"It never seems to stop, does it?" Progae shook his head with a sigh, neither angry nor sad, nor even surprised as he looked down at Leesil's hands. "The blood, I mean."

Leesil barely found his voice. "I had no—"

"Choice?" Progae supplied. "I understand. You followed orders, and undoubtedly were in no position to disobey. . . . None of us under Darmouth's sway ever were. But I wonder about them." He looked down at the ground. "Was this necessary? Did you have to let this happen?"

Leesil stepped around Progae, keeping a careful distance from the man.

He stood on the lip of a shallow and wide depression in the earth, ringed about by a handful of trees. There lay three curled bodies, a woman with her arms wrapped about two girl children.

There was little flesh left on them, their skin pulled tight over bone in starvation's last day before death. The children's eyes were closed, but not the woman's. The rag she'd wrapped around her head didn't hide her thinned hair.

Leesil had slid a stiletto into Progae's skull while he was alone in bed.

His wife and daughters were turned into the streets. The eldest was taken as an additional mistress by a lord who was loyal to Lord Darmouth. There had been no such half-salvation for the wife and the two younger daughters. As the family of a traitor to Darmouth, they'd found no noble or commoner who'd risk taking them in. Leesil never found them and heard only later that they'd starved to death in an alley.

"Couldn't you have done something?" Progae asked. "It's not as if *they* tried to usurp Darmouth."

Leesil still felt blood on his hands and wiped them on his gray vestment, but it continued to run between his fingers. He backstepped until Progae faded from his elven night sight.

Another voice carried through the forest. "We have a tenuous position here, Léshil."

High and lilting, it was touched with a strange accent he hadn't heard in many years. Not unlike the voice of Sgäile, used to the Elvish tongue and not wholly comfortable with a human language.

"Mother?" Leesil whispered.

"You are *anmaglâhk*," came his mother's voice through the night forest.

It was a quiet and hollow statement of fact with no pride in it. She had said this to him long ago . . . not long before he'd taken Progae's life.

He spun about, searching for the voice. There was movement in the trees, but no more than shadowed silhouettes. Lord Darmouth's first mistress, Damilia, who'd conspired with Progae, stepped forward into his sight. She wore a deep green gown and ermine wrap, and a stray lock of auburn hair

hung across her left eye. Her neck was deeply bruised around
the welt left by a garrote wire. Leesil drew back from her.

"Leesil!" A woman's voice called again.

"Nein'a?" he shouted. "Mother, where are you?"

Among the trees, more figures closed in, stepping out into
his way as he tried to evade them.

Latätz, Progae's sergeant at arms, bleeding from a double
wound to the heart. The blacksmith of Koyva, his throat cut.
Lady Kersten Petzkà, wrapped only in her towel, her skin
sallow from a deadly taint in her bath. They had all committed horrendous acts in service to Lord Darmouth or in their
schemes against him. Or both.

But not Josiah.

The little old minister with his white hair and mirthful vi-
olet eyes stepped from the shadows, mouth spread by a
swelled and blackened tongue. He'd never once raised hand
or word against Darmouth. With no suspicion, the old man
took in a young half-elf to train in a scribe's skills. Leesil had
betrayed him to a hangman's noose because of Darmouth's
paranoia.

Leesil raised bloodied hands to shield his eyes and fled.

Farther out in the forest, he caught glimpses of one lone
shadow as it lunged through the trees like an animal on the
hunt.

"Here. I am here," his mother called out through the night.

"Mother?" Leesil called back.

He could find her if he moved quickly, but a second voice
called from behind him. "Wait for me! I am coming for you!"

Leesil glanced back. The hunting shadow raced after him.
He glimpsed a pale face before the figure seemed to dive out
of sight, into the brush.

"Magiere?" he whispered, not wanting to rouse the shadows of the dead once again. "She's here. . . . My mother is
here. We have to hurry!"

He raced on through the forest until a shimmer of white appeared ahead.

A tall, lithe woman sat before an ancient oak with her back turned. White-blond hair hung to the small of her back in a straight, silky wave. Leesil remembered her dress from the last evening of his youth, when he'd fled the Warlands at the sight of Minister Josiah hanging by his neck in the town square. Caramel like her skin, the gown's pattern of fine green leaves seemed like a wild vine printed upon her slender body. He dropped to the ground behind her, reaching out for her shoulder.

Slowly, Nein'a turned toward him.

Her once beautiful face was shriveled dried flesh across her skull. Large and slanted eyes were now empty sockets. She was long dead.

"Too long . . . too late," whispered Nein'a's corpse. "You're far too late for me."

She crumpled to dust before Leesil's eyes.

He couldn't move, couldn't even cry, and knelt there alone in the dark. Dusty grit from her corpse caked in the blood on his outstretched hands.

Magiere landed before him in a feral crouch, sending the dust of his mother billowing up around them. Her irises were full black, teeth extended in a canine snarl.

"Come back to me, Leesil," she said. "Please, I need you."

Wynn ran up the inland road, but once outside the town, she did not know which way to turn. The blue-white mist still plagued her vision, making her steps uncertain, but at least the eddies and currents had stopped moving. Vordana was certainly gone.

And further clouding her thoughts was Chane.

"Leesil!" Wynn called out. "Chap . . . Magiere?"

She could not ask for Chane's help, and she hoped with all her heart that he was on his horse and gone. If Magiere found him following them, she would destroy him, and part of Wynn now understood the dhampir's way.

And still, Chane had come in search of her, to bring her back to sages' guild and the warm comfort of her own life. This was not the action of a monster.

"Chap!" she shouted again.

She stumbled along the road, looking both ways through the dense forest and calling their names over and over.

"Mother . . . ," a voice cried out. "Nein'a?"

It was Leesil.

Wynn took off through the woods. "Wait for me!" she called. "I am coming for you!"

Her short robe caught on a bramble. She stumbled and jerked it free. When she turned to hurry on, she caught sight of something vivid amid the forest's weave of blue-white essence. It was the back of Leesil's glowing white-blond hair, and she rushed toward him.

His amber eyes were the same bright yellow sparks that hurt to look at, but he stared through her vacantly.

"Come back to me, Leesil," she said in a moan. "Please, I need you."

Leesil did not move. Wynn tried shaking him, but she could barely move his body. Scarf missing, his long hair was tangled with tree needles and leaves.

"Too late . . . ," he whispered. "Oh, Magiere, we took too long . . . and she died . . . alone."

He was lost in delusion. Wynn bit her lower lip, unwilling to start weeping again. She needed some way to rouse him, or at least make him recognize her.

Wynn reached into her robe pocket and felt the cold lamp crystal. She squeezed and ground it until its sharp edges hurt her palm. She kept rubbing, hard and quick, making certain its light would burn painfully bright.

"Look at me," she said sharply. "I am Wynn . . . see *me*!"

She grasped his jaw with her free hand, pulled out the crystal, and thrust it directly in front his eyes. The light was intense.

Leesil jerked his head away from her hand and grabbed both her wrists.

"Wynn?" he asked, and then sucked in a sharp breath. "My mother . . . dead. I'm too late."

"No!" Wynn answered, and closed her hand around the crystal to mute its glare. "It was not real. Vordana planted a seed in your mind that your own fears gave shape. Magiere and Chap are out here somewhere and may be wandering in the same state. We have to find them before anything happens."

Leesil looked around the clearing. "Magiere?"

He let her go and got to his feet with effort. Wynn stood, as well, swallowing down nausea as her vertigo surged.

"Which way?" he asked.

"Back to the road, and the town . . . and perhaps you can track her?"

He was still trembling, but he was Leesil again, and Wynn followed as he pushed on through the forest.

Chap ran through a dying land.

Trees and brush wilted before his eyes as shadows ambled through the forest. The world was dying . . . it was his fault. Spirits were wrenched from the trees and the earth to be swallowed by the walking shadows.

Chap slowed among the dead oaks and spruces to look back along his path. There was nothing left alive. The silhouettes came ever closer with a lone figure out in front, a heavy sword glinting in its grip. It stepped out into view.

Magiere wore black armor of scales like those of a massive serpent. Her filthy hair hung in matted tendrils. Her face was as sallow as Parko's, the first Noble Dead she had ever killed. Brother to Rashed in life and afterlife, Parko had lost himself on the Feral Path, existing only for the sensual ecstasy of the hunt. Magiere's irises were full black, not like the colorless crystalline of hungry undead, but Chap saw Parko's ecstatic madness in her eyes.

She roared, no longer recognizing him, and exposed long fangs amid yellowed teeth.

Behind her, the shadows solidified into a horde.

Noble Dead drew near on all sides. Vampires with their pale skin, elongated nails and teeth. Wraiths like black shadows that shifted in and out of physical presence. There were two of the *àrdadesbàrn*, the half-dead of Wynn's continent. And packs of *ghul* from the Suman Empire's northern arid mountains, mortal demons who fed on the living flesh.

There were remnants of living things from the end of the last epoch—the end of the human's Forgotten History. Hulking *locatha*, more reptile than humanoid, and squat goblins with features like hyenas and yellow eyes that twitched.

Some wore tattered clothes or scavenged armor, and most wielded weapons of war.

All eyes were upon Magiere, waiting expectantly.

Chap had sacrificed eternity among his brethren Fay. He had taken the flesh of one lifetime, so that he might fulfill an all-encompassing purpose: to keep Magiere in the light, bound to Leesil . . . to keep her from the enemy's hands and the purpose for which she'd been made. He looked at her standing before this horde like the general of an army.

He had failed.

"Majay-hì." Magiere spat at him.

Chap's sorrow welled up and spilled from him in a wail.

She knew him. And she had become his enemy.

Magiere rushed him, falchion rising and ready to fall. And the horde surged forward, leveling all living things in its path.

Chap stood listless, unable to fight back. The blade fell and bit deep between his shoulder and neck. . . .

Magiere's hungered face faded—but the pain did not.

Chap stumbled and then blinked.

Magiere and the horde and the dead world all vanished.

Around him was the empty Droevinkan forest. Through the trees to the south he saw the manor house and grounds. Something wet dragged across his ear. He jerked away and saw two filmy eyes staring at him in puzzlement.

Shade whimpered as she nosed him again. His shoulder hurt, and she had blood on her muzzle. She licked him, and Chap flinched at the pain running through the base of his neck. She had bitten him and now tried to clean the wound.

He remembered the decayed Noble Dead in the town, the sorcerer, and something piercing through his thoughts like a thorn. He growled at the memory, and licked Shade's head in return.

This simple creature had found him and, without true understanding, had called him back. The delusion remained in his memory, and he could not shake its weight from his spirit. Chap bolted for the town, keeping a pace that Shade could match.

Magiere's cuts and scrapes stung as she skidded to a stop in the town's midway. In her mind, she saw Leesil's wrist as he'd offered himself to her. Where was he . . . or Chap and Wynn . . . or the creature they'd faced?

"Leesil?" she shouted. "Can you hear me?"

All was quiet, and the only movement was the flickering light of the tripod braziers. She ran up the road to the last place she remembered of the battle with Vordana. Her torch and Leesil's punching blades lay abandoned on the ground. She gathered them up.

"Magiere!"

She whirled at Wynn's voice and saw the young sage round the corner from the inland manor road. Leesil was beside her.

Magiere's breath released in relief as she ran toward him. But she stopped short, remembering again the half-real moment he'd tried to make her feed upon him. She couldn't reach out, afraid to step too close. Wynn grabbed her by the arm, surprising her. The young sage faltered a moment, blinking twice.

"Look at me!" Wynn demanded. "What did you see?"

"Don't ask me."

Wynn shook her. "It was all a lie. Vordana's spell took your inner thoughts and turned them on you. Do you hear? It was not real. What you saw never happened."

Magiere looked down into the sage's face. Wynn was so resolute and certain, but Magiere would never be sure. If what she'd experience had come from within herself, then not all of it was a lie.

Wynn suddenly swallowed hard and pulled her hand from Magiere's arm. She turned her face away, as well. Leesil stared up the inland road toward the forest.

"He was lost, like you," Wynn said. "And Chap is still out there. We have to find him."

Magiere reached out for Leesil's hand.

It remained limp in her grip for a moment, and a sharp edge of fear arose in Magiere when he didn't look at her. He said nothing, not even one of his irritating quips tossed out at the wrong moment. What had he seen in the forest?

Leesil finally squeezed her hand with a deep breath, and took his punching blades from her.

"Where is that monster?" he asked. "We can't just drop our guard."

Magiere heard running footsteps and released Leesil's hand, ready to draw her sword. It was only Geza hurrying toward them down the main road. His own sword sheathed, his blue-gray cloak billowed behind him, exposing his leather armor.

"You destroyed it," he panted. "People are waking, and for the first time, I no longer feel the fatigue that comes when I step outside the manor grounds."

Magiere glanced up and down the road. "We didn't destroy anything."

"But you must have. Can't you feel it yourself?"

She shook her head. She'd never felt the slow drain of this place as the others had.

"Maybe," Leesil replied. "But I'm too tired to be sure."

"I did it," Wynn whispered.

All eyes turned on the little sage in her snagged breeches and soiled short robe. Her braid had come loose, and her hair hung in tangled waves about her face as she stared at the ground.

"You?" Magiere asked. "How?"

Wynn remained silent for a moment and didn't raise her eyes.

"After you ran off, I was alone," she said. "I shot Vordana through the eye and fled to the smithy. He caught me in there. I think he wished to toy with me. When he was close enough, I pulled the brass vial from his neck and threw it into the forge coals. It melted and broke open. Smoke rose up everywhere. When it cleared, he was gone."

As Wynn's words sank in, Magiere shook her head. "I'm sorry, Wynn. I'm sorry we left you with that thing. Are you sure he's gone?"

The sage still wouldn't lift her head. Magiere realized

Wynn had been through too much for one night. She should never have come on this journey, but if she hadn't . . . what would have become of Leesil? Of this town?

When Wynn finally looked at Magiere, she cringed away immediately. Her eyes rolled, and she clutched her head. Before anyone could catch her, she toppled to the ground. Leesil dropped down beside her.

"What is wrong with her?" Geza asked.

"I don't know," Leesil answered, and he pulled Wynn up to lean against him.

"I cannot stop . . . seeing," Wynn moaned. "Please make it stop!"

"Oh, damn!" Magiere said. "I'd forgotten her eyes."

"We should take her back to the manor," Geza suggested, reaching down to lift the sage.

"And do what?" Leesil asked. "She can't take any more. We have to stop it, now!"

"How?" Magiere answered too harshly. "She's the only one who understands what happened. At the manor we can at least care for her until she can undo this herself."

"She's not the only one who knows," Leesil said, his voice quiet and cold. "There is someone else. Stay here where I can find you, or bring her if you hear me call out."

The moment Wynn was settled in Magiere's arms, the sage began struggling, trying to squirm away. Leesil was on his feet, already heading toward the inland road.

"Geza, check the woods to the east," he called. "If you see our dog, tell him Wynn is in trouble, and bring him here."

The captain stared at him. "What?"

"Just do it!" Leesil shouted back. "He'll understand."

Geza took off the other way, and Magiere sat in the road, gripping Wynn. The young sage cried out at her, as if Magiere were the source of her suffering.

"Wynn, enough," she said. "Just stay with me. Leesil will find Chap, and we'll make this stop."

Wynn twisted suddenly, wrenching herself to the side. She rolled away to scurry across the ground.

"Ribbons . . . shadows in you," she whispered. "Pulling at me, at my spirit. Do not touch me!"

She backed against the nearest building and curled up to hide her face in her hands.

Magiere crouched within reach, unable to understand why Wynn feared her.

Wynn heard Leesil's voice calling Magiere's name from far away and then felt herself lifted from the ground before she could escape.

She didn't open her eyes—couldn't open her eyes—to watch the writhing black ribbons flowing through Magiere. She knew Magiere only tried to help, but could not stop herself from struggling. All she wanted was to crawl away into the darkness, where those black tendrils in Magiere's essence couldn't find her.

"Wynn, don't!" Magiere snapped. "I'm taking you to Chap. Be still so I can carry you!"

"Magiere!" Leesil called. "Here, across the stream!"

Wynn clenched in panic at the sound of Magiere's boots splashing through water. Then everything turned end over end as she tumbled to the ground out of Magiere's arms.

She felt the soft earth beneath her, and its loamy scent filled her head. She struggled to push herself up and opened her eyes slowly for fear of what she might see.

Through the blue-white mist woven amid the branches and brush, a gleam of white danced down the slope. Wynn dug her narrow fingers into the earth, frantic, ready to scramble away into hiding.

Leesil's hair flashed as he ran toward her. His eyes were

amber stones lit from within. Beside him loped something on
four legs. Shade. Though she possessed her own living inner
glow, Shade's essence was far less than what Wynn saw in
Leesil.

Where was Chap?

Leesil skidded in the mulch as he dropped down beside
her. He glanced back over his shoulder.

"Chap, get down here . . . now!"

Out among the trees, Wynn saw another glimmer of
movement.

At first, it was nothing more than a moving bright spot
amid the forest's essence, but it grew in intensity as it neared.
She had seen Chap during the village battle, and his presence
was as strong as Leesil's, but it was not what she saw now.
Like a brilliant cold lamp crystal, a light loped through the
trees.

As it approached, the very essence of each living thing lit
up where it passed.

Wynn forgot nausea and vertigo and everything else that
plagued her mantic sight.

Unlike all else in her confused vision, she didn't see one
blue-white shape laid over the physical form before her.
Chap was but one image, one whole shape, glowing with
brilliance.

His fur was pure white and each fiber glistened like silk.

He padded toward her.

Wynn remembered studying the properties of light at the
guild back home. The other initiates spun cut crystals on
strings by a window to watch the colors dance on the walls.
Wynn had stared into the spinning crystal itself, as she now
stared into Chap's eyes.

They sparkled like crystals in sunlight.

She felt no wind but saw movement among the trees. No,

not the trees, but their blue-white essence within. It moved and flowed, reaching out . . . to the dog.

Other glows like Chap's were moving inside the trees . . . inside the earth . . . in the air itself. They gathered inward around the dog, above and below him.

Wynn leaned back and closed her eyes against the growing brilliance.

She felt Chap's breath upon her face and sensed his light through her eyelids, and then his warm tongue swept over her closed eyes, one at a time.

Wynn put her palms to the ground, steadying herself as the sensation of falling filled her up and then vanished. She lifted her head to gaze at the world around her.

Before her was Chap, silvery gray and furry . . . and barely visible in the dark.

"That's it?" Leesil asked. "He slobbers on her? Wynn, are you all right?"

She could barely make him out. His white-blond hair was the easiest feature to see, but it looked the same as always.

Wynn wanted throw her arms around Chap, but hesitated. What she had seen began to weigh upon her. The Fay had gathered upon Chap, heeded his call to heal her. Mixed with her shock was an undercurrent of fright that such a creature had been near her all through this journey.

But now she saw only a dog, who licked his own nose and then sat on the ground with an exhausted grunt.

Welstiel stayed hidden among the trees as he watched Magiere and a moderately well-dressed soldier help Leesil and Wynn along the road to the manor. The *majay-hì* was with them, and also an aging wolfhound. He could not hear much of Magiere's words, but she spoke to the soldier in a familiar manner, once clearly calling him Captain. Welstiel's impatience grew.

His dream patron urged him to follow her, but he had listened to those black scales in his slumber for too many years. He was no closer to his goal for it. Magiere's search for her past stalled his pursuit of the jewel of his dreams and the future it hinted at.

He understood why Magiere had stayed in this place. It was her nature to hunt the undead, wherever they were found. But why did she travel farther into this land, lingering in a place where some things still might wait to find her . . . to find him? As he watched Magiere and her companions enter the manor grounds, he decided there were answers he must seek for himself.

His horse was gone, and he began the long walk back to where Chane had pitched their tent the previous dusk. Welstiel was not surprised to find both horses and his traveling companion waiting there for him. Chane sat on the ground outside the tent, his expression guarded. He was feeding his rat a handful of grain.

"I thought it best to get the horses out of sight," he said, as if nothing had happened.

Welstiel looked down at him. "Did you play the hero and destroy the monster to save your lady fair?"

Chane's left eye twitched. "Yes."

Welstiel decided not to press the issue of Chane's disobedience—not yet. Magiere was safe, and with the sorcerer gone, she would continue onward.

"Of course, you made certain Wynn did not see you?"

His companion hesitated. "I am no fool."

Welstiel stepped toward the tent. "It is dangerous to be so close to Magiere. The encounter has left them tired, particularly Leesil and the sage. I doubt they will leave at first light, but they will depart tomorrow. If she continues east, I need to know why."

Chane frowned. "You don't know where she's going."

"No . . . she should have turned north after leaving her village . . . or at least out of this land."

He offered this like a tidbit to a hungry dog, hoping to turn Chane's mind back onto their goal without telling him too much.

"I saw her speak to a soldier from the manor," Welstiel added. "Possibly the captain of the guard there. Did you ever assist your father in an interrogation?"

"Yes."

"On occasion, I helped mine, as well."

"Of course you did," Chane said bitterly. "One more thing we have in common."

Welstiel almost smiled.

Wynn had been given a room in the manor with a large bed and a down comforter. The rare privacy and the small luxuries of a window heavily draped against the cold and a table on which to set her scribe's instruments should have been a pleasure or at least a relief.

Beneath her short robe, breeches, and shirt, she wore a white cotton shift, which she normally managed to keep tucked in. Since leaving Bela, she had not abandoned her clothes to sleep in this loose cotton undergarment. Nights were too cold, and she was far too modest in company. The freedom to do so now, for this one night, should also have pleased her.

It did not.

She had written nothing in her journal concerning the undead sorcerer . . . or more of Magiere's nature, as Domin Tilswith would expect. She did not even warm up her crystal in the cold lamp on the bedside table. Instead, she closed her door tightly and crawled under the comforter, looking about the room's fixtures, so dim and normal in the low light of the single candle.

She had lied to Magiere, to Leesil, to the people here. She took credit for something she had not done . . . to save Chane . . . to keep Magiere from knowing he had followed them here.

There was a knock at the door, but Wynn did not wish to see anyone.

"It's me," Magiere said from outside. "Can I come in?"

"Of course," Wynn answered, but her voice was reluctant. She reached for the cold lamp, lifted its glass, and rubbed the crystal without removing it. Its light grew, brightening the room. As she replaced the glass, the door cracked open and Magiere entered.

She looked uncomfortable, hair down but uncombed, and wore only her loose white shirt and black breeches. A few cuts on her face were beginning to swell.

"Do you have any of the healing salve with you?" she asked.

More guilt for Wynn. She should have at least tended her companions' wounds before crawling into hiding.

"Yes, I'm sorry. I should have thought of that earlier. It's in the side of my pack."

Magiere shook her head. "Don't apologize. We're all tired."

Wynn rummaged out the small tin of salve, as well as a hairbrush. Guilt overwhelmed her discomfort at Magiere's presence.

"I can comb out your hair, if you like. It's full of burrs and twigs."

It wasn't that Wynn distrusted Magiere. She trusted the *woman* with her life, but the other half—the *undead* half—which even Magiere did not truly know or understand, weighed upon Wynn's fears. For the first time, Wynn felt resentful of her calling.

She loved the pursuit of "knowing." Nothing made her

happier than gathering knowledge, but how could she document any of this as if it were some passing scholarly interest? The dark and dead half of Magiere frightened her as much as the pale woman's mysterious and bloody origin.

Magiere glanced at the brush, seemed about to refuse, and then sighed. "Yes, thank you."

Wynn poured water from a pitcher into a porcelain basin upon the table. There was a hand towel folded beside it, and Wynn dabbed its corner in the water. She settled on the bed's edge beside Magiere, forcing her hand not to waver as she cleaned Magiere's scratches and applied the salve. It was good for both healing and pain.

"Better," Magiere said.

Wynn climbed around behind Magiere and began combing out the tangles of black hair.

"How is Leesil?" she asked.

"Resting. All right, I think. I don't think Vordana took much from him in the fight, but we can't be sure. I'll make certain he eats well in the morning."

Wynn stopped brushing to gently pick at a burr with her fingertips.

"You have beautiful hair," she said, though its tendrils reminded her too much of the shadow ribbons in Magiere's essence. "Did Leesil tell you what he saw in the forest?"

Magiere turned about, and Wynn pulled her hands back a little too quickly. She folded them in her lap, holding on to the brush with both.

"No," Magiere answered. "Did he tell you?"

"He was incoherent, like you, but I think he saw his mother . . . dead. He said we were too late, and she was dead."

Magiere closed her eyes. "I should never have let Vordana trick me, never hesitated. If I'd cut that bastard down . . . Oh, Leesil. He's borne too much for me through all this."

She was silent for a moment, and when she spoke again, it was the last thing Wynn wanted to hear.

"What did you see tonight? What did you see in me that terrified you—hurt you?"

Wynn's mouth went dry. "You didn't hurt me, Magiere. It was not—"

"Tell me. I've nothing else but a chamber of bones in a decaying keep. So if you know something, tell me."

"It is not anything that I know," Wynn said, fumbling for a way to explain. "Only what I saw . . . felt."

Magiere sat waiting.

Wynn relented and told Magiere of the black shadow ribbons coiled in her spirit. Magiere barely reacted, gaze wandering the room to anywhere but Wynn's face. Perhaps she had accepted herself as part of the world's darkness. Wynn told her also of Chap, and how the second time she had seen him, he was not two images in her mantic sight, as was everything else. He was one clear luminous presence. When this distracted Magiere enough, Wynn told her of Leesil's sun-spark eyes amid the spirit mist of the world.

"I wish I'd seen him the way you did," Magiere said, and her expression softened. "I didn't really come here for the salve. I wanted to . . . to apologize for what I said back in Bela when you insisted on coming with us. I thought you'd be in the way, but your knowledge and skills have been so useful, and not just in dealing with Chap. Leesil and I, and even Chap, were outwitted tonight. If you hadn't been here, I don't know if either of us would still be alive. The townsfolk are going to give me the credit for this, and they won't understand anything else. And so I wanted to tell you this now and to thank you."

The words were so out of place for Magiere that Wynn's guilt grew again. For all they had learned of what Magiere was, she had no choice in that. She was trying to live a life beyond what had been forced upon her. Yet here she was, thanking Wynn, who was a liar and a secret observer.

Wynn had lied for Chane. Once such an enormous deception was spoken, there was no turning back. The truth would only abolish Magiere's trust, and possibly cost Chane his head.

"Let me finish your hair," Wynn whispered. "Then we should both get some sleep."

Magiere turned around, and Wynn worked the burr from her hair.

"And Wynn . . . ," Magiere said, in her more usual abrupt manner, "no more magic for you."

Wynn sighed, nodding her head. "Agreed."

Chapter 10

At dawn, Magiere left Leesil sleeping in their upstairs room and walked into the main hall to be accosted by Elena.

"Our thanks aren't nearly enough. There is nothing we can do to repay you." The girl grasped Magiere's hands, nearly hopping up and down.

Lord Stefan stood near the hearth. He wasn't so enthusiastic, but Magiere preferred his silence. She'd seen his current expression many times while on the game. Village elders begged for her help, but once she finished, they were far more eager for her departure. Stefan had the same look about him.

Magiere pulled her hand from Elena's grip in embarrassment but tried to be gracious as she asked about breakfast.

"I'll fetch some hot porridge and fresh bread," Elena said, and she scurried toward the corridor.

"Wait a little, Elena," Captain Geza said, and he stood up from his seat at the table, and turned to Magiere. "There is something I'd like to show you before breakfast. Will you follow me?"

Magiere preferred Geza amongst all who lived in this

manor. She followed as he led her outside and across the manor grounds to the stable. In front of its wide doors stood a fine wagon. The long driver's seat was covered with padded leather, and two gray horses were tied nearby. A stable boy was brushing out their lush coats.

Geza gestured to the wagon. "Elena told me you returned the household money and the people's coin. I'm not noble but I'm far from destitute. Stefan is young and foolish, but my success depends on his, so at times I've supported him when I should not. This is my wagon, and I give it to you. Not as a gift but as proper payment, and you cannot refuse."

He stepped closer to the team of gray horses, one stocky and the other more slender and graceful.

"This is Port," Geza said, "because he is so portly. And this is Imp, because she reminds me of my grandmother's tales of fairy mounts. I trained them myself. They will serve you well."

Magiere stepped closer, and Port swung his massive head to look at her. His eyes were clear and calm. Imp reached out her head to chew on her partner's halter. She was beautiful, with a nose like gray velvet.

"These are dear to you," Magiere said to Geza. "I can't take them."

"I heard that your partner detests riding and is still ragged from last night. There are no barges due until the new moon. We owe you—I owe you. Elena is all I have, and I could not persuade her to leave and go back to Kéonsk. If you had not come along . . ."

He sighed, and pulled a small folded parchment from his vestment.

"Take the wagon and team. You earned them. And there is something more I wish to show you now that we're away from the others. You are going on to Kéonsk?"

"Yes."

"Why?" he asked, and when she frowned at his question, he rushed on. "I thought perhaps our fates had been connected. That is why I ask."

Magiere didn't see Geza as a man given to deceptions, but his comment was confusing nonetheless.

"I'm seeking information about my family, my father. That's all. There may be records in Kéonsk."

"I see," he answered, disappointed, and held out the parchment to her. "Then you know nothing of this."

"I don't read well," Magiere said.

"It's from my brother in the southeast of the Äntes province, this province. His lord's fief was taken by a brown-robed man he had never met. Not a noble but with a letter of authority from Baron Buscan. And he is not the only one. I've heard similar from other places within the Äntes province, and in the east of Droevinka, as well."

"Buscan is sending out sorcerers?" Magiere asked. "Like Vordana?"

"I do not know what they are, and Vordana is the only one I've met. I only know what my brother has told me. There are men being sent out to unseat our nobles, one by one, and they have papers from the royal court."

"What does this have to do with me?" Magiere asked, not caring for the direction Geza was leading. She had little interest in the endless infighting of the noble houses.

"Would you look into this when you reach Kéonsk? You and yours stopped Vordana here and might be able to take action others cannot. Just see if my brother is correct."

Magiere wasn't certain how to respond, but her Aunt Bieja lived too nearby for comfort and Magiere found Geza's suspicions unsettling.

"I doubt Buscan would give us an audience," she replied. "Or think us more than a nuisance, but if a chance arises . . ."

Geza inclined his head, satisfied, and he walked with her back to the manor for breakfast.

The morning passed swiftly. Wynn helped pack the wagon, and by late afternoon they were ready to leave. Leesil was silent for the day, and it was obvious to Magiere that his delusion of the night before still plagued him. For her own part, she couldn't rid herself of seeing Leesil offering himself up to her like a sacrifice. Talking would have to wait—but talk they would, for his sake.

As they pulled the wagon around before the manor, Stefan stood in its doorway as Elena came out to see them off. If Wynn was right concerning what Vordana had done to Stefan, he would never again leave that house. Elena looked up at the dipping sun.

"You should really stay the night and set out tomorrow. You will not get far today."

Magiere glanced at Leesil sitting quietly beside her on the wagon bench. He was still lost in his thoughts.

"No, we need to move on," she answered Elena. "Geza says the roads between here and Kéonsk are smooth and dry. We'll keep going into the early evening and gain some ground."

Chap nuzzled Shade once more and ran for the wagon, leaping into the back to settle beside Wynn. He laid his head in her lap.

Magiere offered polite farewells, snapped the reins, and Port and Imp pulled them down the inland road. When they reached Pudúrlatsat and turned east along the main road, Magiere shifted the reins to one hand and grasped Leesil's closest hand with her other. He gripped her palm instantly.

She held on to him until dusk.

Chane awoke precisely at dusk and sat watching Welstiel slumber. He had done the same thing night after night. More recently, his companion had ceased mumbling and thrashing in his dormancy.

Welstiel had become no less an obstacle to Chane's freedom than Toret had been, expecting obedience, though he could not will it as Toret had. Chane had no money and no where else to go, until Welstiel delivered his promised payment and letters of introduction. With such, Chane could seek a new existence, perhaps journey to one of the main branches for the Guild of Sagecraft.

For all Chane's reluctance to be Welstiel's puppet, he had little choice but to obey—for now. And he became more and more curious about the artifact that Welstiel sought.

But behind all this lingered a downfallen moment in the dark smithy.

Wynn had turned him away.

Part of him was strangely full of sorrow, and he was not normally given to melancholy. Wynn followed her conscience, and her clear wish to protect him from Magiere hung constantly in Chane's thoughts. A naïve notion, as he needed no protection, but still . . .

In that moment, the possibility of returning to Bela with Wynn had slipped out before he realized what he was saying. He should not have allowed himself such a fantasy nor pushed it upon her. She was a true intellect and understood that truths could never be forgotten—there was no way to change what was. Like trying to take back words that had already been spoken.

His father's cruelty had taught him to defend himself, to look out for himself above all others. Wynn was the only person besides his mother that he'd ever wished to protect more than himself. He'd failed his mother; he might yet save Wynn.

Welstiel stirred, and Chane cautiously tapped his shoulder. "Are you awake?"

"Yes. We should ready ourselves."

"Do you wish to pack, or are we returning here?"

"We leave directly from the manor. Pack everything."

When Welstiel began assisting with preparations, Chane was surprised. It was clear early in their acquaintance that Welstiel had been raised a noble, accustomed to having things done for him. He struck Chane as lacking in self-sufficiency; regardless of his own noble upbringing, Chane preferred to rely upon himself.

He saddled both horses and strapped the tent over the rump of his own mount. He handed Welstiel his cloak.

"You lead," he said. "I'm still uncertain why you want to question this captain."

"Information," Welstiel answered.

How enlightening, Chane thought, but kept silent on the matter. It was puzzling, too, when Welstiel led them around the town to the east end rather than inland to the manor.

"How will you find this captain?" Chane asked.

Welstiel sat watching the main road through town and occasionally the sparse forest around them. There was little activity past dusk. Then Chane heard a clattering bell off through the trees.

A skinny young boy with thick black hair and freckled skin, not quite in his teens, was herding a group of goats through. The sound came from a crude bell hanging on the collar of the one male in the herd. The boy must have taken his charges out too far, or perhaps they had wandered on their own, and he was returning late.

"Can you charm that boy into fetching his lord's captain?" Welstiel asked. "You seem to have a way with these peasants."

"I will try," Chane answered, ignoring the barb.

He didn't care for these commoners either, but Welstiel's

distaste was more acute. Chane understood the crude minds of peasants and how to use them when necessary.

The boy swung a switch to drive his small herd on to the main road, and Chane urged his horse forward through the trees. He kept his distance so as not to startle his would-be messenger.

"Ho there," he called.

The boy stopped to look him over before answering. "Who are you?"

"Friends of the dhampir," Chane said, gesturing to Welstiel back in the trees. He spoke Droevinkan fairly well but with an accent. "Did you meet her?"

The boy shook his head but his face lit up.

"She's the one who saved us! They say she's white as ghost and can pull down a horse with her bare hands. You know her?"

Chane's eyebrows rose. How quickly truth became legend—and sometimes myth—among the masses. If only they knew who had truly "saved" them.

"Yes, and she sent us with an urgent message. It is of great importance but must be handled quietly, only given to your lord's captain."

"Captain Geza?" The boy nodded. "His Elena handles things at the common house for us."

"Can you fetch the captain but not let anyone else hear you? Tell him the dhampir sent us with urgent news, and he should meet us here, away from any ears. Can you do that?"

The boy looked at his flock.

"We'll keep an eye on your herd," Chane said with a compassionate smile. "This is important, my boy."

The boy straightened himself as though a great duty had been placed upon him in service to this legendary dhampir. He nodded once and was off.

Welstiel urged his horse forward beside Chane's. "At times, you astonish me."

Chane shrugged. "You handled the innkeeper in Bela well enough."

"Greed and ignorance require little more than a flash of coin. This is going to be a more . . . open interrogation. There can be no witnesses, you understand?"

Chane suppressed an indignant retort. "Of course."

They dismounted, leading the horses into the trees but remaining in sight of the main road. The goats wandered by the roadside, and evening rapidly turned to night as the world grew darker.

Chane wondered how this Geza would react to a boy's tale of strange men with a secret message from the dhampir. Had this happened in Chane's mortal life, he would have gathered a retinue of guards before setting foot outside. But Magiere appeared to inspire confidence, and he believed the captain would come alone. Soon a short man in a leather hauberk and gray-blue cape followed the boy up the road out of the town. Chane stepped out, raising a hand to hail them, with Welstiel close behind.

The captain's expression was apprehensive, but he approached with little hesitation and spoke in a lowered voice.

"Young Tenan here says you have a message from Magiere. Has something happened during the journey? She's been gone less than half a day."

Welstiel stepped around Chane. He grabbed the captain's throat before the man could blink. Geza gripped Welstiel's forearm with one hand, reaching for his sword with the other. Before an inch of steel slipped from the sheath, Welstiel snatched his wrist.

Tenan's eyes widened, and the boy turned to run. Chane grasped the back of his neck and pinned his small head against a tree.

"Cry out, and I'll crush your skull," he whispered.

The boy stopped struggling and peered sideways at Geza for help. The captain released Welstiel's arm and struck with his fist.

Welstiel's head barely turned under the blow. He tightened his grip on Geza's throat. As the captain's eyes half closed, Welstiel slapped the man's hand from his sword and pulled the blade himself. He flung Geza into the forest away from the road, and the captain tumbled to the ground, gasping for air.

"Now," Welstiel said, "we need to know where the dhampir has gone and, if she told you, why."

Chane watched the captain lying on the ground, trying to catch his breath in astonishment at being so quickly undone.

"You're after the dhampir?" Geza said between gasps. "She saved this town, and I'll give you nothing to cause her harm."

"Harm?" Welstiel said, and looked to Chane. "Would you please show the good captain what we are capable of?"

Chane snarled. Without hesitation, he lifted the boy from the ground by his neck, so that they both faced Geza. The boy had no time to scream as Chane's teeth wrapped around the slender neck, halfway to the boy's throat. He bit down.

Tenan's legs kicked in the air a few times and fell still.

Chane seldom fed on children. As sweet as their blood could be, they were incapable of putting up a fight. When finished, he tossed the fragile body before Geza, who stared at him in horror.

Welstiel crouched before the captain. "If you think that undead sorcerer was a plague, imagine my companion loose among your people for one night. Or should we start at the manor?"

Geza drew a breath but did not speak. Chane stepped close behind Welstiel, watching the captain with mild interest. The outcome of this conversation was obvious, and all that remained was to see how long it took to play out.

"Without your assistance," Welstiel went on, "we have nowhere else to go. Do you have a son here? A daughter? A wife? I'm sure someone at the manor would cooperate in answering our questions."

Geza's brow furrowed as he rubbed his throat. Chane could tell the man was not accustomed to being helpless.

"What do you want?" the captain whispered.

"I told you," Welstiel responded. "We need to know where the dhampir is going and why."

"And if I tell you, then you and this murdering carrion will go on your way and leave my people be?"

"You have my word," Welstiel said.

"Kéonsk," Geza sighed, dropping his gaze. "She heads to the capital."

"To pass through or to stay?"

"It is her destination, to the best of my knowledge."

"Why?"

"Fief records concerning her family. She's looking for information about her father, and that is all I know. Now leave us in peace!"

Chane was surprised how quickly the captain supplied the answers. Even stranger was his sense that the man spoke the truth straight out, and that his ignorance was sincere. But instead of being satisfied, Welstiel gripped the man by the throat again.

"Records of her father?"

Unable to breathe, the captain nodded his confirmation.

Welstiel slammed the palm of his free hand into the side of the captain's jaw. The man's head jerked sideways with an audible snap, and his body went limp. Welstiel stood up as Geza flopped to the ground, eyes open and head tilted at an unnatural angle.

"What is it?" Chane asked, almost alarmed.

Welstiel had never before lost all his composure like this. He stood shifting his weight back and forth.

"Come," he finally said. "Gather the bodies and get the horses."

Chane did as instructed and rode after Welstiel down the road for a half a league. When Welstiel turned aside into the trees and dismounted, Chane followed. The copse Welstiel had entered was so dark that even Chane had trouble seeing clearly. Welstiel stood deep in thought.

"What now?" Chane asked.

"We need to slow Magiere down. You and I must reach Kéonsk first."

"Why?"

"Just do it!"

Chane had never seen Welstiel so unsettled. "And what do you suggest?"

His companion paused and pointed to the urn hanging around Chane's neck.

"You are skilled with animal spirits, yes? Send something to stop her without causing her injury. The captain said she had been gone less than half a day, so she is not far ahead."

Chane shook his head. "What you ask is a complex process, and at present, the only familiar I have is a rat. I doubt that will suit your purpose."

"Magiere is my only interest," Welstiel returned. "Anyone with her is no concern of mine. Slow her down or I will have to do it myself. And my methods are not as . . . precisely controlled as yours."

Chane blinked. Welstiel knew enough of his private interests to use Wynn against him. A flash of anger and resentment brought harsh words to his lips, but he fought them back.

"Do you have wolf speech?" he asked.

"Do I have what?" Welstiel returned.

"It is what I call it," he explained. "My maker, Toret, told me that each of our kind develops different abilities. Toret lived for many years with another Noble Dead who possessed the power to call upon wolves. Do you?"

"Yes, I can do this," Welstiel answered, and he glowered in distaste. "But it is neither speech nor a kinship with wolves. You can abandon such superstitious nonsense. It is an expression of hungering instinct, cast out to catch the attention of any predator within reach. A base and crude ability which most of our kind develop over time."

Chane pondered this for a moment. In his short time as a Noble Dead, he had not manifested abilities beyond what any undead would have—speed, strength, suppression of pain and physical duress, amongst others. It was curious that one such as Welstiel, so repulsed by anything uncultured and raw, would have developed such an ability.

"Setting wolves upon them," Welstiel said, "is not the precise approach I expected from you."

"I only need one," Chane replied. "And it will be more focused than you imply."

He knelt down and pulled a brass urn, a candle, a silver dagger, and a bottle of olive green liquid from his pack.

"We'll clear a space where I can carve my symbols in the earth for the ritual."

Welstiel became immediately agreeable, and this raked Chane more than the man's previous manner. Welstiel was exactly like Toret in some respects. Polite, so long as Chane did as he was told. They picked a clear space in the copse, and Chane prepared for the ritual as Welstiel cleared the forest mulch with his boot.

"Now, call a wolf," Chane ordered.

*   *   *

Magiere sat with Leesil upon the wagon's seat and drove Port and Imp down the road through the night. It took little attention, as the horses were surefooted and never veered from the road.

Wynn and Chap were still awake in the wagon's back, and the sage had unpacked two cold lamps at dusk. Leesil lashed these to either side of the wagon's front footboard. He leaned back and took an apple slice from Wynn.

"So, you destroyed that creature by melting its urn? Clever."

Wynn didn't respond and continued cutting fruit to hand out.

Chap sat before her with his front legs set wide to balance against the wagon's rock. When Magiere glanced back, the dog licked his muzzle with ears straight up, his full attention on the next apple Wynn peeled.

Magiere hadn't forgotten what Chap had done in the forest for Wynn, though how was still a mystery even after Wynn's tale. What the sage had described was far more astonishing than the simple swipe of tongue that Magiere witnessed. Chap became a larger puzzle each time they learned more of him—most often with no help from the dog himself.

Wynn looked tired and weak, and Magiere wondered how much of this was her ordeal with Vordana, her mantic mishap, or their stay in the village under the sorcerer's draining presence. Leesil had shaken off his fatigue, and this gave Magiere another reason for pause. Vordana had tried to strip his life away, yet he was less worse for wear than the sage.

Then there was Wynn's description of what she'd seen of each of them in her altered sight. Magiere had shared this with Leesil. However, there were more pressing concerns to discuss for what lay ahead.

"Geza showed me a letter from his brother," she began.

"Äntes fiefs are being taken from their nobles by men sent out by Lord Buscan."

"Vordana was not an isolated incident?" Wynn asked, her voice rising. "There are more like him?"

Magiere shook her head.

"I don't know. The replacements carry letters of authority from Kéonsk, but I can't imagine many sorcerers still about in this time—or any time I've heard of. Geza's brother thinks this is happening in eastern Droevinka, as well, and Geza asked us to look into it, though I've no idea how."

Chap lunged forward, threw his front legs over the bench's back, and growled at her. The sound startled Port and Imp, and they pulled up, dancing sideways.

"Stop that!" Leesil ordered, shoving the dog back.

"You know he does not want us on this journey," Wynn said. "Or anywhere in Droevinka, it seems. I suppose he does not want us involved in the captain's suspicions either."

It sounded to Magiere like Wynn had become as weary of Chap's behavior as Leesil or herself.

"All right," Leesil said. "Stop the wagon."

Magiere pulled in the reins, bringing Port and Imp to a halt. "What's wrong?"

"We're not moving another league." He hopped down, circled around the wagon's back, and climbed in to crouch before Chap. "Not until we get some answers from you!"

Chap shifted nervously on all fours, but there was little room left for him to move in the wagon's back.

"Wynn saw you in her mantic sight," Leesil said to the dog. "And she saw them . . . the Fay."

Chap rumbled and glanced at Magiere. She frowned at him.

"He was trying to help Wynn," Magiere said.

"Maybe that's all," Leesil replied. "Or maybe he's in a hurry to get us away from any more information we might stumble upon. Like the fit he threw about the keep near your village. Think about it. Calling his . . . others, kin, whatever. So much power just to banish a simple magic gone awry? Like using a sword when a knife would do."

Even Wynn now stared warily at Chap.

"A very urgent choice, I'd say," Leesil added. "Perhaps to preserve one more new piece in the scheme he's been working all these years."

Chap growled and barked twice for *no*.

Magiere saw Leesil stiffen, and his gaze grew distant. His eyes drooped and filled with sadness. He shuddered and blinked.

"Don't do that again!" he snapped at the dog.

Chap dropped his head, breaking eye contact.

Wynn glanced between the two of them. "What? What happened?"

"Chap's playing his memory game again," Magiere said. "Leesil?"

She watched him drop to sit in the wagon's bed. "My mother gave him to me."

Magiere's stomach turned. This journey—her journey— kept Leesil from searching for a mother who, unlike her own, might still live. Guilt wasn't something Magiere let plague her in the past, but from that night she'd convinced Leesil to head to Droevinka first, she'd had enough for a lifetime. And it felt well deserved in this moment.

"Perhaps he wants to find her, as well," she said quietly, watching Leesil withdraw into his own thoughts. "We'll go north as soon as we finish in Kéonsk, and I—"

"What?" Leesil looked up in confusion. "No, I didn't mean that to sound . . . We'll search Kéonsk, tear the place apart if we have to." His attention turned back upon Chap. "But this deceitful four-footer is going to answer some questions."

Leesil reached into Wynn's pack and pulled out the talking hide. He slapped it down on the wagon's bed before Chap.

"Why do you want us out of here so badly?" he demanded.

Chap fidgeted again. Wynn reached out to the dog, cupping his muzzle in her palm to look him in the eyes.

"I know you helped me because you care for me," she said to him, "but if there is more, then it is time to tell us. Would the mantic sight have faded on its own soon enough?"

Chap gazed intently back at Wynn and yipped once for yes.

"Then why call the Fay?" Magiere asked. "Why the urgency? Why do you want us away from here?"

Magiere had another unsettling moment when Chap looked up at her and began pawing at the hide.

"*Nävâj* . . . enemy?" Wynn translated. "*Bith feith léiras* . . . in wait? . . . no . . . is waiting, watching. *Triâlhi ämvè äicheva tú* . . . leave before it finds you."

Magiere's eyes lit up.

"In Stefan's tale of Vordana's first visit," she said, "the sorcerer said something about being able to 'watch' no matter what Stefan did. I think Vordana tried to drain life from me during the fight and couldn't. He looked surprised, and I heard him in my thoughts. I was what he'd been waiting, watching for."

"Another clan of undead on our trail," Leesil muttered. "Wondrous! More Noble Dead worked up by peasant tales of the dhampir come to—"

Chap pawed the hide again, stopping often to look over its symbols as if trying to find something specific.

"*Spiorcolh aonach* . . . one spirit crime," Wynn said. "No, um, the first spiritual . . . spiritual crime . . . sin? The first sin—*bith feith léiras*—is waiting and watching. *Äm-na iosaj c'tú.* Not time ... too soon ... to know for yóu? Too soon ... for you—for us—to know."

Wynn sat back with a deep sigh of frustration.

"Perhaps our search leads to something he thinks we are not ready to know, and that knowing would place us in danger ... Or the search would reveal us to this enemy?"

"Too late for that," Magiere said. "Considering what we faced in the last village."

Wynn rubbed her brow as if it ached. Chap whined, sniffing at the hide and tilting his snout at her. He hung his head, shifting from paw to paw as his gaze wandered over the hide.

"Don't you start that again," Leesil said. "Wynn, make him tell us—"

"Enough, Leesil!" Wynn snapped, her sharp tone startling even Magiere. "He is an eternal spirit with no use for spoken words—using an animal's mind to handle a written language ... and in a dialect I do not speak well myself. There is something he cannot find the words for."

The wagon lurched suddenly backward, and both Port and Imp screamed out.

Magiere grabbed the bench to keep from being spilled forward onto the wagon's hitch. Port snorted and reared. He thrashed out with his forehooves, and both horses whinnied again in panic.

A large wolf circled into view on the road and rushed in at Port. The wagon lurched again, rolling backward as the horses retreated.

"Wynn ... Leesil!" Magiere shouted as she righted herself. "Someone get my sword!"

Chap lunged forward, front paws on the wagon's bench. He snarled, and his ear flattened at the sight of the wolf.

"Brake!" Leesil shouted. "Pull the brake!"

Magiere saw the wolf harry the horses as she blindly reached back with her hand. The falchion's hilt smacked against her palm, and she closed her fingers around it, not knowing who'd retrieved it. She grabbed for the brake with her free hand.

The wagon lurched to a halt with the sound of splintering wood. Magiere pulled the brake too late. Her grip on lever kept her from falling backward, but that was all, for they'd already hit something.

"Chap, go!" Magiere shouted.

The dog scrambled over the bench as she dropped off the wagons' side, running to get in between the horses and the wolf. It was snarling and snapping at their hooves.

"Get back!" she yelled, trying to attract the wolf's attention.

Chap rushed around her and charged. The wolf turned on the dog, and the two became a mass of growls and teeth. Magiere couldn't strike without risking injury to Chap.

Port and Imp tried to back away, and the wagon's rigging creaked under their struggles. Magiere glanced back to see wagon's corner grind against a tree trunk. Wynn clung to the wagon's side, reaching for a grip on the bench, and Leesil was nowhere in sight. Magiere grabbed for the horses' harness. The wagon twisted sideways and dropped as the outer rear wheel fell free from its axle.

A loud yelp carried above the horses' frantic snorts. Magiere saw the wolf break away and Chap roll to his feet, prepared to charge again. She released the horses and swung her blade, aiming for the beast's throat. It dodged, but her blade tip clipped its left shoulder.

The wolf yelped, and then dashed off into the trees. Chap scrambled after it.

"No!" Magiere shouted. "Let it go."

Chap circled around her, panting, his eyes on the forest where the wolf had fled.

Magiere turned back to the wagon. There was still no sign

of Leesil, but Wynn lay in the road amongst half their belongings, toppled out the wagon's back end. The rear right wheel lay flat on the road.

"Wynn?" Magiere called. "Are you all right?"

The sage sat up, her short robe's cowl flopped over her face. She pushed it back and looked about as if lost.

"Yes . . . yes, I am fine," she said.

"Where's Leesil?" Magiere asked.

Wynn peered about again, climbing to her feet, and Chap ran around the wagon's back.

"Valhachkasej'â!" came Leesil's irate voice from the forest. "I'm in the damn bushes!"

He rose into view from behind the tree their wagon had struck, with dirt on his face and clothes. Stray leaves stuck out in his white hair. He walked stiff-legged as he stepped out onto the road, and held his right buttock as he scowled at Magiere.

"Did you ever manage to set the brake?" he asked through gritted teeth.

Magiere glared at him, though she was relieved that he was all right. "That wolf must have been starving to attack a wagon."

"Am I ever . . . ," Wynn said, head shaking in disbelief, "ever going to have one safe night around the three of you?"

Magiere had no answer.

Chap sat down next to the sage and licked her hand, but Wynn pulled it away. She looked at the wheel lying on the ground. Leesil squatted down and poked at the axle's end. Magiere was about to ask if they could fix it, but Leesil was already shaking his head in disbelief.

"Yes, this makes perfect sense," Wynn continued. "Who else would become stranded in the wilderness by one famished wolf?"

Bitterness was unusual enough coming from Wynn, but

the words hung upon Magiere as she looked toward the woods where the wolf had vanished. There was nothing else to be done, and she began unharnessing Port and Imp.

"Oh, I am sorry," Wynn said. "It is a bit too much to face right now."

"I could use your help," Magiere replied.

Wynn came forward to inspect Port's right front leg. It was bleeding.

"Only the skin," she said. "Proper tending and rest, and he will recover quickly."

"We're here for the night anyway," Leesil said, glaring at the wheel and axle.

He collected their belongings off the road and began setting camp as Wynn dug through her things to find salve and a bandage for Port's leg. Magiere stroked the animal's long forehead, but her gaze was still on the forest.

Chane knelt upon the ground, seeing through the wolf's eyes as he directed its assault upon the horses. He had made the wolf his own familiar and felt what it felt while merged with its awareness. When the dhampir's blade bit the wolf's shoulder, Chane recoiled in pain and severed his bond with the animal.

But he had seen the wagon smash against the tree.

Through his own eyes, he saw Welstiel standing a short distance off, holding his cloak closed about himself, watching Chane with tight lips and eyes narrowed with impatience.

"It's done." Chane panted. "One horse is injured, and the wagon has lost a wheel. No one was hurt, and they are stranded."

Welstiel nodded. "Well done. Can you ride?"

"The wolf is bleeding."

"Will that affect you?"

Chane still felt the pain from the dhampir's blade, but it

was fading. He did not answer and crawled to his feet to repack his components and mount his horse. Welstiel followed his actions.

"Go," Chane said, exhausted and angry.

He did not want his efforts wasted and, once they passed the dhampir in the night, Welstiel would no longer have a need to take matters into his own hands. Wynn would be safe—for now.

"How far ahead are they?" Welstiel asked.

"Perhaps a few leagues or more. I'll warn you when we get close, and we can move off the road through the forest. If we press through the night, we will be long ahead of them by dawn."

Welstiel kicked his horse forward. Chane gripped his reins with one hand and his saddle with the other and followed.

Chapter 11

Leesil awoke well past dawn and felt like he hadn't slept at all. He rolled over beneath the wool blanket to find he was alone.

Magiere was already up and examining the wagon's dislodged wheel. Her hair hung loose about her shoulders, unbraided since the night before when they'd faced Vordana. The small cuts on her face were nearly healed, but the left side of her chin was still tinged red.

The damp air bothered Leesil more than usual, and it was difficult to put on a cheerful front as he got up. They needed to get the wagon fixed and be on their way. He crouched beside Magiere before the axle's exposed end.

"What do you think?" she asked.

"The wheel is intact," he answered. "But I don't see how we're going to lift the wagon enough to remount it."

Wynn and Chap gathered beside them.

"How is Port?" Magiere asked.

"Doing well," Wynn replied. Her eyes were sleepy, and she had not braided her hair either. "The salve helped, and he is not even limping."

"Any ideas?" Leesil asked her, returning to the wagon's wheel.

Wynn led the way into the woods until they found a fallen log. Leesil helped her drag it back. After Magiere hacked it clean with her falchion, Leesil scavenged a stout branch long enough for a lever. They rolled the log up to the wagon, set the branch in place, and all three of them put their weight on it.

The wagon's corner lifted, but when Leesil tried to set the wheel to the axle, it was clear they wouldn't get the axle high enough. More scavenging followed, as they tried to find a way to lift the axle higher. By midmorning, they stopped in frustration for a late breakfast, settling together on a blanket with apples and biscuits.

"If we can't fixed it soon," Magiere said, "We'll have to pack up Port and walk, take turns riding Imp."

"Now wait just a—," Leesil began.

"Listen," Wynn said.

A chattering carried from a distance, almost like the sound of birds. Leesil stopped to listen, and the more he paid attention, the clearer the sound became. The tones took on a distinct tune, and a voice carried lightly above chords both joyful and melancholy.

Leesil got up from the blanket. "Singing?"

The music carried up the road from behind them. The first thing he saw was a small house being pulled along by four mules. It was more of an enclosed wagon with walls and a roof overhead. Dark-haired people hung out of shuttered windows or sat atop its roof or walked beside the wagon. Faded and worn, their clothes were a motley array of colors and patterns.

The man atop the roof strummed a *tàmal*, a narrow-necked four-stringed Belaskian lute, and the boy beside the driver bowed upon a well-worn fiddle. A woman walking beside the mules alternately hummed or sang in a language Leesil had never heard, though it sounded akin to Droevinkan.

"Tzigän!" Wynn said with her usual eager curiosity. "I mean Móndyalítko . . . like Jan and his mother, from the keep above Magiere's village. They have to be."

There were times Leesil found Wynn's need to label everything a bit tiring, but it was more bothersome that they'd run into these vagabonds in the middle of nowhere. He'd lifted a few purses in his days, but only when necessary and not out of habit. Who better to spot a thief than a thief? Any help was better than none, but somehow this seemed like putting out a fire without knowing if there was water or whiskey in the bucket.

The house wagon slowed at the sight of the stranded trio and their broken rig. Leesil made his best effort to appear gracious as he stepped into the road and raised a hand in greeting.

"Can we beg a bit of help?" he called out in Belaskian.

"I don't know about this," Magiere muttered behind him. "There are quite a few of them."

"Do you see anyone else coming our way?" Wynn asked.

Most of the Móndyalítko appeared as openly friendly as had Jan, and in a blink, they climbed from the windows and the back of the wagon in a flurry of chatter. When the fiddle boy tried to hop down and join the gathering, the driver grabbed him by the breeches and pulled him back onto the wagon's bench.

The man from the roof came to greet Leesil, slinging his *tàmal* over his shoulder by its strap. He had a bushy mustache that nearly hid his mouth and trailed to his cheeks like the tips of wings. His hat was little more than a yellow felt sack that flopped to one side, its bottom edge sashed to his head with a mottled blue kerchief.

"I am Giovanni," he said, as if expecting them to recognize him immediately. Only his bottom teeth showed beneath the mustache when he grinned, and he swirled a quick hand through the air at those around him. "Of the Lastiana clan. And you seem to have damaged your home."

Leesil raised an eyebrow as he looked back at their broken wagon. Two men already inspected it closely, one scooting on his back beneath the tilted vehicle.

"We're off to Kéonsk for the autumn festival," Giovanni continued. "The last of the squash and pumpkins are in, and people will pay well for entertainment."

"Really?" Wynn said. "Magiere, could we observe this celebration? Domin Tilswith would be so interested."

Leesil suppressed a groan, and Magiere glared at the sage.

"We could use some help," Leesil said, still keeping an eye on those gathered close to their wagon and belongings. "If you can spare a bit of time."

"When the world puts something in your path," Giovanni answered seriously, "best face it as fate rather than trip like a fool rushing on."

"What?" Magiere said.

Leesil grabbed her hand and squeezed it sharply. "Most kind of you," he answered politely.

Soon five men helped lever the wagon up. When it was high enough, they braced it with cut logs scavenged from the forest, and all grabbed hold to lift the wagon's side again. When Magiere stepped in to assist, several of the men exchanged surprised smiles.

Bit by bit, pushing braces farther under the wagon with each lift, the axle rose high enough for the wheel to be mounted. All the while, the Móndyalítko spoke little of the task at hand, as if each knew what to do without discussion. It was clear to Leesil they were used to dealing with such things as part of daily life. Instead they chatted about the coming festival in the capital, or asked questions of Leesil and Magiere. They studied both with curious amusement, until Leesil grew concerned over Magiere's mounting irritation made plain by her curt answers. Tools were unloaded from the little rolling house and, just past noon, the wagon was roadworthy once again.

Leesil traded some of their apples and extra jerky for a bit of spice tea and a few other supplies, while Wynn chatted amongst the Móndyalítko. Chap was more than occupied with children circling about him. Two young girls tried desperately to get him to fetch a stick, for which he showed no interest at all. But both dog and sage appeared equally disappointed when Leesil announced it was time to move on.

Leesil offered their thanks to Giovanni. "We're grateful you happened by."

Magiere pulled two silver pennies from their purse. "Please take this for your trouble."

Giovanni held up a hand in refusal. "To help a traveler is good luck. This time, threefold."

"I insist," she said.

Leesil tensed. Magiere hated being indebted to anyone, and he worried that she might be insulting them. Giovanni searched her pale face for a moment and then took the coins.

"Our thanks," he said.

"Can we reach Kéonsk by nightfall?" Leesil asked.

"Tonight? No, too far. Perhaps tomorrow."

Concealing his disappointment, Leesil nodded. After cheerful farewells, he clucked Port and Imp into a brisk trot. Wynn sat in the wagon's back, scribbling on parchment as she watched the Móndyalítko's rolling house fade in the distance behind them. She was quiet for a while and then closed her journal to gaze wistfully down the road.

Leesil counted them lucky that the bucket they'd been blindly handed held water instead of whiskey. But with trouble averted, there was little to keep his thoughts from wandering once again back to the nightmare forest and his mother's dust.

Welstiel had ridden hard through the previous night and then slept in their well-hidden tent all day. He awoke precisely at dusk and stepped from the tent with his pack in hand. He needed to scry for Magiere, check her direction and distance, and realized there was neither time nor opportunity to do so outside of Chane's presence.

Watching Chane conjure the wolf's spirit had altered Welstiel's evaluation of the tall undead. Chane's resourceful nature was matched with notable skill, making the creation of a large familiar appear effortless. Welstiel knew better.

Allowing Chane to see how he tracked Magiere would give away none of Welstiel's true secrets. And few others of his acquaintance had studied the arcane arts to the degree that Chane clearly had. He took out the brass disk, turned it over on the ground, and cut the stub of his little finger. Chane paused from packing to eye the brass dish as a drop of Welstiel's fluids struck the center of its dome.

"What are you doing?"

"Scrying," Welstiel answered, and he chanted softly until the droplet shivered and moved west. "We're still ahead of her. We will reach Kéonsk first."

Chane crouched down, examining the disk more closely. "How does it work?"

"You primarily use ritual, but I work my conjury through artificing, creating useful tools. I created one amulet Magiere wears and this brass disk. A drop of my fluids forms a connection. It is dragged in the direction of the amulet."

Chane clearly wished to inquire further but did not. "We should go."

They rode hard through half the night, tiring their horses,

until Welstiel spotted lights ahead. He felt relief that at least he had arrived ahead of Magiere.

Although Welstiel was not fond of Droevinka, his father had served the most ancient house of Sclävên in the eastern province for many years before they had schemed their way into the good graces of the Äntes. He knew well the history of Kéonsk. It was the largest city in Droevinka, less than a third the size of Bela and less developed, and surrounded by a thick wall of rough mortared stone. Its position on the Vudrask River allowed for ease of trade and commerce. Barges from Stravina and Belaski brought goods inland from those countries' main ports.

The stone wall was less than a hundred years old. The castle keep had been constructed centuries before, and the city had slowly spread outward around it. In long-gone days, any prince who managed to take the throne would rule for life, or until the next house waged a successful insurrection. Although civil wars were less frequent then, they were brutal and extensive, and all houses fought to take power. If a weak prince lead a victorious house, the nation had been known to suffer for decades—should he live that long.

Then a gathering was called between the five strongest houses. It was agreed that a ruling grand prince, rather than a king, should be selected by the consent of all. He would serve nine years or until his death, whichever came first. A successful solution overall, though small-scale upheavals still occurred from time to time, especially if an overzealous house tried to keep its prince on the throne rather than surrender power.

The unlanded house of Väränj was a notable exception, and most other houses barely recognized its noble status. Descended of mercenary horsemen in service to the first invaders of the region, they served as the royal guard and city contingent for whoever held the throne. They were denied the opportunity to place their "prince" on the throne or establish a province of their own. They served as peacemakers and policed the nation, occasionally quelling disputes between houses that boiled into open bloodshed.

As Welstiel and Chane approached, they had three choices. The road curved gently, one side going around the city, and the other leading to the riverside docks. A short path led straight forward to the huge arch and rounded wooden gates of Kéonsk's west entrance. Guards in light armor manned the entrance, all wearing the bright red surcoats of the Väränj, marked with the black silhouette of a rearing stallion.

Chane pulled his horse up, and Welstiel turned his own mount in puzzlement.

"What's wrong?"

"Do we need to offer a tale about our business here?" Chane asked. "Or will they just let us in so late at night?"

"I haven't been here in many years," Welstiel answered. "Prince Rodêk of the Äntes currently holds the throne, and we need to see his prime counselor, Baron Cezar Buscan. My father served the Äntes in our final days. I think we can present ourselves as messengers bearing a report. Our appearance is enough to mark us as better than commoners, but do not speak—your accent is too pronounced."

Chane nodded, and Welstiel headed for the open gates.

A young guard with a shaved head and no helmet raised his hand to stop them, a casual gesture of polite protocol and no more. It was past midnight, but this was a large city, so it stood to reason that some people arrived late and others left early. Enormous torches lit up both sides of the entrance, their heads shielded by large cups of iron mesh.

"Your business, sir?" the guard asked.

Welstiel offered his story of bearing reports for the baron, and the young guard shook his head.

"You're welcome in, sir, but Baron Buscan sees no one he doesn't ask for himself. And there are already gangs of nobles from various houses trying to get his attention."

"And Prince Rodêk?" Welstiel asked. "Surely he sees servants of his own house?"

"Not here," and the guard lowered his voice. "He's gone back to Enêmûsk and the Äntes keep. It's rumored there's some family issue at stake. Baron Buscan is the only authority at the castle, and he's not seeing nobody."

Welstiel was perplexed. Rodêk was not at court, and Buscan was not seeing representatives even of his own house. It made no sense, but the Väränj guard welcomed him into the city just the same.

They entered the open cobblestone market area. It was quiet and still, with canvas tarps covering scores of booths and carts that would come alive at dawn with hawkers selling goods to the city's population.

"Do we find an inn?" Chane asked.

"No, we must see Buscan tonight. This cannot wait."

"He'll be in bed."

"Then we wake him. He will see me, in spite of our young guard's account."

They passed beyond the market and entered a district of inns and taverns where the night was not so quiet. Bargemen, prostitutes, and gamblers kept late hours. Welstiel caught Chane staring at a slender woman in a doorway. She smiled and held up a hand, rubbing fingers and thumb together to indicate that coin was needed for good company. Welstiel was thankful his companion had fed on the boy only last night.

By far, the most common inhabitants moving in the night streets were soldiers. Most were small patrols of Väränj, but there were occasional groups wearing the light yellow surcoats of the Äntes. Prince Rodêk had left a behind a visible contingent. No noble house was permitted active troops inside the walls of Kéonsk, though as citizens they were not barred from partaking of the city's offerings. These men appeared armed and fully outfitted for duty, and it would not be the first time a grand prince had considered his own men an exception to the rule.

Welstiel rode directly toward the city center and the gates of the castle. A dozen Väränj soldiers in red surcoats guarded the courtyard's entryway, and more patrolled the ramparts and walls. He remained mounted, approaching at a leisurely pace. A grizzled and scarred man, perhaps as old as fifty, was cursing at two subordinates.

"You," Welstiel called. "Come here."

The old soldier paused midsentence and turned his head. He did not appear impressed by Welstiel's tone and approached slowly, thumping the butt of his spear with each step.

"Yes, sir?" he replied.

"I am here to see Baron Buscan—*now*."

One of the younger subordinates snickered.

The old soldier answered politely. "I'm sorry, sir. The baron doesn't hold audiences at this hour."

Welstiel leaned forward in his saddle and pitched his voice low so that no one but the old soldier would hear him. "My name is Lord Welstiel Massing. My father was Lord Bryen Massing. Do you know that name?"

The man's eyes narrowed, and Welstiel heard his breath catch. He straightened himself with a curt nod.

"Announce me quietly," Welstiel said. "Our business is private."

The old soldier signaled his men to open the gatehouse portal. A few hesitated in surprise but obeyed him. He walked toward the entrance, and Welstiel and Chane rode in behind him.

"If you are known in this country," Chane whispered,

"why haven't we used that ploy all along? We could have traveled in better comfort."

"Quiet," Welstiel answered.

The front entrance was an enormous cedar door three times the height of a man. More portcullis than portal, it opened by cranking upward into the wall on heavy chains. When lowered, the door's bottom edge set into a shallow trough of stone. No one questioned the old guard as he led Welstiel and Chane inward through the gatehouse's tunnel to the courtyard beyond.

In Bela, this stronghold would not have measured up as a castle. It was originally built as a large military keep by whichever house's ancestors had first held this plot of land. It lacked the extensive spread of the Belaskian or even the Stravinan royal grounds, having never been expanded. Perhaps the houses feared it would become a more fortified location, should a grand prince try to keep the throne through force. Still, it was built of solid basalt and granite that had lasted through the centuries.

"Leave your horses here, sirs, and follow me."

They dismounted and tied up their mounts at a rail inside the keep wall. The old soldier led them on through the keep's small and unimpressive main door to the large entry hall. The place was chill and dark, and there was mud on the floor as they stepped in. The sparse rushes in the entryway had not been changed recently. Welstiel had spent too many years living in Droevinkan keeps with his father, and these walls felt distastefully familiar.

"Please wait here, sirs," the old soldier said. "The baron may still be up, but I will need to announce you."

"Of course," Welstiel replied.

He paced, staying clear of the walls and forcing down visions of his father in places such as this. He wanted the entire ordeal to be over. If not for Magiere's foolishness, he would never have been forced to come this far.

"Are you are all right?" Chane asked.

"I'm fine."

"I don't know what you're after in here," Chane said. "So I cannot play out this game for you."

Welstiel straightened. "Be ready to act when I do."

"In what sense?"

"I need to procure documents. Unfortunately, we cannot leave anyone alive who heard my name."

"Then why use the name at all?" Chane asked with some annoyance. "There must have been another way to secure an audience with Buscan."

"We do not have the time to search for him ourselves and kill every guard or servant along the way who sees us. No. We must be granted a private audience, accomplish what is needed, and then leave quietly."

Chane crossed his arms. "Is this Buscan an old friend of yours?"

"Hardly," Welstiel answered. "He has served the Äntes for many years. By the time my father *requested* a specific fief, Buscan granted it, out of fear as much as anything else. Everyone was terrified of my father." He paused. "Was your father feared?"

"Not by the nobles," Chane answered. "Most of those in Belaski found him charming."

The old soldier trotted back down the hall, lantern in hand, and gestured to them. "This way, sirs."

Wynn stayed close to the campfire that night as Leesil and Magiere crawled into the wagon's bed to sleep. Magiere insisted there was room for all, which was true enough, but Wynn preferred privacy for herself and for them. She assured Magiere that she would be fine by the fire with Chap beside her. Leesil and Magiere whispered to each other for a while. Wynn neither wanted nor was able to hear what they said, and shortly they settled quietly to sleep.

Wynn worked a little longer on her account of the Móndyalítko. It was distracting and less disquieting than her notes concerning Magiere. When she looked up from her work, Chap had crawled close, lying with his head on his paws. She closed up the journal, binding the parchments into their leather cover, and scooted next to him across her blanket spread upon the ground.

His crystalline eyes were full of sorrow.

"I wish you would tell me what is wrong," she whispered.

Chap blinked once but offered nothing more. His long fur was becoming matted, and she would need to brush him come morning. Wynn reached into her pack, pulling out a piece of smoked mutton she had saved from the last breakfast at Lord Stefan's manor.

"I do not care for meat," Wynn said. "I was saving this for your breakfast, but you might like it now."

Chap raised his head with a grunt, and she tore pieces for him to chew upon. When the snack was gone, he laid his head back on his paws. Whatever troubled him could not be fixed with a tasty morsel.

"I saw you in the forest before you healed my sight," Wynn said. "You were part of both worlds at the same time, your kin's and ours. I do not understand what you did to take this form, but it cannot be easy to be trapped between worlds all alone."

She gathered his head in her arms. He resisted at first, then shoved his entire face into her stomach.

"You do not have to be alone," she said. "Someday, you will tell us why you are here."

Wynn stroked Chap's head until the fire burned down to glowing coals of orange.

*   *   *

Chane expected the old soldier to lead them to some great conference hall and was surprised when they were escorted into a side passage and up a narrow staircase. At its top was a corridor running both ways. Directly across from it was a plain door. The soldier opened it and ushered them in before retreating, closing the door behind him.

It was a small room of polished wood walls, furnished more comfortably than what Chane had seen of the castle so far. Thick rugs of local weave covered the floor, and a painting of armored cavalry racing though the Droevinkan forest hung upon the rightmost wall. The sight of such artwork in this dismal country seemed garishly out of place.

Candles as thick and tall as his forearm were lit around the room upon small tables or stands of iron. Two large mahogany chairs sat by a small fireplace that must have been constructed in more recent times. Keeps this old rarely held more than the one hearth in a main hall. A small desk sat to the right of the hearth, and a narrow bookcase to its left. On a table beside the chairs were a quill and inkwell.

In those chairs sat a man and a woman. Chane assumed the former was Baron Cezar Buscan. He was enormous in height and girth, and wore a dark blue night robe that stretched around his middle. His bush of a black beard reached his chest, but his head was shiny and bald except for a circlet of dark hair running around back between his temples. His ruddy complexion reminded Chane of his father's wealthy friends who drank too much brandy.

The woman was such a stark contrast that she put Chane on guard. In both his mortal and undead existence, he had known many lovely women. Sitting near Buscan was the most striking beauty he'd ever seen. She stood up to greet the two visitors.

Neither slight nor voluptuous, her small stature was distinctly curved beneath a silk, coffee-brown dress, unusually light for this chill country, cut to resemble a robe and sealed down the front by a long row of brass clasps. A scarlet cord tied about her waist. The first two clasps were unfixed, leaving her exposed from her throat to the tops of her breasts. A teardrop bloodstone hung upon a brass chain about her neck and rested in the hollow of her cleavage. Her dark red hair was not dressed like a lady of court, but hung past her shoulders in a thousand spirals. Green eyes watched Chane below a smooth brow.

She smiled a greeting with one finger tracing the edge of her neckline, causing it to dip briefly.

Lord Buscan rose with some difficulty. He was older than Chane had guessed.

"Welstiel?" Buscan said.

The baron paused too long, eyeing Chane's companion, as if doubting his own eyes. Chane looked at Welstiel and realized what troubled the baron. If it had been many years since Welstiel's last presence in this land, how much had the baron aged since those days to now stand before someone who appeared not to have aged at all?

"It has been so long, we thought you dead," Buscan said. "You look . . . quite well." He gestured to the woman, voice tinged with pride. "Osceline, my consort."

The woman smiled again, her tiny teeth white and perfect. She bowed her head slightly without taking her eyes off the visitors.

Welstiel stepped closer, picking up the feather quill on Buscan's chair-side table to examine it.

"A guard at the city gate told me Prince Rodêk is not here, and that you hold no audiences with other nobles."

Buscan shrugged his bulky shoulders. "Uncertain times require extra precautions. When did you take up this new interest in the affairs of our state?"

"It is late," Osceline said. "Perhaps you could tell us why you've come?"

Her voice was clear and light, like notes from a flute. Chane watched the gently beating pulse in her pale throat.

Welstiel put the quill back down. "I am collecting records pertaining to my family. For the time we served the Äntes, this was the place to begin, as your house currently rules the nation. If you have such, I need to see them."

"Is that all?" Buscan appeared relieved. "Oh, but I fear I can't help you in this. There are no records."

Welstiel folded his hands behind his back and beneath his cloak. The baron's answer was obviously insufficient, as he stared into Buscan's eyes.

"Any records are fewer than fifteen winters old," Buscan explained. "We tried to create a central archive to secure all documents. There was an insurrection by the Mäghyär when Prince Demitri of the Serbóê completed his term. A fourth of the city was razed, along with the judiciary building, and all the records inside were lost in a fire."

Chane couldn't tell if Welstiel was pleased or troubled by this news. Osceline wandered away to the polished round table below the painting.

"You are certain there is nothing left?" Welstiel asked.

The baron shook his head. "If that is all you came for, your journey has been for nothing."

Chane heard a hissing whisper, and turned his head toward the sound. Osceline was chanting, eyes fixed upon Welstiel and Buscan.

Before Chane could call out a warning, Welstiel's hand lashed out from behind his back at Buscan's chest. His hand jerked sideways, missing the baron entirely. There was a short dagger in his grip.

Buscan's teeth clenched, and his brow furrowed in anger.

He lunged for the hearth's mantel, and Chane saw a long war knife resting there in its sheath.

Chane swung out, catching a thick candle upon its stand, and slapped it toward Osceline. The wick snuffed, and the thick wax cylinder struck the side of her face. Her chanting ceased as she toppled against the wall and slid to the floor.

"Now!" Chane yelled at Welstiel.

Welstiel drove his blade through Buscan's back with enough force that the man's head struck the mantel's edge. When Welstiel jerked the blade out, Buscan stumbled back to crumple into the chair Osceline had been using. Welstiel closed on him, but the baron's eyes rolled toward his consort.

"Don't!" he cried out. "Not her . . . please."

Chane was already focused upon the floor beneath Osceline, and he began drawing the lines and figures in his mind to overlay what he saw. As her eyes met Buscan's gaze, she cringed in pain. Anguish marred her creamy features for an instant before they creased with hatred as she glared at Welstiel.

"No!" she shouted, and then her attention fixed on the low thrum of Chane's chant.

Through the encircled triangle Chane envisioned, he saw Osceline's eyes snap closed and her clenched fist raise before her face. She called out a single word Chane didn't catch, and her hand opened, fingers splayed wide.

Light exploded in Chane's vision, as if every candle in the room flared suddenly. Everything turned white, and the pain came too quickly for Chane to suppress. It shattered his focus and the rhythm of his incantation.

He rubbed his eyes, and slowly the dim swirling colors faded from his flash-blinded sight. Welstiel was in a similar state, but Buscan sat limp in the chair, staring up at the ceiling as he struggled to breathe.

Osceline was gone.

Welstiel shoved his blade through Buscan's chest.

The baron buckled under the blow, expelling a groan as air was forced from his lungs. Before his head dropped forward, Welstiel hurried to where Osceline had been. He thumped systematically on the wall's wooden planks. At a hollow sound, he stepped back and kicked out hard.

One plank snapped inward under his boot to reveal a space beyond it. He did not bother to look for a catch to open the hidden panel, and instead tore out the adjoining planks with his hands.

"Go after her," Welstiel said. "She must not speak to anyone!"

"And you?" Chane asked.

"I will deal with the old soldier. Kill her quickly, and join me in the courtyard."

Chane slipped into the passage. Envisioning Osceline's throat was enticing. She was aggressive and sensual. He hoped she would fight.

He stood upon the narrow landing of a dark staircase and opened his senses to smell for blood, life. There were quick footfalls coming from below. Osceline was running, and that made Chane smile. A chase was always a welcome prelude.

The passage steps emerged well below in what appeared to be a prison beneath the castle. Chane stepped out into a passage of iron cell doors. At the passage's end was another hall running left and right. He no longer smelled Osceline and stopped to listen again. All was silent, and then a metal door grated softly.

Chane ran after the echo of metal against stone as he turned left at the connecting passage. At the end of this new path was a door left ajar. He jerked it open to find a chamber with a table and chairs, perhaps a guards' room. Across it, Osceline pulled one last time upon a locked door, trying desperately to open it. She gave up and turned to face him.

Chane was surprised by her countenance. She appeared small and mundane, no longer dangerous and desirable. And tired, as if her spell had taken much from her. Chane felt a twinge of disappointment.

"You don't need to kill me," she said. "I would only do myself harm by speaking a word about who murdered Cezar. My master will be displeased enough as it is."

Chane did not break stride as he stepped toward her, and Osceline held up her hand, palm outward.

A sharp pain sliced through Chane's temples and behind his eyes. His vision swirled to black for an instant. Disoriented, he blinked. The room returned to his sight, but it was hazy. Osceline stood before the door but shimmered in waves like summer heat upon an open field.

Irrational rage rose in Chane to smother all calculated thought. He wanted her dead and no longer cared how. He lunged and grabbed her by the throat.

At first he felt nothing, as if his fingers had closed on air. Then his grip tightened on warm and pliant flesh. Chane blinked.

Osceline's throat was in his hands, her swollen tongue pressing out between paled lips and green eyes frozen wide and vacant. He felt cracked vertebrae under her skin and muscle.

Chane blinked again, and she lay dead on the floor at his feet. He stepped back, a mix of satisfaction and fury clouding his awareness.

He vaguely remembered rushing Osceline as she raised a hand toward him. He snatched her throat, bore her down, and crushed the life out of her. Yes, that was what had happened. She was dead, and he could leave. He returned to the passage doorway but stopped and looked back.

Osceline still lay near the locked side door, and Chane looked down at his own hands.

He remembered the feel of her neck breaking, but he had not bothered to taste her life as it vanished, and he couldn't understand why. Perhaps in his anger and panic to reach her before she could flash-blind him again, his instinct had taken more expedient action.

Not wishing to wander the castle in retreat, Chane back-tracked to the wood-paneled room and down through the passages the old soldier had guided them along. As he emerged in the main hall to head for the front entrance, Welstiel stepped from a side corridor.

"Did you find the old guard?" Chane asked.

"Yes . . . and the woman?"

Chane remembered that he had clearly seen Osceline's body. "Dead . . . I snapped her neck . . . and left her below in the keep's prison."

"Good." Welstiel nodded approval. "We will take the horses and walk them back out. I have seen no other servants up and about. No one will find Buscan until midmorning, as it appears he stays up late into the nights."

He reached out a hand to propel Chane toward the front entrance. Chane found this odd, as Welstiel rarely touched him.

"There is nothing more for us to do here," Welstiel said. "We wait for the dhampir to arrive. When she finds no records and no one to help her further, she will have no choice but to turn back."

A sudden connection occurred to Chane. Welstiel had come to hide records of his family, and Magiere searched for records of her own father.

"No records regarding the Massings," Chane said. "And none regarding her . . . How did that the captain put it, 'her family'?"

He turned and found Welstiel returning his steady gaze.

"Do not forget your place," Welstiel said in a voice

stripped of all emotion. "You are here to serve the bargain we made, and that is all."

Chane's discovery would have to be handled carefully or he risked giving Welstiel further cause for conflict. He nodded calmly.

"We deserve some comfort," Welstiel said in a more sociable tone. "Let us find out if Kéonsk boasts a decent inn. A bath and laundered clothing are in order, as well as comfortable beds for a change."

Welstiel's quick shift to placation left Chane wary as he followed his companion out to the horses. Again he pictured Osceline's body by the locked door with the smooth flesh of her throat still intact.

His own change of habit disturbed him.

Chapter 12

The wagon rolled up to the gates of Kéonsk at midday. Leesil dug through his pack and pulled out an orange paisley scarf. He pulled his hair back behind his ears and tied the cloth around his head. It was so large that the ends hung down to his shoulders.

Magiere wrinkled her nose as if she'd bitten into a rancid pear. "Where did you get *that*?"

"I traded with one of the Móndyalítko for some apples."

"You paid for that with our apples?" she asked. "Where's your gray scarf?"

"I lost it in the forest the night we fought Vordana."

"The color doesn't work."

"Of course it does. My shirt is brown."

"You look like someone lit your head on fire. You'll stand out like a fever blister. Take it off, and find something else."

"I don't have anything else."

"I think it's rather striking," Wynn put in.

"You would," Magiere muttered.

Port and Imp pulled to a stop as a guard at the gate stepped out and held up his hand. His expression was serious. Nine

others stood inside the entrance in varied armor and red surcoats.

"Your business?" the guard asked.

"To the market . . . for supplies," Magiere said. "And one
of our horses injured his leg. We need someone who knows
horses to have a look at it."

The guard lost some of his harsh manner. "The township
of Nesmelórash is a half-day south. It would be best if you
could make it there."

Leesil saw genuine concern in the guard's wary expression, but he knew Magiere wasn't going to turn aside.

"We're heading east," he explained. "Is something
wrong?"

"Pardon," the guard said. "Your business is welcome at
market. But the grand prince is not in residence, and there is
contention over who should take charge until he returns."

Leesil's nerves began to tingle. This guard wore good
quality mail, and the scabbard of his sword bore a family
crest. He was at least a captain, if not a minor noble, and
likely educated, as most guards didn't use phrases like "in
residence." Why was he on guard duty at the city gate?

"What contention?" Leesil asked. "Why isn't someone in
charge while the grand prince is away?"

The guard looked each of them over. Though he gave
Leesil a serious inspection, he paused longest upon Wynn
huddled in the wagon's back with Chap. The sight of her
seemed to further soften the guard's manner.

"Baron Buscan, the city's protector, was assassinated last
night," he answered. "Prince Rodêk left an illegal contingent
of his soldiers in the city, and other houses are using this and
the lack of authority here to raise charges against the Äntes.
It's not safe."

The mention of assassination brought Leesil immediate
thoughts of Sgäile, the elven *anmaglâhk* sent after him in

Bela. He was about to ask if any elves had been sighted in the city and then thought better of it. It was unlikely anyone would see a member of this caste of assassins, as silent and undetected as Sgäile had been.

"Thank you, but we can take care of ourselves," Magiere replied.

With a troubled nod, the guard stepped back and let them in.

On impulse, Leesil called out, "Sir, what is your name?"

"Captain Marjus of the Väränj."

Port and Imp pulled the wagon into the market area. Most booths were closed, but a few people were visible among those tables and carts conducting business. There were also soldiers in red surcoats, like the captain's, patrolling the fringe of the area. Leesil spotted men in light yellow surcoats, as well, who kept their distance from Marjus's cohorts.

"Now what?" he asked. "This is bad luck. An audience at the castle is next to impossible, since there's no one there to hold one."

Magiere watched the soldiers and didn't answer.

"We are most likely going to be here a day or two," Wynn said. "We should find a respectable inn, a stable for the horses, and something warm to eat while we consider what to do."

Leesil smiled. "A capital plan. Magiere?"

"Yes. I see a stable ahead on south side of the market."

It took little time to find a nearby inn, a place called Jêndu Stezhar, the "Acorn Oak," which looked clean and respectable. They soon settled to spooning in mouthfuls of milky potato soup in its common room. The innkeeper was a good-natured gray-haired man who wasn't offended when Leesil requested an extra bowl for Chap.

Since the vision of his dead mother, each time Leesil ate warm food or succumbed to the smallest comfort, he wondered if she had suffered . . . was suffering. Then he looked at Magiere's pale face. He couldn't force her to turn away until she knew what she was and how she had come to exist, or she had exhausted all hope of finding these answers.

He spooned another mouthful of soup, ready to discuss matters at hand, when he gave more notice to a tall middle-aged soldier in a yellow surcoat sitting near them. The soldier had short-cropped brown hair and a thick scar down his left cheekbone, and he was on his third tankard of ale since their arrival.

Leesil was uncertain how much should be said in close proximity to any of the Kéonsk soldiers . . . of any house. He saw Magiere glance in the man's direction.

Innocent Wynn blurted out the first question before Leesil could stop her. "So how do we acquire permission to search records at the castle?"

The scarred soldier looked up from his ale. "Girl, the grounds have been locked down tighter than a cask of autumn wine."

He answered her in Belaskian, and his voice was sad rather than angry. Wynn turned sideways in her chair to see him better.

"What do you mean 'locked down'?"

Leesil tensed. "Wynn, let's not bother the—"

"I mean the house of Väränj has locked the gates. Until my prince returns, no one but a redcoat gets anywhere near the castle. That swine Buscan is dead, may his spirit rot in the earth along with his corpse."

Wynn had spilled their intentions, and there was little they could do to wash their presence from this captain's awareness. It appeared factions within the houses were at odds, as well as the contentions between houses Marjus had mentioned at the city gate. This Äntes captain gulping his ale didn't care for the grand prince's own counselor.

Leesil held out his hand to the man. "I'm Leesil. These are my companions Magiere and Wynn. We've come looking for the names of nobles who held fiefs in west Droevinka long ago. Surely, the Väränj guards will not object to such a simple request."

The soldier laughed but without humor. When he saw Leesil's outstretched hand, he gripped it in greeting. "Apologies. I am Captain Simu of the Äntes cavalry. I don't mean to interrupt your supper, but you may as well go home when you're done."

"We're not leaving," Magiere said.

Simu looked at her and sighed. "Do you understand that Baron Cezar Buscan was assassinated last night? The city's protector—curse him—is dead! Those Väränj mongrel watchdogs haven't the wit to see we're better off."

Magiere leaned closer. "A captain from a nearby fief told us that Buscan has been replacing Äntes nobles as fief holders without giving any reason. Is this true?"

Simu's ale-weary eyes cleared, and he pushed his tankard away.

"Why else do you think he'd be judged a traitor by those of us in the ranks? It is difficult enough to gain note in a noble house. What good does it do when rewards are handed off to the undeserving, simply because they hold favor with the prime counselor?"

The captain hung his head then glanced about the common room before continuing in a lowered voice.

"I'd swear by my ancestors, that temptress with the red curls he took as consort bewitched him. Maybe she's the one who knifed him in the back. Either way, he's dead. Soon as Prince Rodêk returns, I'm taking my men onto the royal grounds until a new protector is selected—and the Väränj be hanged!" Simu stood up and delivered them a curt bow of parting. "Perhaps then I can help you, but for now, no one but a redcoat gets inside the castle wall. Good night and safe passage to you."

As Simu walked out the inn's door, Leesil pondered his words, rubbing his chin with one hand.

"What's in that head of yours?" Magiere asked.

"It'll take a little while to prepare. You and Wynn stay here. Chap, come with me." He dumped his pack out and slung its empty bulk over his shoulder. "Can you put my things in the chest for now?"

"Stop right there," Magiere said. "What are you up to?"

"Trust me," he answered, and started to get up.

"Oh, no," she said, and grabbed the bottom of his empty pack, jerking it hard. "Every time you say that, things end up in a mess."

Leesil pulled on his pack, but Magiere's grip held firm.

"No, they don't—not every time," he shot back. "Magiere, let go!"

"We've enough people—and other things—coming at us in the dark. You're not going anywhere until you tell me."

"What you don't know, you can't get blamed for . . . if it doesn't work. Will you just let me handle this?"

Leesil pulled on the pack again. Magiere held on, and they jerked back and forth, until empty soup bowls jostled precariously across the table. Wynn leaned forward and threw her arms over the empty pack, pinning it to the tabletop.

"Could you two attract any more attention?" she whispered. "Leesil, tell us what—"

A cavernous belch filled the common room.

It drowned out even the murmur and chatter among the patrons of the Acorn Oak. Leesil and Magiere ceased tugging on the pack. Splayed across the table, Wynn looked to Leesil's left, and he followed her gaze.

Several elderly men, pipes clenched between their teeth, sat around a table. The nearest one still had his hand in the air, fingers poised downward as if he'd held something in them but a moment ago. No one watched the battle over the empty pack, for all eyes were on the creature squatting below the old pipe-biter's fingers.

Chap yawned, smacked his jowls, and let out a second burp. He looked up at Leesil, Magiere, and Wynn, and licked his nose at them.

Leesil could have sworn Chap's expression mimicked his own feigned innocence whenever he was caught in something unseemly.

Magiere shook her head in disbelief, and Wynn wrinkled her nose in disgust. The distraction was enough, and Leesil jerked the pack free before either could stop him.

He rushed for the inn's door, and Chap slipped out behind him.

Magiere sat with Wynn in a room upstairs at the Acorn Oak, fuming inwardly at Leesil. Of all the stupid things he'd ever done, she had a feeling this one was going to be near the top of the list. Darkness had come, and still he hadn't returned.

Where would they even begin looking for him?

Most likely in a cell at the local constabulary, if he didn't run afoul of the Väränj. And imprisonment seemed the best of outcomes, compared with what could happen to him now that tensions ran high in the capital over the assassin in their midst.

The room was sparse, with only a bed and no table. Wynn had set up a cold lamp atop their travel chest, and it lit the room in a dim white light.

"He will be all right," she offered. "Leesil and Chap can take care of themselves."

"Yes, but what are they doing?"

Wynn pursed her lips. "I might guess, though I doubt you will approve of Leesil's ethics."

Ethics were rarely a concern with Leesil. He did whatever he thought would be the quickest solution to a problem.

"What then?" Magiere asked. "What do you think he's up to?"

The room's door swung open, and Leesil fell inside before spinning to shut it, almost catching Chap's tail as the dog lunged in behind him.

He leaned against the closed door, panting and hugging his pack, which was far bulkier than when he had escaped Magiere's grasp. He was filthy from head to toe, like he'd been rolling around in the street. Chap dropped to his haunches and sat with his tongue dangling. He looked no better. His entire body was wet, and his legs, belly, and tail were splashed with mud.

Magiere's wave of relief passed instantly.

"Where did you go?" she shouted.

Leesil, still catching his breath, closed his eyes in resignation.

"And you!" Wynn cut in. "Now you decide to help, and this is how you start?"

Magiere's ire faltered, uncertain what the sage meant. Then she noticed Wynn was glaring at Chap and not Leesil.

"You did that on purpose," Wynn continued. "That little scene downstairs . . . that was so Leesil could get away, yes?"

Chap glanced up at Leesil, wrinkled his jowls, and turned away with a low growl.

"Duplicity is not enough for you," Wynn said. "Do you have to be so . . . so disgusting?"

"You're the one who said we were drawing too much attention," Leesil replied between breaths. "Better they look at him than you sprawling across our table."

"Don't try to toss this off on her," Magiere answered. "You're the reckless idiot here. What have you done?"

Chap stood, dripping, and rolled his shoulders, prepared to shake himself. Wynn cut in before Magiere could turn on the dog.

"Don't you dare do that in here!" she said, and Chap froze. "You want to go off and get dirty with Leesil, fine, but you will not share it with us."

Leesil and Chap groaned as the dog squatted on the floor again.

"Magiere . . . just get your sword," Leesil said. "Both of you get your cloaks."

He shoved off from the door and went to kneel at their travel chest. Setting the cold lamp and his pack on the floor, he opened the chest, dug through to the bottom, and pulled out the long, thin box that Magiere hadn't seen since Bela.

His assassin's tools. She felt a hollow grow in the pit of her stomach.

"What do you need that for?"

"Any records to be had," he said, "aren't going to be lying about. I may have to get us around some restrictions once we're inside the castle grounds."

"Inside?" Wynn sat up, worry growing on her round face. "How are we going to get past the gates?"

Leesil smiled. "I'm going to walk right through them."

A chill settled in the hollow in Magiere's stomach.

She snatched up Leesil's pack, digging inside, and withdrew a large wad of red cloth. She dropped the pack on the bed so she could shake out the fabric. It was Väränj surcoat, the emblem of a rearing stallion plain to see. For a moment, she couldn't speak and then drew a long breath.

"Leesil, are you mad? You'll never pass as a castle guard. Your hair—"

"That is likely what this helmet is for," Wynn said, and

she pulled it out of the pack's bottom, looking it over before she gazed at Leesil with sudden concern. "Did you hurt someone for this?"

"Nothing lasting," he answered. "A bit of pressure to the throat, and I left him resting in a doorway. He'll have a headache in the morning, that's all."

"How does this get the rest of us inside?" Wynn asked.

"It doesn't," Leesil replied. "Once I'm inside, I'll let the rest of you in through the bolt-hole."

"I'm afraid to even ask," Magiere said, and she dropped down on the bed beside Wynn. "A bolt-hole?"

"A hidden exit on the river side of the castle wall," Leesil said. "Most fortifications have at least one, in case the place falls to a siege, and they can be opened only from the inside. Tonight, I'll walk in with the guards or even on my own, slip away, and let you in."

"What if you're caught?" Magiere insisted. "You won't end up in some Belaskian or Stravinan jail. You might not make it there alive."

"No one is going to catch me," Leesil said with a hint of resentment. "Just get your cloak."

Magiere crouched down beside him, still angry.

"Listen to yourself! If the need were dire—if one of us had been captured—I might agree to this. But I won't risk your life on a thin chance of finding my father's name. There are other ways. I came here for answers, not for your funeral."

Leesil's brow furrowed. Magiere's frustration made her almost weary, trying to get him to understand that she couldn't risk losing him for anything.

"If you still want those answers," he said quietly, "this is the only way—and don't think of suggesting we find you a surcoat, too. We've seen no women among the guards."

"Leesil, it's not worth—"

"When we head north to look for my mother, I don't want to watch you suffer, wondering what might have been found that we left behind. Now we need to go, before someone discovers that Väränj unconscious . . . or this will all be for nothing."

Magiere looked into his amber eyes and realized what drove him.

She didn't have his cunning and stealth, and she hated his recklessness in trying to acquire what she wanted. But in turn, when their positions reversed, she knew she would cut down anything in his path that tried stopped him from finding his mother.

Welstiel sat in a velvet cushioned chair by a warm hearth. He did not feel cold, so its heat brought no pleasure or relief, but he appreciated sensual trappings as remnants of a mortal life long lost.

Chane relaxed at a small mahogany table, scrawling on paper with a feather quill. They had procured individual rooms in a fine inn, but took their leisure together in Welstiel's room.

For twenty-six years, Welstiel had traveled alone, shunning his own kind. Chane had more in common with him than any Noble Dead he'd ever encountered. A scholar who both understood and practiced the arcane, Chane had also been a noble in life and spoke only when it was worthwhile. In spite of Chane's baser nature, Welstiel was developing an appreciation for companionship.

He felt fatigue creep in upon him. He needed to go off privately and seek sustenance.

"What are you writing?" he asked.

Chane looked up. "Notes on Droevinka and its current political structure. Once I secure relations with the guild, I may continue documenting this region."

Chane's current demeanor made it too easy to forget how savage and brutal he could be. Welstiel felt strangely at peace in spite of the distasteful act he was about to commit.

"I must go out," he said. "Please stay . . . carry on with your journaling. The city is in an uncertain state, and we should avoid too much activity that might draw Magiere's attention."

"She's here in the city? You are sure?"

"Yes, but the visit will do her no good," Welstiel answered.

"You knew this would happen when you killed Buscan," Chane said. "You knew the Väränj would lock down the castle, and the dhampir would not be allowed in."

"I suspected."

Chane swiveled, sitting sideways with one arm across the chair's high back. "But you weren't sure? My maker, Toret, could feed on prey and leave it alive, clouding its memory. Can you not do the same?"

"I have similar abilities, which I once used on your little sage," he replied, and ignored Chane's darkening expression. "But I find the individual must be relaxed, perhaps trust in me somewhat, before it is effective. Such powers grow with practice, and I do not practice often."

Welstiel rose, donning his cloak. "Stay and write. I will not be long."

"You go to feed?" Chane asked.

Welstiel picked up his smaller pack and slipped out of the room.

The common room downstairs was nearly empty, but the inn was located in a wealthy district. Late in the evening, most patrons would retire to their rooms or be out seeking entertainment. The street outside was equally quiet but for a small group of guards in their red surcoats. Only once along his way did he spot two others in their pale yellow, lingering under the eaves of a public house.

Welstiel slipped along the streets until he saw no one in any direction, then turned into the alleys and unlit sideways as he headed for the poor district on the city's outskirts.

Killing did not trouble him. He'd committed several brutal acts back in Bela to lure Magiere. Even as a mortal, ordering executions and using violent means to suppress peasant uprisings had been simply part of his duties. What was necessary was sometimes repugnant, just the same.

Food for a mortal was a matter of absorbing life, in one fashion or another. The body consumed materials it could break down and use. Relishing cheese and bread and bits of roasted mutton served on elegant plates had never caused Welstiel to stop in his life and contemplate the nature of sustenance.

The method of nurturing his new existence was far less pleasant.

A drunken bargeman staggered from a tavern door. Welstiel remained in the shadows of the narrow walkway between the tavern and next building. When the bargeman passed by, he grabbed the back of the man's coat and pulled him in.

Welstiel struck the base of the man's skull with his fist, and his prey slumped to the ground unconscious. Though he hated even touching such a lowborn creature, much less *needing* it, feeding on the better half of society was unacceptable unless there was no other choice. Kneeling down, Welstiel removed an ornately carved walnut box from his pack and opened it.

Resting in fabric padding were three hand-length iron rods, a teacup-size brass bowl, and a stout bottle of white ceramic with an obsidian stopper.

Welstiel took out the rods, each with a loop in its midsection, and intertwined them into a tripod stand. The brass bowl's inner surface was etched with a pattern of concentric rings all the way to its lip, and between these lines were the characters of his conjury. It had taken half a year to fashion it from what little he remembered of working upon Ubâd's vat, a task of years in itself. He had not understood all that he had seen; not all, but enough. Though the cup had not the power of that vessel, it served Welstiel's limited needs. He placed it carefully on the tripod.

The white bottle contained thrice-purified water, boiled in a prepared copper vessel whenever he had time to replenish the fluid. He pulled the stopper and poured just enough to fill half the cup.

Welstiel rolled the bargeman over on his back. So much life energy was lost in bloodletting that little was actually absorbed by an undead who drank it. His method was far more efficient and less debasing. He slipped out his dagger, made a shallow puncture in the man's wrist, and let blood collect on the blade's tip. Tilting the blade, he let one red drop strike the water in the cup.

As it thinned and diffused, he began to chant.

The air around him shimmered as in a desert heat, yet he felt it grow humid, more so than even Droevinka's climate could produce. The bargeman's skin started to shrivel and dry from the outside, collapsing into desiccation. When his heart stopped, so did Welstiel's chant. The bargeman was a brittle shell. Even his eyes were dried sockets.

The water in the cup brimmed to the lip and was so dark red, it would have appeared black to a mortal's limited eyes. Welstiel lifted it carefully from the tripod. He tilted his head back and poured the liquid down his throat.

So much life force taken in this pure form was not pleasant. It tasted of ground metal and strong salt if allowed to linger on the tongue. And then it burst inside him to rush through his body.

Welstiel set the cup back in place with a wavering hand, then flattened both palms upon the ground to brace himself into stillness. As a youth, he'd gone out with the captain of his father's guard to the local tavern and drank his first tall ale. It felt good, until he stood up too fast. What he had just swallowed was far stronger, and he had not yet climbed to his feet.

He waited for the worst to pass.

When he picked up the cup to put it away, it was clean and dry, with no sign that anything had been in it. He packed away the iron rods and white bottle along with it.

The corpse weighed far less than it had in life. He rolled it in his cloak. The river shore was but a short walk, where he stopped long enough to load the body's clothing with heavy stones. When he was certain the dock was deserted, he carried the body to the end planks and let it slip into the depths of the Vudrask.

Welstiel walked back to shore and stood there alone, tainted with familiar disgust and self-loathing. However, capturing every last dram of the mortal's life would sustain him for over half a moon, perhaps longer. It would be a while before he needed to feed again, and this was some comfort.

He closed his eyes and reluctantly gave thanks to the black-scaled patron in his dreams for guidance and assistance. Soon, Magiere would reach the end of her fruitless search and move on, leading him to an artifact that made his own creations mere toys by comparison.

And he would never need to feed again.

He did not put his cloak back on as he walked to the inn. He would have it laundered first. Returning to his room, he found Chane still at the small table, quill in hand, red-brown hair tucked behind one ear.

Across the room was a tall oval mirror on a stand, and Welstiel studied his reflection. His eyes were clear and alert. No sign of fatigue remained in his bearing.

"You seem much improved," Chane said. "I was becoming concerned."

Welstiel suppressed a grimace. Chane believed he had been out feeding at the throat of some peasant. Let him believe what he liked.

He sat again in his chair by the fire. "What have you recorded so far? I spent many years in this country. Perhaps I can provide more detail."

Chane raised one eyebrow. "Truly? What can you tell me of how the noble houses collectively select a new grand prince?"

An unsettling wave of satisfaction passed through Welstiel, from both the pleasure and the scholarly interest on Chane's face. He turned his chair from the hearth to face his companion, and they spent the remainder of the night immersed in Droevinka's political history.

Crouching behind a stable near the castle grounds, Leesil felt his discomfort grow. But this had been his idea. Hair tucked under a helmet, and dirt smeared on his face, he wore the bright red surcoat over his hauberk.

"You look fine," Wynn assured him. "The helmet shadows your eyes, and most of the Väränj soldiers will be tired from longer duty, now that more of them are needed. It is doubtful they all know each other."

Leesil found Wynn's confidence almost as unsettling as Magiere's reluctance. Chap sat next to the sage, and she carried the pack he'd prepared for when they were all inside. Among its contents were his box of tools and a slender rope. His punching blades would draw attention, so he'd left them at the inn, arming himself with wrist-sheath stilettos and a stout dagger in each boot.

Magiere assessed him and unstrapped her falchion. "Put this on. All the guards are armed."

"I'm armed," he said.

"With visible weapons," she growled at him.

"Oh." He strapped the sword around his waist. "I'll show you where the hatch is, but you can't sit by it and wait for me. Someone will see you."

He crept into the street along the castle's side wall and led them to where it met the edge of a corner tower near the river.

"This is where nobles are supposed to escape?" Magiere asked.

"Yes, it's a good choice," Leesil replied, and flattened one hand against the stone wall where he knew the hidden opening would be. "The river is close, which would be the first option. If that is blocked, there's a chance to slip into the city through the nearby buildings. Do you see where my hand is?"

"Yes," Magiere answered, "but I don't see any hatch."

Leesil patted the stones. "Keep your eyes on this spot, and you will. Go back and stay low behind this row of shops on the riverside. I shouldn't be too long."

Chap headed for their hiding spot with Wynn close behind him. Magiere grabbed Leesil's arm, and a tense silence passed between them. She wouldn't let go.

Leesil touched her fingers. "I'll be peeking out that bolt-hole before you know it."

She released him and slipped off to follow Chap and Wynn.

Leesil crept along the river's edge the other way, passing by the castle and farther down to reenter the city. He cut inward to a main road and back toward the castle gates as if he'd come from the heart of Kéonsk. Four Väränj soldiers out front were deep in conversation as he strolled up. The two walking the ramparts to either side of the gatehouse did not even pause.

"Hallo," he said. "Long night?"

One soldier smoking a short-stemmed clay pipe offered it to Leesil. "We been here since nightfall. You heard word about relief squads?"

Leesil took a pull on the pipe. The leaf the man smoked burned too hot. It tasted old and stale.

"No, I was sent with a message for Captain Marjus. My sergeant hasn't been able to find him, so he told me to head for the barracks."

Another solider frowned. "Marjus? That snooty straight-back who talks like he's a lord?" He suddenly cleared his throat as he eyed Leesil. "Pardon if you count him a friend, but he's no such among us."

"Yeah, that's him," the first soldier said, taking his pipe back from Leesil. "Haven't seen him tonight, but that don't mean nothing." He tilted his head to look up to the wall walk-ways. "Positions! Messenger coming through!"

A creaking sound came from within the gatehouse. As the large gate slid upward and opened, the soldier's companions on the ground fanned out, spears ready. Though they'd appeared relaxed upon Leesil's arrival, he could see these men were veterans.

Another group of soldiers met him inside.

"Message for Captain Marjus," Leesil said.

"Try the officers' quarters in the barracks . . . east side."

"Thank you."

After this exchange, Leesil was just another Väränj pa-trolling the courtyard. He walked casually toward the inner keep's east corner, in case anyone was watching. Once he passed out of sight, he hurried around the barracks to the back.

There were no guards patrolling the back courtyard for the moment. All he need worry about were those upon the ramparts, but the night shadows near the wall made it easy to slide along the courtyard's outer edge. He stopped when he'd reached the correct place.

Testing stone and mortar with fingertips, Leesil found no sign of an opening or its catch.

For a moment, he feared he'd misjudged the bolt-hole's location. He had felt it on the outside, but his bearings were disoriented. He forced himself to grow calm. He knew it was here. He just had to find it.

The best escape routes were often exits from tunnels beneath a keep, but the lay wouldn't work for that. The grounds were too close to the river, and tunneling toward the water's edge would create a problem with seepage over the years. Not impossible to deal with, but this place was not large or complex in construction. So the obvious choice would be a simple hidden portal through the wall itself.

Of course, standing there flattened against cold stone in the shadows wasn't exactly the best moment to consider all this.

And he heard footsteps up on the rampart moving toward his position.

Leesil looked both ways, along the wall to his left and to the tower's base on his right. There was a ground-level door into the tower. He slid along the wall, stopping to listen at the door and then slowly cracking it open.

Inside, a ladder led up to a wooden half-platform above. To either side were archways leading out onto the walls. He could hear the soldiers strolling above, but what he sought wouldn't be there. Leesil felt along the tower's inner surface nearest the wall that he knew held the bolt-hole, and low to the ground he found a small cubby in the stone, and within it was a wooden lever. He stuck the toe of his boot into the hole and stepped down on it.

A section of stone around his foot shifted, and he went down on all fours to shove it inward.

The hatch was barely large enough to crawl through on hands and knees, but once through it, he slowly stood up in a hollow space inside the wall itself. He pulled out a cold lamp crystal Wynn had given him and rubbed it once with his thumb. It gave off a dim glow, enough for his elven eyes to make out his surroundings.

There was no need here for the engineers to hide the mechanism for opening the bolt-hole. Counterweights hung from chains that passed through steel wheels mounted in the narrow chamber's ceiling. Short steel rails in the floor led up to where the bolt-hole was. All he need do was trip the lever and tug on the counterweights, and he did so. A small section of the outer stone of the wall rolled inward along the rails, and the bolt-hole was open.

Leesil closed his fist around the crystal and peered around the opening's edge with one eye, first one way then the other. There was no one in sight on the street. He leaned out and raised his hand, loosening his grip on the crystal to let its glow leak between his fingers. He waved it back and forth.

At first, no one came, and he worried that something had happened to the others. Then he saw Magiere creep out of the shadows across the way, leaning down with her eyes toward the city. Wynn and Chap followed behind her.

He put his finger to his lips and helped them into the wall. Then he put his shoulder to the section on the rails, waving for Magiere to do the same. They pushed it back in place, and Leesil set the lever to lock it in position.

"Now what?" Magiere whispered.

"We get out of this wall space and find a rear entrance to the keep."

"What if there isn't one?"

"Then we'll have to find a disguise of some sort for you and Wynn . . . and hope for the best."

Magiere stared at him as if he'd sprouted horns. "You're insane."

She was right, but in the past he'd had only himself to get inside a place such as this.

"Just follow me," he said.

Leesil was first to crawl through the low hatch into the tower's bottom. When he was certain the soldiers atop the walls were far enough off, he signaled the others to follow.

He spotted no entrance along the keep's back. The only other possibilities were the closer side facing the bolt-hole wall or the far side by the barracks. He kept to the bolt-hole wall as they scurried in its shadow. When they were nearer to the keep's corner, he ran across the courtyard to it, and the others followed to crouch beside him.

It was a horrible position. Any soldier upon the rear wall might spot them. Leesil looked around the corner to the keep's near side, but he saw no entrance.

"Well?" Magiere whispered from behind.

He shook his head and led them along the keep's back. Around the corner on the barracks side, he spotted what they sought.

"Good and bad," he whispered. "There's an entrance with two soldiers in front of it."

"Can we take them by surprise?"

Leesil scowled at her. That prospect wasn't appealing, but it was only thing he could think of himself. As long as no one else came along in the middle of it, they might not get killed on the spot.

"Wynn and Chap, wait here," he said, pulling a dagger from his boot and handing it to Magiere, blade first. "When I move, ram this handle into the other guard, dead-center between belly and ribs. It'll take his breath so he can't call out before you put him down."

Leesil sauntered out of the shadows as if he had all night, and Magiere followed his lead.

He smiled lazily as they approached the soldiers, but both men tensed at the sight of Magiere. She wasn't armed, as Leesil still wore her falchion, but the castle grounds were sealed. Anyone not wearing a Väränj surcoat called immediate attention.

"Captain Marjus requested a delivery of stores for the prince's return," Leesil said with an edge of boredom in his voice. "She's to see about space in the cold room and larder. Got the orders right here."

He gestured with his thumb at Magiere, and he stepped across to the Väränj on the far side. Magiere stepped up to the nearer soldier. Leesil's target glanced toward Magiere.

Leesil grabbed the man's arm and neck, simultaneously turning him about and closing off his windpipe.

Magiere instantly rammed the dagger's hilt into the other guard's stomach. Her target buckled over, and she grabbed the back of his helmet, pulling forward and down. She flipped the dagger in her grip, and smashed the hilt against the base of his skull. The soldier toppled to the ground, still and silent with his face in the dirt.

Leesil's soldier struggled for a moment before going slack. He let the man slide to the ground beside his companion.

"Behind the barracks with them," Magiere whispered, and Leesil followed her lead as they dragged the soldiers away to where Wynn and Chap crouched in hiding.

"Wynn, get the rope out of my pack," Leesil said.

"Why?" the sage asked, already doing as instructed.

He cut two sections of rope, and he and Magiere bound the soldiers's arms and legs.

"Where's that ridiculous scarf of yours?" Magiere asked him.

Before he answered that he'd left it behind, Wynn pulled it from the pack.

"I thought you might need it," she said. "In case you had to abandon your disguise."

Magiere took the scarf and split it in half with her dagger.

"What are you doing?" Leesil asked.

"Gag that Väränj," she answered, handing him half the scarf. "Better he swallow it than you wear it again."

There was no time for a nasty retort. With the soldiers hidden among the barrels and crates behind the barracks, Leesil was about to lead them back to the door. He turned back to dig inside the surcoats of their unconscious prisoners, and pulled out an iron key.

"Much quicker than picking the lock," he said, and led the others back to the door.

Once it was open, Leesil slipped in first to make sure there were no servants about. The room was wide and empty, little more than an entryway with another solid door in the right wall. He checked it, found it wasn't locked, and cracked it to peer through at a large kitchen on the other side. He returned to his companions and motioned them into the entry room.

Leesil put a finger to his lips, signaling the others to be silent. He warmed up his crystal and closed it tightly in his fist to hide most of its light, indicating for Wynn to do the same with the one she carried. Leading them into the kitchen, he checked the far end entrance and the one to its left side to be sure no one lingered in the passageways. Then he returned once more to the others.

"There isn't any food here," Wynn whispered.

It was a large kitchen like the few Leesil had seen in keeps and manors of his homeland. Iron pots and pans hung on the wall above a wide and deep cooking hearth. The butcher block looked as if it hadn't been used in a while.

"Over here," Magiere said.

Leesil and Wynn went to her and found a small open pantry with a few supplies, mainly dried foods, but also onions and turnips.

"Someone has been eating," Magiere pointed out, "but I don't see signs that servants have been here in a while."

While this was baffling, Leesil thought they should move on. "Wynn, you said you'd know where to look?"

"Yes," the sage answered, "if this is similar to places I have helped my domin search in the past. Records are usually kept in a large study or office on one of the upper floors or in the cellars or lower storage—or both. Any place requiring effort to reach and with limited direct access."

Magiere nodded. "All right, let's get upstairs."

She seemed tense to Leesil, now that the answers they sought might be so near. Again, he led the way, checking each room and its next exit before bringing the others forward. When they reached the main hall, he wasn't surprised to find it deserted but took a deep breath in relief.

"Is it possible Buscan was the only one living here?" Magiere asked. "There should at least be guards inside near the main entry points."

Wynn looked down the side corridors. Chap nosed along the edge of a stairway leading up.

"Perhaps the soldiers cleared the castle," Wynn suggested, "after the baron was assassinated. Perhaps there is no one left here to protect."

Leesil turned up the stairs with Chap at his side. When he was satisfied that the upper corridor was clear, they began searching the rooms. Most were sleeping chambers that were either kept in fastidious cleanliness or had not been used in a long while. Wardrobes and chests were empty, and almost none of the rooms had chamber pots or water pitchers and basins. One room appeared to serve as a central parlor, but other than a few hand-tooled books and the usual fixtures, it held nothing of interest. When they'd reached the keep's opposite end, Leesil opened a door across from a narrow stairway leading down.

He stood upon a thick carpet in a wood-paneled room, a surprising sight after the stone walls throughout the keep. The place had a warm feel, though the fire was dead. A small desk sat to the right of the hearth, and on the right wall hung a large painting of armored cavalry in the wilderness. The feature that attracted Leesil's attention the most was a spot below the painting where wooden panels had been broken loose. A dark recess showed behind the wall.

"Wynn," he called softly.

His companions came to join him. Wynn hurried to the small desk and was about to open a drawer when she froze.

"What is it?" Leesil asked.

She pointed at a large dark stain covering the back of one chair and backed away from it.

"I think . . . this is where the baron was killed," she said.

Chap circled the chair, sniffing, and he growled. Leesil hadn't given much thought to the murder of Buscan during their illicit entry into the castle. The baron obviously wasn't liked among some factions of his own house, let alone the other noble families. There were plenty of possibilities for responsible parties in this land, but the stain gave Leesil a moment's reflection.

A trained assassin didn't leave evidence in plain view if it could be helped—unless there was something to be gained by early discovery of the target's death. By the size of the stain, the killer's method had been direct and crude. And there was still the strange opening in the wall to be considered.

Leesil wondered exactly what had happened in this room.

"Start searching," Magiere said.

Wynn helped her, and the two nearly took the desk and bookshelves apart. They found nothing of interest beyond a draft of a very old letter that Prince Rodêk had written to his mother. All the while, Leesil studied the opening in the wall.

He reached in and held up his crystal so its light filled the space beyond. A passage of stairs led downward from the small landing.

"There's nothing in here," Magiere said angrily.

"We're done with the upper floor," Leesil said. "We need to head down anyway, and I want to know where this leads."

"I do not understand this," Wynn said, looking about as if to spot something she had missed. "There should be some immediate papers about. . . . For the day-to-day matters, at least. Yet we have nothing. It makes no sense."

Magiere took a deep breath. She tossed aside the books in her hand and nodded to Leesil.

Leesil stepped through the wall first. Chap stayed close behind him, then Wynn, and Magiere followed last. Leesil took his time, studying the walls and steps along the way in the crystal's light. There was little chance of surprises, as this was only a simple hidden passage and not a concealed main avenue to be protected. They reached the bottom without incident, and Leesil judged they'd gone deeper than the main floor. They were underneath the keep itself.

The stairs ended at a plain door, and they emerged into a prison. A row of iron cell doors lined both sides of the passage, and its end connected to another corridor running left and right.

"I don't think we'll find any records here," Leesil whispered.

Wynn hurried ahead before Leesil could stop her, and he had to follow more quickly than he liked in unfamiliar terri-

tory. When she reached the cross-passage, looking both
ways, she paused to glance back before disappearing to the
left.

"Come on," she called. "I think there is a main room
ahead. Perhaps guard quarters or an officer's room . . . or a
way out of here."

"Wynn, slow down!" Magiere called.

"Wait and let me check first," Leesil added.

He was about to go after Wynn when Chap's growl made
him freeze.

A woman's voice drifted from down the row of cells to
their right, away from Wynn's discovered door.

"Dhampir?"

Magiere stepped close behind Leesil, and he felt her hand
settle on the falchion's hilt still strapped around his waist.

"Who's there?" she called back.

From the shadows beyond the crystal's light, Leesil saw
movement. Magiere tilted the falchion back and drew it from
the sheath.

"Who's there?" she repeated.

A young woman emerged into the light's reach, one hand
braced against an iron door, as if so frightened or exhausted,
she needed the support. A brown silk gown cut like a robe
clung to her figure, tied at the waist with a scarlet cord, and
its top two brass clasps were undone. A mass of red curls
hung down her back. A bloodstone pendant rested below her
creamy throat.

She looked at the crystal in Leesil's hand, and its presence
made her wary enough to pause. She appraised him carefully,
and then she turned her attention upon Magiere.

"Dhampir," she said again, her tone a note of music this
time.

Magiere stepped around Leesil with her falchion up.

"Stay where you are and keep your hands still, or I'll slice off anything that moves."

"I wish to help you," the woman said.

Wynn's footsteps approached behind Leesil. "Are you coming? I need help with a locked . . . Oh," she said as she saw the new arrival.

Leesil stepped away from Magiere to the passage's other side. It wasn't much separation, but it was as far as he could stretch this stranger's field of view. He'd learned enough hard lessons in recent days, and didn't care to have this woman able to hold all of them in her sight line at the same time. With Wynn present, her crystal in hand, there was enough light that he tucked his own crystal into his surcoat.

"Who are you?" he asked, sliding farther down the side of the passage.

"You want to help me?" Magiere asked with a bitter challenge in her voice. "How do you plan to do that?"

The woman tentatively lifted her hand from the iron door and then froze with apprehension in her eyes. Magiere nodded, and the woman lowered her hand to her side.

"Osceline," the woman answered. "That is my name. You have questions about the past and look for records—but you won't find anything here. I can help you. I serve the one who can provide your answers."

Leesil curled his hands at his sides until he could pull loose his wrist-sheath straps with two fingertips. A stiletto hilt dropped into each of his palms.

Magiere lifted the falchion's tip higher toward the woman. "You serve someone who claims to know me?"

"More than a claim," Osceline answered, and a smile surfaced briefly upon her quivering lips. "He was there when you were born."

Chap lunged foward, snarling and snapping. Osceline shrank away from the dog, and Leesil took advantage to slip past her in the corridor. She was trapped between him and the others. Wynn grabbed Chap's haunches, but her gaze was on the woman. Magiere scooped downward with her free hand and shoved Chap back.

"You're lying," Leesil said. He wasn't about to let anyone toy with Magiere.

"No, I'm not," Osceline replied. "My master took great pains to recruit Buscan and then sent me to protect his plans. Likely you've heard what has happened here. When word reaches my master, I won't live out the day."

"Who killed Buscan?" Leesil asked.

Osceline's gaze shifted erratically between him and Magiere, as if uncertain how or who to answer to.

"I don't know who they were," she said at length. "They caught me off guard."

"So you were there when it happened," Leesil said. "In the room . . . you saw who did it?"

"I told you. I don't know them . . . who they were. Buscan was familiar with one of them."

"Them?" Leesil pressed. "More than one? And this old friend, did he have a name?"

Osceline glared at him. Her fear seemed to waver as if she knew something he'd missed—or had something he wanted. Leesil realized he'd gone too far. If she knew anything, she was considering what value her knowledge might have.

"I heard no name, and it doesn't matter anymore," she said, turning back to Magiere. "It is nothing compared to you. My master thought you dead long ago, or he would have found you—saved you from the life you've had to endure. Only in recent years did we hear the rumors and whispers . . . that a dhampir walked the wilderness. So, he began setting up his servants to watch for you, to find you. He needed Buscan for this, to help properly place loyal watchers. Now, Buscan is dead."

Leesil saw Magiere's grip tighten on the falchion's hilt.

"Do you know the name of my father?" she asked in low voice. "Is he your master?"

"No," Osceline answered. "My master will explain all himself. That is his wish. I can't tell you any more, except where to find him, but first you make me a promise."

"I'll promise you nothing!" Magiere said

Her voice was a little too loud, and Leesil could see her pain. He wished he could offer comfort, but for the moment, he couldn't take his attention from Osceline.

"Then I tell you nothing," Osceline answered.

Leesil lifted his stilettos into view. Osceline's gaze shifted toward him, but she didn't move another muscle. She saw nothing she considered a threat, and Leesil's own wariness sharpened.

"What is it you want?" Magiere finally asked.

"Swear to tell my master that it was I who found you, I who sent you to him and no one else. Do this and I might regain his favor and my life."

Magiere glanced at Leesil, and he nodded agreement.

"All right," Magiere said. "You have my word, as I've no deity to swear by."

Osceline cocked her head toward Leesil. "Swear on his life."

Magiere tilted her head forward, dark hair curtaining half her face. Her irises flooded black. She lifted the falchion with her elbow cocked back and took a step toward Osceline. The woman flattened herself against the cell door, but there was still no fear in her eyes.

"It's all right," Leesil said.

He saw Magiere hesitate, her attention split between him and the woman. She lowered her blade.

"I swear on his life," she said, the words grating out of her throat. "I will tell your master you sent me. Now spit it out! What is his name, and where do we find him?"

Relief filled Osceline's lovely face, followed by satisfaction. A silent tension passed through Leesil as he wondered if they'd just made some terrible mistake in bargaining with this skulker in the belly of the keep.

"Ubâd," Osceline said, calm and collected. "His name is Master Ubâd."

She stepped away from the door as if there were no longer any threat she need be concerned with. She even turned her back on Leesil, facing Magiere directly.

"You can find him in the wetlands beyond the village of Apudâlsat," Osceline continued. "To the east, in the province of the Sclävên on the edge of the Everfen region. The keep is deserted, as is the village, but he is there. Go to the keep—he will know when you arrive. He is wise and will explain all to you. But do not forget your oath to me."

Osceline turned around and stepped past Leesil without looking back. She walked down into the passage's dark end. Magiere started after her, but Leesil grabbed her arm.

"Let her go." When he glanced back, Osceline was gone. "I believe she was telling the truth . . . for what little she did tell us."

Chap rumbled softly in Wynn's arms as she crouched behind the dog.

"We have not finished looking," the sage suggested. "There might still be—"

"We've found nothing here," Leesil corrected, "and I don't think looking further will change that. We'd best leave while we can."

He saw the ridged clench of Magiere's jaw, and he'd seen how close she'd come to cutting into Osceline when the woman had made her swear on his life. Magiere turned away, heading for the hidden staircase, but her hand slid gently down his arm as she did so. Leesil waved Wynn and Chap on behind her.

He looked back down the passage Osceline had taken as he sheathed one stiletto and pulled out his crystal. There was something wrong here. He stepped farther down the row of cell doors shut tight on both sides.

In three steps, the crystal's light revealed an empty dead-end, and he'd heard no cell doors open.

Leesil backed carefully to the intersection of the corridors, watching every shadow.

He followed the others up to the study, looking back over his shoulder more than once. From the wood-paneled room, he led the way out into the hall and then down the narrow stairs facing the door. This emptied into a corridor on the main floor, and it did not take long to reach the kitchen and step out behind the courtyard barracks once again. Leesil locked the door behind them and refastened the key to the belt of the unconscious guard. Magiere handed him her falchion, and he slipped it into the sheath.

When they returned to the bolt-hole inside the castle wall, the others crawled through. As he stepped back and prepared to slide the wall section on its rails back into place, Magiere grabbed his arm.

"What are you doing?" she asked. "It's time to get away from here."

"I can't secure this from the outside. If we leave it open, the castle could be breached. If something happened, the Väränj soldiers would be blamed."

She was about to argue, and he knew what she would say. Why should they be concerned about the Väränj? But Leesil leaned into the opening and kissed her quickly on the nose to silence her.

"I'll meet you at the inn . . . or beat you there. Now go."

He shoved the stones along the rail and pulled the lock lever into place.

For the second time that night, Magiere waited with Wynn in the room at the Acorn Oak. Dawn approached, none of them had slept, and Chap paced worriedly, glancing repeatedly at Wynn. No matter how the sage tried, she couldn't get the dog to touch the talking hide, much less answer questions concerning the woman in the corridor or this Master Ubâd.

Magiere tried to remain calm, but her thoughts tangled with questions over and over. What if she delayed Leesil's search for his mother only to be led down another dead end? What if Osceline was lying? All Magiere wanted from this journey was the truth, and now that it might be within her reach, she was no longer certain she could accept it.

Wynn watched her from the bed, and Magiere read apprehension in the sage's eyes. Curious Wynn, the little scholar, also feared what they might discover next.

"No matter what happens, Magiere," Wynn said. "You are still just you, and we are with you."

The words were trite but welcome.

Leesil opened the door and walked in. Magiere breathed in relief.

"So you bluffed your way back out again," she said.

"Of course." He wasted no time packing his toolbox and blades in the chest. "I know we're all tired, but we should leave straightaway. We'll take turns at the reins while the others sleep."

"Just like that?" Magiere asked. "We hunt down this Ubâd on the word of a mysterious woman hiding in a castle prison?"

"Aren't you ready?" he returned.

"It depends on whether she was telling the truth or not,"

Wynn said. "We were looking for records of Magiere's father, and this is . . . a convenient coincidence."

"Osceline told us truths and lies, I'm sure," Leesil replied. "As to her 'master,' her fear of him seemed real enough. He'll be dangerous if he commands that kind of submission at a distance."

"We know Vordana was watching for me," Magiere said. "And we know something arcane was required for my birth. If this Ubâd was there, he was involved. If such as Vordana serve him, he'll be dangerous indeed."

Magiere studied Leesil for a moment, and then dropped her gaze, no longer able to meet his eyes. The moment Osceline demanded an oath on Leesil's life, Magiere had wanted to make the woman suffer for it. Leesil obviously thought nothing of such an oath if it got Magiere what she needed. Another added leg to their journey would cause him to wait longer before seeing to his own need.

"I didn't expect to go this far . . . this long," she said. "I'm so sorry."

"Sorry?" Leesil returned. "It may have taken longer than expected, but we might be less than six days from the answers to your questions. Don't be sorry when there's nothing to be sorry for."

Chap growled at him, but no one paid attention, least of all Magiere. There were so many thoughts whirling inside her mind that she could grasp hold of only one and cling to it.

"Wynn, see about the wagon and horses," she said. "Take Chap. Get us something hot to eat for the road, if you can."

"Some hot water for tea, as well," Wynn answered, and she got up to leave, Chap ambling along behind her.

Leesil closed the chest up tight. He started to pull it toward the open door, but Magiere shut it in his way, and he stood there staring at her. "What's wrong?" he asked.

Magiere put her hands to his face, and leaned her forehead against his in silence. Why was it so hard to say a few simple words?

"What?" he whispered.

She couldn't open her eyes as she spoke. "I love you . . . you know that?"

Leesil remained still in her hands. She felt his fingers slide up along her temples, lacing into her hair.

"Of course," he whispered. "I'm the one who came after you . . . dragon."

"No, I have to say it," she said, "when and while I can. And you have to remember . . . no matter what else there is of me to come, that's what you have to remember."

Magiere pulled his face to hers, pressing her mouth deep against his.

Chap watched the city walls fall behind as the wagon rolled out of Kéonsk at dawn, well before anyone could discover the unconscious guards at the castle. The horses were well rested and kept a steady pace, and both Leesil and Magiere sat in front on the wagon's bench.

Wynn was already asleep under her blanket in the wagon's back, and Chap curled up against her. Even sleeping, the little sage's presence brought some comfort, though he felt uncertain what her place was in all this. It would have been far easier to keep his secrets without her constant curiosity about him. He no longer had complete faith in his own actions, but he had come to one decision of which his kin might not approve.

Although he could simply force Magiere from this path, he would not. And it was clear that he was unable to dissuade her. In spite of nightmare visions while under the undead sorcerer's spell, or perhaps because of them, he would help Magiere complete this journey.

At the very least it was the quickest way to remove her from this land and give them all a little more time before events started moving forward too quickly. And if they found Cuirin'nên'a—Leesil's mother, Nein'a as he called her— this might help to balance things as well.

The enemy was aware and watching. This was one of the few certainties left to Chap.

He would go with Magiere, face whatever came of her discoveries, and do what was possible in the aftermath. He would finish what he had started when he had connected Magiere's path to Leesil's.

Chap would have to trust Magiere, and trust Leesil . . . or at least trust in what he had created between them.

Chapter 13

The patron in Welstiel's dreams sensed that he had fed, knew he was stronger, and whispered to him throughout his dormant hours.

The sister of the dead will lead you.

Welstiel was roused by Chane's soft knock on the door. He awoke disoriented, as he always did when communing with the roiling serpent coils. He looked about before remembering they had procured rooms at a decent inn. His door was locked, and he climbed from the bed to let Chane in.

His companion was already dressed in a white shirt and midnight-blue tunic. His height filled the doorway. He took in Welstiel's disheveled appearance and stepped back. "Forgive me. I assumed you were up."

"Come in," Welstiel said. "I will scry for the dhampir. It is possible she has not given up yet, stubborn as she is, but I prefer to keep track of her presence. You will not mind a few more nights here?"

"This isn't Bela, but any city is a pleasant change nonetheless."

Welstiel retrieved the brass dish and his knife, and sat at the table. Replenished as he was, all recent scars from cuts had faded, leaving the stub of his left little finger smooth. He cut it again and allowed a drop to strike the center of dish's dome as he chanted.

The droplet shivered. It slid and stopped a thumbnail's distance down the dome toward the east.

"No," Welstiel whispered, staring at the tiny trail. "Why would she head farther east?"

The direction was more disturbing than the fact that Magiere had slipped away again. Welstiel knew of nothing east of Kéonsk connected to her past. Only he had a history back in that accursed place.

There was no way she could have found a lead to take her there—to him—even if that withered madman was still there after so many decades.

Chane walked over. "What has happened?"

"She is going to Apudâlsat, the village of Water Downs," Welstiel said, only vaguely aware of his companion's question.

Magiere was headed into the Sclävên province. In Welstiel's youth, it was the first noble house his father had served upon arriving in this country, this continent. At the keep near Apudâlsat, on the edge of the vast swamps of the Everfen, Bryen had come home one night with a withered old Suman in shimmering charcoal robes and an eyeless mask.

Magiere was headed straight for Ubâd.

"What are you talking about?" Chane asked.

"Quiet and let me think," he snapped.

Welstiel stared at the droplet's trail. How could Magiere have learned of Ubâd?

Chane crouched down by his chair, following his gaze. "Should I try to slow her down again? Do you need to reach this place first?"

Welstiel pondered this. No, it would do no good to race her to this destination. Such frantic activity would only alert

Ubâd, and Welstiel had no intention of giving his own presence away.

"No, that will not help this time," he answered. "Nothing will dissuade her, but we need to catch her and stay close. Magiere heads for a danger she has no way to deal with."

He looked at Chane.

"From within the shadows, we must protect her," Welstiel added, "as you protected your little sage."

At this pointed mention of Wynn, Welstiel thought he saw a flicker of pain on Chane's face. If so, it quickly passed.

"Of course," Chane answered, and headed for the door. "I will pack the horses."

Welstiel knew his companion's prime concern was the young sage. The mere suggestion that Wynn was in peril was enough to secure Chane's compliance. But only Magiere mattered, and she was determined to seek her answers to a ruinous end. However, Welstiel knew Magiere, and Ubâd did not. She was not easily manipulated. All Welstiel could do now was to be there in the shadows and shield her from Ubâd as best he could.

Chane's preparations would take a short while, and Welstiel sank down on bed, his mind drifting back to a night at the keep above Chemestúk. He looked at the orb of three flittering lights upon on the desk. It had been with him from the beginning of this existence. He remembered fear from long ago . . . fear of his own father.

Several nights after he'd watched his father and Ubâd cut the dwarf's throat and drain his blood into the vat, Welstiel sat in his upper-floor room of the keep, trying to study.

Ubâd repulsed him, but over the many years, Welstiel played the game of master and disciple with his father's lackey, increasing his skill in conjury through artificing. Spells, though versatile, were of such limited nature. Ritual, though powerful, was not as lasting as the making of an object. On his desk sat his most recent creation, a frosted glass globe resting in an iron pedestal. Within it flittered three sparks bright enough to illuminate the room in a dim glow. It required no oil or flame but instead imprisoned conjured elements of the simplest nature. Not Fay but lesser bonded elementals of Fire and Air, subdued to the command of the orb's possessor. If one Fay were the sun, these pricks of light were but winking distant stars in the night sky.

Still, he was pleased with it.

Leaning against his four-poster bed was one of his first creations, a falchion, its blade imbued with an essence deadly to the undead. Given his father's blind trust of the necromancer, Welstiel felt the need for protection. He had learned in private to depend upon himself alone.

Focusing on his notes was difficult with images of the crates' bloodied contents slipping into his thoughts. Magelia was locked in one of the smaller cellar rooms below and would have heard the struggles and wails from her chamber. Before retiring, Welstiel made certain the servants brought her water and food, but he did not stay to see her himself.

He avoided the cellar, as his father had conscripted a stone mason and three workers from a neighboring town to wall off the passage's end and the seventh room. When the workers finished, they would not return home.

A knock sounded on his door, but he did not wish to see anyone. "Who is it?"

"I need to speak with you," came Lord Bryen Massing's voice from out in the hallway.

Welstiel reluctantly arose and opened his chamber door.

His father looked worn and wild, hair disheveled around his pale face. His white shirt was soiled and untucked, hanging loose over his breeches, and he wore no tunic or sword.

. "Are you all right?" Welstiel asked, though it was now difficult to even fake concern.

His father had not come to this room since they arrived at the keep, and his presence was unsettling for some reason. Bryen stepped in, and Welstiel backed out of his way before closing the door.

Bryen approached the desk and perused its contents, though he touched none of it. He stood in silence so long that Welstiel wondered what troubled a . . . man . . . who could commit the kind of butchery done below the keep.

"It's time, my son," Bryen said, his back still turned. "Time for you to join me."

"Join you? It's rather late to be going out."

Welstiel saw him nod distractedly, still staring at the desk.

"Yes, late," Bryen agreed, and reached out to brush the globe of lights with his fingertips. "Late for what should have been done long ago. But you were always so connected to the things of your world. Now, I need you to join me in mine."

Welstiel's disquiet grew, and he stepped toward his bed.

"Do not try to draw that falchion," his father said without turning around. "I understand why you made it, but leave it now. My gift for you makes it unnecessary."

"I do not want your gift." Welstiel shook his head. "I have no intention of becoming like you."

"I . . . Our patron needs you. He whispers his plans, and you play such a part, my son. You are so honored."

In less than a breath, Bryen suddenly stood between Welstiel and the bed . . . the falchion. His irises were clear and crystalline, and disquiet turned to fear in Welstiel. He bolted for the door. One step was all he took before a strong hand gripped the back of his neck.

Welstiel twisted and swung, and his knuckles collided

with cold flesh and bone that did not flinch. "No!" he shouted, swinging again. "Father . . . no!"

Bryen clamped a hand around Welstiel's arm like a manacle, pinning it down. Air rushed out of Welstiel's chest as he was slammed to the floor.

He remembered yelling for the guards, clawing out for the falchion, kicking wildly to throw his father's weight off. The chamber door open again, and Master Ubâd slid in to stand above him.

"Remember, Bryen," Ubâd rasped out. "Forget the old superstitions. You need only drain him so quickly that his essence is trapped as his body dies. That is all. Your close presence as he dies will pull him beyond death and—if his will and spirit are strong enough—he will rise by next nightfall."

Lord Massing's face was savage and cruel. Welstiel saw extending fangs and thickening teeth press his father's jaws apart. They slipped from sight as Bryen leaned down and bit into Welstiel's throat. Welstiel bucked again, still trying to throw his father off.

"Don't!" was the last word he managed to speak.

"Our patron has great plans for you," Ubâd said to him. "A bride and a daughter."

Pain smothered awareness until it, too, numbed in a growing chill that filled Welstiel's body more quickly than darkness filled his sight.

When his eyes opened again, he was lying on the floor of his room in his own feces and urine, stinking like an unwashed peasant after his dying body released its waste. It took moments for him to realize he no longer breathed, and panic made him suck in a mouthful of air.

Breath brought no calm—or any effect at all. His body felt cold and distant as the stone walls of his room.

Heightened anxiety widened his senses. He heard the

thrum of a spider as it worked its web in the ceiling corner. He sat up, clothing sticking to him with filth, and he saw his father and Ubâd by the door, watching him. At their feet was a grimy peasant girl, bound and gagged, eyes wild with fear. How long had he lain in this room?

Welstiel felt the girl's body heat.

The sight of her . . . the scent of her warmed flesh made him feel . . . starved.

"Come, my son," Bryen said. "Instinct will guide you. Put aside thought of last night. There will be time enough for that. Now, you must feed."

Welstiel could not remember his father ever speaking to him with this mild taint of compassion. The night before, he would have given much for a kind word. Now he did not care for anything . . .

. . . only the warm flesh beneath the girl's jaw where it flexed with the soft rhythm of her pulse.

He crawled at first, forgetting the stench of his own flesh, and then scrambled like an animal on all fours, rushing across the room. The girl squirmed in her bonds. She tried to scream through the gag as he fell on her, sinking his teeth into her throat until blood flowed into his clumsy mouth.

Strength and comfort filled him, and then a peace that was wholly unsettling. He stopped gulping and slowly swallowed the pleasure on his tongue.

When Welstiel could take in no more, he raised his head to look down at the body clenched in his arms.

The girl's eyes were open. Her jaw slacked around the gag. Her throat was a torn and mangled mess, and blood had run across her face and soaked into her loose dress. Her heart beat twice and stopped.

Welstiel looked down at himself. His shirt was soaked with blood. His heightened sense of smell took in its coppery scent amid the stench of his own wastes. He dropped the corpse and rolled away to huddle on the floor by the bed.

"What have you done to me?" he cried.

But Welstiel knew the answer. There would be no return to light and life. Nothing in his arcane arts could ever rectify this.

"How could you?" he whispered.

Ubâd glided to Welstiel's desk and poured fresh water into a basin. He picked up clean towels and came to Welstiel.

"Remove those clothes and clean yourself. Your father needs you."

"Get away from me. Both of you."

"Do as he says," Bryen ordered. "Your bride is waiting."

Chapter 14

Winter was not far off, and dense muck upon the roads made the journey to Apudâlsat longer than expected. Or so it seemed.

The first time Wynn insisted upon taking her turn at the reins, Leesil was surprised, and Magiere was openly concerned. Did they think her so helpless that she couldn't drive a team of gentle, well-trained horses?

"I'm not so sure—," Leesil started.

"I have spent more time with horses than you have." Wynn cut him off. "And with far less complaint about them."

Leesil scowled at her and crawled into the wagon's back to give her room to come forward. Wynn climbed onto the wagon's bench, taking the reins Magiere held out. When Magiere stayed upon the seat beside her, Wynn shot her a glare.

"I will be fine," she said in an overly polite tone. "You should take some rest, as well."

"I'm not tired," Magiere answered, eyes ahead on the road.

She had barely spoken those words when Wynn jumped as Leesil wrapped his arms around Magiere's waist.

"Hey!" Magiere snapped, but it was too late.

Leesil heaved, and Wynn ducked aside as Magiere tumbled backward into the wagon's bed.

"Leesil, dammit!" Magiere snarled. "What do you think—?"

That was all she said, and Wynn did not look back to see how Leesil had silenced her. Leesil's mood, if not Magiere's, had oddly improved since the morning they left Kéonsk.

Chap scrambled up on the bench beside Wynn and settled there with a low grumble.

Aside from this one moment, their passage was peaceful, though the nights grew colder and the roads more troublesome as they reached the marshy region of eastern Droevinka. They pressed on for several days, sometimes starting before dawn and not stopping until well after dusk.

Like Leesil's, Chap's demeanor had altered. He was not his old self, begging or grouching about meals, but he had become more compliant. No longer growling each time Magiere mentioned their journey's purpose, he remained silent. Wynn was uncertain what disturbed her more, his change of attitude or his constant watchfulness as he gazed all day into the thickening wilderness. She often tried to discern what he watched at any particular moment. She saw little, hearing only croaking frogs, an occasional plop of something surfacing in a pond or marsh, or the far-off screech of a bird. The stench of a bog assaulted her nose now and again.

Near dusk on the seventh day, Leesil was at the reins when he pointed ahead.

At first, Wynn could not spot what he wanted them to see. Against the gray-white clouds, the distant skyline was only just visible through trees along the open road stretched out before them. Far ahead was a dark knob like the jut of a bar-

ren rock mesa, its top peeking above the trees on a tall hill.
Wynn recognized it as the crest of a keep.

Magiere's eyes followed to where Leesil pointed.

Sympathy wrestled with wariness in Wynn when she saw
Magiere's anxious expression. Each piece of Magiere's past
found so far promised the next to be darker still. It was not
long before they crossed a stone-and-timber bridge spanning
another of the many sluggish streams.

The water was clogged with dead branches and masses of
sprouting reeds, and the road beyond climbed a large rise in
the land. Down a short side path to the right were the remnants of an empty village. Thatch or timber roofs were
pocked with holes or had collapsed entirely. A small stable at
the village's near end had a broken fence. Cottage doors were
ajar or missing.

No one in the wagon said a word as they passed the village of Apudâlsat.

Leesil had earlier said its name meant "water downs village" and the reason was apparent as the main road swerved
toward the keep and met with another bridge. This one was a
long mound of piled stone and packed earth that spanned a
wide pond turned green with floating scum. The village was
situated on a rise in the marshland, with filmy water, bogs,
and quagmires on all sides of it. Once they crossed over, the
road straightened, and the keep loomed before them as they
crested its hill. Leesil pulled the horses to a stop, and they all
climbed out.

Wynn grabbed her pack and approached the keep before
the others finished gathering what they needed. She had
searched a few abandoned buildings and strongholds with
Domin Tilswith, but nothing quite like this. The keep near
Magiere's village was well mended by comparison.

Half the wooden gate in the outer stockade had rotted
away long ago, and the remaining half was dank with decay.

The main building's top had crumbled, leaving large moss-covered stones embedded in the courtyard around it.

Wynn looked back toward the deserted village, but she couldn't see it through the forest. "What happened here?"

"Civil war, famine, perhaps sickness that swept through long ago," Leesil said. "Any of these could leave a fief without enough people to carry on work to support it. And it's certainly not a prized piece of land. Who knows what the main livelihood was here."

Somehow, Wynn did not believe anything so easily explained had happened here. The silence of this place made the cold of the coming night more acute. Though she could not see the village, the moss-draped trees blocking her view carried their own telltale signs.

"Look," she said, pointing, and Magiere came to join her.

An ancient spruce close to the outer stockade was tainted with brown. A few limbs had broken away or rotted through, and the stumps showed the same color turned dark with dampness. Other trees were in a similar state, and tumbled stones inside the keep grounds showed patches of lichen that had faded, only to be plastered down to mere stains. Around the keep of Apudâlsat, death nibbled at the world, leaving marks too recently familiar for Wynn's comfort.

Chap came to join her and growled once as he shoved his head under her hand. She stroked him absently, looking about at the creeping blemishes within the forest.

"We should go inside," she told Magiere. "Osceline said her master would know when you arrived. There is no one waiting for us, and we will learn nothing further out here."

Magiere looked into the forest, hand on sword hilt, and then turned and led the way as Wynn followed. Leesil stepped out ahead of them.

As with the stockade's gate, the keep's huge wooden door had crumbled to scraps that littered the ground and floor be-

neath the arched stone entrance. The pieces mulched to
smears under Leesil's boots as he stepped close.

The light outside was fading, and Wynn unpacked the
lamps, placing the crystals in the holders and settling their
glass covers in place. Handing one to Magiere, she followed
Leesil through the short entryway, and they found themselves in a center hall.

The interior was less decayed but not by much. It was an
old-style keep, with a huge fire pit in the center instead of a
hearth to one side. The walls held archways and doors that
likely led to side rooms and antechambers. Those same walls
reached up to the remnants of an upper floor. The hall's center was open all the way to the keep's top, where an iron grate
would have let the fire pit's smoke escape. Now all Wynn
saw was the dark sky above where the roof should have been
and crumbled stone littering the fire pit and floor. There was
no sign of the fallen roof grate.

Enormous tapestries hung on the walls, their images faded
and streaked with grime and mold. Sections had decayed
through, and some hung in folds by their tattered threads.
One portrayed a battle between forces Wynn did not recognize. She stepped up to another, raising her lamp to illuminate the image of men in long cream robes and head wraps
riding thin-legged, fierce horses.

"I think this is Suman," she said. "There are dunes in the
distance behind the riders. It would cost a great amount to
bring it all the way here. Why would a Droevinkan lord want
such a thing?"

Magiere paced around the fire pit. "The place feels familiar, but I know I've never been here. I've never been this far
east."

Wynn joined her. "You are certain?"

"Yes, I'm sure."

Leesil stopped examining the tapestries and circled the

room to peer through archways and test old doors. Wynn was
about to begin herself, hoping they might still find records or
other information in this place. She spotted the first dead rat
and stepped back.

"Leesil!"

"What?" He hurried over. "What is it?"

Rats did not frighten Wynn, and she had certainly seen
dead ones before.

Instead of being bloated or rotten, the carcass was shriveled. The skin had shrunk around its rib cage and limbs, as if
it had starved to death. In a place like this, where the forest
grew wild and thick, that seemed impossible.

Chap sniffed it and growled.

"Another one," Magiere said from a few steps away.

They scanned the floor, kicking aside debris and checking
the shadowed corners. There were at least a dozen tiny
corpses about the hall, all in the same condition.

"All right," Leesil whispered. "Do I need to say how
much I don't like this?"

Chap whirled about, and his growl rose to a snarl. He cut
loose an angry wail.

The sound resonated from the stone walls, and Wynn tried
to cover her ears. This was Chap's hunting wail.

Magiere set down her lamp beside Wynn and pulled her
falchion. Chap circled them, doubling back now and again as
he looked toward the archways and doors all around.

"Leesil, blades!" Magiere shouted, but Wynn barely heard
her above Chap's noise.

Leesil's cloak was already dropped to the floor. He wore
his studded hauberk and slipped the holding straps on his
thigh sheaths to draw both winged blades.

"Chap, quiet!" he shouted, and the dog's voice dropped
back to a growl. "Where is it?"

The dog bolted toward a small archway at the back of the round hall. Magiere and Leesil rushed after him.

Wynn carried both cold lamps. She ran behind her companions down a narrow passage, more frightened of being left alone than of what they might be hunting. She had seen Chane throw Vordana's brass urn into the smithy's coals, seen it melt, and watched as the sorcerer dissipated into smoke. But the dying trees and shriveled rodents fostered doubt in her mind.

She could not see much with the others ahead of her. Chap's growl abruptly shifted to a snarl, and Leesil pulled up short. Wynn caught sight of Magiere in the jostling lamplight as she turned left. Leesil followed, and Wynn hurried to catch up.

As they passed a side opening in a widening of the passage, Chap swerved and leaped through the doorway. Magiere and Leesil turned, as well. As Wynn stepped in behind them, she glimpsed a blur, little more than a moving shadow, racing away.

She faltered as fright took a sharp hold on her.

A creature like Vordana would never flee. He would not need to.

Someone screamed out, "No, no! Please no."

Leesil and Magiere were in front her, weapons out but poised where they stood. The broken shelves and scattered pots and implements on the floor told Wynn they were in some type of kitchen. Vordana, or any undead, would not plead in fear. She pushed past her companions with a shout.

"No, Chap! Stop it!"

Leesil grabbed her from behind. Both blades were in one hand as he wrapped his other arm around her waist. He lifted her out of the way as if she were a small cat. Wynn struggled to see what they had cornered. The cold lamps jangling in her grip made light waver across the walls, and she could not make out anything beyond Chap but the arch of the cooking hearth.

Leesil dropped Wynn to her feet and grabbed Chap by the scruff of his neck. "Enough, get back."

Chap snarled but obeyed, and Wynn steadied one lamp, holding it up so that its light spilled out beyond the dog.

Cowering inside the barren hearth's hollow was a boy dressed in tatters turned dark by dirt and grime. Gaunt, with filthy brown-black hair to his shoulders, he squirmed to the hearth's far side and pressed one shoulder tightly into the corner. He covered his face as he looked out in horror, only one eye peeking between stick-thin fingers. There were fresh slashes down his arm from Chap's claws.

"Chap, what have you done?" Wynn cried.

Magiere crept forward in a crouch, ready to lunge at the boy, and her voice sounded forced and slurred. "Leesil, let Chap go!"

Wynn turned to Leesil, about to argue, but Leesil stood wary and tense with his gaze locked upon the cowering little figure. Wynn's own anger faded.

The topaz amulet Magiere had given Leesil hung in plain view, and it glowed brightly.

"It is only a boy," she whispered, looking back to the hearth in disbelief.

The boy shuddered continuously as he tried to force himself deeper into the hearth's corner.

Magiere glared back at Wynn. "I don't care what it *was*."

Her irises were completely black, her words barely clear, as if her mouth wouldn't form them correctly. Wynn wasn't certain, but Magiere's teeth appeared longer between her moving lips.

"Think," Wynn insisted. "No one lives here. The village and keep were deserted long ago. Do you not find it strange that he is here alone?"

"Wynn, don't you do this again," Leesil warned.

"No!" she shouted back, and jerked out of his reach.

Chap tried to snap his jaws closed on her short robe's hem, but Wynn backed away to the wall by the hearth. She crouched down along the wall, set her lamps upon the floor, and peered around the hearth's edge. Languages came easily to her, and she had picked up enough Droevinkan now to converse in simple phrases.

"If you . . . attack," she said quietly, "They . . . take your head. Understand? Be still and we . . . not hurt you."

"Speak for yourself," Magiere hissed.

"Magiere, not now." Wynn kept her gaze upon the boy. "What is your name?"

He studied her and finally pulled his hands from his face, glancing now and then at the others. "Tomas," he whispered, as if it were some secret he shared with her.

"Did you eat . . . the rats?"

The boy shrank back, eyes on Magiere. Wynn did not turn her attention away to see what had made him cower again. He shook his head.

"No. My food all dead now. Can't find any but dead ones." His voice cracked. "I starve now."

Pity washed through Wynn.

"No toads, no rats, no snakes, and birds all gone," Tomas whispered, and his eyes half closed in exhaustion. "I sleep. I starve. I sleep more."

His face was so coated with filth, it was dun colored instead of the pale shade Wynn remembered of Chane and the undead of Bela. His gaunt body would not stop quivering.

Wynn dug blindly in her pack, watching Tomas cautiously. She felt the slick skin of an apple, and then another. When she had found three, she pulled them out.

"We have nothing for you," she said, holding out the fruit.

"These come from . . . living tree. Fresh. Perhaps some life in them."

Tomas lunged at her.

"Wynn, get back!" Leesil snapped.

She felt his grip close on the shoulder of her short robe as Chap rushed forward with snapping teeth. Before Leesil could jerk her away, Tomas's narrow fingers seized the apples. One crushed in his grip as he quickly retreated into the hearth. Wynn thrust out her arm in Chap's way, and the dog halted.

Tomas shrank into his corner. Sharp teeth and fangs sank through an apple's skin. His gaze fixed on Chap as he sucked, hunger overriding fear.

"Wynn, what are you doing?" Magiere demanded, stepping forward.

This time it was Leesil who held a hand out to stop her.

"Who did this to you?" Wynn asked.

Tomas looked at her, still sucking hard upon the apple, and his fingers made dents in the fruit from his tight grip. His brow furrowed over wide eyes, as if he did not understand the question. He glanced about the room before letting the fruit slip from his mouth.

"Long time back . . . very long," he said, staring at the floor before he looked up at Wynn again. "Too many before me ran away. He said he would make me stay, wanted to be sure he could do this . . . good practice, he said."

Tomas set his other two apples on the floor. He flattened one hand there to lean in Wynn's direction.

"He drank me—like a rat," Tomas said firmly, as if the comparison had just occurred to him. "Like a toad, like a lizard, like a snake but not a bird, because those are too hard to catch. He made me be like him, Lord Massing, but I fooled him. Young master taught me how."

Wynn pressed her hand against the stone wall as a wave

of cold sank through her, filling her with nausea. She looked up at Magiere.

Magiere crouched low, creeping forward toward Tomas. "Massing? Is that who lived here? Was he lord of this fief?"

Tomas pulled back. He spat at her, pulling his spare apples closer to hold them between his bare feet.

"Stay away," Wynn warned Magiere.

"Warm . . . the warm girl is better," Tomas whispered.

He stared at Wynn and, for an instant, she thought she saw his irises fade to colorless crystalline disks. Tomas held up his mangled apple.

"Even nicer than the young master," he added.

"My name is Wynn," she said. "The young master . . . Did Lord Massing have a son? Tomas, do you . . . know the lord's first name?"

The boy shook his head and licked his fruit. "Don't know, didn't hear, never told. Wasn't here long before they went away. But the young master taught me of rats and lizards and snakes so I wouldn't need no folks from the village. Can't feed on kin, it's not right. Young master taught me."

"Cursed saints!" Leesil whispered. "Welstiel was here, and he had a son? Or was the son? What's the little monster telling us?"

Tomas looked blankly at Leesil. He seemed unaffected by the names he was called and returned to sucking on the apple.

"They left him here," Wynn said. "They abandoned him, and he's been living here on rats."

"You're eating rats?" Leesil asked the boy.

Tomas shook his head. "No more, just dead ones, all dried up the same day. All gone."

"All at once?" Wynn asked. "When?"

"Not long back." Tomas frowned and dropped his gaze

from Wynn's face. "I sleep some nights. Too hungry. I wake, not sure if same night. Don't remember but not long back."

Wynn looked up at Leesil. "The trees are not as far gone as those we saw in Pudúrlatsat, and this boy says the rats all died at once. You know what this sounds like?"

"But you told us Vordana was destroyed."

"His urn was destroyed, and I watched him dissipate, yes."

Magiere still crouched, glaring at the boy, but when she spoke, it wasn't to him. "Welstiel . . . It's been Welstiel all this time."

"We don't know that for certain," Leesil corrected. "All we know is that he was here long ago, and he had family. Or someone or something else using the same family name."

"Tomas, is there a man here?" Wynn asked. "Living . . . close, in the forest?"

The boy leaned toward her, small face filled with urgency. "Don't go in that forest, Warm Wynn," he said, either sadness or fear welling up in his eyes. "There's dead things that still move. Worse than me. That's why all my kin left, long time back, but I couldn't go."

Wynn had no idea how old Tomas was. He looked like a boy of no more than ten, perhaps younger, but he had been here a long time and might be older than any of them.

"What dead things?" Leesil asked.

Tomas shook his head, and Wynn saw his furtive glances toward the doorways at either end of the kitchen.

"I don't think he can tell us much more," she said. "We should let him go."

"Let him go?" Magiere rose up to her full height. "We don't let his kind go."

Wynn stood up, as well, and stepped directly in front of Magiere. "He is a victim—like you! This is not his fault. He does not feed on anyone. We should help him. Leesil, talk to her."

"Haven't you gotten over this nonsense?" Magiere answered. "He's dead and was made to rise up and prey upon the living. He's not an innocent."

Leesil crouched down before the hearth. Wynn balled her hands into fists, ready to jump on him if he made a move toward Tomas. He lowered his blades, both still in one hand, as he spoke.

"You're going have to leave this place and hunt deeper in the forests. That's all there is for you now. We hunt your kind. If we hear you've touched anything but an animal, we'll be back for you. Understand?"

Tomas took in Leesil's words. Brown eyes wide, he nodded.

Leesil tossed his head toward the kitchen's far door. "Go."

Chap's snarl rose sharply. Leesil scooted back to put his hand on the dog's muzzle.

Tomas looked up at Wynn. He cringed, a look of shame on his gaunt little face, and then bolted for the far door and was gone.

Beneath her relief, Wynn was miffed that Tomas had been allowed to go free only when Leesil stepped in. Magiere had not argued with him at all, but she'd brushed Wynn off without even listening to her.

Magiere turned in a slow circle, examining the kitchen. "Welstiel. All this time, all this way, just to come back to him."

"We're still not sure," Leesil said. "We only know he was involved somehow."

Wynn tried to put aside her irritation. "Your Aunt Bieja said there were three who came for your mother. Osceline said Ubâd was present at your birth. If Welstiel was there, as well, perhaps, then who was the third?"

Magiere's gaze ceased roaming to turn upon Wynn. The lost look in her eyes faded, and determination returned. "When we find Ubâd, we'll ask, as it seems he's not coming to us."

As they headed back outside, Wynn's thoughts were upon Tomas, who never had a choice in what had become of him. Much like another she had spent time with in a small room filled with books and old scrolls and peaceful quiet. She looked ahead in Tomas's existence and saw long solitary years in a dank forest.

They should have done more. There should have been a way to take the boy from this place. Though he would never grow up, he deserved something more than what had been left to him in the wake of his lost life. Some day, Magiere—and Chap—would have to see the individual in place of the natural enemy their instincts drove them to hunt.

They emerged in the courtyard, stepping out through the stockade's missing gate, and Wynn's breath caught as she saw Port and Imp in the light of her cold lamps.

Still harnessed to the wagon, Imp had dropped to the ground, legs folded under her. Port's eyelids sagged, his head hanging, and his massive legs trembled. Wynn rushed over to them, and the others followed. Port blinked once at her but did not lift his head.

Wynn gazed about the dark, fear creeping in upon her.

"I do not feel tired," she said. "Leesil?"

He looked around, as well. "No, I'm fine."

Chap began to growl again.

"Over there," Magiere said.

Both Wynn and Leesil turned toward the south side of the stockade as something gray walked forward through the trees. Its face was shriveled in upon its skull, so much so that its lips did not meet over the teeth of its closed jaws. There was no mistaking the wisps of long, white hair clinging to its scalp.

Vordana.

Chane woke the moment the sun set.

They'd been forced by dawn to pitch their tent and hide for the day in this soggy forest, but Welstiel had told him they would reach Apudâlsat shortly after dusk. Wynn might already be in danger, and Chane had no intention of waiting any longer.

"Welstiel, get up. We need to go."

His companion rose, rubbing his face. "Give me a moment."

Chane strapped on his sword, wishing he'd had time to make another wolf familiar, or whatever large animal he could find in this dismal province. "While you're taking your moment, you can explain what we're facing. This sword, and my conjury . . . is that going to be enough?"

Welstiel's silence was more than frustrating. Chane couldn't help Wynn if he didn't even know what waited ahead for them. Indecision weighed on Welstiel's face. He looked older with his hair askew, in a cream shirt that badly needed washing.

"Do you know what a necromancer is?" Welstiel asked.

"I've heard of conjurors who specialize in spirits of the dead." Chane paused. "Is that what Magiere seeks?"

"His name is Ubâd, and he's much more than you suppose. He served my father . . . and helped create Magiere."

Once again, there was more to this than Welstiel let on, and he was giving up what he had to only at the last possible moment. Magiere had been "created"? Chane harbored doubts concerning any undead fathering a child. The involvement of a conjuror—a necromancer—told him little, but it hinted that there was considerably more to the dhampir's origin that Welstiel kept to himself.

"When he finds Magiere," Welstiel continued, "he will be most anxious after all these years. I'm uncertain of specifics, but I suspect it took Ubâd a lifetime's preparation for her birth. He will try to persuade her to follow him for his own purpose. When she refuses, he will not let her—or anyone in her company—leave this land alive."

Chane glared out into the dark. They should have been planning their strategy nights ago, but Welstiel's selfish secrecy left them at a disadvantage.

"I hope you have more toys than a brass disk and a ring!"

He grabbed Welstiel's pack and threw it at him. He was almost certain the ring helped Welstiel to hide his presence from mantic and divinatory magics—or unnatural senses, such as those of other undead. Welstiel was not moved by his outburst and caught the pack in midair.

"You do not know Magiere as I do," he said. "Her powers will be strong when she faces Ubâd. She is resourceful, and her experience grows. And my 'toys' are more useful than you imagine. We will assist from the shadows."

Chane cared nothing for Magiere. He cared only for Wynn.

"I'll saddle the horses," he said, "while you finish your moment."

Leesil's topaz amulet glowed brightly.

Vordana's appearance was no surprise. In the back of Leesil's mind, it had always seemed the undead sorcerer had gone down too easily. Now that they knew what this creature was capable of, Leesil's only worry was how to take its head. How could he fight something he couldn't get close to?

Vordana smiled, little more than a lipless stretch of his mouth to expose grayed receding gums around clenched

teeth. He raised one hand, and Magiere stepped out in front
of Leesil.

"Run!" she ordered.

Wait.

The word filled Leesil's mind.

The topaz jerked upon the leather cord around his neck,
extending in the air before his face. The cord snapped, and
the amulet sailed into Vordana's upraised hand. Bony fingers
closed around the stone, and he smiled again.

Follow me.

The voice echoed again in Leesil's head. He glanced to
Magiere and then Wynn. They clearly heard the words, as
well.

"An escort," Leesil said. "I think Wynn should stay here."

"No," the sage replied, her eyes on the walking corpse.

"It's all right," Magiere said. "You thought you'd finished
him, but you still saved us and the town. That's all that matters."

Wynn looked away. "Wait a moment."

She set one of her cold lamps down, ran to the wagon, and
dropped her heavy pack and the other lamp inside. She returned with a crossbow and quarrel case, strapping both to
her back, then retrieved the cold lamp, holding it out in front.

Leesil nodded to Magiere, and they all stepped into the
trees. Chap was silent, but his hackles stood up upon his
neck. Magiere kept her falchion up, and Leesil gripped both
his blades. Wynn and Chap followed behind him, the dog
staying close to the young sage.

Vordana's clothing had changed, and he no longer wore
the stained shirt from the night Stefan had murdered him. His
umber brown robes were cleaned of the soil from whatever
secret grave he'd crawled from. The state of his own form
was another matter. The sorcerer's skin was more drawn and
shriveled. He was no vampire, and his corpse succumbed to

time, no matter how much life he bled from the world around him. A new brass urn hung around his neck.

He motioned for them to follow and turned back into the forest.

Strands of moss in the high branches hung down to the ground, like dark green curtains between the tree trunks. Vordana passed through them easily, but Leesil and Magiere had to hack a clear path with their blades. Soon their hands and sleeves were soaked from the damp foliage. Without sight of the night sky through the forest canopy, the dark was too thick for even Leesil's night sight. He was grateful for the illumination of Wynn's cold lamp.

Wynn gasped and grabbed the back of his cloak. "Leesil!"

She pointed beyond him, and he froze.

"On the other side, too," Magiere said. "And behind us."

In the half-circle of a sparse clearing, glowing shapes surrounded them. Leesil heard their whispers but couldn't make out their words as they drifted in and out among the trees.

When Tomas said the villagers had left, and he couldn't follow, Leesil assumed they'd abandoned the village and the boy was left behind.

Floating near a tendril of moss was the translucent figure of an aged soldier. His hauberk was slashed open, exposing internal organs that bulged, ready to spill out. Beside him was a short and tattered young woman with a ring around the skin of her throat where a rope had strangled her. She opened her mouth, trying to speak but her tongue was missing.

A scarecrow-thin peasant boy glared in hatred at Magiere. He wore no shirt, and though his visage faded in and out, Leesil saw the ribs and telltale swollen paunch of starvation. Drifting out through a curtain of wet leaves came a pretty girl no older than Wynn, with dangling black curls. She reached out at Leesil, and he sidestepped quickly, though she couldn't possibly touch him. Her throat had been ripped open.

Leesil smelled the strong scent of damp earth and decay as the cold sank into him, feeding despair. He heard Magiere's quick breaths beside him, and he looked back to Wynn.

Her eyes were downcast, watching only the ground before her feet, and she held the cold lamp in front of her like a shield. Her free hand gripped the fur between Chap's shoulders, and the dog pulled her forward.

"Ignore them," Leesil whispered with effort. "Keep moving."

He kept his eyes on Vordana's cloak, trying not to focus upon the misty figures moving around them.

"They're just ghosts," Magiere said.

There was no fear on her pale features, but Leesil still heard the rapid rhythm of her breath. Vordana held up his hand. The topaz dangled in his grip upon the leather string, and its glimmer became a beacon they followed.

Leesil was shivering from the cold when they emerged in a large clearing and saw smoke rising from the chimney of a strange little stone house. It had been built onto the side of a massive granite knoll.

Vordana walked to an oval door in the cottage's front wall and opened it. He motioned them to follow as he stepped inside.

Leesil grasped Magiere's wrist. "Whatever we find here, it doesn't change who you are."

She gently pulled her wrist from his fingers and walked toward the open door.

Welstiel hid behind the stockade fence with Chane, watching through a space left by a missing post. Magiere emerged from the keep with the others. The young sage ran to their team of gray horses, one already collapsed upon the ground.

"Stay close," he told Chane. "If you step away from me, the dog will sense you clearly."

Chane did not argue or even speak, his eyes fixed upon Wynn.

Welstiel hoped he would not have to enter the keep. In this place, his father had come home one night transformed into a Noble Dead, accompanied by the loathsome and conniving Ubâd. It was not long before the people here began dying. When the remainder fled, Welstiel's "family" moved on to offer service to the Äntes. How Bryen and Ubâd had managed to learn exactly where Magelia had lived was still a mystery to Welstiel.

A hollow presence pulled at Welstiel from nearby, and he caught the flutter of gray hair in the forest trees. The undead sorcerer stepped out into view before Magiere and her companions.

"I thought you destroyed that," Welstiel whispered.

"So did I," Chane replied.

The sorcerer held out his hand, and the topaz amulet the half-blood wore shot into his grip. The walking corpse grinned and turned into the forest. Magiere and the others followed. Chane was about to rise, and Welstiel clamped a hand on his shoulder, holding him down.

"Wait until they are in the trees."

A small part of Welstiel pitied Magiere for what was to come, as he had once pitied her mother.

Chapter 15

Magiere was numb with cold as she stepped through the doorway behind Vordana. The dwelling made her skin crawl as if she were covered with insects.

An iron staff leaned against the wall by the door, its surface stained and etched with wear. Rough-cut tables and shelves were loaded with jars and other vessels of ceramic, glass, and metal. In the nearest glass container, Magiere saw cloudy liquid in which fleshy shapes floated. A severed joint of cartilage and bone pressed against the side. She wasn't certain what kind of being it came from, and she didn't want to know. The fire in the hearth burned brightly, but its heat made the place feel tight and stifling.

Vordana walked to the room's back and opened another door leading into a passage.

She followed a few paces back, for the smell of the undead sorcerer made her gag in the enclosed space. The passage was crudely chiseled granite rather than mortared stone. To her amazement, she stepped out its far end and into an enormous cavern.

Torches blazed upon poles stuck in the bare earth, but their light couldn't reach into the dark expanse above.

Magiere stood within a cave inside the granite knoll. The vast area reached back at least a hundred paces. Directly ahead, in the cavern's center, was a thick granite slab resting upon two shorter blocks of stone. Its surface was partially covered by a rumpled white satin cloth. Before it stood a cast-iron vat hanging from a towering tripod over a stack of firewood. Leesil stepped up beside her, looking about the cavern.

"Dhampir . . . ," a hollow voice said. The word wafted through the space up into the darkness overhead. "I had begun to doubt the reports."

Magiere peered into the darkness but could see nothing.

Then, from beyond the torches a figure took form out of the shadows. Its hooded robe was dark gray. Torchlight across the fabric's folds revealed faint markings, symbols that shimmered in and out of sight. Across the upper half of his face was a mask of aged leather ending above a bony jaw.

Vordana bowed to the new arrival.

As the robed figure glided nearer, Magiere saw there were no eye slits in the mask. She wondered if this aged creature could see her, and she held out the tip of her falchion in warning.

"That's close enough."

He stopped beyond the blade's reach. His head swiveled about as if he listened for something. When Chap circled around Leesil's side, the dog was quiet, but his jowls pulled back in a silent snarl. At that instant, the masked face turned directly toward the dog.

Magiere's dhampir half rose enough that her senses expanded. She saw the masked man's chest rise and fall beneath the robe and felt his slight heat. He was alive and mortal for all she could tell.

"You are Ubâd?" she asked.

"One of my names," he answered, ending in a slur than made his voice hiss.

"I have questions," Magiere said coldly. "I'm told you have answers."

"Yes. And I've longed to tell them to you for many years." Ubâd faced his visitors and raised a leather-colored hand to point at Magiere. "Perfect. Your hair, flesh, power. Day combined with night, the living and the dead."

"Get to your answers, old man," Leesil snapped. "I think you know the questions already."

A cluster of ghosts appeared instantly around them. The soldier with the stomach wound hovered near Leesil.

"You're here on the whim of this *thing* . . . this oppressor," Ubâd said to Leesil, pointing to Chap. "I can do little about that, but you are nothing to me. Keep your tongue—or I'll keep it for you."

"Don't," Magiere whispered, and flattened her free hand against Leesil's chest. "It's all right."

She caught sight of Wynn hiding behind Leesil. The sage peered out with wide eyes, still holding her cold lamp, but she looked at Vordana rather than the masked old man. It troubled Magiere that Vordana, who showed all signs of succumbing to decay, had not been destroyed as Wynn had thought.

"How is he still standing?" Magiere asked of Ubâd, nodding in the dead sorcerer's direction.

Ubâd swept a hand toward the spirits surrounding Magiere and the others. "I conjure the dead into my service and have learned much in my life's work. Vordana is loyal . . . and useful. He called upon me for help, and I preserved him."

"And if I severed his head right now," Magiere asked, "would he still be useful?"

Vordana shifted, his robe rustling around him. He, at least, was unnerved by her suggestion or uncertain what the result would be. It was more difficult to gauge Ubâd's reaction beneath the mask, but his wrinkled lips tightened.

"Did you come to discuss the welfare of my servants?" he asked, waiting briefly for an answer and continuing when none came. "How did you find me? Vordana only recently learned of your return to this land."

Magiere felt no obligation to answer any of Ubâd's questions, but in this matter, she had sworn on Leesil's life. "Osceline sent us."

My apprentice? Vordana's voice filled Magiere's head. It appeared Osceline was as firmly connected to Vordana as to her Master Ubâd.

"Unexpected," Ubâd said, ignoring his servant's outburst. "But we have much to discuss, and I have much to show you."

"Who is my father?" she asked. "Is it Welstiel Massing?"

"Too fast, too far," Ubâd answered with a shake of his head, and he turned to glide toward the stone slab in the cavern's center. His robe neither twisted nor rustled with his movement. "I'll show you, and afterward, you will thank me for dispelling this false front you wear. You have a far better purpose to fulfill."

"Answer me, and it had better ring true," Magiere said. "I've no interest or trust in your twisted tales of my past."

He stopped, his back still to her. "Would you trust your mother?"

Magiere's stomach lurched. "You can't fool me with some delusion. Your corpse servant already tried that."

"You misunderstand me," Ubâd replied. "I am no trickster of sorcery. I work with the dead, who are the past . . . and sometimes the future. The past is what leads us into the future, and you might ask your little sage and dog about that. Come here, child. Here is your past."

He gripped the edge of the white satin cloth and jerked it
away.

Lying upon the granite slab were carefully arranged
bones, almost as white as the cloth on which they lay. The
skull was set upon its jaw at the far right and appeared polished and cared for like a valued possession. The skeleton
was human, the bones slender.

Magiere stopped breathing.

Chap lunged forward, snapping and growling. As he
passed through the spirits directly in his path, he flinched
away from the contact. He turned again toward Ubâd as he
circled to the cavern's right side.

"No . . . no," Wynn whispered.

Ubâd gave Chap no notice, but Vordana focused upon the
dog. Magiere heard a resonating chant fill her mind as the
sorcerer fixed his gaze upon Chap. Before she could take a
step, Chap backstepped twice, and his growl cut short. He
shook himself sharply and leaped, landing a few paces from
Vordana, and let out a vicious series of snapping barks.

Vordana didn't retreat, but Magiere saw him recoil, and
his chanting ceased.

"No advantage of surprise this time," Leesil said. "It
seems that won't work on him again."

Magiere stared at the bones upon the granite slab.

"It's not her," she said. "In my childhood, I visited the
grave where my aunt buried her."

"Draw on your awareness," Ubâd challenged. "Touch the
bones, and see for yourself."

"She didn't die here. It won't work that way, and I think
you know that," she rasped, anger feeding her frustration.

Ubâd shook his head with a shallow sigh. "This is not the
same. She is your relation, your blood . . . bones of your
bones. Touch her and see."

Unable to look away, Magiere took a step forward. Leesil

grabbed her arm. "It's a trick," he said. "And even if not, I told you in the graveyard. You don't want to see this. You don't want to see her die in your hands."

The air about Magiere whipped sharply, tossing her hair, and the soldier spirit lashed out at Leesil.

Its translucent fist struck his temple and passed through his skull. Leesil buckled, eyes rolling up as the frenzy grew around Magiere.

Spirits circled them, never touching her, but moving like wind-ripped trails of mist that dove at Leesil. Wynn backed toward the passage as she was struck, two blurred streaks in the air piercing through her chest. The sage crumpled to the cavern floor without even a whimper, and the cold lamp tumbled from her hands.

"Ubâd . . . ," Leesil groaned.

He clung to Magiere's arm but dropped his blades. Magiere spun about, putting herself between him and the withered old man. She pulled Leesil close with her free hand, trying to shield him with her own body. She heard Wynn cry out in pain. Leesil pulled a stiletto from his wrist sheath and held it by its blade between them, where no one else could see.

In her confusion, Magiere looked into his amber eyes, and he whispered to her. "Get to Ubâd!"

Leesil shoved her back and raised the stiletto. When he threw the blade, Magiere understood.

She turned and charged, following the blade's path through the air.

The stiletto tumbled toward Ubâd's mask, but the old man didn't move. Magiere saw Vordana in the side of her view as the sorcerer raised a hand in panic.

The stiletto froze in the air a hand's length from Ubâd's face.

Magiere closed on him, falchion swinging out. Vordana

rushed in from her side, the topaz amulet in his hand, and then he stumbled as growls filled the air.

Vordana fell back out of Magiere's sight, and the stiletto dropped with a muffled thud to the cavern's floor. Magiere heard Chap's snapping jaws and knew the undead sorcerer was well occupied. She stood perfectly still, the end curve of her sword slipped into Ubâd's cowl and pressed against his throat.

"Call off your dead," she demanded. "Or you can join them even quicker."

Ubâd neither gestured nor spoke.

Chap's snarls lessened, and the sound of Vordana thrashing upon the ground faded.

"Leesil?" she called out, keeping her eyes upon her prisoner, but no answer came. "Leesil!"

"I'm all right," he said from behind her, and she heard his ragged breath drawing close.

"And Wynn?"

A pause followed before he answered. "She's up again."

"Dead . . . alive," Ubâd whispered, and his thin mouth pulled into a smile. "They are not as far apart as most think. Not for such as you and me. Do you still want your answers?"

He glided slowly back out her way, not even raising a hand to the shallow cut seeping blood on his throat. Magiere kept her eyes on him as she reached out to touch the skull upon the slab. Images flashed through her mind.

Blue fabric . . . a dress. The one Aunt Bieja had given her. And long, dark hair.

Magiere jerked her hand away.

"No," she whispered, and glanced toward Ubâd, ready to run him through. "You had someone dig up my mother's grave?"

He waved one hand as if the question were irrelevant and then held it out toward Vordana.

The undead sorcerer got to his feet as Chap circled around behind him. Vordana moved cautiously as he pulled a pole torch from the ground and walked toward the cavern's center. Magiere backed away to keep him in sight, and Vordana shoved the torch head into the wood piled beneath the iron vat. Wild flames ignited.

"I can allow you to speak with her," Ubâd suggested, "let her show you who you are."

Magiere's heart pounded. To speak with a mother she'd never known, to hear Magelia even for a moment was something she had never imagined possible. This gift came from the hands of a death-monger like Ubâd. Still, she couldn't turn away.

"Only her and me?" she asked.

Ubâd nodded. "She will be in you. She will show you anything you ask."

"Do it. Do what you have to."

"Magiere!" Leesil snapped. "No."

Torchlight flickered across Ubâd's mask. Magiere wondered at the expression hidden beneath it. Her revulsion grew past hatred.

"Quiet, Leesil," she said. "I'll know if it's a trick, if it isn't her."

Ubâd drew a narrow dagger from inside his robe and picked up one of the loose bones on the slab. The sight of this creature touching her mother's remains made Magiere tense against the urge to cut him down. The dark liquid in the large vat was boiling, and it began dribbling over the side to hiss in the raging flames.

Ubâd held the bone over the vat and scraped it with the dagger's edge. White flecks fell from the blade into the roiling liquid. He set the bone on the floor and reached out his hand to Magiere.

"You share blood and bone. Give me your hand."

Magiere kept her falchion up and held out her other hand. He sliced her smallest finger and squeezed it, until a drop of her blood followed the bone shavings into the vat.

Ubâd began to chant.

The ghosts in the cavern vanished, and Vordana stepped back.

Magiere had one moment to see Leesil's concerned face and Wynn's frightened eyes as the sage crept forward.

The liquid in vat rose, spilling freely over the sides until its sizzle in the flames sent up a cloud of vapor that nearly blotted out the tripod. An image formed in the mist.

She was young and lovely and could easily have passed as Magiere's sister. Her skin wasn't as pale as Magiere's, and her black hair showed no glints of bloodred, but the resemblance was clear: a high, smooth forehead over thin arched eyebrows and a long, straight nose. She was tall and slender, wearing a blue dress that Magiere herself had worn on several occasions. Her brown eyes filled with confusion—and then her gaze fell upon Magiere.

Ubâd's chant grew louder.

The young woman dropped lightly from the air to the granite floor. Her eyes locked with Magiere's, and she held out a hand. Magiere hesitated a moment, then took it. She felt no pain as the darkness of the cavern vanished.

She stood upon a grassy hill in a forest, and through the trees she saw the low huts of Chemestúk. It was early fall, and in the nearby fields cut out of the forest were villagers at harvest, clearing weeds or pulling fat pumpkins and squashes from their vines. One woman caught Magiere's attention. At first she thought it might be the same one she'd seen in the cavern, but this one was shorter and stout of frame, dressed in purple. She stood from her labors and wiped perspiration from her face.

It was Aunt Bieja, but younger, without the years weighing upon her.

Magiere heard the cloth rustle in the low breeze and turned to find the woman in her blue dress standing beside her.

"Mother?" she asked. "Magelia?"

The woman settled a hand upon Magiere's cheek. "Daughter. I know you."

"Magiere," she said back. "I'm Magiere. Aunt Bieja named me for you."

Tears slid down Magelia's face. "You grew up with Bieja? You have been happy?"

Magiere didn't know how to respond. She wanted to touch her mother's tears, to comfort her, but she couldn't seem to move.

"He took you that night," Magelia whispered. "The night you were born, but he promised to protect you. I remember your soft hair. You were born with a head full of black hair, and those dark eyes, not blue like most babies."

"Mother." The word was difficult to even say. "I must know what happened. How . . . I happened."

"Is that why you call me now?" Magelia's face darkened before Magiere, and it was like looking at her own angered reflection in a mirror. "You want to know your father?"

"I need to know."

Magelia's expression softened again. "I don't care, as long as I can see you, touch you." Magelia's fingers dropped from Magiere's cheek to grip her hand. "Come with me, back to the keep."

The grassy hill faded along with the autumn sky.

*   *   *

Magelia had been moved to an upper-floor room of the keep, one without windows. She examined the door from top to bottom, but the lock was solid. The door would not even budge when pulled, and likely was barred on the outside.

She was alone.

For all her fear, she couldn't stop thinking of Bieja, how frightened she'd been the night of the abduction and how worried her sister must be. Wild thoughts of bribing servants to deliver messages ran through Magelia's mind, but she saw no one except the guards delivering her meals. Two always came. One remained in the passage while the other set her bowl upon the floor inside the door. She'd given up trying to goad or question them, as neither spoke a word to her.

The only other person she'd seen was Welstiel, the noble with white patches at his temples, coldly polite. He had been the one to move her to this room.

The room was chill and bare, with a thin mattress on the floor and a washbasin beside it. There was no other furniture.

Her thoughts were broken by the sound of the door's bar drawing back. The door opened, and Lord Massing stepped in, the one called Bryen.

He was tall and used his imposing stature to cow those around him. Looking at his dark hair and pale skin, she thought he might be handsome were it not for the blankness of his expression. The only quality she ever saw flicker upon his face was arrogance.

Magelia hated the sight of him.

Tonight, he was beautifully dressed in black breeches, a tan shirt, and a chocolate brown tunic, with his hair carefully combed back. Behind him stood a young serving girl, clearly terrified of her lord. Magelia didn't recognize the girl, so she hadn't come from Chemestúk. The girl carried a silk gown, a hairbrush, and pins. The gown's color was somewhere between ivory and pale pink.

"Take off that rag you're wearing," Lord Massing ordered. "This girl will dress you properly."

"Not until you get out," Magelia replied. She would not show him any fear.

"You will not speak alone to anyone," he said. "Take off that dress, or I will do it for you."

It was not a threat. She could see that he was simply informing her of the consequences and waited for her to decide which indignity she chose. Magelia began unlacing her blue dress, and the girl hurried to assist her.

Magelia turned away from Lord Massing to stand in nothing but her shift while the serving girl helped her into the silk gown and laced it tightly. The girl then brushed out her hair and pinned part of it atop her head, leaving enough free to curl down her shoulders and the back of her neck.

"Sir?" the girl asked when she had finished.

Bryen nodded. "Yes, much better."

Before Magelia turned around, he grasped her forearm. She didn't bother to fight, as it would do no good. He pulled her from the room and down the passage to another chamber.

Through its open door she saw a large four-poster bed. Upon a small table, a globe rested in an iron pedestal. Lights flickered within its frosted glass. As she stepped inside, a movement caught her attention. Magelia saw herself in a long mirror on the wall by the table.

She looked like a lady, one who might accompany her lord in the keep.

The room appeared clean but had the thin stench of a spilled chamber pot overlaid with a lingering sweet odor she couldn't name. There were two others present as Lord Massing stepped in behind her. She saw their reflections in the mirror with her own and turned about.

Standing near the bed was the masked and robed eyesore called Ubâd. He wore a smile on his thin lips and tucked his hands into the opposing sleeves of his charcoal robe. On the far side of the bed stood Welstiel.

She'd heard him refer to Lord Massing as Father, but Welstiel looked to be the elder of the two. Fine lines surrounded his cold eyes, and his dark hair was white at the temples. Her opinion of him was only slightly better than that of the other two. He was quiet and removed, and he seemed to disapprove of both her presence and captivity.

On a narrow stand beside Ubâd was a strange vessel, not unlike a vase that she'd once seen used for cut flowers. Metallic and yellow red, perhaps made of brass, it was covered in etched symbols. A dark liquid filled it nearly to the top, though its color was unclear in the room's low light. It made her anxious when she realized that the thick, sweet scent in the room came from whatever the vessel held. She tried to back away. Lord Massing's hand flattened against her back. Magelia stepped farther into the room, away from his touch.

Welstiel looked her over, and she saw that his face looked different from before. His dark eyes were flat and emotionless like Lord Bryen's. His skin was pale.

"Is she not improved, my son?" Lord Bryen said. "I had the gown purchased in Stravina and sent all the way from its capital, Vudran, just for this night. I've seen you admire women in this color and style."

Fear began to grow in Magelia.

"What do you want from me?" she asked.

All three men ignored her.

"I have no interest in anything you ask, Father." Welstiel said. "You might as well take her back to her room. Or better yet, release her from this lunacy."

Bryen shoved Magelia toward Welstiel. She caught herself on the nearest post of the bed. A heavy curved sword leaned by the headboard behind Welstiel, and she froze.

"You *will* do as I say!" Bryen ordered, and a semblance of anger surfaced in his voice. "The careful and costly steps of Master Ubâd cannot be wasted. It has taken him a lifetime of preparation for this night."

His voice lowered and softened, but Magelia kept her eyes on Welstiel's face, occasionally glancing to the sword.

"You play a role far greater than you know, my son," Bryen continued. "You will sire our patron's treasured one. A Noble Dead cannot lead its own kind in what is to come, nor can a mere mortal. Something of both is needed. You will hold the esteemed position of father to a being this world has never seen, even in its forgotten days. A herald of what is to come when our patron wakes again."

Magelia's stomach twisted. She didn't understand all she heard, but one thing was clear.

"Do as Master Ubâd instructs," Bryen said to his son. "Drink the collected life of the five that has been prepared for you. Then take this girl and make a child of day and night before which all the world will fall. I know this woman appears to be only a peasant, but she is from old blood, very old, and a singular vessel for this creation."

Welstiel's dull eyes widened.

"You want me to drink more blood . . . and make a child with . . . with that?" He gestured to Magelia. "No! Even when I would have done anything to please you, I wouldn't have done this. I will not touch blood again or touch this woman."

"Young lord, you do not understand—," Ubâd began gently.

"Quiet!" Welstiel shouted. "You are the cause of all this, and I am sick of your poisoned tongue."

He pushed past his father, and to Magelia's surprise, he broke easily away from Bryen's grip on his shoulder.

Welstiel paused when he reached the door. "If you wish to

serve that masked abomination," he spat back at Bryen. "You will have to accomplish it without me."

He slapped the door open with one hand and slammed it shut behind him.

Bryen circled around the bed to the door but stopped short, staring at it. Magelia began inching nearer to the sword.

Lord Massing and Master Ubâd stood still.

"Can I take his place?" Bryen suddenly asked. "Will it still work?"

Ubâd's mask made it difficult to read his reaction, but Magelia knew he was startled. His mouth dropped open briefly, as if Bryen's suggestion horrified him.

Magelia reached the far post of the bed's foot and was about to step toward the sword.

Ubâd finally answered in an anxious voice. "There must be a way you can command him. He is your son."

Bryen looked at Magelia, and she froze where she stood. "Desire cannot be commanded," he said. "And we cannot fail now that we've come so far."

Ubâd bowed his head until Magelia no longer saw his mask, but there was something akin to sorrow or regret in his voice.

"No, we cannot fail," he whispered. "I have heard our patron, stood before him within his dream. I spent my life at his bidding in this task. . . . Prepare yourself."

Lord Bryen let his tunic slide off to the floor, and he removed his shirt. His chest and arms were tightly muscled but pale and hairless. There was no sign of a wound or scar where Magelia had stabbed him with the knife in her cottage. Ubâd lifted the brass vase, and handed it to Bryen.

Magelia tried to make herself small and invisible. She kept one eye on Bryen and inched along the bed's far side.

"When the spirits fade, you must drink immediately," Ubâd told Lord Bryen.

He began chanting in a low voice that slowly grew louder. Magelia felt a breeze pass through the room, though there was no open door or window. The bedclothes whipped up from around the mattress, and she shrank away.

Two softly glowing shapes materialized near Ubâd. They grew sharper and clearer as his chanting increased. They were transparent, but Magelia saw the color of their hair and clothing. One was a lovely middle-aged woman with light brown hair. She wore a tan wool dress and crown of leaves on her head. The other was a savage-looking woman with matted black hair. She wore black armor like large reptilian scales, and when she opened her mouth to hiss at Ubâd, Magelia saw elongated fangs.

Reason told her these were but ghosts, spirits of women already dead, but they looked furious and disoriented. When Ubâd's chant grew to a shout, they began to scream.

Their shapes wavered, and suddenly they meshed into each other and vanished.

Ubâd's chant hammered in Magelia's ears as Bryen lifted the brass vase and gulped the liquid inside. Some spilled out the corners of his mouth and ran in deep red trails down his neck to his chest.

Bryen's pallor darkened until his skin looked healthy. He drank until he seemed able to take no more, and then he dropped the vase upon the stone floor with a clang. He wavered, clenching his mouth closed as if the draft threatened to rise back up his throat.

Ubâd's chant ended, and he slumped into the wall with exhaustion. "Now," he managed to say.

Bryen circled around the bed.

Magelia rushed to grasp the sword. The sheath slid away as she spun around, swinging the blade with both hands.

Bryen's glazed eyes were fixed hungrily upon her. The sword's curved tip nicked his right shoulder and dragged across his chest.

He cried out in pain and shock. Magelia stumbled under the weapon's weight, her swing pulling her toward the wall. As she tried to bring the blade up again, he stepped inside her reach and backhanded her across the face.

Magelia's vision flashed white and then black, and she felt herself falling. Something scraped along her fingers as the sword was jerked from her hand. Her returning vision jumped again as her head struck the mattress. She felt Bryen on top her, pulling apart the silk dress. His skin felt different from when he'd dragged her by the wrist from her own room. It was now warm, nearly hot. Blood from his chest wound smeared across her exposed torso.

She struggled but couldn't move under his weight, and he did not waste time in pinning her arms. When he pushed himself into her, the pain was explosive.

Magelia remembered nothing more until a numbing cold called her back from unconsciousness. Bryen stood at the foot of the bed, staring at her with an expression she had never expected.

Fear. His features wrinkled in pain as the icy cold in the room deepened around Magelia.

Bryen's features turned blank with shock as he whispered, "No."

His face grew lined, and the color in his skin faded.

Through the burning pain between Magelia's legs and the chill all over her skin, she watched Bryen begin to age.

"Ubâd!" he cried out, his voice cracking like an old man. "Why did you not tell me the price?"

"Because you would not sacrifice your son," came the hollow answer as Ubâd looked away.

"And you would sacrifice me?" Bryen asked, his voice now just a rasping whisper.

"We cannot fail," Ubâd answered.

Bryen grew *withered* beyond old age, his hair falling from his head. His skin dried and shrank upon his bones, and then split like old bleached parchment.

Magelia closed her eyes, not wanting to see any more.

She did not know how much time had passed when she stirred again into consciousness. It was dark, the room lit only by a strange globe of flittering lights. Welstiel stood over her at the side of the four-poster bed.

"Are you all right?" he asked.

She sucked in one shuddering breath by way of an answer. She would not let these things holding her captive see her cry. Every part of her body felt bruised, and she could not sit up.

"Help her," Welstiel said, looking across the room.

Magelia rolled her head with great effort. One of her bedroom guards stood at the other side of the bed. He reached down to lift her.

"Carefully," Welstiel added.

Magelia was limp with pain and exhaustion as she was carried to another room with a large bed and a painted white wardrobe. The serving girl who'd dressed her earlier was hurrying about, filling basins of water and bringing towels. Magelia was laid on the bed, and Welstiel stood nearby looking quietly distressed, but he did not touch her.

"My father is gone, and I am lord here," he said. "You carry his child, and no one will hurt you. This girl is here to care for you, to help you. If you need anything, she will bring it."

In the days and nights that followed, she was not allowed to leave the keep. But she herself had changed. She could not explain the open sorrow mixed with gratitude she felt for

Welstiel's belated concern. Her dependence upon Welstiel grew more pronounced until she almost feared the very shadows of her room outside of his presence. She slept during the day, so that she could spend her waking hours in his company rather than alone.

At times he required privacy, but for the most part, Magelia found he didn't mind her presence, so long as she never touched him or spoke too often when he was occupied. As her body began to swell with child, he took greater efforts for her comfort, even ordering cotton dresses with loose bodices, so the child would not be constricted.

Welstiel moved himself to another room and ordered the furnishings of his old one to be taken out and burned, including the four-poster bed. He kept the globe of flittering lights but never returned to that room again. Master Ubâd was allowed to remain as long as he kept out of Welstiel's way.

"Why don't you get rid of that abomination?" she asked Welstiel one night.

They sat in his new room as she embroidered a blanket for the child. Welstiel spent many hours there making strange objects, etching symbols in them as he whispered in a soft voice she could never quite understand.

"Because you might need him when the child comes," he replied.

His answer was so unexpected that she faltered. The old Magelia would have threatened to run him through with a sword if he allowed Ubâd anywhere near her baby. But she feared he might leave if she were disagreeable, and then she would be alone in this place.

"Why would you think this?" she asked. "There is a good midwife in the village."

Most recently, Welstiel had been working on a thin brass ring. It required a great deal of his time. One evening, it took almost the whole night for him to carve one tiny symbol with his steel stylus in the string of marks running along the inside surface of the metal. The only other object of his that she found curious was a glowing topaz resting near his leather-bound books.

Welstiel looked up from his ring in mild annoyance. "The child you carry is not natural. Therefore its birth cannot be expected to be natural. We may yet have need of Master Ubâd's knowledge."

Magelia nodded and went back to her embroidery. She would find a way to keep Ubâd from this child.

Welstiel slipped the ring on his finger. The glow of the topaz upon the desk suddenly went out, and Welstiel nodded in satisfaction

"Perfect," he said to himself. Magelia didn't ask why this pleased him.

As she grew heavier with child, he became concerned that she needed exercise and fresh air. He walked with her about the courtyard in the early evenings. Sometimes he brought the globe so that he could sit and read while she continued her walk, but she did not mind this as long as he stayed within sight. She was never certain if his concern was for her or the child she carried.

One night as they walked, he was more preoccupied than usual.

"Is something wrong?" she asked tentatively, as he did not like his private thoughts invaded.

"No." He seemed to speak to himself more than to her. "In my sleep today, I had a dream. I didn't know that I could, as I have had none since . . . since shortly after I came here."

"A nightmare?" she asked with concern.

Welstiel looked at her. He shook his head with a frown, as if embarrassed to be discussing a personal issue. He made a passing remark about repairs to the courtyard wall and then paused to lift one hand to the white patch at his temple.

"What is it?" she asked. "Are you ill?"

He didn't answer and stood there whispering to no one. He came back to himself and escorted her inside.

After that night, Welstiel changed in small ways.

He was never unkind, but their limited conversations became almost nonexistent. When he did speak, it was only to ask about her health and the baby. Some nights he appeared more rested, but often he would come down in the evenings looking exhausted, as if he hadn't slept at all. On those nights, he would whisper to himself and rub his temples as if a persistent ache troubled him.

For two more moons, Magelia's stomach swelled, and the baby kicked inside her. She found the sensation pleasant and spoke to the child, as there was no one else left for her. She didn't care who its father had been. This child was hers, and hers alone.

Welstiel mixed elixirs and drank them and spent more time chanting in the nights. His state of mind improved. He seemed to gain control over whatever plagued him, but his interest in the child increased.

One night as he worked in his room, she entered without knocking to find him sitting at his desk with a bloody bandage wrapped around his left little finger. He dropped something into a bowl on the desk, and the liquid inside hissed and bubbled. She came up behind him, and he was so intent that he didn't notice her. Next to the bowl were the beginnings of a pendant with a tin backing and a stout bloodied kitchen knife.

She looked down and gasped. The object hissing in the bowl was the top of his little finger. Acid began eating away the flesh.

He was startled by her touch on his shoulder, and he whipped around. "Get out," he ordered. "I am working."

Magelia fled to her room, holding her stomach. The old Magelia, the fierce Magelia, began to whisper inside her that she might need to protect this child from more than Ubâd.

The night her pains began, Welstiel behaved like the politely concerned man she had known in the early to mid-months of her pregnancy, before his dreams. He had the man-at-arms, whose name she never learned, help her into bed, and he called the serving girl to assist her.

"I will bring the midwife," he said.

"Her name is Betina," Magiere told him. "She brought me into the world."

Even through her labor pains, she could not help smiling at him. He was going for the midwife himself instead of sending one of the guards. The pains grew closer together, but she did not cry out. Sometime after he left, she rolled on her side and looked to the doorway.

Master Ubâd stood there, as if watching her through his eyeless mask.

"Stay away from us," she said.

He glided slowly down the hall beyond the door's frame and out of sight.

Welstiel seemed to be gone too long, but this was Magelia's first child, and the labor took time. She felt the child coming and needed to push. The shock of pain when she tried to do so made the room dim, and she screamed.

The serving girl ran to her side. "What is it, miss?"

Before Magelia could answer, the child inside pushed downward on its own accord, and she screamed again.

Welstiel hurried into the room, and the midwife, Betina, followed close behind him. He was carrying a small bundle in a bloody, tattered blanket.

"What is that?" she whispered.

"Get out!" he ordered the serving girl.

The young woman rushed from the room, and Magelia was alone with Betina and Welstiel.

The child pushed again, and the pain was so sharp, she couldn't speak or breathe. Tiny knives seemed to cut her from inside, like the child was clawing its way out. Betina was standing over her, and the woman's face was white, as if she had been through an ordeal or was ill.

"Magelia," she said. "Hold on, my girl. Let me see what is wrong."

Welstiel set his bundle down and crouched beside Magelia near the bed's head. She felt a rush of wet warmth between her legs and thought perhaps her water had finally broken.

Betina gasped, and Magelia knew she was wrong.

"Am I going to die?" she whispered to Welstiel.

"Yes."

"Did you know?"

"I suspected."

"You must protect the baby," she begged. "Keep it from Ubâd."

He looked into her eyes and then reached out to grasp her hand. It was the first and only time he had ever touched her.

"I have planned for this," he said. "Ubâd will never have this child . . . if he is convinced it is dead. If you love your child, you will help me."

She didn't understand what he meant, and her mind went white with pain as the knives began cutting again. After what seemed like an eternity, she felt the child slide from inside her into Betina's hands.

"Is it all right?" she asked, growing weaker.

"A girl," Betina answered. "A healthy girl with your black hair."

She wiped off the newborn, wrapped it in a soft cotton

cloth, and laid it beside Magelia. Though still blood-smeared, the child was beautiful.

Welstiel stepped around beside Betina, who looked down upon mother and child with a forced smile.

He reached out and snapped her neck with his hands.

Magelia thought she had slipped into a nightmare as Betina's body dropped from his hands to crumple on the floor. Welstiel retrieved the bundle he had entered with and opened it. Inside was a dead baby girl with dark hair. Its throat had been cut.

"What have you done?" she whispered.

He pulled the brass ring from his pocket and slipped it onto his finger. "Ubâd will come soon. When he does, tell him that I did this. Tell him I murdered the child to avenge my father, and then I fled. He will come after me, but he will not find me."

She glanced at the ring, which had made the topaz's light wink out when he'd first put it on in his room months ago. Magelia didn't understand what it meant, but Welstiel was certain of his ways for dealing with the sightless old mage.

"I have things to collect for the child," he said, "and then I promise to take her out of here. If Ubâd believes the child is dead, he will not return."

He picked up her baby, and Magelia reached out. Welstiel paused long enough for her to touch her daughter, and then he turned away to wrap the child in a clean blanket. He placed the murdered infant at the foot of the bed.

"Tell Ubâd, Magelia, and your daughter will be safe."

"My blue dress," she whispered. "Save it for her."

He nodded, and that was all. When he stepped to the door, he looked both ways before slipping out.

Lingering moments passed, and Magelia fought to keep her eyes open, to hold out until her enemy showed his face.

A blurred figure of dark robe appeared beside her bed. His

cowl drooped down as he looked at Betina's body and then the dead child upon the foot of the bed.

"Welstiel," she whispered, "to avenge his father. You will never have my daughter."

Ubâd became nothing more than a dark shape in the dimming room, but his rolling moan of anguish brought her relief. "Where is he?" the mage shouted.

"Away," she whispered. "Away from here."

Magelia's eyes closed, their lids too heavy to keep open.

Magiere felt her knees strike the cavern floor. Above the cauldron, Magelia's face materialized with a sad smile, and then the apparition was gone.

"You murderer," Magiere whispered at Ubâd.

She lunged to her feet, swinging the falchion at him. Suddenly, he was gone. When she heard his voice behind her, she whirled to face him.

"You feel for her, and you should," he said. "But think, dhampir. You were born from life and death, day and night. Think of the preparation necessary, all the sacrifices made for you to rise up in this world. You are years behind where you should be in your power and awareness, but you have come back to me of your own choice. This was not mere chance."

"You did that to her, and then you just let her die."

The dim torchlight in the cavern brightened, and she knew her irises had gone black. Canines elongated in her mouth, and she felt her nails harden as if they rooted themselves in the bones of her fingers.

"You want to see how far my power has grown?"

Vordana stepped in behind Ubâd, a wary expression on his sunken face. Magiere could hear Leesil nearby, behind her, and Chap circled out to her right.

"Listen!" Ubâd commanded. "You are as you are, and nothing can change this, so embrace truth. Our patron will

place you above all others, and all you must do is accept who
you are . . . rather than this deluded guise you cling to. Take
your place beside him."

Magiere felt her control returning. She understood nothing of his words, and she cared little at all for whatever patron, deity or otherwise, this creature thought she belonged
to. She held her form, not allowing her dhampir aspects to
fade.

Ubâd no longer appeared shadowy and intimidating.
Magiere saw but another petty, self-serving conniver—like
Welstiel—who had also helped to kill her mother. On im-
pulse, she turned to glance at Leesil.

He watched her, punching blades gripped in both hands.
Long white-blond hair tucked behind his oblong ears, his
slanted eyes were wide with suspicion at the sight of her.
Then his features softened as he saw she had not lost herself
to savagery this time.

"You are Magiere," he said, voice firm. "Nothing can
change that. And I know you. You belong with me—not
them, not . . . whatever they serve."

He glanced toward Ubâd, lifting his blades ever so
slightly, poised between advancing and holding his ground.

Magiere sense his fear just below his anger, as if his own
emotions flooded her. Something in Ubâd's words ate at him,
something more than the old man's deluded fanaticism and
hunger for power. Magiere took one step back from the
necromancer and his dead servant.

"Time to leave!" Leesil snapped.

He whirled forward, swinging his blade at Vordana's
throat. The sorcerer dodged back as he'd done in their battle
in the town street. Leesil followed with a full spin of his
body, and his left blade cut through Vordana's shoulder.

"Chap!" Leesil yelled.

Vordana stumbled, clutching his shoulder, and Chap

launched himself into the sorcerer. Wynn had closed in, unslinging her crossbow to load it. Magiere turned on Ubâd, striking for his throat with her falchion.

Again, he was suddenly beyond her reach.

Magiere slashed once more, and this time saw shimmers swirl in the air around Ubâd. His form grew hazy and transparent, and then he stood back a step's distance from her. The air around him settled, but not before Magiere saw the streams of white vanish, like the spirits who had assaulted Leesil and Wynn.

Ubâd was using the spirits to escape her, and somehow they carried him wherever he wished without a word.

The ghosts reappeared.

Their forms and shapes blurred as they rose in a flurry about the cavern. The air grew colder by the moment. The young woman with the rope-burned throat flew through Wynn. The sage cried out and dropped the crossbow.

"Stop it!" Magiere shouted.

Two white blurs dived down at her, and she tried to twist out of their way. One struck her shoulder, and the other flew through her stomach as she tensed.

Magiere felt nothing.

There was no pain or chill agony as she'd expected. They had no effect on her.

The girl with the dark curls and torn throat materialized out of the air, and then blurred again as she flew through Chap. He didn't yelp but rolled off Vordana and backed up in confusion.

A soft smacking sound echoed from the back of cavern beyond the altar, accompanied by heavy, plodding footfalls. Two figures emerged from the shadows, and Magiere recoiled at the sight of them.

Dressed like mariners armed with curved swords, their skin was tinged gray and green. One was missing an ear.

Most of their hair had fallen out, leaving bald patches of decaying flesh. Their faces were devoid of thought or emotion as their mouths opened and closed sharply. No sound came from their throats. Their brackish lips smacked together, over and over. Wynn scrambled across the cavern floor, holding her chest as she retreated from them toward Leesil.

Vordana rose to his feet, disoriented, and clutched at his shoulder wound. He turned toward Leesil, who ducked away from another stream of white mist in the air. Magiere knew he couldn't evade these spirit creatures for long, and Wynn was clearly at a loss. This conflict was nothing like what they'd faced before. None of Leesil's skills or Wynn's knowledge would save either of them.

Magiere grew frightened as she feinted toward Ubâd with her blade point. She had to do something. She would not let Leesil or Wynn die in this cave. When she saw the air shimmer around Ubâd again, she lunged forward with her free hand, and it passed through the place where he'd just stood.

Her hand appeared to slide through him one instant, and as she blinked, he was one step farther away. She didn't stop, and her hand closed about his throat. Pivoting around him to face the others, she put her sword arm around his narrow chest with the falchion at his throat.

"Call them off!" she ordered. "All of them, or I'll slit your throat."

The ghosts stopped, as did the decaying mariners. Vordana turned toward her.

He was watchful and still. The wound Leesil had inflicted seemed to affect his focus more than Magiere expected, but his words sounded in her head.

Harm him, dhampir, and you'll regret it in ways you can't imagine.

"Leesil . . . Wynn," she called. "Both of you, run! The ghosts can't hurt me, and neither can Vordana."

Leesil turned on one foot to face her in disbelief. "No. You're the one they want."

"Get Wynn out of here!" she shouted. "These spirits can kill her and you, but not me and not Chap. Get to the wagon, and we'll meet you there."

With her eyes, she willed him, begged him to listen. Even once Vordana regained his focus, he couldn't drain her or Chap as he could Leesil or Wynn. In this fight, her partner could not help her. He would only be an added worry—but he could save Wynn, and thereby give her and Chap space to fight.

Chap barked once loudly as if to yell, "Yes!" and he snarled again at Vordana.

Leesil glanced at the dog and then back to Magiere. He seemed to understand. With an anguished expression, he backed away and grabbed Wynn by the arm as she gathered up her crossbow. He dragged her along, running between the two rotting seamen and through the passage to the cottage.

Chap circled around Vordana. The sorcerer tilted his head from side to side, trying to watch the dog and yet keep Magiere in his sight.

Magiere saw only one way to escape this standoff. She hoped Chap could pull Vordana down before he tried to worm his way into her mind again.

She pulled hard to slash the falchion across Ubâd's throat.

As her arm tensed, his bony hand snatched her wrist, and a swirl of white enveloped them both.

The spirits didn't come for her. They threaded themselves through Ubâd's robe, not surfacing again. She saw one meld into his exposed forearm, and his grip tightened on her wrist until she couldn't move it at all.

Ubâd's other hand flew outward, and a cloud of white powder showered in an arc from his fingers toward the cauldron.

A flash of light exploded throughout the cavern. It faded to black as Magiere's arms were thrown aside, and she lost hold of the old mage. Magiere toppled back, falling to her haunches upon the cavern floor.

She blinked twice as she got up, swinging the sword before her. Her sight cleared, and she saw Chap pacing the cavern in a panicked rush, sniffing the ground and peering into the shadows beyond the torchlight.

Ubâd, Vordana, the ghosts, and the corpses with their sabers had all vanished.

Chap ran for the passage, turned, and barked. Magiere stopped long enough to kick over Wynn's lamp, grab the crystal, and shove it in her pocket. Then she followed as the dog dived into the dark passage out.

She ran through the small house, past the jars of floating body parts, and reached the front door. The iron staff that had rested beside it was gone. When she stepped outside, Chap traversed the open ground, scenting the earth for a trail. There was no one else in sight.

Shapes glimmered among the trees, and Magiere saw ghosts disperse into the forest in all directions.

Chap began barking wildly. He ran a short distance to the tree line and turned around to look at her. Magiere went after him, and Chap cut into the forest, slowing only to let her keep up.

A dim phosphorescent shape stepped from behind a tree into the dog's path. Chap skidded to a stop with a low rumble growing until it made his whole body quiver.

The ghost of a small girl stood before Magiere, and her lips parted.

"Follow me."

The words were spoken in Ubâd's hollow voice.

Chapter 16

Welstiel and Chane stepped into the forest and found themselves surrounded by the ghosts of the dead. Welstiel had expected this as they entered Ubâd's area of influence. Neither of them could be injured by these spirits, as they were both already dead, but he had neglected to inform Chane.

A transparent man dressed in rags flew through Chane's body. Chane thrashed wildly, backing into a moss curtain and drenching himself.

"Ignore them," Welstiel said. "They cannot harm us."

Chane turned on him. "Wynn passed through here!"

His endless distress over the sage was beginning to unsettle Welstiel. "I doubt anyone with Magiere was harmed. Ubâd would not do anything to dissuade her from reaching him."

Chane drew his sword and slashed aside the wet strands of moss.

More ghosts slipped between the trees as they pressed on. A few lashed out at Welstiel, but he ignored them. The chill sensation of their touch was unpleasant, but no more than that. Still, Chane flinched away from them as he cut a path, leading the way. Soon his sleeves and cloak were soaked through.

"You're veering west," Welstiel said. "Turn more north."

"Do you know where we're going?"

"Yes."

The cottage of piled stone attached to the massive granite outcrop appeared before them. Welstiel stopped amid the trees and called Chane back to wait with him. Magiere would have reached the cavern by now and faced the old necromancer.

Welstiel wondered what half-truths and ploys Ubâd would use to put her off guard. The plan for Magelia's special child had never been completely revealed to him. He would have spared Magiere this, but only to keep her focus clear. Whatever Ubâd planned would lead Magiere down another path.

She would refuse Ubâd, just as she had refused him.

"Enough waiting," Chane said, the line of his mouth tight. "They could be trapped in there."

"Do you suggest we walk in with a pleasant greeting?"

Chane did not answer.

Shouts came from inside the cottage, and its door burst open.

Ghosts whirled out of the forest in a maelstrom that obscured Welstiel's view of the cottage. He heard running and the slashing of brush and moss. Streams of spirit mist in the outside air went wild and rushed toward the sound.

Chane lunged forward, but Welstiel grabbed his cloak and pulled him back. He gripped his companion's shoulder tightly. Ubâd depended on spirits as his eyes and ears. Such arcane emissaries would not find Welstiel or anyone he touched while wearing his ring of "nothing."

When the air cleared, the cottage door stood open. Far to his left Welstiel heard the thrashing of brush and spotted the sage and the half-blood scurrying into the forest. Two more figures appeared in the doorway and headed into the forest.

Welstiel sensed no tingle of life within them as he reached out with his awareness.

Chane glanced at Welstiel as the decayed men passed into the trees.

"Reanimated dead," Welstiel whispered. "Ubâd's skills have become more diverse."

Another pair appeared in the cottage doorway. One wore a leather mask, and the other's skin was stretched tight and gray across the bones of his face.

"Ubâd?" Chane whispered, gesturing to the first man.

Welstiel barely nodded. He shivered off trepidation, suppressing the terrible memories conjured by the sight of his family's old retainer.

Between the necromancer's leather mask and cowled robes, it was difficult to imagine what he might look like underneath, but his withered jaw and hands were as Welstiel remembered. As ancient as he had always seemed, he had aged no further in twenty-five years. He carried a long iron staff that appeared far too heavy for his stature.

Ubâd spoke to his companion, and Welstiel's senses expanded sharply to catch the man's words.

"I will lure the dhampir off," he said, "and see to it that she takes her place with us. Find the half-elf and kill him. The sage, as well, though it is doubtful she would last a night in the forest."

"And that bothersome dog?" asked his companion, holding his shoulder as if it pained him.

"He will stay with the dhampir . . . and I will deal with that misbegotten mongrel sent by our patron's oppressors. His meddling ends tonight."

They both stepped into the trees and then separated.

Chane made to go after the undead sorcerer, sword

gripped tight in hand. Welstiel stopped him, but kept his voice low.

"The dhampir and the *majay-hì* have not come out yet. Stay close where I can hide you from their awareness."

"The dead are wandering every corner of this forest," Chane answered. "That dog is not going to pick me out. I must go!"

Welstiel realized Chane was not going to help him protect Magiere. Perhaps that was best. If Ubâd's undead sorcerer overcame Leesil, he would return to his master's side. And that would make Welstiel's own task far more difficult. Chane's only thoughts were of his little sage now in Leesil's company.

"Go," he said, "but do not let her see you."

Chane was off into the trees and out of sight.

Welstiel looked back at the stone house just as Magiere and Chap rushed out. Her eyes were completely black. When her lips parted in a deep breath, he saw her elongated canines. His confidence in her wavered. Had he underestimated Ubâd's poisoned whispers? Would Magiere give in and follow the necromancer's path?

She was in a fully enraged dhampir state, yet she paused in the open space before the house. She waited calmly as the *majay-hì* sniffed the earth. It turned, barking wildly at her, and ran a few paces in the direction Ubâd had taken then paused to look back. Magiere broke into a run and followed the animal into the forest.

Welstiel followed, as well.

Chap slowed to let Magiere to get ahead of him. He trailed her as she crashed through the dense forest after the child ghost. His concern should have been for her alone, but Leesil and Wynn were at the mercy of Ubâd's minions. Magiere was almost beyond his sight, and he paused in a hollow between the moss-laden trees and closed his crystalline eyes.

Hear me, my kin. Come to me.

He reached out, again and again, sensing for an answering touch of spirit in the wilderness. A presence grew around him, and he opened his eyes.

Enormous oaks and firs crackled and rustled as their limbs reached outward into each other's embrace. He heard something akin to whispers that did not come from Ubâd's spirits. Tiny movements made leaves and strands of moss quiver, and he felt the many lives of the wild surrounding him, turning their awareness inward upon him within the half-circle of sentinel trees.

A yellow speckled lizard crawled slowly across a spruce's wide trunk, its tail twice the length of its body. The tail dragged behind the reptile in a lengthy curve like a mouth in the bark below the glittering eyes of other creatures in this massive tree's shadowed upper reaches.

Why do you call us . . . now that you have abandoned us in our need to go your own way?

Chap bowed his head as the lizard's tail slipped out of sight behind the trunk.

I stand by her. I stand by my choice. And nothing you hope for has been lost as yet. But the others . . .

A flurry of skittering filled his ears like tiny claws and paws racing through the forest canopy in agitation.

Chap padded back and forth impatiently. *And the half-elf? He still serves his purpose, to keep Magiere from the reach of the enemy . . . and perhaps more.*

A telling silence was the only reply, and he pressed further.

Let life bar death in this place. Hold off the restless dead. Hold them for even a short while. Keep the sage and the an-maglâhk safe.

Whispers and rustles in the leaves grew louder.

Chap knew his kin hated this forest of death. He rumbled in anger at their indecision.

Without her companions, the dhampir will fall to the enemy. Hold back the spirits of death, or what we seek will certainly be lost.

Whispers faded to silence.

Chap felt a wind, gentle at first but growing in strength, until it whipped at his fur. He heard cries in the dark that mingled with whispers from the trees and the skittering of life among them.

White mist whipped among the branches around the hollow in which Chap stood.

The grizzled soldier and scores of others took half-form in the air as they swirled together above him. More and more of the forest's wandering ghosts were pulled in. The girl with dark curls and torn throat rushed past him, caught in the gale. And all began to blur until they became nothing but translucent glowing streaks.

The whirlwind expanded until its circumference touched the dark branches above. The threads of white mist split and tangled in the forest canopy. Bit by bit, the wind died down to a breeze.·

When the rustle of Chap's fur ceased, there was only the dark above him. All trace of the spirits had vanished, trapped by the forest.

Relief filled him. Leesil could find a way to face almost anything else that came, and Wynn might yet survive this night.

Chap waited no longer and bolted through a space in the sentinel trees. He thrashed through tangled branches and curtained moss, until he broke into the open and followed the scent of Magiere.

                    *   *   *

Leesil was well into the forest when the first ghost assaulted him. He dodged only to be struck in the back by another. Icy pain made him stumble to his knees, and streaks like vapor in a wind exploded from his chest. When he rose, ducking through the trees to escape, he lost track of Wynn. When he circled back, she was nowhere in sight.

Breathing brought pain as he backtracked to find her, but a hideous form flew toward his face.

The man looked as if he'd been stretched until his bones were broken, and his arms and legs hung in the night air, distended from his shoulders and hips. Madness twisted his features as the spirit melted to a white blur and struck Leesil's torso.

The cold was so severe that the breath clogged in Leesil's chest. He tumbled to the wet ground trying to expel the chill from his lungs.

Leesil clawed up the trunk of a tree to his feet.

He had lost control of this journey, and he couldn't fight what his blades couldn't touch. He and Wynn would die here. The ghosts wouldn't stop until the very life was frozen out of them. And what would become of Magiere, left alone in this world?

Leesil drew in a painful breath. A gentle breeze crossed his skin, pulling at the branches and dangling moss around him. He looked for any place he might run, remembering the rush of air in the cavern when Ubâd's guardian spirits had attacked them.

The breeze built to a wind . . . and then a gale that whipped his hair into his eyes as he clutched for a handhold on the base of a low stout branch.

Spirits all around thrashed frantically—but not at him.

The anger in their warped features transformed into fear. The broken man opened his slack jaw in a whispering scream as the wind dragged him away into the forest.

Translucent figures flew past Leesil on the air. Within moments, the forest around him emptied of all but the dark branches and wet foliage and long strands of moss.

The wind dropped with a last gust that pulled at his hair.

Leesil looked about, uncertain what had happened. His first instinct was to call out to Wynn, but he stopped himself. If anything else lurked here, he would give away not only his own position but possibly Wynn's, as well.

He silently cursed himself as a fool.

He never should have agreed to Magiere's reckless gambit. The four of them shouldn't have separated. He tried searching again for Wynn, but he had lost his sense of direction. Every step in these marshy woods looked the same as the last.

A spark of light in the distance caught his attention. It blinked in and out as it moved among the trees.

Leesil's fear melted in relief as he remembered Wynn's cold lamp. Then he spun behind an oak as that same relief vanished. Wynn hadn't been carrying her lamp when they'd fled the cavern. And the light was an orange yellow tint rather than crystal white.

He crouched as the glimmer came around the side of an oak. The figure carrying it took shape in Leesil's night sight.

Grayed and shriveled skin took on a sickly yellow cast in the glow and revealed eyes that bulged in sunken sockets. The topaz amulet Leesil had lost was still clutched in his bony hand.

Vordana held his shoulder where Leesil's blade had sliced through.

Leesil smelled the walking corpse even at a distance and remembered how that cut had broken the sorcerer's focus in the cavern. Vordana had a weakness in his decaying flesh that other undead did not.

Leesil crawled quietly along the ground, keeping his

quarry in sight. The topaz glowed in Vordana's presence like a beacon. The sorcerer stopped to look about in puzzlement, and Leesil turned his course to move out ahead. He found thick brush between two trees and crouched there, gripping both blades.

Vordana wandered, turning slightly to his left, and Leesil bit his lip in frustration. Then the sorcerer curved back upon his original path. Waiting in the darkness, Leesil gauged the distance as his target neared.

Ten paces, five, two . . .

He sprang up and forward, driving his right blade in below Vordana's collarbone.

A soft metallic click came just before the sound of severed bone scraping against steel, but Leesil kept his eyes on his opponent's face. The force took Vordana off balance, and Leesil followed on the momentum.

Vordana's back slammed against a tree as the blade's tip drove deeper. The impact brought a shower of water drops cascading down upon both of them from the branches above. The dead man's putrid stench thickened from the wound, and light dimmed as the topaz fell from his grasp.

Leesil raised his other blade to hack into Vordana's throat, and the sorcerer's filmy eyes widened. A chant rose behind Leesil's thoughts, filling the back of his mind. He changed the second blade's swing, taking the quicker path into Vordana's stomach. As the blade sank in, the chant swelled to a shriek, then ceased.

Vordana's mouth gaped. Leesil jerked the blade from the dead man's gut to draw back and strike for his neck. A wave of fatigue struck him, and his blow faltered.

The blade's edge clipped Vordana's wounded shoulder, and the sorcerer flinched. His bony hands grasped Leesil's arms.

Fatigue flooded Leesil's body so quickly that his legs and

arms quivered as he fought to stay on his feet. Vordana's voice filled his head.

Your life is my strength, half-breed. What a meal your elvish blood is.

Vordana's words were filled with malicious joy, but there was still fear in his skeletal face. Focus appeared to take great effort on his part, but Leesil felt his life being ripped from him by the walking corpse. He needed to break the undead's concentration, but he felt himself growing weaker.

Leesil let his legs buckle and the blade slide from Vordana's chest.

As he dropped, he twisted his wrists so that the blades came over the top of Vordana's forearms. Something hard jabbed his back through his hauberk as he hit the ground. He gave it no notice, and summoned all his strength to pull one leg up to his chest.

He used the weight of his own fall combined with the undead's grip. When Vordana began to topple toward him, Leesil kicked out into his abdomen.

Vordana rose up in the air, filmy eyes widened in surprise.

As the sorcerer flipped over Leesil's head, he slashed his blades outward in a last effort. Vordana slipped from sight, and Leesil lay prone and sweating on the wet ground.

Breath came with difficulty, as if his chest had no strength to rise and fall. Something still poked his back where he lay. His mind cleared, and he felt fingers still gripping his forearms inside the wings of his blades.

Leesil rolled to his side.

Bony hands were tightly latched on to his arms, but they weren't joined to anything. Only half the sorcerer's forearms remained, ending in cleanly sliced gray flesh and bone.

Leesil thrashed as he rolled to his knees, trying to dislodge the undead's hands. Their grip wouldn't release.

Vordana rose and stared at his own severed arms. No

blood poured from the man's dead flesh. No tears of pain or anguish fell from his milky eyes. His voice called out through Leesil's head.

Bastard . . . half-blood!

Leesil kept fighting to breathe. How in this hellish land could he kill such a monster if its severed parts still obeyed its will? Taking its head was hopeless.

He slipped his left blade tip under the thumb of Vordana's hand still clinging to his right arm. Weakness rushed through his body, along with pain, as he felt Vordana begin to drain his life again. He slashed the digit off, and the hand fell away.

It hit the ground, fingers clawing air, and Leesil saw something shiny beside it.

His legs gave away under him, and he fell so quickly that his blade tips slid into the ground.

Half-pressed into the wet earth was a small brass urn, its top sealed with a whitish filling that might have been wax. Its chain had been split in half. The soft metal clink Leesil had heard at his first blow into Vordana's chest had been the chain severing on his blade's edge.

Leesil raised his head and saw Vordana coming for him. The sorcerer didn't seem aware that he'd lost the urn . . . didn't see it lying so close. Leesil knew he couldn't defend himself much longer, and he had to end this. If not by finishing this walking corpse, then at least by driving it off—as Wynn had once done. He shoved himself upright on his knees, and wavered as he lifted both blades.

Vordana hesitated at the sight of sharp steel in the air before him.

And Leesil swung downward, letting go with all his weight behind the blades.

His left blade missed and buried in the soft earth up to his fist.

The right struck true.

A snapping puff of vapor issued as the urn split in half. It smelled of pepper and the scent burned in Leesil's nose, making his eyes water. The sensation of his life draining away ceased.

Leesil's fatigue started to fade, little by little, and he looked up at Vordana.

The sorcerer clenched exposed teeth as he stared at the urn's halves to either side of Leesil's blade.

No . . . no . . . no . . .

Over and over, the one word filled Leesil's head as he struggled to his feet.

Ubâd!

Leesil lunged at Vordana. Whatever the urn preserved of the sorcerer's presence, its loss had undone his ability to prey upon the living.

Vordana's filmy eyes turned fully white. They collapsed inside their sockets, and Leesil slashed. Vordana raised the stump of his arm to shield himself. The blade hit, skidded along bone, and tore away rotting flesh.

Ubâd! Master, save me!

At this outcry, Leesil's fear sharpened to replace his lost strength. He couldn't let the withered mage save this creature. Vordana's grayed flesh shriveled further and split in places to reveal yellowed bone. The undead sorcerer decayed before Leesil, but it was not enough to satisfy him. He chopped down into Vordana's head.

The sorcerer crumpled to ground, still writhing with a spilt in his skull, and Leesil fell upon him, striking again and again.

When Leesil finally stopped, he was panting in exhaustion. He rose to his feet, wavered there, and stared down at the unrecognizable remains of Vordana's head. With one kick, he scattered the rotted pieces into the forest.

"Come back from that, if you can," he gasped out.

Now he had to find Wynn . . . and Magiere and Chap.

A high-pitched scream carried through the forest from a distance.

"Wynn?" he whispered hoarsely.

Leesil snatched up the still-glowing topaz, and stumbled through the trees.

Wynn knelt upon the ground, clinging to a tree trunk with both arms as the gale died away. She stayed there, shivering for a long while, before she could open her eyes.

The glimmers of the ghosts were gone, and she had fled so quickly, there had been no time to pick up her cold lamp from the cavern floor. Even the moon was hidden somewhere above the thick forest canopy. All she saw was the silent dark forest.

No ghostly translucent spirits. No thin trails of white in the air that pierced her with cold pain. And no Leesil.

"Leesil?" Wynn whispered.

He was nowhere to be seen, and she had no idea which direction she had run—which direction to turn and search for him. The sound of Wynn's own rapid breaths filled her ears, and she willfully slowed her breathing before it dizzied her.

"I am not lost," she told herself.

If she could not find Leesil, then Magiere and Chap would come. Chap could track her . . . if those two had escaped the cavern.

Magiere had been so angry when the communion with her mother had ended. Ubâd's suggestive words of her greater purpose only fed fuel to her rage. Wynn so often felt frightened both for and of Magiere that it was becoming a familiar state. She wondered what confidence Magiere and her mother's spirit had shared.

Her thoughts were cut short by thrashing in the forest.

Neither Leesil nor Chap would ever make so much noise. Perhaps Magiere? But wouldn't Chap lead her in a more stealthy fashion?

Wynn grabbed her crossbow and quiver from the ground and crawled around the tree trunk away from the sound. She peered out, and a dark figure moved haltingly through the forest.

She fumbled with the crossbow, trying to cock and load it. The figure pushed through a tangle of low branches, not bothering to hold them aside from whipping at its body and face.

Even in the darkness, Wynn saw the darker hollow of its mouth open and close with no sound but the wet smack of its lips coming together. She made out the long curve of steel in its grip. It was one of the dead seamen who had appeared in the cavern.

Wynn quietly slipped the quiver's strap over her shoulder and raised the crossbow, ready to step out and fire if it came close. A rancid stench surrounded her over the forest's thick smell. She turned at the rattle of branches behind her.

The second seaman's face pushed through a curtain of moss, green strands tangling on the stained teeth in its open mouth. Filmy eyes stared blindly ahead as it slashed at her with its saber.

Wynn screamed and clenched the crossbow's lever as she fell along the tree's side.

The garlic-soaked quarrel struck the dead seaman's stomach as his saber split bark where she'd crouched a moment before. The first seaman closed in from the other side, its clumsy feet stomping the wet earth.

Wynn scrambled on all fours, dragging the crossbow behind her. When she tumbled beyond the next clump of trees, she got to her feet and began recocking the crossbow. The way these things moved, she should be fast enough to stay out of their reach. As she was about to pull out another quarrel, she looked back and nearly screamed again.

They were charging after her.

Wynn turned and fled. She heard more thrashing in the forest close behind as her short robe caught in low brush. Feet skidding in mulch, she jerked herself free.

Something grabbed her cowl from behind, and this time she cried out.

Wynn turned upon the grip, swinging her crossbow as a club. Its bow snapped off in pieces as the weapon collided with her attacker's head. The smell of putrefied flesh welled up around her.

His skin was gray and darkly splotched. Eyes without pupils stared blankly ahead, as the seaman raised his saber and brought it down at her head.

She held up the crossbow stock with both hands, and the saber cracked against it.

A deep voice call out from nearby. "Wynn! Where are you?"

"Leesil?" she called back. "I'm here! Please help—quickly!"

She struggled with the dead seaman, trying to hold him off.

A fist shot past her head from behind, striking the dead man's face, and he fell. But the corpse's grip held on Wynn's cowl, and she was jerked along, spinning around to fall backward to the earth.

The cowl ripped from her robe, and she rolled to hurry away on hands and knees. As she looked back, wiping dirt and muck from her face, she saw the dark silhouette rising up over the downed seaman.

In his hand he held a longsword.

Wynn froze in confusion. The figure standing over the

seaman was too tall, and his hair was dark. Even in the moonless night she caught the pale tone of his skin.

Chane turned toward her.

The moment Chane heard Wynn scream, he abandoned silence and raced toward her voice. "Wynn! Where are you?"

A loud crack sounded ahead where her voice had come from.

"Leesil?" she cried out. "I'm here! Please help—quickly!"

She had mistaken his voice. Welstiel had warned him not to reveal himself, but Chane didn't care anymore.

He opened his senses, smelling the air and feeling for life among the trees as he ran. Wynn was close enough to hear, and that was close enough to pick out her living presence in this place where anything animate was dead or undead. He felt her easily, but there were also two spots of cold emptiness he sensed near her.

He ripped through the forest's tangle and saw her.

Wynn held up the broken crossbow, blocking the saber pressing down at her. The dead man had her cowl in his free hand, and she could not pull away.

Chane rushed in, striking with his fist over the top of Wynn's head and into the corpse's face. Its grip on Wynn's cowl held. As she spun about, dragged after her attacker, Chane threw himself forward rather than fall on top of her.

A rotting stench filled his heightened sense of smell, and he gagged as he fell on the man. Chane quickly rolled to his feet, and turned to look for Wynn.

She scurried away on all fours, her cowl ripped away. Wiping dirt off her face, she stared at him blankly.

"Chane?" she whispered, and then her eyes widened as she looked down at his feet. "Chane!

The prone corpse swung its saber at his legs.

He caught the blade with his longsword and stomped on the corpse's wrist. Bone snapped under his foot, and the saber came loose. He rammed his own sword though the corpse's chest and felt the blade sink through into the earth. The thing beneath him thrashed awkwardly, even with the sword through its body, attempting to grab his leg with its free hand.

A troublesome creature. Chane wondered what it would take to put an end to this. He snatched up its saber, raising it to hack the corpse's head from its shoulders.

He heard the hiss of a blade from behind, followed by a cry of pain from Wynn. He started to turn as Wynn shouted, "Another, behind you!"

Pain pierced Chane's back. He looked down to see the point of a curved blade protruding from his rib cage. His own black fluids spread through his torn shirt and vestment. He suppressed the pain and slammed his elbow high to the rear.

He felt it crack into something that whipped back from the blow. But the attacker behind him held on to the saber's hilt. Chane lunged forward sharply, sliding his body off the blade. Fluid loss would eventually weaken him, and he couldn't leave Wynn unprotected. As he turned around to face this new assailant, he glanced toward her and faltered for an instant.

Wynn's legs buckled under her as she dropped to her knees with a strange frown. She stared at him in bewilderment.

Blood ran out her collar down her severed sleeve.

The undead must have slashed her with its saber before running Chane through. Chane lost all awareness of his own body, and even the lingering faraway echo of pain in his torso vanished.

"Don't move!" he shouted at her.

He swung at this second corpse's neck with the saber. The

dead man blocked with his own blade. Chane had no idea what it would take to put these things down. Welstiel had called them "reanimated," and Chane hoped they were as mindless as that might imply. While this creature's expression showed no self-awareness, it had enough survival instincts and lingering memory to wield its weapon.

Chane feinted, and as the creature followed, he kicked out into its knee. Its balance faltered, and he swung for its neck. It blocked again but not quickly enough. The blade bit through fetid flesh and stopped on bone. When it showed no sign of slowing, Chane dropped his weapon and lunged at it with both hands.

Before it could draw the saber back, he threw his arms around its neck, toppling it over. As they hit the ground, Chane pulled his knees up and pinned the corpse. He gripped its head and wrenched sideways.

Its head tore free in his hands.

He tossed it aside, grabbed a saber from the ground, and ran to the other corpse—now clutching at the longsword still pinning it to the ground. One hard blow was enough to sever its head, and the body ceased moving.

Chane tossed the saber aside and stumbled toward Wynn. He knelt before her, working quickly to open the blood-soaked collar.

"What are you . . . What are you doing?" she whispered.

Wynn's round, olive face was streaked with dirt. Her long braid had come loose and light brown hair hung down her shoulders, some of it matting in her blood.

"Be still and quiet," Chane said. "I need to see how bad the wound is."

He pulled back the left side of her robe to expose an ugly tear in the soft flesh between her shoulder and collarbone. Though the saber's tip had slashed open her sleeve, it had not cut into her arm, as well. He slipped off his vestment and cloak and tore away both his sleeves. Lying on the ground, the cloak seemed to move of its own accord. His rat crawled from the pocket and skittered off into the trees. He did not try to stop it. Folding the sleeves together for a makeshift bandage, he pressed it against the wound.

Wynn let out a cry, and Chane almost pulled away. But she could not stand to lose any more blood.

"This needs to be sewn," he said. "Where's your pack?"

She didn't answer but reached out with her right hand as if checking to make sure he was real.

"I told you to go."

Wynn looked so shattered, frightened, that Chane could not help pulling her around until her uninjured side rested against him. She went rigid at first but then shifted closer, pressing her face into the crook of his neck. He kept pressure on the bandage and felt blood soaking through to his palm as he put his other arm about her shoulders. He rocked her back and forth.

"Everything will be all right," he whispered. "I'm here."

Chapter 17

Magiere struggled to push aside what her mother's spirit had shown her. Of all the faces that passed through her mind, from Betina's, to that of the infant with its slit throat, and to Bryen's, one face wouldn't be suppressed.

Welstiel—her brother.

She pressed on through the forest, focused upon the child ghost leading her to Ubâd. The undead of this place served his whims, assaulting anything he wished—except for herself, and perhaps Chap—and remained a danger to Leesil and to Wynn. The most certain way to end that threat was to find Ubâd quickly and kill him.

With every step, Welstiel's face lingered in her thoughts.

Magiere looked back to check on Chap.

There was no one behind her. Even with her night sight open wide, she saw no sign of his silvery shape in the forest.

But she couldn't lose track of her guide, so she kept moving. Relief came when the dog burst from the brush to lope beside her.

As the ghost girl slipped around a tilting spruce, she hovered in the air, waiting for Magiere to catch up. The ghost shimmered and vanished as Magiere stepped into a clearing with Chap at her side.

Across the open space stood Ubâd, an iron staff resting in his grip with one end upon the ground. His head turned toward her, and Magiere wondered how he was aware of her through the eyeless leather mask.

"Now we can speak alone," Ubâd said.

"I didn't come to talk."

She headed straight for him without breaking stride, swinging for his head with the falchion.

Instead of gliding away, or fading out of reach as he'd done in the cavern, he leaned the staff forward to catch her blade. Steel and iron clanged sharply together, but Ubâd's arm didn't give an inch under the force.

"Stop this!" he ordered. "I spent a lifetime, my lifetime, in your creation only to believe you murdered at birth. There wasn't time enough to begin again, and all was lost. But when rumors were heard of a hunter in the land, I regained hope. I have waited too long and suffered too much."

"Suffered?" Magiere drew back her sword. "You speak of your suffering, after all you've done? After what you did to my mother?"

"You have no venom for Welstiel? This is his doing. I searched for years . . . years, to take vengeance. Without his interference, you would be standing by my side . . . standing at our patron's side."

Magiere's hatred swelled, and her teeth hardened in her mouth. She struck downward, so he couldn't block without lifting the staff. Ubâd shifted left, swinging the staff upon its grounded end, and deflected the blade.

Rage brought strength, and Magiere lunged, faking left. When Ubâd shifted away, bringing the staff back around, she leveled her swing. The falchion's tip slipped in behind the staff's slant and sliced through his robe at the waist.

Ubâd faded back, winking in and out like a ghost, and lifted the staff from the earth. Its top end dipped, sweeping her sword aside. He used both hands to bring the staff's bottom end around at her head. Magiere ducked away as it narrowly missed her jaw.

"Instead of conversation, you wish for instruction," he mocked.

She glanced to his stomach. The robe was too full to tell if she'd reached his flesh, and the fabric too dark to see if it was stained with blood. He didn't appear injured.

Magiere's self-control began to waver. Hunger burned up her throat and into her head. She swung again, pressing in on him.

"You feel the hunger, yes?" Ubâd asked softly. "Like your great father, you've already learned to control it."

Chap lunged in behind Ubâd. Magiere hadn't seen him circle around, and the dog snapped at the man. With the same spin of his staff, Ubâd cracked her blade aside with one end while the other slammed into the dog's shoulder. Chap tumbled away but sprang to his feet again.

"You master it now, as your source of strength," Ubâd continued, "instead of being driven before it like a slave."

Ubâd blocked her repeatedly. One swing of his staff clipped her forearm so hard, it made her stumble, but she barely felt the pain and instinctively pushed it down. However Ubâd managed such a heavy and unwieldy weapon, he easily kept pace with her. And his unnatural ability to shift places like a ghost left Chap's teeth closing upon empty air. Magiere's instinct warned that he was only toying with her.

He lashed at her with words harder than the iron rod. "You were born of life and death to be more than either. Both will bow before you . . . if you accept who you are. You cannot hide from yourself any longer."

Magiere shuddered as if his words were the cold sweat
upon her skin.

As long as she clung to hunger and hatred—the same that
this madman claimed were her birthright—she could keep at
this all night and face exhaustion afterward. How long before
Ubâd would tire of this play and his preaching? How long
before he turned to something more within his talents?

"You have no one else," he said more quietly. "No one but
me who understands these things. There are so many more
questions you have that only I can answer. To find your
place, your family . . . I am all that is left to you."

Ubâd's block was slower this time.

Magiere threw her weight behind the sword and into his
staff. He was forced to exert more effort, and his attention
fixed firmly upon her. In an instant, he screamed out and
stumbled.

As Ubâd twisted about, Chap jerked hard upon the man's
ankle clenched in his teeth. Magiere grabbed the iron staff's
end with her free hand and thrust with the falchion. The blade
split through the robe and into Ubâd chest.

He screeched, and the staff jerked from Magiere's hand.
As she pulled on the falchion to free it, the staff cracked back
across her temple, and she lost awareness of the world.

There was no pain at first, but it rushed into her skull as
her sight returned.

She looked up into the dark sky above the clearing and
felt wet earth beneath her. There came two sounds as if from
a great distance—Chap's growl and strange whispered
words of a twisted language she didn't know.

Ubâd was chanting.

Magiere flopped over to her hands and knees.

Strange guttural words issued from Ubâd mouth as he
swept the staff's end at Chap. The dog whirled away, and
Ubâd rammed the staff's end into the ground.

"Khurúj," he shouted, *"fê nafsê htalab!"*

These words didn't match those of his chant. They rolled from his mouth in a familiar manner like a demand to someone Magiere couldn't see.

A shudder answered from the earth.

Magiere stood up as best she could, uncertain whether to assault Ubâd once again or to back out of the clearing. Chap let out a snarl that mixed with a mournful yowl. He rushed at her, skidded to avoid crashing into her, and then began shoving at her legs with his head and shoulders. He was trying to drive her back toward the trees.

Ubâd repeated his strange words in a commanding shout. *"Khurúj, fê nafsê htalab!"*

The earth rolled beneath Magiere's feet. As she started to fall, light gathered all around her. Something lashed around her arms and legs, and she was lifted from the ground. Before she saw what held her, she spotted Chap running across the clearing's floor as a crack in the earth extended to race after him.

Blue-white light lanced upward from the split. It congealed and took shape in the air, forming into long tendrils that moved with a life of their own. They lashed out at Chap, winding around his body and neck. The dog was wrenched back from his flight and lifted in the air within their coils.

Tendrils curled up around Magiere's limbs, as well, like ropes of living light.

"The dead may be my preference," Ubâd said. "But I can still conjure and summon other things, such as the collective spirit of this forest."

Magiere fought to move her arms. If she didn't kill Ubâd, what would become of Leesil and Wynn?

"Are you prepared to be rational?" Ubâd asked.

Anger faded from her into numb loss. When she spoke, her mouth moved freely, teeth receded to their normal state.

"My companions . . . Leave them be . . . and I'll listen to anything you wish to say."

"How generous," he answered mockingly. "I will be your father, your teacher, your only family. You have no other. Vordana has finished your half-blood by now, and my other servants have fed on the sage."

Leesil's face filled Magiere's thoughts, and she grew cold inside.

Ubâd lied. It had to be a lie.

Anger and hunger swelled in her as Ubâd turned toward Chap.

"As for this mongrel puppet of the enemy, his meddling ends now."

Welstiel sensed Magiere's presence and followed her. Around him, the trees were strangely empty of movement. It was not Magiere that he saw first, but a blue-white light filtering through the forest. As he drew closer, it moved and grew. Welstiel hurried on as quickly as silence allowed, and what he saw almost made him bolt into the clearing.

Tendrils of blue-white light sprouted from the cracked earth, snaring both Magiere and Chap. She hung in the air, tangled within them. The tendrils had to be shaped from summoned or conjured elemental material, but their nature was unknown to Welstiel. Ubâd had never shown this ability in the years Welstiel had suffered the man's presence and tutelege. Urgency made him take another step forward before he could stop himself.

Welstiel had no prepared tool or artifice to deal with this. Conjuring elementals of this magnitude was beyond anyone he had ever known.

He clenched his fist, frustration and panic eroding his self-control. As Magiere and Chap struggled, the tendrils shifted to grip them, responding to their movements. Ubâd turned his attention toward the *majay-hì*, and the tendrils tightened around the animal.

Welstiel took another step, moving close behind a tree at the clearing's edge.

These tendrils were a mass of elemental matter, but without any will of their own. They responded to commands from the necromancer.

Sightless Ubâd had no natural vision that Welstiel knew of behind that leather mask. He relied upon some arcane method to see the world around him. Welstiel had one possession that could deceive all detection but physical senses. He had created it long ago to escape with Magiere when she was a child.

Welstiel sat upon the ground, his legs crossed, as he stared at his ring of nothing.

It had been created to work passively upon the wearer, without the need for willful activation. It was all he had, and in this moment, he needed its influence to grow.

He removed the brass band, holding it level between his fingertips like a conjuring circle engraved in the air. As he murmured softly, he focused within the circle to pass his consumed life force into it. Exhaustion crept through him, but he held his concentration until it felt as if he had lingered there far too long.

Ubâd had to sense Magiere's presence in order to assault her. Welstiel would hide that presence.

Fatigue sharpened suddenly, and Welstiel felt a ripple of tension in the air expand outward from the circle of brass.

Anger built inside Magiere, along with fear of loss. Leesil couldn't be dead. It was a lie.

When Ubâd turned upon Chap, she meant to shout, but the words came out hoarse and low. "Touch him, and I'm finished with you."

Ubâd paused, one hand in the air.

"I'll tolerate your words," she said, "but you'll do as I say—or you can go find one of your corpses to chat with."

Ubâd turned back to her. "You do not care for helplessness. What if I told you that freedom is yours to take?"

Magiere had no wish to play any more of these games. She had hope in Leesil's arms, in his eyes. If she lost him, there was nothing left but death and blood—and both would be Ubâd's.

"Get to the point," she answered.

"I gave you the answer, if you had listened," Ubâd said. "All existence is composed of the five elements, and life itself is no different. These tendrils that bind you are made from the element of Spirit summoned from the forest, and life clings most to that element. You can feed upon life. Freedom is yours, and you have but to consume it."

He stepped close enough that when Magiere looked down at him, she saw the creases in his leather mask.

"Take the life from the tendrils. Consume it like the Noble Dead you are. With its pure form pressed to your flesh, you need only will it so . . . and be free."

Magiere grimaced as she looked at the glowing blue-white tendrils curled about her arm. She felt their slick warm touch upon her as if they were solid. To her eyes, they appeared no more material that the ghosts of the forest and cavern.

What Ubâd asked sickened her.

To give in to hunger? To feed like the undead that she and Leesil hunted and burned to ash? Whether by touch or blood down her throat, it meant becoming one of them. It meant becoming all that Ubâd claimed she was rather than what she wished to be.

Only once had she ever done this. Leesil had been her willing victim, though she'd been unaware of his sacrifice until it was nearly too late. But if Ubâd lied and Leesil still lived, he would be alone against this madman and his minions if she didn't get free.

Leesil's life . . . or the life she wanted to live?

Magiere let her hunger rise.

It spread through her whole flesh instead of just her throat and head. She felt it move like the black ribbons Wynn had seen with her mantic sight. Hunger coiled through her limbs toward the tingling life touching her skin through the tendrils.

And nothing more happened.

Magiere stared wide-eyed along her arm, torn inside between anguish and relief. Her body wouldn't consume the life it felt there. Perhaps it couldn't do so at all.

And she couldn't free herself to help Leesil.

Whatever she might be, Ubâd didn't know as much of her true nature as the twisted mage thought. She looked down into his leather mask, unable to speak. What could she possibly say to him that would gain her anything?

A sudden tension in the air passed over her—through her—like a wind pushing at a dangling leaf.

Ubâd stumbled back, and Magiere saw that he'd felt this strange sensation, as well. The staff slipped from his grip to thump heavily on the ground, and he slapped both hands over his mask. As he slid backward, he stumbled and fell hard, his arms flailing.

Magiere didn't know what had just happened, but with Ubâd down, she thrashed to pull her right arm free, the falchion still in her grip. The tendrils held, but they didn't clench tight at her struggle.

"Dhampir?" Ubâd whispered, an edge of fear in his voice. He crawled upon the ground, feeling along it with his hands for something, perhaps his lost staff.

Magiere watched in astonishment. Ubâd was now truly blind.

The glow to the far right of the clearing brightened, and Magiere looked up.

Chap still hung in the air, but he wasn't the same. His fur appeared whiter. The brighter he grew, the more the tendrils' glow softened. Those cords of blue-white sagged until Chap's paws touched the earth. As he scrambled free of their touch, the glimmer in his coat faded, flowing back into the earth from where it had come, and he ran to Magiere.

At Chap's movement, Ubâd rose on his knees. His masked face turned sharply toward the dog, and he raised a hand in the air.

Chap froze, and Magiere feared the old man had regained his sight.

Ubâd turned back and forth as if still blind. He was following the sounds of the dog's movement. Chap crept toward Magiere.

She took a deep breath and blew a shrill whistle through her lips.

Ubâd flinched, spinning toward her on the ground, but his head turned erratically as his outstretched hand came back to his ear. The piercing sound masked Chap's movement from his hearing.

Magiere looked down and saw Chap brush against the tendrils holding her.

His coat glimmered to white wherever it made contact. He licked the tendrils, and they buckled more quickly than his own had done. Magiere dropped to her feet. At the sound, Ubâd faced her directly, and his hands shot out like weapons.

Chap scurried away to the left while Magiere shifted right. Ubâd froze in confusion and slowly withdrew his hands as he cocked his head, listening.

Magiere raised her hand, pointed to Chap then Ubâd, and curled her fingers to motion the dog forward. She began to steal inward toward the kneeling old man as the dog closed in quietly from the other side.

Ubâd's head twitched from side to side. Magiere saw his mouth open and heard his breathing quicken. He straightened himself, raised his hands in the air, and slapped them down against the ground as he shouted.

"il'Samar, li-yigdim êyäk khädim fa-ta'zêz ana alän!"

Magiere stopped, turning to both sides to catch whatever new trick Ubâd tried. There were still the empty cracks in the earth, and nothing more rose from them. Chap was nearly within lunging distance, and Magiere moved in again.

"il'Samar!" Ubâd shouted once again. "Come to your servant and aid me!"

Magiere abandoned silence and lifted the falchion high.

The night around her deepened, until even her night sight couldn't penetrate it. She blinked, thinking her eyes had somehow shut. She felt her eyelids open and close, and yet still everything remained black. Slowly the night shapes of the forest reappeared, and there was movement in the trees.

Magiere turned from one side to the other and saw it everywhere.

The dark in the spaces between the trees undulated. It circled the clearing.

In each turn it seemed to come nearer, passing through trunks, branches, brush, and moss strands like a turning ghost made from the night itself. At first it looked like the ground had risen up in moving waves of black earth. Then Magiere saw it slowly sharpen into clarity.

Those rolling mounds were coils, each one larger than the height of a man. They glinted from a strange dull light that came from nowhere, and she saw their surface. They were covered in scales like a mammoth serpent, writhing around her in the forest with no beginning or end and no space between.

"Great patron," Ubâd continued with arms once more in the air. He leveled one hand out toward where he'd last heard Chap move. "I bring you the minion of your enemy to devour!"

His other hand reached out toward Magiere.

"And the child you desired, for when you awaken from your long slumber . . . May it come soon."

Chap turned about, running back and forth. The low cry issuing from his jaws sounded almost human in its anguish. He ran to Magiere's side of the clearing, scrambling back and forth between her and the coils in the forest.

The coils reached the clearing's edge, sliding within the trees, but they came no closer. When Magiere peered carefully, she could see trees beyond them. They were not wholly real, yet Chap was in a state of panic.

And Ubâd supplicated himself.

Was this what he served . . . what he had made her to serve?

"il'Samar . . . ?" Ubâd said. "I feel you with me. . . . Will you not take her, after all the many years of my labor?"

Chap ran around Magiere and charged for the necromancer.

Ubâd's scream filled Magiere's ears even before she turned to see the dog strike. The animal atop Ubâd was still the long-legged and silver-blue figure who'd been with her and Leesil for years, but all that she'd learned of him in recent months vanished in that moment.

Chap's jaws snapped closed on Ubâd's throat, choking off the man's wail. The dog's victim thrashed at him as Chap began ripping and tearing flesh.

A voice filled Magiere's head as if it came from all around her.

High . . . in the cold and ice. Guarded by old ones . . . oldest of your predecessors.

The words slipped into her mind, deep and resonating, and suffocated all other thoughts. She felt their vibration in her whole body, and she looked out to the roiling coils in the forest.

Sister of the dead . . . lead on.

Chap's snarls halted to be replaced by rasping pants.

The voice faded from Magiere's mind as the coils faded from the forest. All that remained around her were the dark spaces between the trees. She looked down to where Ubâd lay and cringed.

She had seen horrible things in her life. The mangled mess of the necromancer's throat was no worse an end than she herself would have given the man. It was the sight of Chap she found so unsettling.

He paced with his back to her and stared into the trees. His low rumble came out in gasps, and his sides rose and fell in rapid pants.

"Chap?" she called quietly.

The dog spun about with a snarl. The fur upon his muzzle, throat, and chest was soaked dark red, and with his jowls pulled back, his teeth were stained, as well. His brow furrowed around wide, wild eyes. He stood looking at her between glances toward the trees, as if he expected the coils of dark to return. And underneath his feral appearance, Magiere saw him quivering.

Chap was terrified.

Magiere had never seen this in him before, and it made her look warily into the forest and then back to Chap again. She wasn't even certain he recognized her, but she held out her hand, palm up, not trying to reach but waiting for him to catch her scent.

Chap's jowls pulled back slightly. He took a slow step toward her and stopped.

"That was what you've been keeping from us," she said softly. "Or what you have been keeping me from?"

After a stretched silence, he barked once.

There was no time for more questions.

"Leesil . . . and Wynn," she said. "Can you find them?"

Before he answered, Magiere felt a sudden tension in the air pass over her. It was the same sensation she'd experienced just before Ubâd had gone blind.

Chap lifted his head, ears cocked as he stared steadily into the trees. The quiver of fear had left him, and he was poised. He gave her one look with wide clear eyes in his blood-spattered face and bolted into the forest.

For an instant, Magiere was at a loss as she ran after the dog, about to call out for Chap to stop. Then she heard his hunting wail ahead of her.

There was another Noble Dead somewhere in the forest.

Welstiel's strength was all but drained, but he kept whispering and watching, feeding the ring to keep Ubâd blinded until the necromancer was finally dead. Exactly why the *majay-hì* had gone mad, he wasn't certain, but he had seen the coils of his dreams appear in the forest. The shock of that sight had almost broken his concentration.

All the long years, the black-scaled coils in his dreams had taunted him with hints to what he sought. Something that could change his sickening existence. It seemed the patron in Welstiel's slumber had been with Ubâd for far longer. Perhaps it had even been this patron that his father had so often muttered to in the dark. When the voice came, not in dream but in the night itself, it had not spoken to Welstiel or even to Ubâd. The necromancer's groveling was ignored, and he was abandoned.

Welstiel had heard the coil's words.

Sister of the dead . . . lead on.

The voice in the night had spoken to Magiere. And the words were similar to those it had whispered into Welstiel's dreams.

As he stopped chanting and slumped upon the forest floor, he slipped the ring back upon his finger before his shaking hands dropped it. A piercing wail issued from the dog, and it raced into the forest with Magiere following. With the ring's sphere of influence contracted to its wearer once again, there was nothing to limit the *majay-hì*'s awareness. It had sensed something more out among the dark, wet trees.

Chane.

Welstiel was surprised by how much this thought disturbed him. He tried to rise but collapsed again upon the ground.

Magiere pushed herself to keep up and didn't call out to Chap.

A short distance into the trees, the dog ceased wailing but continued to run. Magiere trusted Chap's judgment in a fight against the undead. If he chose to run in silence, he had a reason.

With Ubâd dead, perhaps Chap had picked up on Vordana or another of the necromancer's minions. If such still moved and searched in the forest, there was hope that this meant Leesil and Wynn were still alive.

She ran on and on behind Chap, using her blade to slash away anything in her path that she couldn't force her way through. When Chap stopped ahead of her, Magiere slowed as she approached him.

He was alert and tense, and stepped forward through the brush between two oaks. She followed, sword at the ready.

Chap paused as they entered a clearer area and stared at the base of a tree across the way. Magiere followed that gaze.

The sight was unreal, and it took her a moment to believe she was not seeing some vision like the coils in the forest.

The headless bodies of both undead mariners lay before her. The neck stump of the nearest one was ragged and torn, its head nowhere to be seen. The other lay farther off, a longsword impaled through its chest, pinning it to the earth. Its head had rolled away from its body.

A man with red-brown hair and a handsome face knelt upon the ground, holding someone in his arms. Magiere saw his profile and remembered the last time she'd seen him in the sewers of Bela.

Chane.

The person he held moved and sat up.

Magiere looked into Wynn's frightened eyes.

The sage's shoulder was bleeding badly beneath a makeshift wad of cloth Chane pressed against it. Magiere had no idea what was happening here, but she didn't care. She stepped forward with her falchion out.

"Get your hands off her!"

At the sight of Chap and Magiere, Chane scrambled out of the way, reaching for the longsword embedded in the headless corpse.

"No, Magiere," Wynn called. "He saved me. He came to help me."

"Came to help you?" Magiere's rage increased. "Wynn, get back!"

She charged toward Chane as he jerked out the longsword and turned to face her. Black fluids stained his shirt around a tear in the fabric. She thrust under and up, breaking inside his guard and slicing him across stomach with the falchion's tip.

Chane gasped at the touch of her blade and retreated. Magiere knew it would burn him as a mortal weapon would not.

"Stop it!" Wynn shouted.

Chap rushed by and launched into Chane with snapping teeth. Both dog and vampire toppled back across the wet ground. Magiere followed, waiting for an opening to pin the undead down by running him through. He saw her, kicked up, and caught her in the jaw, then pitched Chap away so hard that the dog rolled off into the brush.

Chane rose up, shifting his gaze between his two opponents. Magiere sidestepped, watching for an opening.

"Wynn is correct," he said. "I only wanted to save her from these walking dead."

"Liar!" Magiere snapped, and she felt her canines extend as she shook her head. "You're nothing but a killer . . . and you're getting tired."

Chap was on his feet again, but he limped upon his rear left leg. He growled again, watching Chane's every move, and hobbled closer. The calm in Chane's light brown eyes faded, and he looked at Magiere in anger.

"So are you," he replied.

Magiere charged Chane, swinging for his head. He dodged, spun, and swung back. When she blocked, he let his blade slide off hers.

He turned so fast, she could barely follow. Instead of slicing back with the sword, he slipped inside her guard and slammed his fist into her cheek. Only Rashed, the Suman undead of Miiska, had ever struck out with such force. Magiere went down.

A moment later, he was standing above her, sword gripped in both hands, its tip pointed down at the center of her chest.

"No!" Wynn shouted, and the sage threw herself over Magiere, kneeling with one palm raised toward Chane. "Please, do not hurt her."

Chane hesitated, lowering the blade as he stared at Wynn.

Magiere reached up and grabbed his wrist. He tried to jerk

away, and his own effort pulled Magiere to her feet and
Wynn tumbled away. Magiere thrust her sword up through
the circle of Chane's arms.

The falchion's tip bit into the soft skin below Chane's jaw,
tearing his neck open as it slid out over his right shoulder.
Black fluid spat from the wound. He toppled back, and
Magiere fell on top of him, flattening the longsword between
them. She rolled left, blade up, and swung down on his exposed neck.

Chane's head shot off his body and rolled through the
mulch.

She remembered Wynn shouting . . . Chap snarling . . .
but all she could do in the moment was breathe until her self-
control returned.

Wynn crouched by Chane's body, pulling at his shirt as
she sobbed. The bandage had fallen from her wound, and she
was bleeding again.

"No . . . oh, Magiere, no," she whispered.

"Stop it," Magiere told her.

Wynn looked up with wild eyes. "You murdered him, as
if he were nothing! What are you, Magiere? You think you
are better than him? You are worse."

Enough anger swelled in Magiere that she almost slapped
the sage. The little fool had put her trust in a monster. Then
she remembered Wynn's earlier words, and her anger became cold suspicion.

Chane had come to help her.

"How long has he been following us?" Magiere asked.
"How long have you known?"

"Since Stefan's village," Wynn shouted, dirt smearing in
tears upon her round face. "I did not banish Vordana—he
did! He is the one who saved us from an undead you could
not overcome. But I was afraid to tell you . . . because you
might have killed him."

Wynn dropped her head upon Chane's chest.

Magiere stood up and backed away.

"You lied to us? Betrayed us? All those nights you curled up with Chap, you knew an undead was trailing us. You even knew who it was—and you didn't say a word?"

She trusted few people, and she had trusted Wynn with her life and Leesil's.

Chap ceased growling and stood watching them both. He looked to the south and whined as he trotted toward the heavy brush. When he barked once, Magiere joined him, peering out into the forest.

Leesil came toward them, at times leaning against or catching himself on a tree trunk or low branch. Relief washed everything else away for the moment, and Magiere hurried to him. As he grabbed for her, she pulled him close. He threw an arm over her shoulders for support.

"I'm so glad to see you," he said, half-breathless. "I lost Wynn."

"Are you hurt?" she asked.

"Just weak. Vordana caught up to me."

She looked back the way he'd come. "Where is he?"

Leesil lifted his other hand, waving off her concern. "He's back there somewhere . . . most of him, that is. We won't have to see that awful grin of his again."

Magiere pulled his face in close to hers without a word. Leesil, always so constant, who kept her in the light.

"We have to find Wynn," he said.

Magiere pulled him through the brush, and he took in the scene of the decapitated mariners, and Wynn with her face resting on the chest of a headless corpse. Leesil pulled away from Magiere, catching sight of the head beyond the body.

"What in—? Wynn, you're bleeding. Is that Chane?"

The sage lifted her face, but she didn't look at him. She had ceased weeping and stared vacantly into the dark.

Magiere had no pity for her. She had betrayed them.

"We have to burn the bodies," Magiere said.

Wynn blinked once and grabbed Chane's sword. She could barely lift it, but she pointed the blade out, and her shoulder started bleeding harder. "You are not touching him!"

Leesil's eyes darted back and forth between the sage and Magiere, unsure what was happening. Chap whined loudly, and barked twice.

"No?" Leesil said, looking to the dog. "No to what?"

Magiere kept her angry eyes on the sage as she joined Chap once again.

She heard an eerie scream in the distance, and a hissing sound much closer. A glimmer flew through a tree only a stone's throw into the forest. It was the child ghost who had led her to Ubâd.

"We don't have time to burn bodies," Magiere said. "Ubâd is dead, but his servants are still out there. We need to go."

"They're coming back?" Leesil said. "There was wind earlier that seemed to drag them all away."

He stepped slowly, either in fatigue or in fear of startling Wynn as he neared the young sage.

"Time to leave," he said quietly.

Wynn's effort failed all at once as the sword tip dropped to the ground. Leesil picked up the blood-soaked bandage at her feet. He pressed it into her shoulder, closing the torn short robe over it.

Chap led the way, holding his rear left leg off the ground now and then as he loped ahead. Leesil was beside Wynn, and it was difficult to tell who held whom up as they hurried. Magiere followed last, watching both ahead and behind.

She spotted open space ahead out ahead. They were almost free of this marshland forest, filled with its apparitions of the dead and scaled coils of night. A wail rang out through the trees behind them, growing louder, closer, and Magiere looked back.

The grizzled soldier with the stomach wound rushed through the air toward her.

"Run!" she shouted. "The forest ends just ahead."

Leesil glanced back, caught sight of the ghost, and gripped Wynn's shoulders, propelling her forward. Magiere drew her falchion, flashing it in the air as she tried to catch the spirit's attention.

More illuminant shapes appeared among the trees. Spirits dived through her but caused her no pain. When she thought her companions neared the forest edge, she ran after them. She wished only to be away from this place and the discoveries of this night.

Leesil, Chap, and Wynn had broken through the tree line and waited in the open. She ran for them, and when she passed the last tree, the wails behind her grew. Leesil caught her in midstep to steady her, and they both turned to look back.

Angry spirits passed through high branches and back down again. They wailed and cried out, but none passed beyond the forest's edge.

Behind Magiere was the old ruined keep, and she saw their wagon and Port and Imp waiting outside the stockade. She wished for at least some dull relief, but she felt nothing at all.

"Wynn's shoulder needs attention," Leesil said.

Magiere couldn't look at the sage. "You see to it once we're under way."

As the others trudged toward the wagon, Magiere looked back to the spirit-laden forest. With all that had happened there, she'd forgotten one who hadn't been saved. Leesil was more worn than she was, Chap limped, and Wynn was wounded. There was no time to go back for one who'd been left behind.

Magiere turned away toward the wagon with sudden shame, her mother's bones left in a tomb of granite.

Welstiel did not know how long he'd been unconscious, but the night was fully dark, and he felt no approach of dawn. Ghosts wailed all around, and he tried to shut out their clamor. Weakened and tired, he climbed to his feet and re-membered Ubâd was dead. He stepped into the clearing for one last look.

There was blood on the ground—he could smell it—but there was no sign of the necromancer's corpse.

Welstiel gazed into the tree line all around him.

Perhaps one of the minions had retrieved the body, but he had no intention of investigating further. Not at the risk of being discovered while depleted and alone. His role here was done. He would find Chane, scry for Magiere, and leave this place for what he hoped would be the last time.

He walked slowly through the dank forest, opening his senses to the night. He wanted to avoid being seen by any-thing living, should Magiere and her companions still be nearby. Nothing living entered his awareness. What he did smell was the stench of decay and putrefaction.

The scent grew stronger as he walked, until he had to withdraw the willful expansion of his senses as he stepped into a small clearing.

There were the two bodies of animated dead he had seen earlier this night—and Chane.

Welstiel stood there for a long while.

Finally he stepped closer, looking down at Chane's fallen sword and at the black fluid soaked into the collar and front of his fine white shirt.

Chapter 18

Leesil drove the wagon into a bustling village before dusk on the second day after leaving the ruins near Apudâlsat. The sight of an inn with soft smoke billowing from its chimney brought some small relief.

The past two days had been filled with painful silence. Magiere sat beside him on the wagon bench, ignoring Wynn and speaking to him only when necessary. Wynn was curled into a ball beneath her blanket in the wagon's back and often seemed lost and far away even when her eyes were open. Leesil had applied salve to her wound and bound it as best as he could, but the worst of her injury wasn't to her body. She hadn't spoken since leaving the clearing and Chane's corpse.

As yet, Leesil was uncertain what had transpired between Magiere and the spirit of her mother. They needed time alone for that, and a night's separation would be best for Wynn and Magiere. He climbed down from the wagon, found the innkeeper, paid for two rooms, and arranged for the care of Port and Imp. Then he returned for their belongings.

"There's a hallway in the back of the common room," he told Magiere. "Take the first room on the left while I settle Wynn in the next one. Chap can stay with her tonight."

Magiere looked at him without blinking. She glanced down at Wynn's form curled in the wagon's back. Without a word, she climbed out, grabbed their trunk by herself, and carried it inside.

Leesil climbed into the wagon's back and crouched down beside Wynn. He was still exhausted from facing Vordana, but he could carry her if need be.

"There's a soft bed waiting. Can you walk?"

Wynn stirred but didn't look at him. "I can walk."

Hearing her voice was encouraging. Leesil stepped off the wagon and reached up to grasp her by the waist and lift her down. Chap ambled along beside them to the inn. His limp had lessened over the passing days.

Leesil settled Wynn on the end of the bed in her small room. It had a straw mattress, but by its bulk, it had been recently restuffed and would be suitably soft. The innkeeper left hot water in a small lidded pot, so he added tea leaves from Wynn's pack. While he waited for them to steep, he pulled back the bed's old quilt.

"Let's take your boots off and get you settled."

He helped with the boots, and she obeyed him without a word. He checked her bandage, pulled the quilt up around her chin, and then knelt down close to her face.

"Magiere did what she had to. I'd have done the same."

"No, you wouldn't have," she whispered, staring up at the bare rafters in the ceiling.

"Yes," he said firmly. "Chane wasn't some undead boy living on small animals in the wild. He tried to kill Magiere in Bela, and he tried to burn Chap alive. I'd have punched a blade through his throat without a second thought. That is what we do, and you're the one who asked to join us."

Wynn rolled away from him, and it was a long moment before she spoke. "Will she send me away?"

"No. She would never abandon you here," he said, and

reached out to stroke the back of her hair. "And I wouldn't let that happen either. You're part of this now, for better or worse, but you'll have to earn her trust again. In time, perhaps, she'll be back to growling at you."

He hoped this was true, though he knew Magiere judged Wynn's lie of omission as a betrayal. However, he believed in second chances. How could he not, given the ones that he'd had himself? Sorrow over this rift with Magiere was only part of Wynn's anguish. The loss of Chane, whatever he'd meant to her, wasn't something for which Leesil could offer comfort. Wynn was young and new to their calling, and Leesil still didn't know if this was the right life for her.

"Get some sleep," he said. "Tomorrow we hurry west out of this land and then north. It will be hard traveling through the winter, but when we reach my mother's people, all that knowledge you're so proud of will finally be useful."

He stood up and put some water into a bowl for Chap. Then he poured tea into two tin cups sitting near the pot. One he left by Wynn's bedside, and the other he took with him. He gave Chap a tilt of his head toward the bed. The dog hopped up on the end and curled into a ball, watching the sage intently.

"It's going to be all right, Wynn," Leesil said. "I promise."

Wynn didn't move. "Good night, Leesil."

He stepped into the hall and closed the door with a sigh. Comforting Wynn, though complicated, seemed simple when compared with opening up Magiere's thoughts. And getting her out of this land was the most urgent thing on his mind.

Chap curled against Wynn's feet as Leesil closed the door. He was satisfied but not relieved.

For all his fears—more so, the fears of his kin—Magiere had faced Ubâd without faltering. He had kept his faith in her, and she had not failed him. The Fay would have to accept that he had made the correct choices in the end.

There remained the apparition of the enemy's chosen form—the black scaled coils in the forest—and this still sent waves of panic through his spirit. It had not been Magiere's journey into the past, after all, that was quickening the coming days. After an age in the mortal world, the enemy was already aware, reaching out from within its slumber to gather new servants. It had been waiting, watching for Magiere.

And it had spoken to her.

This last event troubled him deeply, though he did not know what it meant. There would be more trials ahead, some worse than those of this past season. He would be with her—and Leesil, another whose spirit was dark and yet chose to live in the light.

Chap heard Wynn's breath deepen into a slumbering rhythm. He cared for this little sage but was as surprised as Magiere that a Noble Dead had shadowed them. This undead had come too far without him knowing. More disturbing, the sage had hid it from him. She would have to be watched.

Chap closed his eyes and let the quiet of the room, filled only with Wynn's soft breaths, settle around him. All else was too much to consider now, and there was time enough for one more quiet night of warmth.

Magiere sat in an old chair in the corner when Leesil entered their room. He didn't speak at first and, instead, handed her a tin cup. The smell of mint tea filled her nose before she saw the leaf settled to the cup's bottom. She put the cup down on the floor without tasting the tea.

She was quiet as well, but not angry at him. Was she even angry at all anymore? This left her bereft, as anger had always been her strength.

Leesil looked about the room. "It's too familiar. We started this journey in a small inn not much different than this."

"Yes," Magiere answered, and now that he spoke, she didn't want him to stop. It made all things better just to hear his voice. "It's over. There's nothing left to find."

He held his hand out. She'd always liked his hands, so tan and slender.

"Come sit with me," he said.

She came to the bed with him, wishing they were curled beneath a blanket by a campfire instead. It felt strange to be indoors.

"Tell me what your mother showed you," he said.

She longed for them to speak more freely of the things that mattered, but old habits ingrained by earlier years together were hard to break. That he simply asked seemed new and pleasing, and he deserved to know. If he was to link his life to hers, he needed the truth as much as she did.

He listened in silence as she told him everything. From her father drinking the blood of the five to Magelia's rape and Bryen's death. She told Leesil of Welstiel's involvement and the murdered infant, and how he'd had carried her away while Magelia bled to death.

"Oh, Magiere," Leesil whispered.

"There's more behind all of this," she said. "Ubâd sacrificed a lifetime of effort to create me. And my mother showed me that something whispers to Welstiel. Ubâd referred to it as his patron. But I'm not what they think . . . what Ubâd thought I would be."

She told him of the tendrils that had trapped her and Chap, and how Ubâd had tried to force her to feed upon the forest's summoned spirit within them, to drain life from them.

"It didn't work, Leesil. I am not what he thought."

"You are Magiere," he said as if it were an obvious fact.

When she spoke of the black-scaled coils that appeared at
Ubâd's call, Leesil looked about the room as if watching for
something.

"Whatever it was," she finished, "it abandoned Ubâd and
spoke to me. 'Sister of the dead, lead on,' it said."

Leesil was silent, lost in thought, almost as if he'd not
even heard this strange message she'd received. He took her
hand, not yet looking at her, and Magiere's thoughts would
not stop turning.

"The coils' voice . . . could it be what whispered to Welstiel in my mother's vision?"

Leesil frowned. "Welstiel."

"I am his sister," she said.

"And he tried to use you, no less than that old death-
monger. If he comes near you again, I'll take his head."

His protective manner both warmed and annoyed her. She
pulled her hand away, took off her boots, and crawled up to
lay on the pillow.

"And what makes you think I need your protection?" she
taunted him, but he didn't smile. "It's over, and we can head
north to find your mother. . . . I'm sorry this took so long."

"I'm sorry the answers you found were worse than the
questions." He scooted up to lie beside her. "For better or
worse, you've learned where you came from. But it's not
over. Something started here, and I fear it will follow us."

There was no hint of the humor in his amber eyes that she
had grown so accustomed to.

"Ubâd and Vordana are dead," she insisted. "As well as
Chane. There is no one left here to get in our way as we look
for Nein'a."

Leesil stared up at the ceiling, then sat up to look at her
with a hard expression. His voice was flat and full of
warning.

"When rumors of a hunter of the dead reached Ubâd, he

placed servants in fiefs throughout the Äntes and Sclävên to watch for you. They're still there, and whatever this black coiled thing was in the forest, we must get you out of this land."

Magiere knew all that he spoke of before he said it. She wasn't blind to what they'd uncovered and didn't yet understand. But she wanted to pretend for one night that it was over. She looked into his face, and he seemed to know how disheartened his words made her.

Leesil closed his eyes, and Magiere saw him swallow hard. He placed his dark hand on her pale one.

"I helped you all the way to the end of your search," he whispered. "I need to get you out of this land quickly, so now will you follow me to the end of my journey?"

"Of course . . . how can you even ask that?"

He was so somber. Leesil could usually be counted upon to lighten the mood, even when his methods were in poor taste. He lay back with his face near hers, and she reached out to touch his cheek.

"Tomorrow," she whispered. "We'll start at first light . . . all the way to the end."

Then he smiled. "And I love you, my dragon."

Epilogue

Welstiel dragged another half-conscious peasant through the trees and dropped him next to the other two, all of them bound and gagged.

It had taken two nights of weary travel to find a place where he could accomplish what was now necessary. Within the hilly outskirts of a village off the main road, he'd found an outlying cottage. He had waited anxiously as dawn approached, and a man and his two tall sons left for their day's labors.

The sun had almost breached the horizon, and Welstiel felt a warning sting upon his skin. When the men were out of sight, he rushed into the cottage and struck down the middle-aged woman preparing clothes to be washed.

He filled his teacup brass bowl with purified water and drained the woman to a husk to replenish his energies. Then he settled to wait out the day until the men returned near dusk. One by one, he'd dragged them back into the forest, back to Chane's corpse.

In a shallow hollow he had dug in the earth, barely deep enough for a grave, he laid out Chane's body and carefully adjusted his head in place. A lowly end for one who had been born a noble. Yet the importance of a proper burial, according to one's station, was another superstition to be dismissed.

Welstiel dragged the father to the grave, drew his dagger, and slit the man's throat. He tossed the dying man into the grave atop Chane's body. The two sons quickly joined their father, all bleeding out their lives, like loved ones of ancient days who chose to die with their fallen patriarch rather than live on in sorrow.

He settled upon a nearby downed tree with folded hands, leaning his elbows upon his knees as he stared at the piled bodies and waited.

Welstiel rubbed his temples and tried to clear his mind. Half the night passed as he sat in vigil. He looked upon Chane's face again.

"Are you awake yet?" he asked.

Chane opened his eyes.